THE RUINS

THE RUINS

Mat Osman

Published by Repeater Books

An imprint of Watkins Media Ltd

Unit 11Shepperton House

89-93 Shepperton Road

London

N1 3DF

United Kingdom

www.repeaterbooks.com

A Repeater Books paperback original 2020

2

Distributed in the United States by Random House, Inc., New York.

Copyright © Mat Osman 2020

Mat Osman asserts the moral right to be identified as the author of this work.

ISBN: 9781912248674

Ebook ISBN: 9781912248728

Printed and bound in the United Kingdom by TJ International Ltd

MIX
Paper from
responsible sources
FSC
www.fsc.org   FSC® C013056

For Anissa

Side One

The First Footprint in Fresh Snow
In the Ruins
Dead Beats
Mythical Beasts
The Day After the End of the World
Daughters of the Daughters
Some Monsterism

Side Two

Clear Your History
Tiny Lightning
Are We Going to Be Alright?
Slowing of Light
OU Kids
Eosophobia
This is What We Get Instead of Love

I stand stock still, as if I'm full to the brim with petrol, full to the very edge with flames twisting around my feet. The snow falls at night here but this evening is so bible-black that the only sign of the surrounding snowfall is that sound itself has died.

felt on the piano strings, padding in the bass drum

I can see the faint outline of the deck, then all is abyss. I stand, frost crackling under my boots, and spread my arms wide to lean into the wind. The pressure holds me there, precisely balanced, leaning, forward, downhill, into the night.

woodwinds: lacuna, solo

I feel I could dive, swooping between the starburst of fat, soft flakes and the silent pines, over the sleeping lakes and dead roads, all the way to the end of America.

strings: andante, acceso, glissando

I let go…

Chapter One

I was about to start the earthquake when the phone rang. It wasn't to be a big earthquake — I was thinking of two, maybe three hundred dead. You need some level of uncertainty to keep these things interesting, and I planned enough damage to mean that the repairs would run throughout the coming summer.

I'd set the epicentre to strike at the riverside suburb of Sild, a snaky tangle of slender wooden townhouses that surrounded a chapel topped with a typical Umbragian corkscrew spire. I'd rigged a blender motor to the district's supporting central strut. I would try a whole minute on full power for the initial quake and then dial it down by two thirds for the aftershocks.

I was nervous. This wasn't my first natural disaster — the flood that had washed away the clifftop village of D'reter and the fabled Ten-Hour Fire were both recent projects — but what they all had in common was their unpredictability. That was the joy of them too.

I stood in the doorway to make a last inspection of Umbrage while it was still intact. It was sleepy in the twilight and the hillside suburbs that abutted my bedroom door were veiled in a thick mist. I made a mental note to turn down the concentration of water in the dry-ice machine to back it off a little. Traffic systems were in their post-work lull; the funicular puffed dwarf clouds ceilingwards as it struggled up the back mountains and a couple of the cable cars still looped over the busier districts, but there was a pleasing air of calm and anticipation. Which was ruined by the ringing of the home phone.

I assumed it was a sales call. I couldn't remember the last time it had rung before this week. In fact, the last time I'd paid the bill there hadn't been a single incoming call listed, and only three outgoing ones (all from me, to my mobile, trying to work out exactly where in the flat I'd left it).

I let it ring and tried to concentrate again on the earthquake. The radius was hard to calculate and that made the damage little more than guesswork, and I don't like guesswork. But the phone rang on and on. Twice this week it had rung, both around this time of day. I tried to ignore it but some mental subroutine was counting the rings — *twenty-five, twenty-six* — and it played havoc with my focus. You need proper concentration to pull off a successful disaster. During the fire of '92 the smoke alarm went off, bringing concerned neighbours to my door — *thirty-one, thirty-two* — and while I was trying to persuade them that nothing was amiss, and trying to keep nosy eyes from peeking inside, the whole quadrant from the Drill Pits to Ulls'ton was burnt to a cinder. I double-checked the support struts — *thirty-nine, forty* — and made sure the plug switch was on — *forty-three, forty-four* — before conceding defeat. Now it felt vital to get to the phone before whoever was calling rang off. I had to crawl under the legs that supported the Darks of Mol before I could reach it.

"Hello?" My voice was cracked with non-use. It had been days since I'd spoken to anyone.

"Hello? Oh thank god. Adam. Adam?" An American voice: female, youthful, worried.

She spoke again. "Adam?"

I realised I hadn't said anything.

"Yes. This is Adam."

"Great. Wow. I've been calling a lot."

"Sorry, I don't usually answer this phone." Everyone who counted had my mobile number, and there were precious few of them. "Could I ask who's calling?" I flicked the flywheel on the blender motor and it spun with a pleasing hum.

"It's Rae." A pause. "Brandon's Rae? In California."

I flicked the wheel again. The spires of Sild arrayed in front of me were as delicate and brittle as icicles. They were far from the epicentre but their rigidity would make them vulnerable.

I didn't recall a Rae, though it had been a couple of years since I'd spoken to my brother, so she might be new. An image flashed in my mind though, a picture attached to a Christmas email from him, ages back. Brandon and a girl, her all teeth and blonde hair, the two of them atop a mountain somewhere encased in bright, unlikely skiwear.

"Rae, hello. I don't think we've…" I didn't think we'd anything. Met, been introduced, whatever. "How are you?"

Mist was pooling in the glens of Dras, an isolated suburb on the low ground to the right of the bathroom door. I upped the ceiling fan by a degree and watched it dissipate.

"Not great, Adam. I have some news. I've been trying to get hold of you for a week."

"Yes, sorry, like I said, I don't usually answer this phone." The flywheel ticked to a stop.

"Anyway, you're here now. OK. So… so, your brother is dead."

I have a habit, people tell me, of saying the wrong thing at times like these, emotional times. I get flustered and blurt out something that is, I'm later informed, inappropriate.

I took a breath, mirroring hers, and imagined myself in a film. What would a character in this situation say?

"Oh Rae, that's awful. Awful for you." Had I overstressed the word "you"? "When did it happen?"

The ceiling fan was at too high a spin now and the mist was being driven down the slope to the sea in an annoyingly unrealistic way. I switched it off.

"About a week ago?" She sounded unsure. "Your English police called me on Saturday. I've been trying to track down anyone over there who could go identify the body." She paused, two long breaths. "I don't know anyone there."

"He was here, in Britain?"

"Yes. He was killed in…" I heard her flick through some papers, "Motcomb Street, London W11." She pronounced it "double-you one-one".

"He's in London?" I corrected myself. "He was in London?" That seemed more unlikely than his being dead.

"Yes," she said.

"Why?" As far as I knew Brandon hadn't been back in London, or Europe even, for nearly twenty years.

There was a sadness to her voice now. "I don't really know, Adam. He disappeared about three weeks ago. Pfft. No note, no message. Our car turned up at San Francisco airport with five hundred dollars' worth of fines. I doubt it's even worth that. I haven't heard a single word from him since the day he left. Then the police called and said he's been shot by masked men in this Motcomb Street."

Masked men. My first thought on hearing Brandon's name had been that this was going to be just another one of those can-you-get-my-money-back-from-your-twin-brother calls that I'd been fending off since we were teenagers, but this sounded like something else entirely.

She was talking faster now. I recognised the feeling: when something has been tumbling obsessively around your mind for days but you've not spoken to a soul and you have to let it all come pouring out.

"The last I saw of him was ten days ago. He didn't pick Robin up from school, which isn't much of a surprise. And he didn't come back that night. Again, big deal, right? You know how he was. But after three or four days and his phone still switched off I began to think it wasn't just a lost weekend. And I started to feel guilty. Y'know, what kind of girlfriend doesn't call the emergency rooms and his friends the minute he's not back? But with Bran…"

She paused again. It was probably my turn to say something. "I know, I know."

"I went to the police after a week. Can you imagine how embarrassing it is to sit in a police station, reporting your husband missing after seven days without any contact at all? They asked me, 'Is it possible that he's just left you?' And to be honest it was kinda fifty-fifty. Or maybe seventy-thirty. They're asking whether he has ever done anything like this before and I'm trying not to count the instances out loud." She let out a long sigh. "And then this fucking limbo. It's so weird, not knowing if you've been abandoned or not. You don't know what to wish for, d'you know what I mean?"

I didn't really. "Masked men?" I asked.

There was rustling and then she continued, voice faltering only slightly. "According to CCTV evidence Mr Fitzroy entered Motcomb Court at 6.15pm, crossing from east to west, when a white Toyota Rav4 pulled in from the Delia Street entrance. The vehicle pulled up in front of Mr Fitzroy and two men, dressed in dark suits and masks, got out. They exchanged words with Mr Fitzroy and then the driver produced a firearm and shot him twice in the chest. Both men then went through his pockets before getting back in the vehicle and exiting via Delia Street. Mr Fitzroy was found by a passing pedestrian and then driven by ambulance to St Mary's A&E centre but was declared DOA. Passers-by stated that the two men were white, in their forties, and that the driver filmed the shooting before driving off."

"Who is Mr Fitzroy?"

"It's Bran, he changed his name, back in LA." She sounded annoyed. "For his acting career." Then her voice softened. "You didn't know?"

Even after over a decade of non-communication between us, people assumed Brandon and I had some kind of mental bond. It's the identical twin thing. People expect a connection that — for me at least — has never really existed.

"I'm sorry Rae, I don't think I've exchanged more than four emails with him in fifteen years. I couldn't tell you the first thing about his life. This is all very new to me."

When she started speaking again her voice was slower, more careful.

"No, *I'm* sorry. I always assumed I was the only one he kept in the dark. I didn't know he was so secretive with you guys too. You do know that you're an uncle, right?"

"Wow, no, not a thing. Recently?"

Five thousand miles of telephone static couldn't hide the edge to her voice. "Robin's *ten*."

"Ten. OK." I wasn't quite sure what to do with this information. "Um, say hi from his Uncle Adam?"

Her description of the killing was bothering me. "You said it was filmed? I've not seen anything on the news." I hadn't watched the TV for days though.

"I know. There's been nothing online either. Obviously his name didn't mean anything to the British press." She paused. "He'd have hated that."

She was right about that. As a kid Brandon had studied his weekly *Melody Maker*s and *NME*s like they were court reports. He knew every in and out of the music world: chart positions, gossip, break-ups, fights, alliances and feuds. And from day one he had assumed that he would join their number, that in ten years' time, now seven, now five, some kid would be studying the news of his exploits as eagerly as he himself was doing with the Smiths or the Bunnymen. What had followed had been, for him, a perplexing series of near misses and wrong turns. He formed and broke up bands methodically and I would only hear from him when a gig threatened to be particularly ill-attended, or when the presence of an A&R man necessitated as many warm bodies in the room as possible, even if they were as unimportant as me.

Twenty-five came around and some kind of stability beckoned. The Nineties were a boom time for London bands and his, a four-piece called Remote/Control, finally began to clamber up the foothills of recognition. There were articles in magazines, gigs attended by people who weren't just close friends, and singles that you could actually buy in the shops. They had everything bar real success. So as Rae said, the idea that his name still meant nothing to anyone here, even on the occasion of his being gunned down in the street, would have infuriated him.

As she talked it became clear that Rae was something more than one of his usual girlfriends. Back when Brandon and I lived at home, and were forced into interaction, I never bothered to learn the name of whoever was hanging off his arm that week. His relationships were usually measured in days rather than weeks (and, in one spectacular instance, hours) and I lost count of the times I picked up the phone to the sound of a girl's sobbing, or yelling, or worse. After we left home — me to university, Bran to a band — every time I'd seen him for family occasions he'd brought a different girl with him. Rae didn't sound like one of them. She'd been with him for fourteen years. Fourteen years, through about ten different homes, and they had a kid — this was quite a step up for my brother. They even owned a house, in Tahoe City, a tiny mountain community right on the edge of California. She sounded remarkably nice too — slightly loopy, but nice. Our conversation kept flipping between the practical — what to do about his body, who to call, was she OK for money — and the gossipy. One second I'd be talking death certificates, the next we were gabbing away about my family. I ended up on my back under Umbrage's lower foothills, listening to the click of the ceiling fan and Rae's voice, and it was hypnotic, like a radio play. She had a voice that drew you in and made you press the phone a little closer to your ear to shut out the rest of the world.

"So will you do it?" The question made me resurface. I couldn't remember exactly what we'd been talking about.

"Do what again, sorry?"

"Go to the police station, or I guess by now it might be the morgue, and identify the body? I can't leave Robin. Or afford the air fare for that matter."

"Sure," I said, grateful that she wasn't asking for me to pay for her to come over. At the back of my mind was still the suspicion that this, like so much involving Brandon, was some kind of scam. "Give me the number and I'll see what I can do."

There's something disconcerting about finding yourself in a setting that you've only known via television before. The police station and the interview room were at once deeply strange and totally familiar. The policemen used phrases that I'd heard on screen and I wondered if this was life imitating art or whether TV researchers had picked them up and used them for colour. I kept thinking that it must be strange becoming a policeman and having this weight of fictional behaviour rattling around in your mind. Certain people — the police, medical staff, lawyers, for example — shouldn't ever let you see behind the scenes.

At first, out in the waiting room, it was fine. The officer on duty was unsmiling and curt with the people ahead of me and the place had a satisfyingly professional aura to it. But once I'd explained who I was and why I was there, I was taken back into the shabbiness of the private areas. It reminded me of those occasions back at school when I'd be sent to take a message to a teacher in the staff room. I used to hate seeing them that way. Smoking, shoes kicked off and reading the paper. I preferred to think of them not having an internal life at all.

I followed the case officer, a gangly, jug-eared man whose clothes hung off him like a kid in hand-me-downs, who told me to call him Jonjo. We walked through the detritus you find in offices everywhere. Noticeboards with sign-ups for five-a-side football and jogging clubs. Doors open onto a messy kitchen, someone reaching deep into a fridge. Colleagues in the hallways nodding or stopping to pass on some bit of information, leaving me standing there feeling foolish. It all felt pretend, curiously am-dram. We finally found our destination: a harsh windowless room with nothing in it bar three plastic chairs and a TV and video, both of which were chained to the wall.

"I wouldn't have thought that was necessary, here," I said to call-me-Jonjo, who was fiddling with the leads.

He looked up and saw what I meant. "You'd be surprised".

I've often been told I don't talk enough. And it's true that if I make an effort to analyse a conversation and calculate my share of the words involved I'm usually on the low side, but when I've tried to counter that by being more loquacious the results are worse. Instead, I've worked on those things that I understand typify a "good listener". I try to maintain eye contact, especially with men because it seems that women can find prolonged eye contact intimidating, and I frequently make subtle interjections to indicate that I am following and enjoying the conversation. (Though this can be problematic. In an effort to appear sincere I vary my responses, rotating through "yes", "I see", "uh-huh", "of course" and subtle head-nods. The problem comes when I'm making sure that my responses seem suitably random and I find myself concentrating on a realistic sequence of replies, rather than on what the person is actually saying.)

And here, in the police station, it was even harder. I wanted to be helpful but I knew absolutely nothing of Brandon's recent life. Jonjo sounded downbeat about the whole case and I got the feeling that I was another in a line of disappointments for him. I suppose originally it had been a crime with everything going for it, like something from a film, but it was gradually revealing itself to be both prosaic and difficult. And my answers were only annoying him more.

"What was your brother doing in London?" He was sitting alongside me, at right angles, probably to give the impression that this wasn't an interrogation.

"I have no idea, sorry, I didn't even know he was here." He looked hangdog.

"Had he contacted you at all?"

I'd searched through my emails the previous night. "No. The last time we had any contact was three years ago when he sent me an email on our birthday." (It was actually four days after our birthday, but I doubted that was important.)

He looked through his records.

"He was killed just a couple of streets from your flat?"

I nodded.

"Do you think he was on his way to see you? Did he know the address?"

I'd discussed this with Rae.

"No. And yes. Or, maybe and yes. He certainly knew the flat; it was our aunt's before it was mine so he'd been there many times. As for visiting me, I doubt it. It would have been the first time in many, many years, but I suppose it's possible."

"You weren't close?"

"No, not at all."

"Do you know of anyone else in the area he might have been visiting?"

"I'm sorry, no. I have no idea who his friends are now."

He laid his pen down and scratched behind his ear. He didn't pick it up to write anything else down.

"Enemies then? Someone who might want to do him harm?"

"Like I say, I haven't seen him for a while, but unless he's had some kind of mid-life conversion I would say yes, there will be people he owes money to, women he's cheated on, husbands of women he's cheated with, and about a thousand other people who he just plain annoyed."

This perked him up. "Names?"

"As I keep saying, I have no idea, I've had nothing to do with his life."

"What about this girlfriend, Rae?"

"What about her?"

"Well, he ran out by all accounts, left her holding the baby." He turned back a page. "Well, not really a baby. But still she sounded pretty pissed off to me."

She hadn't sounded pissed off to me. She'd seemed more resigned.

"I really don't know. Yesterday was the first time I'd even heard her name."

He showed me the CCTV footage of my brother's death. "Strictly speaking, this should wait until after you've identified him, but seeing as you two are... y'know... I think we can safely say he's him and you're you, if you know what I mean. You'll still have to go to the morgue though, sign some papers."

It took him a couple of goes to get the tape running. "There aren't too many that run off VHS any more. We should really get this transferred to DVD but we haven't had the time, sorry." He didn't sound particularly sorry.

The tape showed a set of garages that ran perpendicular to an estate just around the corner from Trellick Tower. I knew them well enough. They were a shortcut through to Portobello that I'd sometimes take if it wasn't too late in the day. After dark they were populated by dealers and I usually took the long way round. Jonjo fast-forwarded through the footage, the occasional jerky, hooded ghost crossing the screen, until he got about an hour in.

"Right, just about here." He slowed the tape.

I couldn't tell if the footage was black-and-white or if it had just been a particularly grey day. There were ten seconds of nothing and then Brandon entered the screen from the left. He was probably coming from Portobello or the tube. Even if it hadn't clearly been him you'd have known that something was off-kilter, like one of those "what is wrong with this picture" games. He was wearing an unlikely cagoule over a suit and tie and carrying a cane which he swung with every step. He looked purposeful, a man with somewhere to go, and he didn't glance up or around him.

He was about halfway across the space when a car pulled in, coming from the same direction. A white SUV, very bright on the screen. Brandon looked round. He stopped and peered at the occupants. The car stopped and both doors opened simultaneously. Two men stepped out, their faces obscured.

"Are those..." I started.

"Donald Duck masks," said Jonjo.

On the screen Brandon looked unconcerned. He stood with hands on hips. Only when the driver pulled something from his jacket did he open his mouth. There was no sound on the recording so all that you saw was the driver raising his hand and Brandon falling backwards onto the ground. There were no histrionics, no writhing, no blood. One minute he was upright and the next he was a bundle on the floor and the two men were going through his pockets. From the way they tilted their faces towards each other it looked as if they were talking. They seemed supremely unconcerned. Then, as quickly as they'd arrived, the two men walked back to the car and drove off. The tape wheezed on and we sat there in silence for a while, looking at the row of garages and a dark smudge that was the last of my twin brother.

The officer clicked it off.

"So."

"So?"

"So. The car was bought that morning in Leeds with a fake ID. One man, tall, British, shaved head. That's all the seller remembers. It was left at the Heathrow long-stay car park a couple of hours later. There were no witnesses of course; anything that has the whiff of drugs or gangs around there goes quiet very quickly."

He turned the light back on.

"You brother had his American driving license in his pocket, a notebook and a couple of grams of cocaine."

"A couple of grams? Is that a lot?" I asked.

The officer looked at me quizzically, as if he was seeing me for the first time. "No, it's not a lot."

"What's with the masks?"

"The Donald Duck thing? We wondered that, obviously. It doesn't mean anything to you?"

I shook my head, trying to imagine a situation in which Donald Duck had a life-or-death significance. I couldn't.

"It's just his reaction to the men," said the officer. "Two men jump out of a car in duck masks and start walking towards you. I mean, what would you do?"

I played it in my mind. "I'd run like hell."

"Me too. But Brandon acts unsurprised by it." That was true. The hands on hips, the tilt of his head.

"You think he knew them?" I asked.

"Do you?" He rubbed his face. All at once he looked exhausted. "So we've been hampered by not having the faintest clue who this Brandon Fitzroy was, or what he was doing there. It's taken us nearly two weeks to find anyone with a connection to him."

I was a disappointment to him, I could understand that. To go from no clues to a partner, kid and identical twin in a couple of days must have felt like a breakthrough. He looked frustrated, stuck.

"OK, OK." He rearranged his papers. "If you think of anything, call me."

I knew this bit from the TV too, so I waited for his card. He stood to go.

"Don't you have a card for me?" I asked.

He made a gesture, palms out. "I've run out, just ask for me at the switchboard."

If the police station was disappointing compared to TV then the morgue was a major let-down. It was tiny, overlit to the point of migraine, and smelt like a portaloo. It was kept cold so both I and the technician had our coats on, as if we wouldn't be staying long. He was unaccountably jolly. "I normally ask for some ID at this point," he said, pulling back the sheet from my brother's face, "but I don't think I need to this time."

One frustrating thing about being an identical twin is that it's just not as strange as people assume. I could see the interest in the technician's eyes. His thought processes were so clear that I could have written subtitles. *Is it strange seeing your own face staring up at you from a slab in a morgue? Did you feel some psychic jolt the moment he died?* All that rubbish.

I looked down at Brandon's face. I couldn't tell if it was the chemicals in his bloodstream or just that life had caught up with him, but he looked old. There were spider veins cracking across his cheeks and dark half-moons under his eyes. My first thought, before anything else, was that he was beginning to look like our father. It used to annoy me that Brandon's lifestyle didn't show on his face. At those rare family occasions where he made an appearance it would be clear he hadn't slept. He'd be crumpled and nicotine-stained with squally moods and scattergun conversations, but he still looked youthful, at least as youthful as me. I hoped that if his lifestyle didn't have to be paid for physically then at least it might be karmically (and however he spun it in his sporadic emails from LA it was clear that he'd been driven there as much as choosing to go, which gave me a warm, but guilty glow).

But here under bluish light he looked every one of his forty-five years. The bags under his eyes looked like permanent features, not the occasional visitors mine were, and his skin was sallow and blotchy. Maybe this is how age comes to you when you've lived the life he had: all at once like the bill at the end of a meal. Or maybe I was just being harsh — no one is going to look their best in such circumstances.

My second thought, I'm ashamed to say, was that he had a really good haircut. We both suffer from thick, pure white hair that stands up at odd angles and constantly threatens to run wild. Somehow he'd managed to tease this mess into a rigid quiff. Even here, after a couple of days zipped inside a bag, it stood as proud as a ship's prow. I thought I should leave a second or two before I spoke, to give the impression that this process was in any way moving; such things are expected. I forced my mind elsewhere, to a problem with the flow of one of Umbrage's rivers, and gave it a full ten seconds' thought.

"Yes, that's him."

"Do you want a couple of minutes alone?" The technician's eyes shone.

"No, no that's fine."

"OK, do you know where we're to release the body to?"

"What?"

"You're arranging the funeral?"

"I… I didn't expect to. I think his girlfriend…" But of course she was in America, and broke, and pissed off with Brandon. "I'll need to talk to her first."

He eyed me dubiously. "OK, but as soon as possible please, we're backing up here."

There was some confusion over his possessions. They'd assumed that Rae was his next of kin, but my arrival, coupled with my twinhood, had apparently trumped that. Three policemen argued behind the counter over which of us had the better claim, more for something to do than out of any real sense of moral dilemma I thought, and eventually they handed over three small see-through bags with his things in. I signed for them.

"One wallet containing three credit cards in the name of Brandon Fitzroy, one expired. American driving license, same name. One twenty-dollar bill and £85 and change."

"One British passport, also in the name Brandon Fitzroy, recently renewed."

"Three plectrums... or is it plectra?" one of the policemen asked. He got no reply.

"One notebook, full."

"One key."

The policeman looked at me as he handed this over. "Any idea what this might be a key to? We still don't know where he was staying." The key was heavy, with some kind of red woven tassel attached. The fabric was etched with a ribbon with letters picked out in gold: ATSOTM.

"No idea," I said. It was stuffy and over-bright in the office and I was getting a headache. Two hours is about my limit with strangers without having some kind of cataclysmic withdrawal, and the thought of the sanctuary of my flat was tugging at me. I left with promises to phone them if "I thought of anything", which sounded needlessly vague.

Outside on the pavement I felt that relief that even the most law-abiding of us has after contact with the forces of law. It was a blustery day with a constant threat of rain and people hurried by with their heads down. I found an empty doorway from which to text Rae. It was midday — 5am in California — so I didn't want to risk calling.

"Do you know what ATSOTM might mean? It's on a key that was in Brandon's pocket. Might be to do with where he was staying."

Her reply was immediate. "No, but I can search. Skype in half an hour?"

I took the bus. I was feeling oddly excited about talking to her again. I couldn't remember the last time someone needed something from me, and the haul of Brandon's possessions had the pleasing mystery of a video game before you'd worked out the rules. I laid the items on a newspaper on my lap in the back of the bus and studied each in turn.

The key was heavy and dark, but something about its neatness made me think it was modern. There were three plectrums (or plectra, who knew?). An Oyster card. Credit cards in the name of Mr B. Fitzroy but with signatures as abstract as Pollocks. £85 in notes and some change. And a much-used notebook: one of those Moleskine ones that snapped shut with an elastic strap.

I started with the notebook right there on the bus. If you read it the right way up it was a jumble. Fragments of what I assumed were lyrics jostled for space with notes and reminders and the occasional deft sketch. On one page you might find CALL SAUL/KASPARs GUY/ LP PRESSER transmuting into much-crossed-out poetry and rapid drawings of limbs draped over beds or bird wings. Some pages were nearly empty, some infuriatingly opaque.

Finding the opaque winning out over the comprehensible, I started to skim through and found that, at the back, the writing changed. At some point he'd turned the book over and upside down and started again, writing what looked like a diary. On these pages his writing was small and neat and it looked unedited compared to the lyric stuff — the text ran for five or six pages without a correction or a hesitation. I started to read. It was typically Brandon: flighty, overblown and unconcerned with anyone else in his life. I felt guilty reading it and snapped the book shut.

Back at home I risked the lift. The flat was technically my aunt's, a council home for life due to her disability, but she'd preferred the countryside and I'd been looking after the place for years. When she died I'd packed and waited for the notice of eviction, but it never came, so I kept myself to myself, avoiding the neighbours and coming and going when no one else was around.

As soon as I got inside I could feel that something was wrong with Umbrage. The sounds that it gave off all had their particular rhythms, and the combination of motor whirrs, ticking clockwork and water pumps gave the city a sound as unique as a fingerprint. I listened carefully until I could pick out what had changed. A snag in the cable-car mechanism that led up through the kitchen hatch meant that something was clicking impotently in the engine room, and I thought it might take a little while to fix. It preyed on my mind as I opened up the laptop.

I'd used Skype a couple of times before to explain something about Umbrage to modelmaker colleagues, but still it was a shock to see my face on screen. I looked pale and darkly lined, like a photofit. Rae, in contrast, shone from the screen. I tried hard not to stare. She looked healthier than Brandon's other girlfriends, with a crown of staticky blonde hair that flared white through her laptop camera, and big, loopy features. There was something of the farm girl to her too: that band of pale freckles and a hot flush to her cheeks. Her voice didn't sound city-ish either.

"God, thank you so much for doing that. Was it awful? How did he look?" Her eyes darted around the screen and I realised she was checking for differences between the face she saw and Brandon's.

I started to say something and then stopped. How *had* he looked? "It was… it was OK. His face hadn't been touched in the… incident, so he just looked like he was sleeping. He can't stay like that for long, apparently, so we'll need to discuss the funeral at some point."

She waved that away. "That can wait. So, ATSOTM. At the Sign of the Magpie. It's some fancy hotel-stroke-private club out in the East End. Too cool to be on Tripadvisor or anything but there's a Japanese design blog that Bran was subscribed to. He's used it for places to stay before so I had a look through and I think I found it."

Another window opened on the laptop and I clicked on the link. It was a gallery of low-lit photographs of a place that looked like a Victorian library.

I dangled the key in front of the camera. "Same kind of look. Is it the sort of place Brandon might stay?"

There was an edge to her voice. "It looks like the kind of place he'd *love* to stay, if he could afford it. I couldn't find prices anywhere online and you know what they say about 'if you have to ask'. It's more likely that he's charmed some girl who was staying there and squirreled himself away with her."

She gave me the address, some place out in east London that I couldn't picture. I waited. I felt like there was something she wanted to ask me but I couldn't imagine what. I laid out his things in front of me. "There was a journal too, among his stuff. I can send all of it on to you."

She ignored that. "Did you read it? Does it say what he was doing there?"

I fidgeted. "I read a little, just to get a sense of what he was up to. Lots of it is lyrics and stuff, things I don't really understand, but the back is more… structured. I didn't read much. It seemed private."

Her eyebrows shot up. "Private? He's dead. I give you permission to read it, if that's what you want."

I didn't know what to say. I just stared at his things in front of me. Notebook, passport, cash.

"So tell me about the part you *did* read at least."

I tried to formulate a reply. Her eyes flicked across my image on the screen and then her shoulders rounded. "I see. You have read it. How bad is it?"

I struggled to find the words to describe the coldness of his tone or his elation at leaving her and their son behind. She nodded, more to herself than to me.

"Listen Adam, I'm under no illusions what your brother could be like, none at all. On Robin's third birthday I was called away from a party where I was looking after twenty screaming toddlers, on my own — to bail him out of an Oakland jail. And Oakland was five hours away. I had an afternoon of dropping moaning children all over Vegas while he sent me a ton of WHY AREN'T YOU HERE YET messages. So, just read it, if you can. I'd rather know than to sit here wondering."

"OK, I need a coffee first. It's long. Meet back here in ten?"

She gave me the shortest of smiles. "It's a date."

It took nearly an hour to read it all out. Brandon's handwriting was tiny and haphazard and often there would be an inked arrow leading to some other piece of text. Some of those pieces were connected, some were tangential thoughts that he'd thought absolutely, positively had to be laid down for posterity at that very moment, and some of it bore no obvious connection to anything else in the text. It was like walking in a maze; side paths turned out to be main streets and thoroughfares were dead ends. I didn't know what to say to Rae after we'd read everything. All the time we were reading, asking each other to decipher words, trying to figure out where the body of text led next, it felt like a game. I knew that the names had lives attached but it was only when we reached the last line, and I found myself back in the darkened living room, the automatic lights of Umbrage casting skyline shadows on the bare walls, that I reconnected the face on the screen — open, wild-haired and blank — with the Rae from the text. I was conscious that my voice and Brandon's were the same. It must have made it sound doubly real to her.

"Look... sorry." I said, immediately unsure of why I'd said it. "He's just... a dick."

She looked at me. "Yes. Yes he is." She looked as untethered as I was feeling.

I wanted to change the subject. "Those three names at the end." I flicked back. "Kimi, Saul and Baxter. Do you know them?"

"I know of them. They're the rest of the last band he was in: Remote/Control? I don't think he's had any contact with them for the last fifteen years either, though. Kimi ended up being pretty famous, she's the chick with the voicebox? The other two I don't know much about."

The chick with the voicebox. I knew who she meant. A singer I'd seen on TV a couple of times, a stately, high-fashion woman with a robotic voicebox doing exactly the kind of modern music that I don't like. I couldn't remember whether the voicebox was something she needed or an affectation.

"Shit, it's nearly three. I have to go pick Robin up." She looked into the screen. "No fucking car you see. It's back to the bus for me." She looked disconsolate for a second and then started laughing. "Sorry, not your problem. None of this is your problem."

I could feel the loneliness coming off her like heat. "Well genetically I suppose it is my fault," I said. "It's my exact genes that have done all this to you. Just in a slightly different vehicle."

She gave a wan smile.

"Let me help." I said. "I can go visit this At The Magpie place and see if there's anything I can find out. Someone there might know what he was doing here or who might have it in for him."

"Are you sure?" Something in her voice said *please, please, please*.

"Of course, I had nothing planned anyway." That wasn't strictly true. The earthquake was pencilled in, and something had been blocking the aqueduct that snaked between the water city of Sorent and the Darks of Mol, but I wrenched myself back to the present. "It'll be fun," I said uncertainly.

"Thank you. Will I see you when I get back?"

I checked the time; it was nearly midnight. "I don't think so. I'll Skype you tomorrow?"

This time the smile was broader, "Of course — night night." Then she stopped. "Can I ask what is that in the background?"

I'd angled the laptop away from Umbrage, towards the one unencumbered wall of the flat, but in laying out Bran's possessions I must have brought more of it into view.

I flattened my voice in expectation of scorn. "It's a model. Of a city."

"Oh, model trains?" she said with a note of forced interest.

"No, not really, just a model." I wondered how much of the city she could see.

She beamed, showing her teeth. "Oh wait, I know about this. Bran told me ages ago. This is the thing that you've been building since childhood, right? Can I see?"

"It's not that interesting, really."

"Oh go on. I'll show you my place if you'll show me yours. Go on, walk me through it. Please."

No one new had seen Umbrage since an estate agent back in '98. "OK, just quickly though." I took the laptop in my arms and angled it downwards. I tried to imagine what she was seeing and how it might look to a newcomer. The two halves of the city were at about chest height, cleft in two by the serpentine Dropwall ravine. The left-hand side housed the newer city of 'Rage which sloped away steeply and by the time it reached the back wall, nearly thirty feet away, grazed the cornicing around the ceiling. The camber meant that 'Rage's highest roads had to snake back and forth like San Francisco's, with vicious hairpins at each end and houses and churches clinging to the hillside in serried ranks. A funicular puffed its way effortfully through the steepest section. The right-hand, older city of Umb was more classical and its gentler slope allowed for a tidier structure. Shadowy plazas emanated languor and thin lanes radiated off them like arteries. In the centre was the oldest part, where some of the buildings dated back to my childhood. They were rudimentary compared with the intricacy of the later buildings. Architectural styles criss-crossed and cross-pollinated on both sides. Onion-domed churches abutted cave-like cubby-holes carved from a roseate sandstone, and slender, timber-fronted shops threw long shadows over a shady park ringed with painted caravans. I walked through the ravine showing Rae each side, then turned the laptop back to face me. She was wide-eyed.

"It's just… wow. If I didn't have to go I could spend all day looking at it."

I turned the laptop back to face me again.

"So. Many. Questions," she said with a lop-sided smile.

"Fire away."

"Is that all of it? Some of it seemed to be spilling into other rooms."

"Nope, there's a water-city called Sorent in the bathroom, and a couple of suburbs in the bedroom." Actually the bedroom was totally taken over bar a single futon, and even that had two-thirds of its length hidden under the platform that held the Darks of Mols, but revealing that might make me seem obsessive.

"How long did it take?"

"Well, Brandon was right, I started back when we still lived with our parents, but most of that is gone now. It's been thirty years on and off."

"Is there anywhere left for you to actually *live*?"

"The bedroom's half clear. And the shower. There's a bit of kitchen too." I pointed the laptop back towards the collection of units that passed for a kitchen.

She chuckled. "It's amazing. That's not a good enough word for it. There are no people, though?"

"No, they're too hard to make. That's where your imagination has to come in."

She considered this. I hadn't expected her to take it so seriously. Model-making is one of those things that seems to split the sexes entirely, like cricket or being able to browse in Boots the Chemist.

"People are too hard to make," she said finally. "Would they spoil it?"

As I'd done a hundred times, I imagined the tracks and paths and motors I'd need to make Umbrage a proper, populated city. "No, not at all, but the machinery to keep the transport and electricity and steam-powered stuff running needs a *lot* of work. If it was working thousands of figures too I'd be snowed under. It takes up most of the day as it is."

She smiled at that. "Could Robin see it? He just loves to make stuff and I always wondered where the urge came from. It certainly wasn't from Bran — he'd get a guy in to change a fuse — and I can't draw or make things at all." She placed her hands face up on the table and examined them critically.

Robin. My nephew. Something new in the world. "Sure," I said, "I don't see why not."

She gave me a searching look. "He'd appreciate it, I promise, I can just tell."

"OK, next time we talk."

She gave me a grin that seemed to come out of nowhere. "See you later, investigator."

The First Footprint in Fresh Snow

My brother's notebook, pages 1–11. These are all of the pieces that Rae and I read that night. I've relegated the parts that I felt were extraneous to footnotes.

Treachery, like all adult pleasures, is best taken slowly.

I step out of that front door for the very last time, out into the held breath of pre-dawn, and gulp down lungfuls of crystalline mountain air. It's too early for traffic, too early for the birds even, and the only sounds are the crunch of my footsteps and the catch of my breath: kick drum and snare in a lopsided beat. I head downhill, my footsteps in the snow writing a sentence with no full stop. First steps out into a morning's unsullied whiteness, woman and kid and home and possessions sleeping safely behind me, and I know that there will be no corresponding set of footprints ever returning. Each step an arrow pointing straight into a new life. The last time I'll ever be *here* and *here* and *here*.

I parked Rae's car a couple of streets over last night where there was no danger that the engine might wake the household; even betrayal has its logistics. I brush snow from the windscreen, unglue the wipers and scrape away the ice with a credit card. One of Rae's cards actually, one of the three that I drained of funds last night, not that there was much credit left anyway.

Here, close to what they laughingly call a town, there are just hints of sound: the bomb and glide of sparrows, snowmelt's fingers stretching towards the lake, coffee pots bubbling behind triple glazing. I open the

Jetta with the actual, physical key, like someone from the twentieth century, and wind the windows down. Needle-sharp air on my skin as I let off the handbrake. The movement is almost silent, just the creak of rubber on snow and I push off down the hill with one foot in the car and one on the ground, like Robin on his scooter. It accelerates, dumping snow from its roof, and the key waits in the ignition. I let the speed build, pull the door closed, and wait for the junction at the bottom where it should be too early for any traffic, unless the snowploughs are out but I would have heard them surely, and anyway it wouldn't be the worst way to go, crushed under the wheels of one of those municipal behemoths, so when we hit the corner, snowblind and moving fast, I finally turn the key and the engine coughs and catches and the back wheels skid — taking my stomach with them — and then straighten and the radio springs into joyous life and the timing is perfect — an omen if I believed in such nonsense — and I am away and free and gone.

Treachery, like all adult pleasures, is something you have to learn the taste for. It's like blue cheese, or Tom Waits, or a single malt. These are things that are terrifying when you're young because at their hearts they're poison. But you grow a little and you twist and harden and you learn a taste for a little poison; it's an inoculation against the hard stuff. Treachery, nicotine, asphyxiation: little deaths. That's what leaving my home and never looking back feels like. It's delicious and venomous and it rings with the sting of a neat gin.

I flick through the radio waiting for something dumb and fast — unlikely in the pre-breakfast show hours — but then I strike gold with the soul station over in Truckee. I wind the windows down and howl to the last sliver of moon as it slinks away. It's ten miles to the interstate where the snow is already gritted to water and the tyres hiss with pleasure.

The trick is to keep moving. Stillness is where doubt settles, so you keep the car rattling just over the speed limit and the music just a fraction too loud. Don't think about later today, and Robin sitting on the curb outside school, his head turning hopefully at the sound of each new car. Don't think of Rae noticing my bag gone, and then doing anything but checking the wardrobe for empty hangers because then she'll *know*, rather than suspect, that I'm not coming back. Just switch lanes, switch stations, smoke and sing. Break the treachery down into easy-to-swallow portions.

Mountains give way to flatlands. Snow to scrub. The soul station submerges in static so I switch to Oldies Radio out of Sacramento and sing along to "The Wanderer" and "Why Do Fools Fall in Love". Backwoods diners are replaced by motorway services with their near-indistinguishable list of dining options. It's like computer game scenery — *procedural*, they call it — where the combinations of a few finite units are varied each time to give the illusion of richness. Robin, my son, who still at this moment is unaware that the conversation we had as I picked him up yesterday is the last we'll ever have, could read some underlying logic to these constellations of outlets. On an unfamiliar highway he'd press his forehead against the window and study each grouping of McDonald's and Coffee Beans and Red Lobsters until the pattern became clear to him. Then, minutes before the next forest of signs, he'd make his prediction, whispering under his breath, "Burger King, Dairy Queen, Dunkin' Donuts, Starbucks" and he'd be right nine times out of ten. Strange kid.

When I'm far enough from the orbit of my soon-to-be-ex family I pull over and do a couple of lines in the restroom of a coffee shop about as close to San Francisco as it is to home. Here's the last point at which I could turn back. Half-life. Wave or particle. For the moment I'm Heisenberg's cat. Until someone peeks in my box I'm both doting partner and abscondee (and I'll leave it to you to guess which is life and which is death).

The air here still twinkles with Alpine clarity but there's a rumour of the tropics in the wind riffling the garbage bins. A place that fits snow chains sits amidst a perfumed orange grove and in the mini-mall you can buy bikinis and showshoes, parkas and flip-flops. Cars towing snowmobiles park up next to VWs bedecked with surfboards. I sing *everybody knows this is nowhere* to myself. Nowhere: the American speciality. Thoughtless non-places where the outlets spore and everywhere looks like the back side of somewhere better.

I drink a final cup of the tepid brown water that Americans call coffee and dump my cellphone in a bin. If this were a film then this would be the moment you saw a light go out on an electronic map, as agents crowd around the screen, yelling *we've lost him*.

Back on the road the Jetta feels too small to contain me. I want to go spinning off in all directions. I open the windows as wide as they go and turn the radio up higher. Will I be missed, back in Tahoe City? Robin and Rae will miss and hate me in equal proportions, but I have to scour them from my mind, they're gone, they're the Old World. There will be a few other people who'll mourn my non-appearance. I brought a spoonful of glamour to the school gates. The appearance of a dad always added a frisson of excitement. And when he was an exotic, British dad, with, it's whispered, a *past*, and enough of a personal sense of style that he didn't just rock up in a fleece and jeans, well that was all the better.

After Sacramento the road widens and something lifts from me, not a weight exactly, but a fog from my mind, and the day looks bright and newly washed. I take sleepy NorCal suburban roads so as not to fall into the pull of San Francisco. I skirt the meat of the place and drive instead through empty streets of lumber companies and taxi repair places and strip malls and storage units until I'm on the coast road to SFO with a whole life dwindling to a point in the rear view mirror and Belinda Carlisle on the radio.

A million years ago, when I made this journey the other way — London to California like a million crappy screenwriters and wannabe actresses — I sat next to a mumsy Texan in elasticated slacks and bug-eyed glasses. She watched as I methodically destroyed every remnant of my London life. I worked studiously on photos, letters, bills, address books, alternating between scissors and my bare hands, until the tray table in front of me was a snow scene of personal confetti. When I finally called the stewardess over to *take this rubbish away and burn it please could you love?* Mumsy peered over the glasses and said, in that honeyed Southern accent that disguises a multitude of unpleasantnesses, "Oh sweetheart. You can't run away from your troubles you know?"

Back then, when I thought that extreme old age (she must have been at least forty) brought wisdom, rather than, as I now know, fear, I took this warning seriously. But if anyone on this flight is foolhardy enough to try that shit now I'd tell them, "Sure you can, you're just not trying hard enough". I've successfully run away from my problems a few times now. The running isn't difficult, it's the never looking back. Never. You can't take anything with you; a scorched-earth policy. Robin, Rae, Tahoe, car payments, friends, lovers, bars, neighbours, record collections, email addresses, mementos, clothes, memories even. Not just gone but never existed.

I'm first on the plane, which is in itself a first. I upgrade on a whim — what's one more debt among the hordes — and this time my seat-mate is a Belgian, in chemicals or something. I celebrate another no-turning-back point over Newfoundland, once Britain is closer than the US, raising a glass of champagne to the silent mountains and tiny lights. Again I feel something slip away. Downhill, downhill, downhill. I pull the laptop out somewhere over Greenland, relishing being a lone pool of light among the sleepmasked bundles around me. I didn't bring a piano keyboard but nowadays it's not too hard to make a decent-sounding track with nothing more than a laptop and some imagination. I sketch something out in Pro Tools. Rizla-thin drums drawn across a grid like some Bletchley Park codebreaker, a synth line created by drawing a parabola over a lined screen. I scatter notes at random: snowdrops peaking their caps through frost. Then I run the whole thing through a couple of effects, pulling everything together, pointing things in the same direction. One note is a stray, wandering away from the scale, and I'm about to delete it when I remember an old jazz dictum that Kim used to quote. "Do it once and it's a mistake, do it twice and it's a motif". I copy-and-paste the note to every verse and soon that's the phrase you're waiting to hear. I finish up as the microwaved breakfast cools towards edibility and listen back as the window screens go up, with morning just a powdering of sugar on the horizon. It sounds pretty good. I title the file The First Footprint in Fresh Snow and save it in a blank folder. The new world starts here.

(There's a sketch on the next page. Thin black trees and a path of footsteps across a blank wasteland. When the writing starts up again it's in black ink and in a smaller, less certain hand.)

At Heathrow I channelled Kim Philby. He was a particular hero of mine as the patron saint of life-burners. Here was the Picasso of betrayal: its Einstein, its Elvis.

23 January 1963. "The Night Has a Thousand Eyes" on the radio, "Walk Right In" and "Go Away Little Girl". Philby steps out of an interrogation carried out by an old friend and colleague, and knows, deep in his heart, that he's done. The jig is up and his life's work — a traitorous double agency at the heart of the British establishment — is about to be revealed. He doesn't pack. He doesn't say a single goodbye. He moves fast, and is smuggled by cargo boat to Odessa then flown as a hero to Moscow.

My parents knew Philby a little, he'd been to the house. There was a picture of them all in the back garden at Goring with the lawn chairs arranged just so, everyone facing the guest of honour. Even in a straw hat and with that long frame folded into a deckchair, there was a sooty glamour to him — that submarine smile and the air of somewhere to be. What fucking chutzpah, what fucking control, what fucking *balls* the man had. Thirty years a living lie. Thirty years sending a simulacrum of himself out through the corridors of power. Just a piece of the man but still one with more than enough charm to come within an inch of running the whole damn Secret Service. (Even the Ruskies couldn't believe that Philby was real; no one could split himself so completely and let nothing bleed across surely? Like all betrayers their problem was that they saw betrayal in everyone.)

23 January 1963 he steps off the plane at Chkalovsky military airport to the salutes of fifty serious Soviets, the rest of the world still sleeping, and he pushes that leonine head out into the deathly Moscovite cold, breath like smoke, trumpets sounding through a far-off PA, the clack of heels and snap of salutes, *behold the man*. For these hours, until the West finds out how long and well and thoroughly it has been fucked, there are just these few witnesses to his transfiguration — the butterfly becoming the caterpillar — as flamboyant, boozy, bed-hopping Philby is revealed in dowdy glory to be an older kind of man: secret, serious, free.

(There's a sketch here of Philby — I had to look him up online. It's a pretty good likeness, and there's an asterisk beneath it. Later on in the book there's the below text, I'm assuming it's what is supposed to be linked.)

(I wrote to the man actually. Jan 1988 — the slightest thaw in the Cold War and a friend of Dad's, who'd met him at a Government reception in Moscow where he'd been wheeled out to talk cricket and salt wounds, gave me his address, knowing I was a fan. I sent him a care package:

Fortnum & Mason tea, a half of Glenmorangie, shortbreads and a Wisden. I tried a letter but it gushed so instead I added a note asking the only question I really wanted answered. *What would you have done if they'd never found out?)*

They should blindfold visitors to London until they're through the suburbs — it's just embarrassing. The route through west London is fifteen minutes of scruffy back gardens, parking spaces and dumping grounds.

Treachery, like all adult pleasures, is a long game. I counted off names on my fingers. Robin and Rae, Tahoe and America. All those nameless bodies. Gone, like a dandelion clock. Pffff. And then I counted again. Kimi, Saul, Baxter and Dillon: those four owed me and the one who thought they owed the least would pay the most. I was going to take all the dross of the last twenty years: the drabness, the boredom, the successful friends and the successful enemies, the shopping lists and the PTA conferences and the bad TV — I would take all of it and spin it into gold.

How? Just watch me.

Chapter Two

There are moments in life about which everything turns. Moments when your points get shifted across and a hundred tons of life's train go thundering down an unexpected path. In engineering we call this *sensitive dependence on initial conditions*, and I've spent my adult life making sure that my initial conditions were as unchanging as possible. My parents died steadily and expectedly. My romantic relationships were slow-blooming and long-dying: a series of dissolves between interchangeable scenes. Sometimes I find myself remembering a holiday or romantic meal with perfect clarity except for one detail: I can't recall who my companion was. That meal of vine leaves and fresh figs on a Grecian rooftop — Rachel or Lisa? A sleigh ride through trees festooned with icicles has a friendly blur at my side in the memory. My health is good, my work is dull, my bank balance is stable. If you'd asked me at sixteen how I might turn out I wouldn't have known the specifics — Umbrage, my bonsai business, aunt June's flat — but the shape of my life is quite as I expected it. Quiet and uncomplicated. Lonely sometimes, but not unfulfilling. Like a human suburb, I've situated myself far from the places where life-changing events might happen. So I'm not sure what led me, there amidst the beeswax and panelling of a hotel lobby, to pretend to be my recently deceased twin brother.

I'd slept badly. Normally the rhythms of Umbrage's machinery act like a lullaby on me, but the thought of coming back into contact with my brother's world was unsettling. There would be mess, and drama, and people with obscure motives. The day after Rae's call I worked on the city, carefully not thinking about the task ahead.

Once I'm within Umbrage a change comes over me. My hands move of their own accord. Problems arise and are solved and the outside world fades to shadow. Two days previously I'd been at a car boot sale where, on a stall of foxed paperbacks and mismatched crockery, something glittered like a smashed disco ball. An old case bulged with nearly a hundred unused camera viewfinders. They were clever little mirrors that were adjustable via screws set in their sides and something in their angles suggested a structure to me. Back at home I screwed them onto a circular wooden base in a concentric spiral like the chambers of a shell, positioned so that each mirror fed the next until any light that shone on the outer mirrors appeared dimly on the opposite side. Then I connected a motor from an old music box and extended the handle so the whole wheel of mirrors could be wound and set in motion from outside. I spent the morning mounting it in a cobbled central square that until now had been populated only by carved wooden benches, each in the shade of its own bonsai'ed Chinese elm. Inside the new structure's outer ring I rigged intricate trellis-work from dental floss and glove-leather, and linked it back to the central spindle. A figure placed in one of the outside chambers faced a glass, mirrored box, his reflection nowhere to be seen, and I set the mechanism running. The forks of the music box were bent and blackened with grime but they lent the tune a haunted air. There, sixteen chambers later on the far side of the wheel, the figure was reflected in an empty chamber, life-size and clear. I let the mechanism run down and the space between the notes lengthen as the story of the building began to revolve in my mind. I wrote in *The Book of Umbrage* in the same way I'd been working: undeliberately, the hand leading the mind.

Umbrage is a city without mirrors. To catch a glimpse of your reflection is thought to be unlucky, unseemly even — it straitjackets the soul as surely as a prison cell. No pool of water, from the humblest bird-bath to the eel-ponds of the Autumn Palace, is ever allowed to settle. Instead fountains ruffle surfaces and wind machines drive ripples across millponds. Metals are prized for their patina: Umbragians relish rust and verdigris the way other cultures might prize the sheen of precious metals. There is just one place in the city where mirrors are allowed: The Carousel. It sits in Dromedare Square, draped for the majority of the time in velvet, but Umbragians do their best not to look at it even in its shroud, as if the hidden mirrors still exerted some photonic pull. It runs for an hour in the morning for any citizen to ride for free. Some days queues snake back to the city walls and mornie-cake sellers do a rapid trade along the waiting line. Other times there are only two or three riders in a week. Like much in Umbrage there seems to be reason to these surges and lacunae; they are a faddy, capricious people.

The Carousel's process is simple. You step inside while it's still moving, as the chime of the Fork Organ sets the morning air ringing. Your wrists go through the leather cuffs that dangle from the ceiling and you the grab the thin twine. It tightens automatically and your arms are hoisted aloft, hands apart. You position yourself in front of a mirror. Nothing. You are reflectionless, vampiric. Instead angles throw your reflection around the whorl of mirrors. The Carousel spins, darkens and then your reflection appears — or rather a reflection appears — because someone has entered the chamber directly opposite and their image has made the inverse journey to yours. Your twin reflections pinball through the maze, reversed, upended, magnified, diminished and righted again. This time it's a woman, older, dressed in the grey swaddling of a wet nurse. Her pose echoes yours: arms wide, palms facing. The Carousel spins and the metal tines chime a note like a deadened bell. Pulleys do their work somewhere deep in the mechanism and your wrist is guided upwards and forwards. The woman's image follows exactly. It's you but not you, moving in unison, a slow dance. The floor turns ninety degrees and your double does the same. You turn to see your profile; she does too. The left-hand cuff loosens and you watch her wrist fall to her side as you feel the weight of your own. You are a stranger.

For people who have never seen themselves in a mirror The Carousel can be a kind of miracle. I'm the most beautiful girl say grizzled dockmen, thick-knuckled hands stroking a face more beard than skin. I'm so old say teenagers, so tiny say giants, so lucky say the lame. And it adds a spoonful of spice to one's day.

Umbrage isn't huge and its citizens cross paths regularly so it's not uncommon to bump into your reflection. There I am, trained songbirds trilling from my outstretched arms in the Sea Market. See me in the crowd over there, looking over my shoulder before disappearing into Brothel Alley — naughty me, I never knew. There I am passing sentence, there I am washing dishes, there I am coughing up blood in the gutter. Retirees in the zinc bars under Dromedare Square say that people who visit the Carousel often are the best kind of citizens: friendly, generous, forgiving."

Once I was done with The Carousel the day ahead had lost some of its terror. So I was to go to a strange place and question people I didn't know about my brother's death. What of it? I steeled myself for Brandon's kind of people. When we were young he was always friends with the most troubled kids: boys whose fathers were euphemistically "away", girls with scars. Mixing with them, even in passing, was fraught with danger, but I tried to tuck these fears away. I was just a messenger, a tool for Rae to find out some information that she deserved.

I walked right past the place the first time. I don't know the East End well and even with the map printed out it wasn't what I'd been expecting at all. There was no sweep of drive or dressy doormen. It was only on my second trawl along a litter-blown side street that I noticed that a sign that swung in the morning breeze depicted a magpie. It hung above a set of grimy red doors set back from the street like sunken eyes. There was no name but the knocker was a brass bird. I rapped it and after a moment's silence a voice emanated from somewhere overhead.

"Ah, Mr Kussgarten. I was beginning to think we'd lost you to the charms of Blackburn again."

Wherever the camera was, it wasn't obvious. The doors swung open onto a passageway that looked cool and dark after the fug of the streets.

And there, on the stairs, I decided that I wouldn't say that I wasn't Brandon, at least not yet. The decision ambushed me but thrilled me too. And it brought a deeper thrill: the idea of telling Rae later.

I took the stairs as slowly as I could, trying to adopt Brandon's swagger, as much to mask my own nervousness as anything. I took a breath as I turned the final twist of stairs. They opened into a dark, wood-panelled room with high ceilings and a whiff of beeswax. The light had the liquid tremor of candles though I couldn't see where the glow came from.

A figure peeled himself from the gloom in the corner. A trim, waistcoated man with geometric facial hair and an air of glee. He came striding towards me wearing an expression of obvious pleasure but then at the last moment paused. He gave me a quick, but obvious, once-over — hair, clothes, shoes — the way women do to each other on the street. His lips parted and then stopped.

"Mr Kussgarten, what a pleasure. We were just starting to get concerned. No bags?"

I looked stupidly at my empty hands.

"No, no, nothing."

His eyes flickered across my face and I forced myself to hold his gaze.

"Excellent, well, the room's just as you left it." He reached over to take my coat and I snuck a look at the name embroidered into his waistcoat: Kaspar.

I tried nonchalance. "Sorry Kaspar, just a bit of a lost weekend, if you know what I mean?" I'd practised that line on the way up the stairs.

He laughed. "Well we all deserve one of those every now and then. The room's not been touched as you requested, but the bar and kitchen have been restocked. Is there anything you'd like sent up?"

I was about to say no when I realised that I had no idea where I was going. The lobby had at least three exits. I pushed my hand into my pocket and said, "Well here's the thing Kaspar, I left my key at a friend's."

He laughed again. "No problem, follow me up and I'll see about a new one for you later."

We took a doorway between two bookcases and then walked up a spiral staircase steep enough that I was staring into the backs of Kaspar's knees as we climbed. Then along a picture-lined corridor that sloped first downwards and then up again. I was just feeling like my claustrophobia might kick in when he stopped outside a small door and fished out a key.

"Home again, home again, clippety-clop." His voice had a tuneful sing-song air. He did an odd, almost military clicking together of his heels and headed back the way he'd come, promising to return with a new key.

The first room was huge. You could have held a masked ball in there. Murals in dusty pastels busied the walls and a mazy parquet floor ran the entire length. It looked like a Victorian reading room: the kind of place where you could imagine Marx and Darwin nodding to each other as they passed beneath the book stacks. Everything was worn. The floorboards were a rich chocolate at the room's edges but straw-pale in the centre. The furniture was solid and old and frayed and every surface was encrusted with things. Books were folded open over every chair arm, guitars leant against any vertical surface. Piles of stuff — sketchbooks, T-shirts, newspapers — collected at the edges, and it was hard to tell what was part of the idiosyncratic interior design and what was Brandon's. There was an orrery — a very good one — that Brandon would have neither appreciated or recognised, and a technical looking turntable with exposed valves that I suspected might be the most expensive thing here.

The room opened out into two more spaces on the same floor: a kitchen-cum-diner where wood panelling hid some high-end German appliances and cupboards full of Fortnum & Mason groceries; the other room was stone-floored and spacious like a chapel, with a walkway running around the second storey and an ornate skylight. There were instruments here too but arranged to more of a plan. Guitars sat patiently in stands and keyboards were arranged into an open-sided square. I fingered a tune on the piano as I passed — something from childhood lessons — and the notes were clean and rich. The floor was covered in chalk markings. There were chord charts, much crossed out and altered, caricatures in Brandon's hand, and a wheel of symbols that took over the central few feet. I skirted around them, careful not to smudge anything.

In the corner rose another spiral staircase, with turns tight enough to make me vertiginous, which led to a bedroom with a windowed, pyramidical roof. The bed was made but that was the only note of order. Clothes covered the floor in a way that made it impossible to tell whether it was carpeted or not. Candles had spilled continents of wax across the end tables and everywhere cabinets and drawers sat open.

I perched on the edge of the bed in a pool of puny mid-morning sunshine and let my heart rate return to normal. There was an open laptop on a draughtsman's table in the corner and I clicked on the Skype icon. There were no entries in the contacts tab so I tried the name Rae had given me last night: *Voodoorae*. There were two seconds of ringtone and then an unknown face filled the screen. It had wide-set eyes, a tangle of dirty-blond hair and wet lips. The face ducked out of sight and then bobbed up again, eyes popping, leaving me with a view of that same room from which Rae had talked. Then it bounced tiggerishly back into view.

"Hi dad," he said, and then was gone again.

So this was Robin. I should have asked Rae what she'd told him. He must know that his father was away, but beyond that?

I tried to keep it noncommittal. "Hi Robin." He examined me, tilting his head from side to side like a bird. What do people talk to kids about? "How was school?"

"Dadd-eeee," he whined. "It's seven in the morning. I haven't been yet. Are you in England?"

So she'd said something. My stomach lurched but I told myself *we're only talking, it's just a game.* "Yes, London, look."

I stepped back to give him a view of the room, feeling foolish as I did; it could have been anywhere.

"Awesome," he said, not really looking. "England is one of the oldest countries in the world and once ruled half the world, including here." He said this in a rush of words.

Another voice came through the speakers. "Robbie, who are you talking to?"

"It's daddy, I'm telling him about England."

Rae swept into view, hair up in a towel. She looked at me on the screen and her eyes flashed. Warning or apology, I couldn't tell.

"He knows all about England darling, he's English, and anyway, I told you never to answer calls on the computer." She gave me a what-can-you-do smile.

He stuck out a lip. "It said Brandon on the screen. That's daddy's name."

"I know, but remember, you never know if someone is who they say online."

"I can see him, it's daddy," Robin replied, joyful with the power of his own logic.

"Yes, well, I need to talk to him."

"OK." He disappeared and then stuck his head back into view. "The guards at the Tower of London are called Beefeaters."

Rae sat. "Sorry about that, he did a project on England last semester and Bran…" She looked behind her. "Bran helped him with it." She rubbed her neck. "And I'm really sorry about the other thing, the dad thing. I've not told him yet."

I breathed out as I felt the weight of the lie. Our connection was so fragile that I couldn't think of a way to tell her what she was doing was wrong without breaking the spell.

"Might it be better to tell him? It's only going to make it harder later, surely?"

She looked forlorn. A silence grew until she nodded to herself, eyes on the floor. "You're right, I know. It's a mess. But we could just do with couple of days when our whole world doesn't get turned upside down again. Sorry." She opened her eyes wide and stared at me. Then she craned her neck to see the rest of the room. "So, how is it?"

"It's… different. I mean, it's beautiful, and it's huge, and obviously expensive. And, the people here think I'm Brandon."

She raised an eyebrow.

"I didn't actually lie, they just assumed. I'm not sure why I didn't say anything but maybe I can find out more this way."

"They don't know that he's dead?"

"Nope, I did a quick online search last night and there's nothing. Neither of his names get a hit in the last five years."

"That's so weird. I thought gun crime was really rare over there."

"It is. I think they've decided it's drug-related and washed their hands of it."

She made a face. "What he had on him wouldn't have lasted an evening, I can't believe it's anything to do with that."

She bit at a cuticle. I'm never sure where to look in these situations. At that little bead of camera, so on their screen you appear to be paying attention? Or at their on-screen image?

"But how are *you*?" I asked.

She looked like she was actively considering the question. "I don't really know. When I thought he'd just left me it was OK. I mean it was horrible and humiliating and I wanted to curl up and die, but it was at least a recognisable thing, you know? People leave, people get left. Perhaps not as brutally as Bran did but it happens. But this is something different. I can't be angry at him when he's just been *shot dead*. I can't mourn him when he ran off like that. I don't know if I'm supposed to hate him or pity him and fuck knows what I'm going to say to Robin. It all seems so arbitrary. I'm on hold."

I wasn't sure what to say. She was checking out the room over my shoulder.

"Do you want the tour?"

"I do. Is that totally shallow of me? I should dry my hair first."

"Well you look great from here. Like a blonde Cleopatra." Her fringe drooped damply over her eyes and gave her a mischievous look.

She laughed. "Cleopatra. OK, Anthony, I'll dry after, lead on."

I walked her around the apartment, holding the laptop out like a waiter with a tray. I put on my best British voice. "We start in the magnificently appointed drawing room, with its Queen Anne furniture and hints of chinoiserie. Note how the proportions are to the classical model, maximising the light through an etched-glass skylight." I made her laugh a couple of times and it felt good.

In the music room I angled the laptop down to show her a chalk diagram. It was a spiral divided into seven sectors, Latin and alchemical symbols in each intersecting box.

"Woah. Stop. What the hell is that?"

I brought the screen closer so she could see it more clearly. "It's a Sigillum Dei Aemeth. One of Brandon's teenage obsessions. He had one drawn out under the rug in our bedroom until mum found it. It's what John Dee used to summon angels."

"John Dee?"

"A magician." Her face clouded over. "Not a Vegas magician, but one of those guys from history, Elizabethan I think. Like a magician and scientist and spy and politician all wrapped up in one. His old house was down the road from ours in Mortlake and Brandon convinced himself that we were long-lost relatives. That's why he called himself Brandon Dee in the first band he had."

"He did?"

"He did. Until everyone started shortening it and calling him Bran Dee, so he went back to Kussgarten."

I walked the laptop up to the balcony where two mannequins, naked apart from a pair of enormous matching headdresses, were positioned so they were staring out of the mullioned windows. They were made with real feathers, the top a replica of a bird's head — a hawk I thought — with a beak as smooth and black as beetle wings. The feathers continued down the back like hair; they'd reach your waist. The eyes looked wet like drops of ink but when I touched one it was dry and cold.

"Woah again," said Rae, "What are *those*?"

They were intricately made; the feathers were oily and iridescent and scalloped into a rippling pattern. The point at the end of each down-curved beak was needle sharp. I touched it with the pad of a finger and felt how easily it would draw blood.

"Fabulous. Put one on."

I turned the screen to face me. "I think they're just ornaments."

"Try it, go on."

I lifted the closest. It was heavier than it looked and had a kind of Latex skull-cap sewn into the underside of the head. I pulled it on. It was neatly balanced, the river of feathers down the back perfectly countered the heft of the beak. The beak curved down to bisect my vision, giving everything a stereo effect as if each eye was working separately from the other. I tilted my head from side to side, immediately feeling somehow avian.

Rae gave a shiver. "That's really something. Is there a label?"

I turned the other one over and examined the skullcap. A silk label had a hand-written note on it: kussgarten 17/4/10. Underneath was a crest and the name Fogerty & Baptiste. I read it to Rae. "Ring any bells?"

"Nope, sounds British as hell though."

She wanted to see a couple of things twice: the contents of the fridge and the bathroom cabinets. When I sat the laptop back down she was silent as she towelled her hair.

"So, what d'you think?" I asked her.

"Well it's fucking amazing, of course. I have literally no idea how he was paying for it. But that's all guy stuff in the bathroom, and the food in the fridge is his taste too, so it looks like it really is his place rather than him leeching off some girl." She patted her hair flat. "I'm guessing there's a safe. It's going to be weird if you have to ask for the combination though."

I thought about it. "I'm not sure it'd be that weird. I turned up after a week away, without a key. My hair is different, I don't know anyone and they accepted all that without a qualm. Brandon's flakiness might be an advantage here. Hang on."

I picked up the old-fashioned rotary handset. The numbers bore pictures of magpies and the old rhyme "One for sorrow, two for joy". I dialled 2 and a voice answered, "Mr Kussgarten?"

I calmed myself. "Yes, stupid thing but last time I was here I changed the combination on the safe, it was late, I was a bit paranoid, y'know?" Kaspar made sympathetic noises. "Could someone come and reset it?"

"Of course sir. Did you want some dinner at the same time, we have that sushi chef over from Kyoto if you weren't in a hurry for the safe?"

"Sure, whenever, I don't need it now, I was just thinking ahead."

"We'll be up in an hour." And he was gone.

"Just thinking ahead?" said Rae once I'd put the phone down.

"I know, I know," I said, "That might be the single most un-Brandon-like sentence ever uttered."

"Maybe. How about, 'No thanks, I think I've had enough'?"

"That's good. Or, 'I should turn in, I've got an early start in the morning'."

She had a face that you wanted to see laughing. Even on a laptop screen her animation was plain and her smile was like switching a light on. She ran her hand through her hair and, as if she'd read my mind, said, "God it's good to laugh. One sec." She looked around her and then got up to close the door. "Another thought. Where do *you* hide your stuff in hotel rooms? I mean your money and your passport, sure, they go in the safe, but the other stuff? Y'know: drugs, toys."

"You've forgotten who you're talking to. I haven't stayed in a hotel for twenty years and I haven't had a drug in longer than that."

She shook her head. "Sorry, force of habit. You're really not much like him are you?"

That gave me a swell of pride.

She went on. "OK, when I stayed in a hotel with Bran, which was once in a blue moon, then he'd always hide his stuff behind a picture on the wall." She looked around again. "Which could be kind of a problem there though, because it's like a fucking art gallery."

"Well, I've got all day," I said, "shall we start in the bedroom?"

Instantly I was blushing but she laughed, "Now you *do* sound like him. Let's do it."

It didn't take long. The third picture we tried, a Victorian portrait with the phrase I FEEL SO EXTRAORDINARY written across it, had an envelope wadded into its frame. I laid it on the bedspread so she could see.

"Open it, open it," she said, with the excitement of a kid at Christmas.

I ungummed the flap and pulled out the contents. Most of the space was taken up by bundle of cash, American notes wrapped in red paper bands.

"Fuuuuuck," whispered Rae, "Look at all that. How much is it?"

I started to count it out onto the bedspread. "Fifty, one, fifty, two, fifty, three…"

Rae only spoke once while I counted, as I reached ten grand, when she let out a long, "No way."

In all there was $27,550 there. It sat piled up in neat rows on the bedspread as Rae paced around her living room. I caught flashes of her as she passed the screen. "Thirty fucking grand, thirty fucking grand in cash and I spent last night unpicking some other kid's name out of a school uniform I got at the thrift store." She kicked against something under the table and the picture wobbled. "How long has he had this, how long?"

"I don't know Rae, sorry, I…"

She interrupted. "I know you don't know Adam, sorry. I wasn't really asking. It's just…" She threw her hands up. "I don't know what thirty thousand means to you but to us it's… everything. It's the mortgage for five years. It's a holiday for Robin that's *not* just to my folks' place. It's a car. Hell, it's two cars." She slumped back down. "It's being able to sleep at night. Where the fuck did he get it?"

I didn't know where to start. A couple of things bothered me though. "It *is* dollars. So he probably didn't get it here. Unless he was planning to send it home?"

She snorted. "You could put that right at the top of your list of unlikely Brandonisms. 'I've just made a bunch of cash, let's send some home.'"

I rooted around in the bag and pulled out four empty wrappers. "Looks like there was more here too, originally."

Rae was very quiet after that. I ran through some scenarios but in truth I had no idea what Brandon might have been up to and after the third theory had trailed away Rae said she had to get back to Robin. I stared at the screen after she'd gone. Should I send her the money straight away? I had no real use for it, though I had no idea how the room was being paid for and I didn't dare call Kaspar again. I resolved to get her bank details when we next talked.

I went through the rest of the apartment, not really certain what I was looking for. Each time I walked around it something new seemed to appear, as if it was changing behind my back. Kaspar came up with a handyman and the sushi, and I sat on a piano stool to eat. Colourful little squares of chilled flesh: reds and pinks and yellows like pools of paint on a wooden easel. It tasted subtle to the point of blandness. I took a Diet Coke from the fridge and a packet of crackers and stuffed them in my pocket. I needed to get back anyway. The timer on Umbrage's various processes would be winding down about now. Soon after that the lights would fail. It didn't strictly matter: few of the automated systems suffered from a shut down, but the idea of the city in darkness always made me antsy.

I packed a few things: Brandon's journal, a book on John Dee that he'd scribbled notes in, and his laptop. I was halfway out the door when I thought of his clothes. Kaspar's up-and-down earlier had been a warning that looking facially like Bran might not be enough. I went back to the carved oak wardrobes in the bedroom and came across the only part of the flat which had any kind of order to it. It was show-home neat: suits gave way to jackets, then a brief stretch of trousers yielded to a long section of shirts while a dull rainbow of knitwear made up the far side. Below, in the drawers, was underwear and beneath that pairs of shoes in a rack. Everything looked brand new and the overbearing smell was of leather polish. It was too much choice, much too much. Some mathematical part of my brain that is forever spinning away in a quiet corner whispered to me the possible combinations. Ten suits times twenty shirts, plus a handful of jumpers. Multiply in the ties and even without the shoes and belts you had 12,000 outfits. Enough for every day of the rest of my life.

I picked something from the middle of each section. A grey suit in some heavy, densely patterned material over a pink shirt with cuffs as starchy as cardboard. I pondered the ties. I'd never seen Brandon wear one but they were probably here for a reason. In the end I decided against it purely because I couldn't guess what colour would go with the grey and pink. I spent ages trying to get the cuffs to work before I realised they needed cufflinks so I settled for rolling them up under the jacket. The shoes were beautiful: sensuous, curved things the colour of calves' liver. Though they looked new they fitted without rubbing and I blessed our shared DNA. In the mirror I didn't look like Brandon but I looked like *somebody*. I felt the weight that decent clothes give you, that air of substance. It had been a good idea.

In the lobby again I felt Kaspar's gaze flicker over me. I thought, for a moment, of lizard's tongues.

"Off again so soon? Are we expecting you for drinks later?"

It was already nine o'clock, but Brandon would keep later hours than me.

"I don't think so. I'm seeing a friend. I may stay over."

"Of course. Jay was supposed to be coming tonight, would you like me to reschedule?"

Who was Jay? "That'd be great Kaspar, I'll be back early tomorrow morning."

He smiled at that so I tried a Brandon wolfish grin. "Well, early for me."

He looked down at my feet. "Are those the Lobbs?"

I'd read the name inside the shoes upstairs, thankfully. "They are, well spotted Kaspar."

He gave a sigh. "Beautiful, beautiful things."

Umbrage was running down but it was nothing drastic. The tracklights on the far wall were just dropping below the screen that simulated the onset of night, and the hillside funicular was throwing a looming shadow that slid across the back wall. I sat in the ticking semi-gloom and ate a bowl of cereal. My heart-rate spiked when I thought back through the day. There had been a slip of dislocation whenever I'd used one of Brandon's phrases or actions. It was lying without anything being untrue, a grey area between realities that made me uncomfortable. And Robin too. That felt strangest of all. The tug of his eyes on me, his waves of need: these weren't things to be toyed with. Rae would tell him, soon surely, and make a liar of me.

I washed up my cereal bowl and lowered the blinds against the street-lights outside. The shimmer from Au-Hav's monastic caves would be my nightlight. I pulled the sleeping bag hood tight over my head and tried to think of nothing at all.

The call woke me from a deep sleep. I had a momentary lurch of something like falling before I remembered where I was. I checked the clock — just gone 2am. Umbrage slumbered all around me. I fumbled open the laptop. "Rae?" I tried to focus on her face on the screen.

"Yeah, listen…" She sounded excited, then saw my befuddlement. "Shit, it's the middle of the night there."

"It's OK." I turned on a side light. "What's up?"

"Sorry, I needed to clear my head a bit. That money on top of everything else was just a bit… A bit much. But I've been out, and dropped off Robin and I think I'm a bit less crazy now. So, I got to thinking about the music Bran said he wrote, on the plane over. That First Footprint in Fresh Snow thing?"

"Sure."

"Well it wasn't on his laptop, right?"

"I don't think so. I've never seen an emptier desktop."

"Well he sounded pretty pleased with it so I thought I'd google it."

"And?" I took a sip of water.

"One hit. A SoundCloud page. An artist called The Band of Rain. And one track."

"The First Footprint in Fresh Snow? Is it his?"

"It is, and there's a whole essay with it too. He says that it's liner notes for the track but it reads more like a brain dump. I started to read it but then I thought we could look at it together. I didn't think about the time, sorry."

"God no, this is intriguing."

She visibly relaxed. "It is, isn't it?"

I took the laptop through to the kitchen and made myself a coffee. There was something restful about Umbrage at night: the sound of tiny waves and the *click-click-click* of the last running tramcars. I settled down on the one free chair and typed in BAND OF RAIN FIRST FOOTPRINT. Rae was right, it was easy to find it once you knew what you were looking for. There was a thumbnail picture of a magpie where I supposed a portrait of the artist would normally be, and a link to the track, shown as the undulating peaks and troughs of a waveform. I pressed play.

"You're listening first?" asked Rae.

"I thought I would." I had to fiddle to get the volume turned up and once I did the track didn't sound as beautiful as Brandon had described it. It was sparse and tinkly and utterly formless.

"Do I have to listen to the end?" I asked her, "Does it do anything else?"

"Not really. I think that's the point. It's quite pretty, don't you think?"

"I suppose. I don't really get his music though, never did. Shall we read?"

"OK, it's the link below." I could see her excitement. "On three, two, one…"

It felt oddly intimate sitting five thousand miles apart but sharing a moment, our eyes running over the same phrases. At one point we both reached for our coffee mugs at the same time, eyes on respective screens, and the movement jolted me back to the present for a second. She looked at me, raised both eyebrows and we went back to it. I finished first and watched her read. Her face was endlessly mobile and I could tell when she'd reached certain sentences by the set of her features. At one point she put both hands flat on the desk and whispered, "Oh for fuck's sake." But mostly she just frowned. She had the corrugated forehead of a child, more overloaded than angry.

When she finished she looked up and saw me watching her. "God, did I look like a loon? Bran always said that my lips move when I'm reading."

I risked a compliment. "You looked fabulous."

She gave me a sideways look. "Sure. So… what do you think?"

That wasn't hard to answer. "Honestly? I think he's insane."

In the Ruins

The track has been taken down from SoundCloud but I kept a copy of the text beneath, which I've replicated here.

There was a page torn from Dan Mellor's biography of John Dee folded in my back pocket. I kept it for a passage that I'd always liked, which read, "John Dee could see the workings of the universe. While his contemporaries, charlatans to a man, cast runes and conferred over piles of chicken innards, Dee had only to glance heavenwards to read the future writ large across the heavens. Nature lifted her veil for Dee as for no other man." I knew the feeling. Sometimes in the depths of a comedown, or late into a night's driving with the oncoming lights smearing to contrails, the sky would shudder and, for an instant, I could see the machinery. I was close to that feeling now: London and the blur of jet lag was bringing it on. I walked and walked until the city's rhythms caught in my throat: the impatience and fury, its willing blindness. I stopped for miniatures of Gordon's gin from corner shops and smoked ciggies in doorways that were more graffiti than wall, until the jet lag washed over me in waves and the air began to throb. Propped up in a pissy alleyway I waited for the familiar arc-weld flash. For an instant the sky writhed with information. I stood as still as possible and watched the tangled skein of new constellations appear. The pulse of wi-fi networks and the spiralling tracer shells of mobile data. Dark blimps of state surveillance and the ghostlights of encrypted traffic. Interference. Phase shifts. Everything was transcribed into the air. The smog of censorship and the lightning strikes of Russian malware. Then it was gone, nothing more than a bruised purple on the backs of my eyelids and the sense that every pavement was a rut.

I retreated to a nothing hotel near Paddington. Magic FM too loud in an empty restaurant, plastic cups in plastic wrappers and a view straight into a telesales office. I dozed and surfed, surfed and dozed.

Thank god for the internet and its deep oceans of data. Back in the day finding contact details for three people you hadn't seen in fifteen years would have been some private-investigator-level sorcery, but now by lunchtime I had personal numbers for all of the band, and a work one for Kimi. The question now was which of the three was least likely to slam the phone down on me? Saul was the one with whom I'd left on the best of terms, but that was relative, and he had a vindictive streak that could happily burn bright over fifteen years. Kimi would be trickiest, what with her shields of management and her complicating level of fame. That left Baxter. I'd probably done him the most damage, and technically I still owed him a great deal of money, but he had a sentimental side to him and he might be the likeliest to swallow some kind of redemptive bullshit narrative. I gave him a call.

It rang for so long that I was expecting the answering machine so when he answered, sounding muddled and distant, it threw me.

"Hello, who's this?"

I cleared my throat, I'm not sure why. "Baxter? It's Brandon. Brandon Kussgarten."

He let out a long whistle. "Is it now, is it indeed?"

"In the flesh," I said, and then reconsidered, "Well on the phone anyway." I hadn't planned what I was going to say. I'd been expecting to be on the receiving end of the conversation but he seemed content to sit in silence. "I'm in London, Paddington actually, and I wondered if you wanted to go for a beer."

His laugh came a second too late. "A beer eh? Sure, sure. But I'm afraid I'm not in town at the moment, sorry, I'm in Mali for a couple of days." He was trying to keep the pride out of his voice as he said this. God knows why.

"Christ. Mali? Why would you go to Mali for a couple of days? Why would you go to fucking Mali at all? You haven't gone all Damon Albarn on me have you?"

"It's a business thing, I'll tell you about it some time. Meanwhile, I'll be back on Thursday and we could catch up then if you like. Is this your number?" He read out a string of digits.

"I don't know, it's a new phone."

"Well I'll call you then. God knows what time it is here, I feel like I only just got to bed."

I needed to get something from this call that would keep the wheels spinning. *Downhill, downhill.* "Wait, before you go, do you have a number for Kim?"

Could I sense his interest prick up at that? He certainly sounded less sleepy now.

"Try Universal and ask for Roxy, or call Dark Talent, the number is online."

This might be a fob-off. Him and Kimi were always pretty tight. "Yeah, I have those but I was hoping for a personal number."

"I bet you were," he snapped, but then some humour returned to his voice. "I can't help you with that unfortunately but Roxy's usually pretty good. I've got to go but let's speak on Thursday." He yawned, making me feel sleepy.

"Wait," I said. The moment of truth. If I was back for a while I had to know where I stood. "How's Mel? And Gabe?"

Jump-cut flashbacks: Mel's tattoo stretched taut as she arched her back in front of me. Black-painted nails down my arm. Dressing room beer bottles spinning across the floor. My hands in her hair. I'd had to trawl through his Facebook to find their son's name, I knew he'd appreciate me remembering.

He yawned again. "They're good. Mel went back to school, took her PhD. She's Doctor Moores now if you can believe that. Gabe's fifteen now, got his own band."

I waited. No hint of recrimination. Mel must've kept quiet. I was almost disappointed.

Hotel TV. Worse than that, British hotel TV. Comedians who weren't funny, drama that wasn't dramatic, porn that wasn't sexy. When I switched off the programmes the welcome message remained. GREETINGS MR/MRS ? I propped myself up on the pillows to check something on my phone and the next thing I knew the maid was banging on the door and it was dark outside. I came to with that brief moment of existential angst unique to strange hotel rooms, where you can't remember where, when, or on a particularly bad day, *who* the hell you are. It made me yearn for touring and the day's schedule slipped under the door: a statement that it was someone else's job to make sure you woke up and got on the bus. What I'd give for that level of pampering today.

I checked my phone. One voicemail: Baxter again. He'd had time to process my being in London. His voice was that estuarial drawl that Home Counties kids adopt when they get to London to avoid getting beaten up on night buses, an affectation that had turned into reality for him. "Fucking hell Brandon but I assumed you were dead or something. That was like getting a call from the afterlife. Anyway listen, I've texted you Kimi's number. Sorry, but I had to check that she was OK hearing from you but she is, God knows why. She's playing tomorrow night at the O2 so don't forget to mention that if you talk. And *please* remember about the voicebox, it's a bit of a shocker the first time, but you get used to it pretty quick. See you later on."

Everything felt gluey and gummed up and there was a slow ache working its way through my limbs. The TV was showing the same shows as earlier. The rain had eased and the streets outside had an inviting sheen to them. London looks best after a storm — don't we all?

Here's a phrase I haven't used in twenty years: *and have one for yourself*. A lovely thing, as rusty in my mouth as "pavement" and "lift" but London pub etiquette obviously hasn't changed because the Pole behind the bar accepted it with a serious nod. In the States it was a dollar a drink but that just felt like a loosely applied tax. Here it was more like largesse and I liked that. The pub was populated by a series of lone men in cheap suits who were working hard on missing their trains. I had a couple of pints, a couple of chasers and then phoned Kim from the bench outside. Baxter had been right. I'd heard her voicebox on talk shows but it still came as a shock in real time. I had to remind myself this wasn't a machine I was talking to.

"Hi, is that Kim?"

A moment. A pause like you'd get on an international call.

"Brandon, Bax said you might call."

I had to bite my tongue to stop my go-to pleasantry, *you're sounding well*, from slipping out.

"Yeah, we've been catching up," I lied, "Old times and all that. He mentioned you were playing in town tomorrow."

Another moment.

"What do you want Brandon?" Something in the box's software was overstressing the two syllables of my name, making it come out *Brand Don*.

"Nothing." I sounded guilty, even to my own ears. "To say hi? To see how you were?"

"So," she said. "Hi."

She unfroze a little after that. We talked a while: places we'd been, the few friends we had in common. I told her I'd seen her show in LA at the El Rey Theatre but she never asked why I'd not come backstage. I asked after her dad, hoping he was still alive the last time we talked. We parted on OK terms: her to rehearsal, me to another drink.

It had been a good six months between my hearing about this British singer called Kimi on the radio in LA and realising she was the same person as plain old Kim Balloch, erstwhile Remote/Control bassist. The first time I came across her new incarnation was at a casting call up in San Fernando somewhere. The ultra-specific brief — "at least six foot, grey hair, no facial hair/tattoos, between thirty and forty" — made the audition room a truly terrifying sight: twenty versions of myself, like a malfunctioning hall of mirrors. I tuned in to my neighbours' conversation about this freaky singer with a voicebox and some kind of obscene Japanese outfit who'd been on *Conan* the night before. They talked for a while but it came down, in the end, to LA's two eternal questions: Would it sell? And would you fuck it? They both thought yes, so I filed it away into the mental box of "things I should check out" and then forgot about her. But half a year later, 10pm in a K-Town bar with five TVs on but no sound, there she was on *Letterman*. The famous performance with the dancers wrapping ribbons around her like a maypole, and something about the tilt of her head plunged me back into a Dalston rehearsal room on the night of auditions for Remote/Control's bass player, and watching this girl, tall, but an inch under it being ridiculous, ducking her head through the door with a gig bag on her back. And immediately thinking *please be good please be good please be good* because she had some little kernel of cool, and when she played it was with a kind of rigid funkiness, concentrating hard on the fretboard as a goofy grin spread across her face.

I told the barman to turn up the TV and we caught the last five seconds, her ironic bow and Letterman beaming, "Kimi, ladies and gentlemen, isn't she just something?" After that she was everywhere. Partly it was me catching up, and partly it was just her time, her imperial phase. Little trace of the girl I knew remained. The Kimi whose album was number three in the UK, and who was modelling for Dolce & Gabbana, was aloof and spiky. Of course the voicebox put her at one remove anyway.

I pieced together her story from breathless broadsheet articles and bemused tabloids. In an interview with *Time* magazine she talked about "five years in bands where you didn't breathe fresh air for a minute a day". It was true. The venues, the studios, the vans, the rehearsal rooms, the house parties, the pub meetings: all came with a nicotine smog so ubiquitous that it hardly registered. She'd gone to the doctor with a persistent cough (instantly, automatically I felt a sympathetic scratch in my throat) and was being operated on the next day, with no time even to go home and change. A week later she returned minus a large chunk of her vocal chords. The options then for the de-voiced were grimly sparse. There was sign language, which was elegant but about as commonly spoken as Esperanto, or you could go for one of those Stephen Hawking-style speech synthesizers which rendered you inexpressive and slow. Kimi had other ideas. She swerved the doctors and the medical suppliers and instead started talking with digital instrument manufacturers. She piqued their interest, this stately, earnest girl with her almost-mohawk and dirty laugh, and together they started to build something brand new. It had something of the vocoder to it, but with a subtlety that they'd tweaked over iteration after iteration. It was hard to work out exactly what it was doing when I heard her interviewed. Her speaking voice could be clanky and flat but then the software would turn a cough or a laugh into a pretty, electronic crescendo. On record it was extraordinary. Her voice would often start out nondescript but then, halfway through a track, split and curdle and bifurcate and loop around on itself and rise like a line on a graph from a whisper to a scream, then back down from hard roar of aero engines to the chatter of sparrows.

My emotions, watching her success, ran like this: jealousy, anger, fear, rising jealousy, scorn. The jealousy was simple: she was on *Letterman*, being called one of the most interesting artists of the new millennium. I wanted to be on *Letterman*, being called one of the most interesting artists of the new millennium (and if it wasn't to be me I certainly didn't want it to be someone I knew). The fear was simple too. I'd also seen intimations that Saul's new band, an Ibiza-ish dark trance duo were, actually, whisper it, quite good. I'd ignored those rumours but now an obsession gripped me. The other three members of Remote/Control would go on to have wildly successful careers, leading to journalists making the connection and writing about the band where (nearly) every member had gone on to be a star. I'd be a frontman version of Pete Best, famous for not being famous, a pub trivia question. One night I dreamt an entire *Vanity Fair* article on Remote/Control, complete with family trees, sidebars and unearthed early pictures. The final line was, "Ironically the guiding light behind the band, and the man who broke them up, is the only one not to go on to success in the following twenty years".

Luckily Saul's duo turned out to be one of those permanently lower-league bands whose promises of a bright new dawn always turned out to be false. Kimi too, after her spectacular rise, now seemed to be on a gentle, but consistent downwards slope, destined to be downgraded from First Class to the Business Class irrelevance of being merely "interesting", and Baxter was as invisible as he'd been on stage.

The thing is, I saw my hand in her rebirth. Back in the early days of Remote/Control Kimi was a tangle of worries. She was even insecure about her insecurities. She stooped and lingered in corners as if that would hide her away and she dressed in the most identikit of indie camouflage: hooped fisherman's tops with ragged 501s and DMs. With hair curtaining her face and sleeves pulled over her hands even her mixed heritage was hidden. On our third rehearsal, as I was planning how the band was going to look on stage, I sent Baxter and

Saul to the pub and sat her down. She sat on a flight case, kicking her heels like a kid.

"Look Kimi, you're nigh on six foot, with shoulders wider than mine and skin like suede. You look fucking amazing but you hide it all away and the more you try to suppress it the more it sticks out. And anyway, why are you trying to hide? I mean, you look fantastic."

I pushed aside her fringe, conscious as always that I had to reach up to do so. She had a great face, oval and smooth and unscathed, like a dark version of one of those ruminant Flemish portraits. I pulled out an *NME*. "Look at these fuckers trying to get noticed." We flicked through the pages and looked at the bands. Student types dressed up as anything but themselves: bovver boys, punks, sailors. "You look a million times better than them without even trying, so imagine if you tried."

She nodded dubiously.

"Here's the rule. What are you most self-conscious about? Your height? Your skin? Your weight?"

She almost howled. "What's wrong with my *skin*?"

"OK, so not that then. Your height then."

She gave the tiniest nod. "Well you know what guys are like."

"Fuck 'em. Which guys? At gigs?" The four of us had been out a few times together checking out the soon-to-be opposition, which was just as important as practising as far as I was concerned. The Camden music scene was as inbred and status-obsessed as a country-house shooting weekend and I'd noticed heads swivel at the bar as the self-styled arbiters of indie taste tried to fit her on their social scale. The scene was so white and middle class that a Glaswegian would stick out as unspeakably exotic. Kimi was something else entirely. "Fuck them all. They're terrified of anyone who has an inch of originality. Next rehearsal, heels."

"You're telling me how to dress?" She stuck out her bottom lip but her tone wasn't aggressive.

"Not telling you. Do what you want. But if you're dressing for the plankton that prop up the bar at the Underworld then that's got to be worse, no?"

She gave a grunt.

"Just think about it, OK? And what else? Your hair?"

Her natural hair, which I'd only seen once, was a wild scribble of near-afro but she spent hours every day trying to discipline it into the dead Sixties fringe that was *de rigeur* among the Camden girls. "Set it free." I said.

I never again gave her any kind of direction but I ruled that band like a Roman emperor. If you make 'em scared enough of the thumbs down they'll do the heavy lifting for you. It was just, "Cool shoes Kim," or a raised eyebrow at anything too fucking Inspiral Carpets and they soon got the message.

Of all of them it was Kimi who took the look and ran with it. I've got a picture of us at one of our last gigs (artfully cropped to disguise the fact that the audience would have fitted, and I use the comparison deliberately, in a small lifeboat). Kimi's in side profile, her hair shaved roughly around the ears giving her a kind of artless, floppy Mohican, and her bottom lip juts out as she concentrates on the frets. She's wearing a Vivienne Westwood blouse — vintage they'd call it now — shorts and stockings, and a pair of scuffed white heels, and she looks so perfectly, oddly, right that it gives me a pang of regret for days past (and then I stop myself because regret is the most worthless of emotions. I won't have that shit in my house).

As for the others: Saul had that infuriating model physique and he looked good in anything. He stayed at mine if he missed the night bus home and he'd often pick some old piece of clothing off the floor in the morning and ask to borrow it; invariably it looked great on him. Baxter was a lost cause. The rule was to shove him at the back and tell the lighting guy to pretend he was a mike stand. But Kimi? I looked at her then, on Letterman, the heels like tower blocks and her hair a slo-mo explosion and thought to myself, "I made that".

I was on the wrong side of the ring road around Tower Bridge when the phone rang. It was "someone from Kimi's office". Not her manager, not even the tour manager but "someone". Could be an intern, could be some phone monkey. Yes, she understood Kimi had said that she was available to meet up for a drink. Where could she send tickets for the show? No, I didn't need to come in and collect them, they'd send a bike, and before I could ask anything more she was gone.

I'd not been to the O2 Arena before. The name alone should have given it away as a big deal, as should the passes, which looked like something you'd need to get into a merchant bank. I took the DLR. The front was all window so I let the stage set of the city churn past. I had a companion, a boy of about nine or ten, with a flatly elegant face, who was pretending to drive the train, anticipating every corner with a roll of his shoulders, and I could see Robin in his fierce concentration. He didn't return my smile.

After years of California what struck me about London was the sheer randomness of it all. Blank slabs of tower block sat atop untidy warehouses that bordered Seventies estates that gave way to Victorian terraces that leant up against industrial estates. Every second building bristled with scaffolding and lone churches stood amidst the scribble like lost children. Every clack of the tracks muddled the genre. To the left the streets were dressed for a Jack the Ripper documentary, to the right for a dystopian sci-fi epic. By the time we got to Crossharbour there were five or six people with Kimi t-shirts on, and as we were funnelled towards the gig the throng grew bigger.

It took half an hour to find the VIP entrance. From there on every corner was festooned with signs: catering, production, security, stage. I felt a shiver of envy. Kimi was playing places big enough that you might get lost in them. It took four goes before I found someone who was expecting me — *to see Kimi right? The guy from her old band?* — and he walked me through the building's innards and left me at a section marked ARTISTS ONLY. Fair enough. I pushed through set after set of double doors, like a nurse on the way to theatre, but at the end of the corridor even my AAA pass became useless. A security guard in a headset said *wait here* and it was fifteen minutes before another of Kimi's goons came to get me.

She looks good. Really good, not just photo good. I wondered if she'd had work done. I feel for this generation's female stars: they have their own photoshopped selves to compete with rather than just a younger, sluttier generation. She looked older now, but not old; touched by the hand of time rather than beaten half to death by it, as I'd been. Her dressing room was as bland as you'd expect in a multi-purpose, credit-card-sponsored, almost-out-of-town arena. It could have been the changing room of a recently built leisure centre, or the council chambers of a middling Midlands town. The only exotic thing in there was her. Her hair was choppy and russet in a kind of expensive version of a cheap home cut (or a cheap home version of an expensive look, I couldn't tell). And she had that stillness a lot of tall girls have. I could imagine she'd be invisible to cats and security cameras.

"Hey." Someone was pinning up her dress so I gingerly threw my arms around her. She felt gym-toned. "Looking good."

"You don't look so bad yourself." The voicebox flattened all cadence out of the phrase. It could have as easily been sarcasm as sincerity. "Are you back in London?"

"Just for a bit. I have some business over here, and a couple of recordings to finish that needed the London touch."

"Wanted to add some grey, huh?" Her laugh was as perfunctory as a LOL.

"Yeah, a bit of low cloud cover. Your album sounds amazing by the way." I'd YouTubed a few tracks on my phone and got the gist. "*Love* the title track." I didn't, but it was so deliberately obtuse that it would be her favourite.

"Oh thanks, yeah that was a bit of a struggle actually."

"Really? Well you must have worked pretty hard to get it sounding effortless."

A costume girl, mouth full of pins, orbited her, every now and then appraising her work. "Arms," she said and Kimi took up a Jesus-on-the-cross pose.

"So you're still recording?" Even through the voicebox she sounded dubious.

"Well this is going to be my swansong, after this it's bye-bye music. I'm going to concentrate on acting." I willed the words to be true.

"Really? I didn't think anyone actually did that. I mean, the business might retire you, but who actually turns their back on it? No one." The assistant, taking a couple of quick pictures on her phone, moved round to work on the other side. "Name me a performer, a singer, who has actually, while they still had a following, just said *fuck it* and walked away."

This was new, her pushing back, probing. Later on I thought of Captain Beefheart, but at the time I couldn't think of a good example.

"Peter Green?" I ventured.

She snorted, a sound that bypassed the voicebox and took me back fifteen years. "Yeah, he's a good object lesson. Go crazy, join a cult, lose all your money and then only come back to it thirty years later when no one is interested?"

The assistant stood back and examined her.

"How's your mum?" she asked.

They'd met once at one of the Brighton gigs. I had a sudden recall of my mother, hair wet with drizzle at the station taxi rank, telling me, "Be nice to that girl Brannie, such a bonny thing."

"She died a couple of years back I'm afraid, she always asked after you actually."

A makeup girl went to work on her lips and Kimi pantomimed *wait a minute*.

"Actually, now you can't talk, maybe I can run something by you?"

People worked on her while I talked. She was repositioned: folded into a chair and her makeup done, pulled back up, arms raised so it was like talking to an animated crucifixion. I'd have found it distracting, but she'd developed that blindness to staff that people get when they're a constant presence. My mind flicked to the only time we'd had sex. It was after the third or fourth Remote/Control rehearsal, where, after what I thought was a perfunctory, but perfectly serviceable performance by me, she'd propped herself up on an elbow, looked at me seriously and said, "Well, we won't be doing *that* again."

What would it be like now? I imagined a team around us as we fucked, ministering to her like a Formula One pit crew.

I talked to her about this and that, just babble really, to get the tiresome business of getting used to each other's presence out of the way. There was a tour schedule blu-tacked to the back of the dressing room door. She was due in China in two days so if I was going to reel her in it'd have to be soon. She made her mouth small so the makeup girl could colour her lips with a delicate paintbrush and said, "I have to be quiet for a minute. Tell me something."

"I have this theory," I heard myself say, "that fame has a singularity." She tilted her head an inch.

"Think of all the images of you. The video, the photos, the fanfiction, the broadsheet puff-pieces, the tabloid gossip. Every fan-drawn felt-tip masterpiece, every South Bank show, every Pornhub tribute."

She made a face and the makeup girl scowled at me.

"Add it all together: the time it takes up, that's your figure. Once that time exceeds the time you've been alive then *boom*! Your singularity has been reached. This Frankenstein's monster, stitched together from fragments of your life, is now bigger than you. The image lumbers out into the world, dragging you along behind it. If you get Madonna-big then it's like King Kong, holding the real you in its hand. What do you think, are you there yet?"

She gave me a blank look as someone handed her a sheaf of papers to sign. And then she was patting down her lipstick and the band were wandering in and you could feel the nip of anticipation in the air. Someone turned on a TV screen with the sound way up, so we could see the crowd, and the girls with Kimi's last-but-one haircut pressed up against the barrier, because of course we were too far from the stage to hear the noise but even over the miniscule TV speaker that hubbub of voices made my blood leap in excitement and I pretended not to see her little nod my way to the tour manager, before he was calling out "band only from now on chaps, let's clear the room." And plenty of people stayed: makeup and girlfriends and assorted hangers-on but it was clear my time here was up, so with a quick "Have fun out there" I was gone.

I was yards down the corridor when the tour manager came puffing after me. "Hey, can you hang on a sec?" He disappeared back into one of the side rooms and came out with a pass. "Sorry, bit of a mix up, can we swap that laminate?" He handed me a new pass that read BACKSTAGE. "We've run out of AAAs, sorry — this one'll get you into the party though. See you later."

Back in the arena, uncosseted by my backstage access, it was bright and chilly. From the side I could sense an invisible line about halfway back in the hall. Up until there the punters looked like punters. T-shirted, sweaty, drunk. But after that it got older and balder very quickly. I stood by the sound desk, seeing if there was anyone I knew on the crew, and all around me stood, well, *ordinary* people. Thomas Pink shirts with sleeves rolled up to the elbow. White wine in plastic cups. Some half-hearted clapping along. Lots of texting and selfies.

I pushed forward to see what the real fans were doing. Twenty yards from the stage it was just row upon row of upraised cameraphones and tablets. You couldn't see the stage. You couldn't see the band. Instead you could watch a thousand little Kimis from a thousand infinitesimally different camera angles, moving in perfect harmony. She was caged — hidden even — by her own image. I made for the left-hand side of the hall and watched the show on the big screens.

It was pretty slick. Kimi didn't do much on stage so a lot of the excitement was outsourced to the band and the lights. The stage was backed by what looked like architectural models — blank white boxes in rudimentary building shapes, like one of my brother's home-made cities. But they were lit in a whirl of overlays so that one minute they were lonely tower blocks, three lights out of a thousand on, the next they were temple walls. Then they were a kid's building blocks and the band became giants. It was pretty effective. It had sweet FA to do with the music, but in a shed like this, what does? Most of it was your common-or-garden "look at the size of my budget" kind of thing but with an unmoving Kimi at its centre the effect was quite something. She was the point around which everything turned, the eye of the storm. The band danced and gurned — the guitarist was particularly unbearable, throwing out riffs with the kind of pained expression you'd make lifting a sofa — but it didn't really matter because in a space where nothing was still you were drawn to the only constant thing. Kimi, voice deep in the mix, but far away from any of the noise. It made me ache to be this side of the stage barriers. I missed the power and freedom of being on stage; the way a word or a movement could wring tears or laughter from strangers. Nowhere else, nowhere since had joy been so easy.

The end, when it came, was an anti-climax. "This is the last song we're going to do", some perfunctory *no*s from the audience, and then an encore of her biggest radio hit and the best track on the new record. It seemed like the final note was still echoing as the lights came on and the cleaners appeared with their brooms. By the time I reached the bar the metal grill was firmly down. It took nearly twenty minutes to find the after-show, which was populated by as motley a crew of hangers-on as I'd ever seen. Before I opened the door I was worried no one would recognise me, once inside I prayed they wouldn't. There was a stunted, funereal atmosphere in the room as speakers set in the ceiling played *The Best Of Kimi* and I wondered where the band were. Kimi herself would be lazing in some inner sanctum but you'd expect the fucking bass player to be here, snaffling the free sandwiches and hitting on people's daughters. Everyone was on their phone checking whether anyone they knew was having a better, better-connected time of it.

I was on my way out when my phone buzzed.

WHERE R U?

WHO IS THIS?

KIMI R U COMING 2 THE PARTY?

THOUGHT I WAS AT THE PARTY. IN THE GREEN ROOM
DID ALAN SEND U THERE? NO COME 2 DRESSING ROOM
I grimaced.

HE TOOK MY AAA

HAHA HANG ON

There was a five-minute wait.

MEET US @ STAGE DOOR COME IN THE VAN

Here's another sign of where Kimi's at nowadays — the van was parked *inside* the venue. On the level below the stage roadies were dismantling the set. Doors the size of house-fronts were open to the night air. Outside in the cold, their heads wreathed in icy breath, huddled a group of fans with that sixth sense for where the action might be. The van was idling and I tapped on the driver's window. He took off his headphones.

"I'm going to be coming back to the party with the band." As I said it I knew it sounded unlikely.

He nodded. "Not a problem buddy, just have to wait until they get back here and give the OK, OK?" He closed the window without waiting for an answer and I saw a couple of the waiting fans laugh. They eyed me professionally, trying to work out if I had any more access than they had. A couple of the band came down, towelling hair and rifling through bags. The annoying guitarist went out to chat with the throng while the other two took the van's back seat and jumped straight on their phones. When the guitarist returned he made a wide circle around me.

The fans alerted me that she'd arrived. There was that slight increase in air pressure then a chorus of *Kimi*s. She'd changed into some kind of elaborate African thing with four-inch cork sandals and she spent nearly ten minutes taking pictures and chatting with the fans, as I stood and smoked and fumed.

Finally she swept back, giving me a look that I couldn't read, and said, "Coming."

I jumped in behind her.

The hotel where they were staying was a gas. In one of those Shoreditch backstreets where Georgian townhouses and tatty warehouses co-exist there was a wooden door tucked into a dark alcove. No one knocked but the door swung open anyway and we trooped up a staircase narrow enough to force us into single file. It was shadowy to the point of ridiculousness; if there were any other guests here I couldn't tell. A neat man in a waistcoat popped out of a vestibule.

"Miss Kimi, we watched the show online. Triumphant."

He was helping her out of her coat and she reached out to read the badge on his chest. The voice box clicked into life. "I climbed the Eiger in three hours. Ask me how?"

They had the look of a couple enjoying a private joke. "How, Kaspar? How did you climb the Eiger in three hours?"

He sighed. "I had my puffa jacket pumped full of helium. The walk was so gentle that I barely left tracks in the snow."

Kimi applauded quietly. "Bravo. Kaspar, this is Brandon, an old friend of mine."

He reached out a hand. "Hello Brandon, welcome to At The Sign Of The Magpie."

If, for my many and varied sins, I were to be reincarnated as an estate agent, this is how I'd describe the suite of rooms in which Kimi had ensconced herself. A period front door with a "speakeasy-style" viewing hatch gives way onto a hallway that you could play a decent game of tennis in, lined with Japanese *makura-e* prints. This leads to a living room with the dimensions and general ambiance of a ballroom. Its generous proportions hold a devastatingly tasteful range of furniture: the chairs are Eames and Chippendale, the couch is Beaux Arts, even the side tables are sourced from a Loire Valley chateau. The kitchen boasts a Meneghini Arredamenti refrigerator that could hold a whole cow, a climate-controlled wine room/humidor and a coffee machine that uses up more chrome than a 1950s sedan. (Note, nothing as vulgar as a hob or an oven — this is not a room for cooking.) Next door is the chapel, 1,500 square-feet of reclaimed Portland stone with a wrought-iron mezzanine gallery that originally graced the Bedlam hospital, just a couple of miles from this site. The staircase leads to the bedroom, which doubles as a gallery for some of east London's best new artists and has a dual aspect balcony out onto the Shoreditch streets.

I guessed the whole thing had been created by knocking through disparate buildings that, between them, bore signs of this area's many guises. You could see traces of Hugenot weaving rooms, Jewish tailors, Bengali fabrics and YBA-style shock art. It was a great place for a party. Musical instruments for the show-offs, a kitchen full of booze, and lots of alcoves for the addicts, both chemical and sexual. If I hadn't had work to do I could have done myself some serious damage in there.

A party, like any other power relationship, is a lattice of interweaving forces; you just have to ride them. I didn't sit by Kimi on the couch (too needy) but I didn't head for the groups out in the bedrooms either. Instead I worked an elliptical orbit, wedging myself into arguments with at least three groups of people, more to keep my hand in than anything serious, and I let my circles and Kimi's overlap. It was like those games of simultaneous chess that Adam used to do at exhibitions: walking from board to board, on tiptoe sometimes to see his opponents' pieces, almost vibrating with focus. I was convincing a slow-witted bassist that the Pistols were simply the Stones with all traces of black removed — *"Their Satanic Majesties" for the Apartheid set, innit* — while telling some vegan ding-dong that owning a pedigree dog was worse than eating meat — *Himmler bred dachshunds, that should tell you everything* — while floating a theory that every generation gets the drug it deserves. All this while cocking an ear to Kimi's gang and their discussion about whether some fashion designer's suicide bid had been serious or not.

At one point I went to have a line and sat in a bedroom whose fur throws and tented ceiling made it look like Ghenghis Khan's harem. As I pondered the right way to approach Kimi the bed started whispering. *Sssssilver ssssssurfers on sssilver sssurfboards.* A girl poked her head out, looked fretfully around the room, her neck a periscope, and then hid back away. I got out my notebook and sat on the edge of the bed. The covers were pulled up over her head but I could see a few strands of sodden hair and hear serpentine whispering. *Ssssons of sssilence sssing sssongs of sssadness.* A hand pounced from under the covers and unerringly encircled my wrist. *Sssshew-stone shows you, sssshow-stone shews you.* I left her to whatever trip she was on.

As the night spiralled inwards the herd thinned. The twenty or so we'd been at first waxed and waned. Guitarists invoked early morning flights and got Kaspar to order cabs to Manor House and Hounslow and other such monstrosities. There were walk-on parts for stragglers, hangers-on's hangers-on, friends of friends, enemies of enemies, but by 4.30am it was just me and Kimi and the seemingly indestructible Kaspar. We huddled closer to the little alcove around the log fire. The pool of light it threw felt like a whole universe: a bubble of life and laughter in the deep space of cold, unfriendly London. We took it in turns to put on records, each one feeling like the best thing ever made, at least for the moment. I played Scott Walker and Laura Nyro, Kimi the Knife and ESG. She was casting some website on a laptop and texting as she listened. It was a no-frills chatroom with cam windows open. I kept sneaking glances at her in the screen-light. She looked remarkably fresh-faced; whatever industrial petrocarbons her team had used on her hairdo were holding solid and her makeup gave her a healthy glow. It was fucking infuriating.

"Look, read, watch." She ran her finger under a line of text. I needed my glasses.

"What site is this?"

She made a face. "Narconauts. Shit name, interesting site. It's all these amateur chemists synthesising their legal highs at home. This is where they come to try them out."

"In public?" In a couple of the windows similarly screen-lit faces worked their way wordlessly through some Olympic-level gurning.

"Yeah, to share the knowledge." I followed a couple of faces on the screen. Glasses, T-shirts and low-level facial hair were the fashion choices *du jour*. I watched the centre one for a while, a plump white guy in a T-shirt that read HIGH ON LIFE... (AND DRUGS). He was playing air drums to something we couldn't hear.

"What's fatty's story?"

Kimi expanded his screen. "Dwight, from Melbourne. He's on a mix of 5Me-O, which is a synthetic DMT I think, and some cannabis oil."

"Can we talk to him?"

She checked his info box. "Says so. Hey Dwight? DWIGHT?" He nodded but didn't stop drumming. Kimi leaned closer to the mic. "You good, man? Having fun there?"

"Sure, sure." His voice was bitty through the speakers. "Coming in waves about six, seven minutes apart. Temporal slips, some strobing, a tiny bit of paranoia." He shrugged it off and executed a long snare roll on the desktop. "Fun trip."

I turned away from the screen to speak quietly. "Do they ever OD?"

She made a side-to-side gesture with her hand. "Not too often. They follow guidelines. It's all tapered microdosing, recovery periods, basal temperature monitoring, y'know."

That figured. "There's a lot more health and safety involved in getting wrecked nowadays. I guess that's why the site is so empty then."

She gave me a blank look.

"Oh please, why d'you think people go to air shows?"

We settled into a companionable silence. She'd put on the second side of *Hounds of Love* and it was washing my emotions back and forth. "So Kim, I want to talk to you about something."

The Sphinx would have found her expression inscrutable.

"I'm going to make a record."

She gave me a smile that was 85% pitying, 15% scornful. "Of course you are. What else can you do?"

I nodded. "I know. But I need some help."

She reversed the percentages of that smile. "Of course, that's the other thing you do."

"Not with the music or anything. That's all up here." I tapped my head. "But with the publicity."

She started to roll a joint and looked at me from under the crest of hair. "That's a shame Bran. Because gear, studio time, that kind of stuff I can get you for free. It's a buyer's market out there. But publicity, that *costs*. And, not to put too fine a point on it, the kind of publicity a forty-year-old musical also-ran who didn't get too much attention back when he was pretty and on-trend, the kind of push that would need, I'm not sure you could afford." She licked the edge of the Rizla. "Even if I wanted to help. Which I really, really don't." She fixed a look on me. "Talent's not enough. Everyone needs a story nowadays Bran. And yours is the oldest, dullest story of them all. No offence."

I don't think anyone has ever said "no offence" to me without it meaning the exact opposite. A twist of fury rose up and I tamped it down. Let her have her head.

"I know that. You think I spent the last twenty years not watching which way the wind was blowing? But what if I have a story?"

Her face was blank. "I'd love to hear it. I'm a six-foot-tall, sexually ambiguous singing bass player with a robotic voicebox and I still can't get playlisted. What in God's name have you got?"

How did she make the synthesised words shimmer with scorn? I lined up shot glasses and poured a row of grappas.

"OK," I said, "How 'bout this."

I downed a shot. "So, a washed-up, over-the-hill musical... what did you call me back then?"

"Also-ran." Her smile was the warmest it had been all evening.

"OK. So a washed-up, over-the-hill musical also-ran called Brandon Kussgarten is murdered, gunned down actually, in an east London street, one of the very streets where Jack the Ripper's victims were found. The whole thing is captured on grainy CCTV: Brandon in his suit, the killers in their costumes. Great visuals. Very Michael Haneke."

I fingered the lapel of my Tom Ford herring-bone and took another shot.

"The police find a white-label album on his body. It's a copy of his just-completed, not-yet-released final record."

The room was stuffy and for the first time I noticed fingers of dawn creeping around the blinds. I was parched and I felt the warning signs of a stammer coming on.

"The police appeal to fans, to musicologists. They think there might be clues to his killing hidden in the lyrics and imagery, in the chord sequences even, but they can't understand them."

The joint sat unlit in her hand. Her expression was unreadable. "Deliberately?" she asked, "I mean the clues are purposely hidden on the record? Or is it unconscious?"

There, then, I knew I had her.

"The latter I think. If Brandon knows that he's going to be killed then it takes on the air of a publicity stunt, and we don't want that, do we?" Stressing the "we". Reeling her in.

She twisted the end of the joint and shook it. "Yeah, that'd get some attention. It'd get some attention without my help though, surely?"

Of course I'd considered it. I'd prefer not to rely on anyone else to make this work, but I knew this century's news cycle was unforgiving. If I were to be killed on the same day that Bowie died, or some terrorist atrocity were to take place (just my luck), then I'd need some earthly representative to nudge my story back on track.

"Possibly. Probably. It's not really a risk I'd like to take. If it slipped through the cracks it would be… y'know?"

"A waste." She lit the joint and passed it straight over. "So, what would Brandon want from me?"

What did I want? The unearned slice of her fame perhaps? The part of her success — a very large part — that came from nothing very musical at all, made up in equal parts curiosity, empathy and desire. Payback for a debt she didn't think she owed.

"Not much. A statement, afterwards. Timed for impact. *Sad loss, towering talent, almost unbearable sexual charisma*, that kind of thing."

Again her snort bypassed the voice box.

"Of course if you were to contribute to the record, that might be helpful." Not unhelpful to her either. A quick search had shown that she'd sold out three O2s back in 2004. The gig I saw, a singleton, had been draped upstairs to mask empty seats.

"Vocals? Or bass?"

It was my turn to snort. "Vocals. Any fucker can play bass."

I got up to change the record. The walk from the circle of light around the fire to the turntable felt like a journey from a Norse epic and I heard the far-off hooves of approaching comedown. It was time to shunt those thoughts into a holding pattern and get this done.

She gestured for the joint. "Where's the money in all this? It's not like a dead man can tour, and, unless you've missed it, that's where the cash is nowadays."

"We're not in it for the money though, are we, you and I?"

She shrugged. "You might not be. Money's the reason I'm making records and you're not. You need money just so that you don't need money."

"Well it might get you a front cover or two. And there's the publishing."

"And it's for real? Brandon's not going to pop up and say, 'Hey, that was just a postmodern joke but you should all buy my record anyway'?"

I let the run-out groove do its thing a couple of times before I shook my head. "No pain, no gain." It was the first time I'd thought seriously about this idea, and what it meant. Each word hardened some thought I'd had into something you could hold. A plan. She examined me sadly and then put a finger to my lips.

"I don't want to hear anything more about it tonight. But I promise I'll think about it — the statement, the singing, everything." She looked tired. She said something to herself quietly, like a reminder and I didn't catch it.

"What was that?"

All the amusement was gone from her eyes. "I said that if you can't shine then you might as well burn."

Kaspar materialised from out of the gloom, I hadn't heard the door. He whispered, "Your car is here Mr Kussgarten."

I raised an eyebrow at Kimi. I hadn't asked for a car.

She gave me a look that was almost tender and said, "You still don't know when you're not needed, do you Bran?"

Chapter Three

"Is he for real?"

After so long reading the text, coming back to Rae on the screen was like waking from a dream. The liner notes had caught me up in my brother's logic again. There was something almost hypnotic about his rhythms. The words bore you along so gently that you hardly noticed that what he was saying was nonsense. Visible Wi-Fi networks. Having yourself gunned down to sell a record. It was insane, but it was consistently insane, and his confidence made even the unlikeliest ideas seem feasible. But one look at Rae crushed that idea. She pressed her hands against her temples as if she were holding herself together and her mouth had retreated into a thin line. For me Brandon had been practically a fictional character for the last twenty-five years. I knew him through hearsay and snippets of media. But this was her life: her partner, the father of her son, the body she woke up next to each day. I reminded myself that he'd only been away for a fortnight. And Robin. How could you explain something like this to him? A pulse of guilt swept over me. I'd enjoyed reading Brandon's notes. I liked the feeling of Rae and I sharing something, and I'd read to the end like it was a novel.

I tried again. "He can't be serious, surely? This is just a story." How would it feel walking out of your front door knowing that you would never be coming back again? Waiting for the end: the slam of a car door, your name called across waste ground, masks, guns, your hands in the gravel.

Rae twisted a strand of hair over and over around her little finger until, even over the camera, I could see the tip swell and purple.

"Rae?"

Her lips moved soundlessly and then she looked at me for the first time. "I don't know Adam, really I don't."

I couldn't read her emotion. Anger? Fear? Resignation? I tried again.

"I mean what good is it? To him? Even if this were to come off, and the record were to be a hit, it would just kill him not to be around to see it." Poor choice of words, I know.

Rae shook her head gently, her finger still entwined in her hair. When she started talking again her voice was low.

"Look, obviously Bran's not a selfless person. If he were to somehow have a hit record and front covers and people talking about him, which is all he's ever wanted, then you're right, it would just destroy him to miss it. You can't rub other people's noses in it if you're dead. But…"

She tilted her head back and stared at the ceiling. I could see her neck muscles flutter.

"I think you're underestimating quite how far he would go just to say 'fuck you'."

"To who?"

She spread her hands. "To everyone. To his contemporaries. You can't imagine the depth of his hatred for those guys. While he was writing songs in our garage, or playing 'Thug #5' in some crime drama, they were busy selling out. They were doing corporate gigs and car commercials and reunion tours and dating models and generally living the life he thought he was due. He didn't even *exist* in that world any more, and every year he moved further and further from it. And then this."

She pulled her hair back into a ponytail, distorting her features. "It's not just that his death would be a rebuke to those guys, proof that you could make it without selling out, though he'd love that. He'd have *died for his art*, Adam, imagine how shallow that would make the others look. But also it would transform the last twenty years of his life. He'd become a music *enthusiast*, and for him that was the worst insult possible.

But if this record were to take off then all that would be transformed. He'd be reappraised. All those shitty years would be the raw material for his resurrection."

There was a proper silence then. Rae was lost in some furious thought and I tried to pull her back.

"OK, but even if he did go through with it then something went very wrong. There was no music on the USB stick. There's been nothing on the news. He wasn't even found anywhere near the East End."

Rae blinked as if she was waking up. I watched the tight curl of hair she'd been twirling unfurl.

"Where he died isn't one of these Jack the Ripper places?"

"No, it's miles away."

She looked around herself. "But it can't be coincidence either. Some of it seems right, doesn't it?" She clicked away at her keyboard. "Gunned down… grainy CCTV… the suit, the costumes."

I nodded. "But even if it got a bit messed up, surely it's the most important things that are missing? The record and his identity. Without them this is nothing."

She looked at me blank-eyed.

"Let me go back." I was thinking on my feet. "Let me go back and poke around some more. I didn't know what I was looking for that first time. For a start if there is anyone there who was mixed up in his killing then I'm going to scare the living daylights out of them." I felt a churn in the pit of my stomach. I couldn't stand the silence and the desolate look on Rae's face. "And maybe the record is finished. Maybe it's *there*."

She sighed. "I don't care about that Ads."

But an idea was germinating: find the record, get it released, give the proceeds to Rae and Robin. I heard a far-off chime and Rae looked around.

"Shit, that's the delivery," she said, embarrassed. "No time to cook what with, y'know, all this." I could hear Robin thundering down the stairs, chanting *pizza's here pizza's here pizza's here*.

The three of us ended up eating together. I chipped a microwave pizza out of my fridge's ice-box and we ate and chatted around our respective monitors. I'm not good with small talk but Robin filled every gap in the conversation with a hotchpotch of questions, jokes and stories from school. Rae was quiet though, and a couple of times Robin complained that she wasn't listening. He watched her constantly, checking how his thoughts landed and whether he was making her laugh. And although she was lost in thoughts she reached for him often: to flatten unruly hair or brush crumbs from his shirt or, as we ate dessert, just to hook a little finger around his. She sent him to wash up, but not before he'd whispered something in her ear. She came so close to the monitor that her voice had a fuzzy warmth. "Can he see the model?"

I remembered the few kids at school I'd let see the beginnings of Umbrage. It had never really worked; the city looks like a toy but its beauty is in the way it runs itself, and kids don't like to sit and watch, they prefer to get their hands dirty.

"What would I tell him? I bet Brandon's never mentioned Umbrage."

"Say you built it as a kid? That it's been waiting there all this time? God knows Bran had bigger secrets than that."

I felt sick but I wasn't sure if it was the deceit or the idea of Brandon claiming ownership of Umbrage. I could hear Robin on the stairs again and I nodded at Rae. She mouthed a silent *thank you* and left us to it.

Back before Modelcon 2010 I bought a second-hand endoscope from a Ukrainian eBay store. The idea was that I could check out blockages in the water-pipes that kept Umbrage's fountains and springs running, but the picture quality was better than I'd anticipated. You could run the 'scope through the streets and output the footage — via a spaghetti of interconnecting cables — onto a laptop. Robin understood the idea straight away. It took him all of five minutes to get the feed up and running on their own TV back in Tahoe. He pointed Rae's laptop at it, and there was Umbrage, reflected and reversed, digitised and trans-Atlantic.

I unspooled the endoscope slowly and talked him through the alleyways and chambers, the plague pits and opera houses. We started with one of my favourite places. I crawled under the two decorators' tables that support much of the south-western quarter and started filming inside the council chamber. I built it back in '94 from the shell of a violin that I found in a Ladbroke Grove skip. The f-holes let in sinuous, solid bands of light, thick with dust motes, and I found that the stories of things that had happened there came easily to my lips. I told him about battles both bureaucratic and bloody, of sieges where councilmen were reduced to boiling the leather binders of the Great Books for morsels of protein and of week-long sessions on complex points of ancient procedure.

I threaded the endoscope through the streets around the Chamber, streets that were perpetually in shadow and flanked by blank-faced buildings that housed homesick sailors and lost immigrants who went months without hearing their mother tongue. Robin listened avidly. In the silences between stories, as the endoscope trickled down cobbled alleyways I could hear his breath in my headphones, as comforting as the sea. In a way this was better than having him here. There was no childish running around or stray limbs. Robin, like me, might be best at one remove.

The stories and the streets doubled back on themselves, knitting themselves into something dense and protective. How long would Robin have listened if Rae hadn't interrupted after two hours with her soft, "Enough now"? I could have gone on forever, letting the stories build and intertwine to a soundtrack of the boy's breath and the scratch of the endoscope. He fled the screen with an over-the-shoulder, "Thanks daddy that was awesome," and left me there stranded, the room coming back into focus as Umbrage receded like the tide. My flat was small and stuffy after we'd toured tree-lined avenues and airy chambers; everything was too bright and too real.

I did a couple of chores. The Great Tree bonsai that topped the vivaria looked listless and I found a blockage in its undersoil pipes. Two of the work-barges at Sorent were tangled and I unpicked their tethers with tweezers. All the time I let the Tahoe feed run on the big screen rather than the laptop. I heard Rae come back before I saw her. The soft pad of slippered feet, like a cat. She sat at the screen.

"Thank you for that. Him and Brandon had been butting heads all month and that's the happiest I've seen him for ages. I feel like that would be a better final night together than the one they actually had."

I wanted to ask when she would tell him what had happened, and where it would leave me, but she looked so raw that I resolved to save it for another time. She came closer to the screen and I felt her gaze slip past me.

"Where do you go to?"

"Who?"

"You. Bran. Men. Where are these other worlds you disappear to? I used to watch Brandon when he was at the piano, writing, and I'd wonder 'where *are* you now?' You could call out his name. You could burn down the house. And he still wouldn't notice a thing. I envy that. To be able to dismiss the real world." She made a face. "It's such a luxury."

She looked past me, out at the lights of Umbrage. The windows of the Shade Dorm were light-sensitive so as the artificial dusk took hold their shutters clicked closed one by one. Each sounded like a long-exposure camera shot.

Cl-lick

Cl-lick

I didn't know if Rae could hear it. She kept on talking.

"And then it becomes more real than this world. That other place where records live, and stories and people you don't really know."

More shutters fell into place. A sound like baseball cards in a bike's spokes. *Cl-lickcl-lickclclcl-lick*

"Bran gave it all up. Me. Robin. This place. His friends. His life. Dismissed it all like closing a tab on a browser. Because there was a more important place than this one."

The last shutter closed. A lonely sound. A row of blank windows looked back at me.

"Were we there at all? Were we ghosts? Were we in the way? Where the fuck *was* he?"

Her gaze was somewhere over my shoulder. She didn't sound angry at all.

"Where do you all go?"

I had no answers for her. She kissed the screen absent-mindedly as she stood and then she was gone.

Street lights flicked on across the city. The sound of Umbrage's systems had a drowsy charm, but all at once I didn't feel like sleeping here. The sleeping bag, the instant noodles, the taped-up windows: it felt so claustrophobic after the wide-open spaces of Rae and Robin and Tahoe. I wanted to have something for them next time we spoke.

So instead, the next day, I woke in Brandon's bed at The Magpie. His pyjamas. His toothbrush. I explored the bedroom, trying to feel my brother's movements about the place. Books were folded open on the nightstand. A biography of a musician called Dennis Wilson, a field guide to British birds and a book about molecular chemistry that I couldn't imagine him reading. The drawers didn't yield much: headache pills and hair gel, plectrums and books of matches. I looked again at the long rail of clothes. Nothing in the pockets, nothing in the bottom drawers.

I dressed pretty much at random. Soft wool trousers as wide as a sailor's and an off-white shirt with a rounded collar. Did they go together? I'd have to ask Rae. The bathroom cabinets were stuffed with products but they were all branded with a magpie so I guessed they weren't his. All except a battered white metal tub of hair wax. I examined the lid. Trufitt & Hill, St James'. Two grooves were dug into the wax; my fingers fitted perfectly. I experimented in the mirror until I had an approximation of the hairstyle that I'd seen on the slab. I looked again in the mirror. Me but not me. The clamp in my stomach that had been tightening since I woke loosened a notch. I have to second-guess myself in social situations anyway, examining my responses before I make them, trying to twist them into the kind of thing a normal person might say. It's a form of impersonation I suppose, so the idea of taking on Brandon's personality didn't seem too much of a stretch. If you're not going to be yourself then you might as well be someone you know. I smoothed back a stray lock and whispered to my reflection, "Hi, I'm Brandon." I took it down a notch. "Hi… Brandon."

I walked through the apartment again trying to feel like it was mine. I sat in the music room and tried to make sense of the diagram on the floor. Triangles within circles, words in what looked like Hebrew. Astrological symbols. There were names written around the edge — BAXTER, DILLON, KIMI — but two or three had been rubbed to clouds of chalk-dust. I filled in some of the blurred lines, my hand feeling the weight my brother had used, his confidence. There was noise that tracked through the apartment occasionally. Something like traffic, as if there were an invisible highway running through the air. I'd mentally blocked it out and it took me a minute to realise the phone was ringing. It was Kaspar.

"Mr Kussgarten, I hope I didn't wake you, the motion sensors indicated you were up. Two quick things: I just wanted to check we're still invoicing Miss Kimi for your bill."

Miss Kimi. From the band. I calculated: now I could send the money from the safe to Rae. "That's still the deal Kaspar, yes."

"Excellent," he said. "And Jay is on his way up, I said that was OK."

There was no mention of a Jay in Brandon's notebook. "Oh of course, sure. Did he say what he wanted?"

Kaspar laughed. "It's what you want that matters."

Jay turned out to be a fresh-faced, tiny-eared man, without a hint of a line and busy, sharp features. He had one of those faces you only really see in cities: so thoroughly international that it was almost a race in itself. His eyes were relentless and quick, his hair curled tighter than carpet. If he'd said he was Somali, or Malay, or Israeli I would have believed him. His foot tapped so incessantly that I had to check he wasn't wearing earphones.

"Good to see you man." He shook hands sombrely. "Get myself a Coke?"

"Sure, help yourself."

He busied himself in the kitchen, obviously at home. He found ice, limes and a chilled glass (at which he shouted through to me, "Bruv! You remembered"). He sat down opposite me, took a sip with exaggerated relish, and then started pulling packages from his pockets.

"The TLAs are the same as last time, you said you liked 'em right?" He went on talking before I could answer. "The coke is new, someone I've bought from before but not for a while so we'll have a little taste just to make sure." He winked. "And I'll chuck the Adderall in for free. It's my kid brother's and I can't stand him when he's on it. Little smartarse."

"Oh, yes… that sounds fine," I said. He was cutting something up into two granular hillocks, and then corralling it into long lines. I tried to dampen my nervousness and curl myself into Brandon's actions. He rolled up a note and handed it to me. "See what you think."

I'd seen this done on TV, how hard could it be? I leant in, my new quiff almost brushing the table, and scooted the note along the line as I breathed in. I got most of it up. It felt pretty much like nothing. Slightly cold, slightly chemical. I nodded approvingly.

"Yeah?" said Jay, taking his line.

"Yeah."

"It's not too rough is it?"

I felt an unpleasant, salty drip at the roof of my mouth. "It's very nice."

He leant back. "So that's £350, unless there's anything you need more of?"

The notes from last night were still on the table. I counted them out.

"No, no extras, I'm trying to have a quiet week."

He smiled quickly at me. "I hear that fam. And the passport? That on or off, because it might take a day or two?"

Could I ask what passport he meant? Probably not. Brandon's had been found on him, and if he was serious about dying then he wouldn't have been needing a spare. "Can we put that on the back burner for just now?"

He gave a nod and started packing up. "There was that other thing, my CD?"

I tried to look noncommittal.

"What did you think?"

I thought about possible answers. "I'm sorry Jay, I totally forgot."

Anger flooded his features for the shortest of moments: blink and you'd have missed it.

"Again, fam?" Then he laughed. "It's OK, I know you'll get round to it. Really wanna hear what you think, whether you can hook me up."

I expected cocaine to be more spectacular. Once I'd closed the door behind Jay I monitored my internal state. Elevated heart rate? A little, but nothing concerning. Sweaty palms? Sure, but that was ordinary. It was closer to the feeling of a double espresso than anything else. I reopened the laptop window back to Rae's but she wasn't around. I checked my email. In the end I decided to do some woodworking. Last night Robin had asked me about two bare patches of earth that sat either side of the Coloffy Bay. They were waiting for a bridge that I'd never gotten around to building. I'd tried a couple of ways of spanning the water but they always seemed drab set against the curves and peaks and the little infoldings of land.

But there were a pair of wooden horses on the mantelpiece that kept catching my eye. They must originally have been mannequins for equestrian artists because they could be posed in various ways. They were perhaps as high as a hand, and lacquered to a sheen so deep it was almost purple. Every time I passed them the unbroken curve from tail to back to mane pricked at me. They'd caught Brandon's attention too. In his notebook there was a page of sketches of horses, each one a little more abstract until the bottom of the page was just a simple, fluid line. If you doubled that line — repeated it in reflection — the shape would be undeniably bridge-like.

I whittled and chipped away and used the weights from a set of antique scales in the music room to work as counterbalances. Once I was done the two horses faced each other, nostrils and forelegs touching, with a path of steps running from tail to nose. I imitated Jay, scraping off a neat pile of the cocaine onto the glass table and then used a credit card to crush it into the finest powder. It went down more easily this time and the lukewarm drip at the back of my throat felt like the push I needed to get back to work. Now if you tugged gently on the weights then joints rotated and the horses reared back enough to let the tallest ships through. The next time I looked up it was 6pm. There was still no sign of Rae or Robin so I stretched out on the floor, letting my throbbing back subside, and then sent down for a burger and chips.

After I'd eaten I tried the laptop again. It was a bright morning in Tahoe and Rae had taken the computer out onto the porch. The backdrop looked fake at first, with snow-dusted pine cones and far-off mountains. I half expected bluebirds to swoop down and rearrange Rae's robe. A mug of coffee steamed in her cupped hands. She was flicking between two windows silently but her face was never still; she was rehearsing whole conversations, her lips moving noiselessly through expressions of surprise, laughter, confusion, flitting across her face like weather. It was maybe five minutes before she noticed me.

Her eyes widened. "Shit, how long have you been watching me?" Her hands did their independent thing, tucking hair behind ears, smoothing down her T-shirt.

"Not long, you looked engrossed."

"I was." Her attention drifted back to the surface and her face lit up. "You're back at the hotel?"

I talked her through the morning. Jay and Kaspar and how little I'd found in the rooms. I wished I'd asked Jay about the passport now because when I mentioned it I could see her mind working. I wasn't sure what she was hopeful for. That he hadn't arranged his own death, or that he had? At one point she said, "I'm trying very hard not to take his death wish personally but it's kind of difficult."

I changed the subject. "Oh hey, I did coke." I wasn't going to tell her but there was something so easy about the setting that it felt safe.

She raised an eyebrow. "Did you now? First time?"

"Yes, I'm starting my misspent youth at forty-two."

"So, how was it?"

"Um… less, extreme than I expected. I was going to say that it had no effect whatsoever but I realise I've done a week's model-making in four hours so I might be wrong about that."

"Interesting. Using a coke-rush to do something creative rather than just talking bollocks." The English phrase sounded quaint in her accent. "It'll never catch on."

She pulled the laptop closer so she could look at me more clearly. "So, how are you really doing? Are you holding up?"

"I think so, yes."

"Because I was thinking this morning that I'm not sure if I could do what you're doing."

"What, stay at a five-star hotel and mooch around making models?"

"Seriously though? You're still fine doing this? Drug dealers and deception, I don't think it's what you're used to."

I thought about it. "Honestly, I'm enjoying it a little bit. It's like *Total Recall*. You know, a holiday in someone else's head. I'm Arnie on Mars."

"You're a pretty unlikely Arnie."

"I know, I know, you make a good Sharon Stone though."

There was a silence where we both tried to remember exactly what Arnie and Sharon's relationship had been.

"OK, but if you want to bail any time, tell me."

"I will, but I won't if you know what I mean. Anyway, yesterday with you and Robin was great." My heart was jumping in my chest.

"You're good for him you know. I caught him on the phone telling a friend how amazing his dad's models are."

The idea of my being discussed, even by a child, even under someone else's name, was fantastical. "When are you going to tell him?"

She shrugged. "I don't know. Whenever. I feel like we have enough on our plates at the moment. That's terrible isn't it? I can do it now if you're uncomfortable."

I considered it. I wanted her to tell him but I didn't want this feeling to end yet.

"Maybe not. It's no worse than Father Christmas. But won't it make it harder to tell him later?"

The transatlantic lag made her pause yawn in front of me.

"For me, yes. But I think for him, no. It might even help."

Rae had work to do so she perched the laptop on the windowsill looking out over their garden. I found myself, hands unmoving on another piece of Umbragian hardware, watching the slow changes in the landscape there. A crow worked its way intently across a snowed-in playing field, occasionally cawing in triumph at some piece of insect booty, and giant 4x4s crunched on snow chains between the shops of the main street, but minutes went by without anything to indicate that the image wasn't a screensaver. I swore I could smell ozone and pine. Work, company, beauty: who could ask for more? After an hour Rae gave a satisfied sigh.

"Done, for now anyway." She turned the laptop around and grinned. "OK, I have to let down Robin's school trousers. Talk to me."

Something she'd mentioned before came back to me. "You said Brandon was an actor?" I could see it. There was something declamatory in the way he talked, even as a kid. He delighted in sitting up with the adults when my parents had parties at the house, mimicking the way they spoke, swearwords and all, like a miniature adult, and my parents' friends, drunks to a man, would applaud this spectacle.

"Well when I say an actor I actually mean an extra." Rae said with relish. "In four years he had seven speaking parts, and one of those was cut. The trouble is he started too well. *CSI Las Vegas* had a part for an English rock star who is found OD'd inside a locked and drug-free hotel room. That was his first audition. He was OK too, it's not like the role was too much of a reach and even I could see he had some talent. But after that, nothing. He ended up doing work as an extra but he couldn't help himself — he'd always argue with someone or try to improvise a line — and he ended up even getting blacklisted from that. The weird thing is that he finally got a load of work in 2007, when the actors' strike was on, so he'll appear in the background of all kinds of things. It always freaks me out a bit. I'll be watching something with one eye and out of nowhere he'll be staring out at me."

She held the trousers up and examined them critically.

"The funny thing is that I think he might have been good if he'd got himself some kind of lead role. He could switch personalities as easily as changing clothes, and he could really do accents. If you introduced him to someone then ten minutes later he could impersonate them, and not just the voice, he'd have found some tic or habit of theirs that would just capture them. But he hated being told what to do and that's about ninety-five per cent of an actor's life."

It sounded like she was speaking from experience. "And you?" I asked, "Did you act? Is that what you were doing in LA?"

She tucked a stray strand of hair behind her ear. "The tiniest, tiniest bit. I actually came to LA as a model, but my agent got me a couple of parts. Nothing you'd have seen."

"You were a model?"

She laughed. "You find that implausible, Prince Charming?"

I blushed. "No, god, you totally look like you could have been a model. I mean, you look like you could be a model now, but you just don't seem the type. You're too normal."

She looked mollified. "Thanks. I guess. I wasn't very good. It's hard being told ten times a week that you're not pretty enough. And I hated getting dressed up." She gestured to her outfit — a robe and sweatpants.

The noise swished through the flat again. It sounded mechanical rather than electronic and it had me checking out of the windows for helicopters, but it was something else, something closer. I made a note to ask Kaspar about it.

We sat in silence for a while. I felt like Brandon was doing what he always did: dragging me along behind him. I wanted a way to get ahead of him. "Maybe we should set down what we actually know?"

"Sure, go for it."

"So, that morning, Bran gets up, packs a bag and drives down to San Francisco."

"He was already packed actually," said Rae. She'd moved back into the kitchen and was alternating between me and a saucepan of something steaming on the stove.

"So you knew he was going somewhere?" I couldn't imagine why she hadn't told me this before.

"No, he always had a bag packed. A go-bag. You know the idea?"

I didn't. She rolled her eyes. "There's a whole community of people online who have a bag of essentials packed and ready by the front door ready for the inevitable collapse of society. When we get a black president or gays can get married or mental patients are barred from automatic weaponry. Y'know, obvious signs of the apocalypse. You have to be ready for your new life in the woods, whittling homesteads and hunting the weak, so everything you might need fits inside this one, quick-to-grab rucksack. It was usually medical supplies, weapons, water purification tablets, that sort of thing. Him and Robin both had one actually."

"It doesn't sound very Brandon," I said. It sounded rather creepy and genuinely appealing. Mentally I'd already started ticking off what I'd include.

"It wasn't. He gets antsy if he's out of sight of a liquor store. But I think the idea tickled him. You know how he was about packing light."

"So you didn't expect him to leave?"

She looked straight at me. "Well, I'd learnt not always to expect him home, but no, I wasn't expecting him to… to disappear."

"Do you think it was a spur of the moment thing?"

"I honestly don't know. Silly, isn't it? I've thought about it a lot and I'm not sure what would be worse. That he'd been planning it for months and I was too blind to see the signs. Or that on a totally normal day he could just get up and leave us without so much as a backwards glance."

I thought about the diary stuff we'd read and imagined how it must feel to hear his elation.

"And anyway. If I had known he'd left, then the last place I would have expected him to go was Britain, London even. Although…" she stirred the pot, "he *had* been talking about the band a bit in the month before."

"Was that unusual?"

"Oh god yes. He never talked about his past. You would think he'd been hatched from an egg the day he came to the States. I'd never have known he was in a band if someone hadn't recognised him in a record store once. It was one of the things that attracted me to him when we first met — he didn't seem to have any baggage at all. It was always about tomorrow and the things we were going to do together. But in the last month or so… you know the story about Dillon's remix?"

I didn't.

"OK, once I did know about Remote/Control, then a couple of times a year, when he was very wasted, he'd start moaning about this fucking remix." She gave me a concerned look. "You know what a remix is, right?"

I laughed. "I'm not a hundred, I'm aware of the concept of remixes, yes."

"OK. So they get to remix a track by this guy Dillon."

"A band called Dillon?"

"A guy who was a band, or a band who only had one member or something. Kind of famous in the States but from the same scene as Bran. All that matters is that it was his track that they mixed."

Rae's emotions lit up and darkened her face like clouds. It was hard to concentrate on what she was saying rather than just watching her.

"This was when they'd had a couple of singles out and they we're being talked about as the next big thing. As Bran told it everyone started sniffing around and a major label asked them to remix one of their artists. The original wasn't very good, and that apparently wasn't just Bran being superior, the thing was just trash. So him and the keyboard player — Saul I think — decided to give it a total overhaul. They stripped out the drums, dumped the bass and replaced them with something a bit more modern. But once they started tinkering they couldn't stop. They got rid of the keyboards and the guitars until they were left with pretty much a whole new track and Dillon's vocals. And then they thought, 'Why stop there?' So they gutted the vocals and kept one phrase, this aside from the beginning, one of those fake-studio bits where the singer said, 'Let's do this thing'".

Something about that phrase rang a bell, something from the radio. "I know that track," I said. I googled it in another window as Rae talked on.

"So they submit this mix to Dillon, hoping he won't mind that they've basically erased his track and they get a big fat *no*. Dillon is not amused, but by now Bran doesn't mind the rejection because he's beginning to think that their track, the stuff that he recorded, is actually pretty good. So they call it their new single and start playing it to people. And everyone loves it. The band's been at a low point and then suddenly they have this track that everyone wants. Bran re-records the 'Let's do this thing' bit so they don't get sued and they hawk it around a few places and then they get a call from the record company who say, 'Hey, we played your mix to the guys at NBC and they love it. They want to use it for *Sunday Night Football*'. So everyone's stoked. This is a massive break. They're on this tiny little indie label in Britain but now they're going to have the equivalent of ten thirty-second ads for Remote/ Control every Sunday night on the most watched channel in America. It's all gravy until the lawyers call. They've been sorting the paperwork and they ask Bran why his track is credited to Dillon Marksman."

Rae took a sip of water. There was a kind of triumphant horror to her tone. "It turns out that when they registered the track, or whatever it is you do, the writing credits had been Dillon's because it was a remix of his song."

"But now it's ninety-nine per cent Brandon's work?" I asked.

"Sure, but still a hundred per cent someone else's property. So Bran contacts Dillon to try to get the rights and this sets off warning lights. Dillon asks around and instead *he* puts it on his new record, licenses it to NBC and sells a couple of million." There was a kind of amused wonder to her voice now.

"Didn't Bran sue?" I could only begin to imagine his rage.

"He tried, of course. But the record company didn't care whose track it was as long as they were selling it. In the end he took a couple of grand which was basically to shut him up about it."

"So? What changed?"

Rae tasted a spoonful of mashed potato and added some milk.

"A court case. Another British band in the same situation but more recent, they sued that… who's the gay singer? Keeps crashing his cars?"

I didn't know.

"Him anyway. They did the whole 'even though it's in your name we wrote it' thing and apparently settled out of court for a bunch of cash. The lawyer who won the case was in *Billboard* saying that this opened the floodgates for other bands and Bran was on the phone to him about ten minutes later. He even went to see him in New York."

"And did he have a case?"

"Yes and no. The lawyer guy said that technically the track was theirs but Bran had settled, so it was too late for him. But this other guy, Saul. He never settled. Instead he played in Dillon's band for a while and Bran always hated him for that. *He* could still sue, apparently but he's totally gone off-grid. I know Bran had people over there looking for him, and it takes something pretty big for Bran to even talk to people back in the UK. But maybe he took things into his own hands?" She absent-mindedly fed herself a mouthful of mash.

"OK, he comes here possibly to see this Saul guy and convince him to sue?"

She turned the gas off. "Maybe. But there's no way that the money is from that. These things take forever. And anyway, this record sounds like something he'd been planning for a while. And if he was serious, y'know, with Kimi, then he wasn't going to need money anyway."

"Could it have been meant for you and Robin? For when he was dead?"

She scrunched up her mouth. "I seriously doubt it, don't you? That little speech you read me yesterday didn't sound like someone worrying how we would cope, did it?"

She didn't look particularly heartbroken, but she was quiet for a while. I couldn't square the scene there — the sleepy town, the loving family, her gentle nature — with the Brandon I remembered. I let the silence grow.

"You know it's not you, don't you?" I asked her.

"What d'you mean?"

"He's done this to everyone. He left home this way, left our folks this way. He's left girlfriends this way too." I didn't want to say that this wasn't the first call I'd had like this. The whole getting gunned down by men in Donald Duck masks was a new twist but she wasn't the first ex to call me (though mainly they had, until we spoke, no idea that an ex is what they'd become).

"I know, I guess," she said, "it's just very hard not to take personally."

"How long until dinner?" I asked her.

"Ten minutes?" She called up, "Robin, wash your hands, dinner in ten."

"OK, let me tell you a story."

I told her the story of Laura Sheldrake. I was sixteen and Laura was, I calculated, the perfect girl for me. Out of my league but not by so much that it was laughable. Pretty but not beautiful. Smart but not superior. Friendly but not indiscriminating. I don't think at the time that I gave any thought to the idea of chemistry between us; she just seemed nice, and possibly attainable, and that was enough. My campaign to win her over, seen from the twenty-first century, might look close to stalking: I learnt her likes and dislikes through sticking close to her and her friends throughout the school day. In those pre-Facebook days this was a long-winded process. It took three months of watching her favourite films and listening to her favourite records before I was confident enough to ask her out.

The plan was simple. Drinks at The Ship, the pub in Brighton laxest with under-age drinking (which I'd already scoped over the previous two weekends, buying pints and making eye contact with every one of the bar staff in turn). Then to see Siouxsie and the Banshees at the Brighton Centre. I had no strong feelings about the band one way or the other (besides being slightly intimidated by the singer) but I was confident that their pre-eminent place on her school bag — above even the Cure — meant that she was a fan. Beyond that I had nothing. No expectation, no plans. I assumed that if she said yes I would be thrust into the brave new world of boyfriendhood, a world that I couldn't imagine in even the broadest detail. So I asked.

The hitch: she already had tickets. Of course she already had tickets. Had I not seen the bag? The twist: she'd still love to go for a drink first. Which is how I found myself sitting ostentatiously at the window table of The Ship, Laura clearly on display for any classmate who might walk past, as a girl stopped in the street outside at the sight of me, wordlessly entered the pub, took my as-yet-untouched pint from the table, and threw it in my face.

I'd never seen her before. She was pretty, older — at least eighteen — and quite clearly not finished. She turned to Laura and examined her with disinterest.

"Is this the latest?"

I was too busy wiping myself down to answer so she jabbed a finger at Laura.

"You want to know how fucking far down his list you are?"

Again, she didn't wait for an answer. Whatever it was she wanted she wasn't going to waste any time about it.

"You're behind his girlfriend, his other girlfriend, the girl from Kenyon's who he got pregnant last year, his ex-girlfriend and, if I wasn't just about to tell him to fuck off forever, you'd definitely be behind me."

She looked Laura up and down and turned to me. "Fucking hell, you're losing your touch."

Then she leaned in so close that I could see the brush marks in her lip-gloss, and said, "Fuck off forever Adam."

It was beautifully done. If it wasn't me having the drink thrown in my face I might have applauded. Certainly you could see people at other tables loving the show. I wiped my face, looked at Laura, and told her, "I have never seen that girl before in my life."

"Well she's definitely seen you."

The penny dropped. "Brandon. My brother, Brandon. My twin brother Brandon?"

She looked dubious. She must know of Brandon but I'd not talked about him.

"My *identical* twin brother Brandon?"

"She called you Adam though."

There was that. That was new. I'd been on the receiving end of scenes like this before. The aforementioned girl from Kenyon's for example, or, more frighteningly, a gang of football fans who claimed I'd "led a charge" at them at the Goldstone, but each time a library card had proved I wasn't the brother they were looking for. This one had called me Adam though.

The date pretty much ended there, as you might imagine. She said she understood and suggested we leave early to catch the support band but once we were inside she disappeared and next week at school it was as if we'd never spoken.

The drink-throwing girl was of course one of Brandon's. The name change, he explained the next day, had been because she'd been warned off him by some well-meaning friend, so when they'd met at a party he just used the first name that came into his head.

Still today I'm wary of strangers. Once in a blue moon I'll earn a double take and I'll know something bad is coming. Usually a rant. Or an accusation. Or a demand for child support. Once, memorably, a fork jabbed in my arm. I've learnt not to try to explain. I simply take it and walk away and add it to my brother's tab.

I'd told that story so many times that it came out automatically, but it was fun to watch Rae react. It was like she was at the cinema. She laughed at the funny bits, covered her eyes when it got embarrassing and tried to look sympathetic at the end (though she obviously found it hilarious).

There was a faint noise and, still laughing, she said, "Oh Lord, one second."

She disappeared from view. Over the speakers I could hear the bubbling of the pot and a bird singing outside. When she returned she was hand in hand with Robin.

"Look who's finally awake," she said.

"I wasn't actually *sleeping*. Just thinking. With my eyes closed," said Robin, heading straight for the fridge. "Hi daddy."

"Hi Robin. Your mum was telling me about your go-bag."

He loomed into view, his mouth overflowing with biscuits. "Wanna see?" he said, spitting crumbs.

"Sure."

He was gone for a couple of seconds and then hauled a rucksack onto the table in front of him. He undid the clips at the top, still chewing away, and pulled things out at random, pressing them blurrily against the screen: a couple of comic books, a compass, a pair of broken binoculars. There was a Meccano set still in its box, some Top Trumps and a Russian fake-fur hat with a plastic picture of Lenin on the crown.

"Wow, you're pretty prepared," I told him.

"I guess. You're supposed to have knives or a crossbow but I'm too little. And I put a load of food in there but Mom took it out."

Rae's voice came from somewhere over his shoulder. "Because you had sandwiches in there not even wrapped, and cake and fruit and you left it there for weeks. It was beginning to smell."

"You're *supposed* to have food. It's what it says online, in case all the shops are gone or everyone's become a zombie."

Rae poked her head around to look into the screen. "See? See the ideas it gives them?"

Robin didn't look too distraught about the possible dawn of an undead apocalypse. I tried to help. "Your mum's right about the food Robin, if it went off it might attract bears."

"And that's why I should have a crossbow," he said, with an air of triumph, and vanished from view.

I could see Rae's back shaking with laughter as she dealt with the stove. "Never argue with an ten-year-old."

"So what now?"

Rae pulled her hair back and fastened it with a band. "Well, the people there at the hotel, were they surprised to see you?"

I considered this. "No, not at all. They did have some time to prepare themselves though but the room looked as if they were expecting someone to come back to it. They had messages for me and everything."

She nodded. "I guess go through them? Who contacted you?"

The messages were in my coat pocket. I took them out and read the names. "Baxter, Saul, Tony, Baxter again, Tony again, Phil, a couple of clothes shops, Baxter again, Saul and a car rental place. Nothing interesting, I read them."

"No girls." She looked quizzical. "You aren't censoring for me are you?"

I angled the messages towards her. "I'm reading them just as they're written, look?"

"OK. I guess there's one obvious thing."

Was there? I couldn't see it.

"No Kimi. The others have all called. But not Kimi. Maybe she wasn't expecting you home?"

Rae's eyes flicked back and forth as she was reading something written on the air. "First up, I think you should make sure they don't know that you're back."

"Tell the guy downstairs not to tell them? What reason would I give?"

"You could…" She started and then smiled. "It's Brandon. If he asks why, tell them it's none of his fucking business. That *is* what he'd do."

She was right. I could hear that sentence from his mouth with a drawl of pleasure. I tried it out. "It's none of your fucking business."

She shuddered. "Worryingly accurate."

I dialled Kaspar. "Hey Kas, if anyone calls I'm still away on my lost weekend and you don't know when or if I'll be back."

"You're still away, I don't know when or if you'll be back."

"Thanks Kas." I went back to the screen. "OK, what now?"

"Call them and listen to how they react?"

I wasn't sure that I was the best person to do that. I have a hard time reading other people's intentions and moods, or so I've been told. "I don't think I'd be great at that. How about speakerphone?"

"Totally. I was already feeling bad about making you do this alone. Do we start with Kimi?"

I thought about it. "No, let's start with Baxter. He seems the least likely to be caught up in all this and I think I might need to be eased into being Brandon." I was already sweating at the idea of pretending to be him. With the staff here it had been fine, they'd made assumptions, and I'd gone along with them. This was deliberate deception though.

We set up the speakerphone right by the computer monitor so Rae could hear everything. "Here goes," I told her, and she crossed her fingers on the screen.

He picked up after a couple of rings.

"Baxter, it's me, Brandon."

There was no pause before his rush of words. "Where have you been? Actually don't answer that, I'm sure I don't want to know, but you really can pick your times. Have you been watching the message boards?"

I was instantly out of my depth. "No," I made a face at Rae, "I've been pretty busy."

"Well you should. I thought about it and instead of announcing I'd found this thing in a yard sale like I said, I thought there might be a more subtle way of doing it. So I contacted Frank Isaacs." He paused there and I surmised I was expected to know who that was.

"Good thinking," I said.

"I know, right? You know what a gossip he is. I did this whole spiel: found something at a library auction, probably nothing but if it is what I think it is then it's the find of the century blah blah blah. Told him I needed someone with impeccable credentials to have a look at it, flatter flatter flatter, and so on."

"Great," I said.

"Yeah, but he got super excited and he's dropping hints everywhere. I've got *offers* Bran, serious offers, and we don't have the fucking thing, do we?"

Rae's look was as blank as mine.

"I guess not."

"So, when? Is your guy ready?"

I gave a hopeless look towards Rae on the screen. She scribbled YR BRAN TUFF IT OUT on a piece of paper.

"No, he's not ready. Don't fucking hassle me Bax. He'll be ready when he's ready."

He sounded anguished. "But it's so much money. Isn't that what you wanted? What we wanted?"

"Sure, but I won't be fucking hassled, especially by you Baxter." I had no idea why I'd added that.

"Fuck, I know, sure. Look, please ask him to hurry. It's ready. Six-figure ready. I'm still coming to yours tomorrow, right? I've got a couple of things you'll need."

I grunted. I wanted desperately to be off the phone. "Sure. Tomorrow. See you Bax," and hung up.

There was a tightness in my chest. Impersonating Brandon physically pained me.

"Way to go!" Rae was cheerleader-bright. "The first conversation's always going to be the hardest and I think you were suitably asshole-ish to pass. He sounded properly told off, don't you think?"

I did. He'd tucked away his anger pretty quickly.

"What d'you think he was talking about?"

I'd been winging it so hard that I'd barely taken in a word. Rae fiddled with something off-screen and then played the conversation back.

"Something from a yard sale that's worth a ton of money? He mentioned a record too, could it be the one he told Kimi about? Though they seemed agreed there was no money in that." She played it again. "Who's Frank Isaacs?"

"No idea. It sounded like someone he assumed Bran knew."

"Wow, you were convincing." Her fingers flew across the keyboard. "Isaacs, Isaacs, there's a load of them. Baseball player? I don't think so. Academic? Oral surgeon? How about this one?" She slipped on a pair of reading glasses and I caught her glancing to see if I was watching. "Frank Isaacs is the author of *Teenage Genie — The Strange and Beautiful World of Brian Wilson.*"

I gave her a blank look.

"Brian Wilson? From the Beach Boys? Oh god Brannie would have killed you. He was obsessed, totally. Knew everything about him."

"So, could it be something of his? Something rare?"

She thought for a while. "I guess, maybe. A record? But what do they need Brandon's guy for? And more importantly who is Brandon's guy?"

I read through a couple of Beach Boys web-forums but there was nothing that seemed to come back to whatever Baxter had been talking about. Robin had reappeared, sitting watching TV in the background, and Rae moved onto other chores now. I watched the effortless elegance of her hands, like two creatures independent of her, straightening, smoothing, tightening, stroking. They were never still, moving across Robin and his possessions — lunchbox, backpack, duffel coat — like an endlessly economical language. A language with a million words but each one saying *I love you*. I felt a jolt of desire. Not for her, or at least not just for her, but for their life. *I want*, I said to myself, words I never say. *I want, I want, I want*. I wanted to keep watching but the alarm buzzed on my phone. Umbrage needed attention.

On the tube something pulled at me that I didn't recognise at first. An undertow: like homesickness but not for home. As we rushed beneath the city — Farringdon, Holborn, Bond Street — it grew stronger. A tide tugging at my depths, calling me back to The Magpie and the big-screen link to Tahoe. At home, Umbrage looked flat in the grey afternoon light — just a model for once. I pulled out The Book and tried to write some magic back into it but everything I wrote petered out. I wished Robin were here to see it from another angle or that the city's crooked backstreets were illuminated with The Magpie's crackling energy. I made tea and toast and watched the transport system make its circuit, always back to where it began. The wires of the blender motor hung down. It was still plugged in — one press of a button would be all it took to start the earthquake up again — but it felt petty somehow. Upheaval and destruction; instead I saw Rae's face as we read Bran's description of his leaving. And then the idea was there, unexamined but correct, right there in my mind. I called the hotel, holding the shape of Brandon's mouth clear in my mind. "Kas, daaarling, I was wondering if you could arrange moving a model for me."

"Shouldn't be a problem. Her name? Address?"

It took me a second. "Not that kind of model, unfortunately — this might be a little trickier."

It took me nearly twenty-four hours to get Umbrage ready for transport. As the city had grown and taken over more of the flat I'd had to make it portable so that districts could be reconfigured. The plumbing and electrics were built into the underside of the land and I had detailed technical drawings of how they fitted together.

While I slept Kaspar had rounded up a team of movers for me. They were a gaggle of architecture students — little more than unpaid interns really — at one of those huge practices that employs a thousand men in complicated glasses to build airports and skyscrapers. They were at home with large-scale models, but I got the feeling that this was a nice change of pace for them. They scurried around the room at The Magpie, quietly conferring with each other as they reassembled the city around the staircase in the music room. When the first level of supports had been fitted I got Kaspar to send up pizza and we sat among the struts and ate.

"We did the model for a whole planned city in Northern China a year back. Ten thousand housing blocks, arenas, malls, bridges. The whole thing was wired up for night-time too. A lot bigger than this but nowhere near as much fun."

The guy talking seemed to be their leader, or maybe just the mouthiest of them. He was leaning on a plywood plinth that they'd made for the Dread Palace of Psma. They'd reconfigured the huge new-town sweep of the Huslings, where the majority of the city's residents lived, into a comma-shaped slope that wound its way around the carved posts of the staircase. Most of Danaan, the sacred quarter, was relocated up in the balcony itself and the stained glass highlighted different locales throughout the day in suitably religious ambers and purples.

While they worked I played "First Footprint" again through the big speakers. I'd taken to listening to it over and over, letting it seep into the walls of the apartment. I still couldn't quite hear the beauty that Brandon and Rae found in the music, but I'd grown fond of it. One of the students, a shaven-headed boy in a jumpsuit, stopped and listened for a while.

"Pretty. Is it one of yours?"

The "no" was on my lips before I thought about it. "Yeah, just a demo though."

He listened, eyes darting between the twin speakers. "The quality's pretty good. SoundCloud?"

I remembered the name from the google search. "That's right."

He was over by the laptop. "Can I get the link?" he gestured.

I nodded and he opened up the page and wrote something down in a notebook. "Just one comment? That's a crime. Hang on, let me add something." He typed away and then gave me a shy smile. "Right, back to the world of dreams, huh?"

When he was back in the main room I went to see what he'd been talking about. It took me a while to understand the set up, but underneath the song's waveform there were two square icons. I clicked on the leftmost one. It was a picture of the student, black and white, nicely lit, with a time-stamp and his comment — *beautiful track, beautiful man* — and a winking emoticon.

I looked back into the main room but he was crouched over one of the easternmost guard towers, an oxyacetylene torch spitting in his hand. I tried the second icon. A black square for a picture and one line of text. "Really? This is worth dying for?" It was dated nearly a week ago.

I texted Rae CAN YOU COME TO THE SCREEN? and she was there in seconds. I showed her the comment and she was silent for a second. Clouds formed on that pretty forehead. She typed again.

"The commenter? They've commented on another SoundCloud track, look. Click through. Different song, same comment. Oh. And there's more text."

I did as she said. A page opened up with another song, another waveform. Malevich was the artist's name, the track title "Mythical Beasts". And in the track description, a link. I opened up a second tab as the track began to play and the link ushered in page after page of raw text.

Mythical Beasts

This is a copy of Brandon's text. It starts and finishes halfway through a sentence, as if it had been cut from some larger piece. One paragraph in the middle was repeated... I've cut it back.

...waking up to a smatter of construction noise and rain. My feet hung out from the bottom of the bed and the furniture looked like a child's. In the bathroom I risked a look in the mirror. Me and my reflection: now there's a broken relationship. Irrevocably broken (as we learnt never to say at relationship counselling). At least when I was young the mirror and I had some laughs. Sometimes we argued, especially after a long night, but we always made up. She'd send me off into the good night with a spring in my step and song in my heart.

But now we can't stand each other: *look what you're doing to yourself, don't you care how I feel?*

"Let's start again." That's what I wanted to say, as I took it all in. The eggy pouches under ruined eyes. Blotches and abrasions. The downward drift. Sandtraps and deep rough.

"Let's start again, darling." Of all life's tricks the ageing process is surely the nastiest. It should be the other way around. When you're young you have everything — that's when you could afford to look like a bombed-out city. It's when life begins to crumble that it'd be good to have dumb good looks to fall back on.

Last night's conversation with Kimi was still with me. I examined what I'd proposed as if it weren't my life at the heart of it. It still made sense. Before the show I hadn't known exactly what I was going to say to her, besides floating the idea of some swansong record. But the gig had bored me. Worse, it made me feel like a fucking music critic. *Four stars out of five. Triumphant return to form.* Her music was dragged along in the wake of a relentless business logic: spring was the perfect time to sell the act to summer festivals, so new material would have been ready by March, whether it was any good or not. The setlist never left you stranded more than two songs from a hit. The merchandise was a tasteful collaboration with Christopher Kane and the catering was vegan. I wanted to do the exact opposite of what she was doing. Something brutal and pure and final and complex, that couldn't be chalked up to greed or ego because I wouldn't be around to see it. I thought about a couple of my more recent songs through the prism of my murder. How would they sound as messages from beyond the grave? Some tracks couldn't handle the increased gravity and imploded. That was fine, it proved they were weak. But some did the opposite: they blossomed under the pressure and swam with double and triple meanings. Coal became diamonds.

A hint of tune scampered around my head. Those dream-born melodies are easy to lose. A stray song on next door's radio or thoughts of the day ahead can wipe them right away; it's like having some kind of skittish animal in the room. I hummed and picked out notes on the laptop. First the melody, then the chords; trying to catch the interplay of sadness and joy.

When I had a version of it — not the spun gold of my dream-song, but I've learnt not to expect that — I tried the simplest, four-on-the-floor beat behind it. Too insistent. I rolled the treble off, until it was something heard at a great distance, from behind thick walls. Once it was suitably amniotic I sang snatches of lines I'd written in my notebook. HEAD SHOTS. ONE FOR SORROW. DEAD BEATS. Phrases snagged on certain rhythms and unravelled, changing chords coloured the words, stories peeked out from nowhere. I sang and edited. Cut a section that didn't work. I took a break, had a line, a drink, and then laid it down in one take. I'd listen properly tomorrow.

Downstairs. The lobby was empty bar a be-headphoned cleaner pushing a hoover about. I waited at reception with the tune rattling around my head until I got someone's attention — a crewcut Indian guy in a too-tight waistcoat.

"Can you recommend a good pub nearby?"

He looked at his watch. "The bar here will be open in half an hour."

Together we looked at the drab section of lobby that was designated "bar". Four stools in front of a long cupboard with a locked, roll-top blind covering it. Three screens showing daytime TV.

"I don't think so, do you?"

He pursed his lips. "Plenty of pubs around here." He considered them. "All the same."

I only phoned Kaspar to ask if he knew of a decent place to drink in the area, but the pleasure that my call appeared to give him sent an idea spinning.

"Mr Kussgarten. Lovely to have your company last night. I've been thinking about what you were saying about Hockney and Warhol all morning."

A good concierge is like a good hooker — technique trumps sincerity — but Kaspar seemed to have both. I must have been wrecked last night to try to talk about art though.

"Are you well?" he asked.

"Yes, fine. I was wondering whether Kimi's apartment is going to be free after she leaves?"

I could hear music playing in the background.

"It is yes, she's got one more morning here, might you be joining us?" The guy was *good*. The note of hope in his voice sounded almost genuine.

"I am, it's a beautiful space."

"And for how long would you be interested in?"

I needed to see Saul and Baxter. That would be a couple of days. And the other thing. I'd need a gun, some watching time, a certain kind of man. "A fortnight I think."

He didn't pause. "That's certainly possible, would you like me to hold it for you?" He sounded positively giddy at the thought.

"Please, how much is it a night?"

"A fortnight would be £11,000."

Fucking London. Think of a number then double it. I tried to sound unconcerned. "Good, OK."

"Do you want me to send the car for you and your luggage?"

I had so much to do. "I'm not sure I have the time to do the move," I told him.

"You don't need to be around for the heavy lifting."

I laughed. "That's the story of my life Kaspar."

I was keen to keep moving — *downhill, downhill* — but my emails to Saul had gone unanswered and he had no truck with mobile phones. I texted Kimi to see if she had a way of reaching him but she'd never needed to get hold of him in a hurry. One bit of news though. When I told her that I was taking her old room she said I could hang on to the recording gear that she'd had installed there.

"I had a guy coming round to pick it up today but it'd just go into storage until we're back. You could use it for your 'comeback record'."

It ought to be impossible to make a software-created voice drip with sarcasm but she did a pretty good job of it.

So I went shopping. Twenty years in California had led to me letting my sartorial standards slip a bit. My rule in Remote/Control was written on every band communique: NFS. No. Fucking. Sportswear. It offended me to see those fucking tubs of lard sweating about the place in their Nike trainers as if the uniform did the work for you. I used to tell Baxter, who had had a penchant for shell-top trainers and all that three-stripe nonsense, "If I see you dressed in that gear doing anything but jogging then you're out of the band. (Pause). And if I see you jogging then you're out of the band anyway."

I headed to Mayfair to reinvigorate my tainted-by-the-Yanks wardrobe. People say that we don't have a service culture in Britain, that only in the States do you get genuine warmth and interest from your retail drones. That might be true in fucking Uniqlo, but if you look like you might drop a couple of G on a pair of shoes you'll get all the lickspittlery you could desire. I went to St James for the bespoke costumiers with their discreet crests above the door, and the bell-pulls to get in and chauffeurs idling their Maybachs on double yellows while the kid played Angry Birds in the back seat. I spent the afternoon being measured and calibrated and came home with the promise of a whole new wardrobe by the end of the week. (The usual three-to-four month waiting list is, like everything, just a matter of how silly you want to be with your money.) I paid for everything with cash. You can't beat the physical act of handing over your money — seeing it depleted brings home the alternative ways it could have been spent. Next month's Tahoe mortgage money didn't even cover the price of one shoe at Lobbs. The money Rae and I had put aside for finally having the roof fixed *almost* paid for a bespoke jacket. When the world is coming to an end you have to get your priorities straight.

Kaspar texted: the room was ready. It took the cabbie three goes to find the hotel again, it didn't seem to register on the sat-nav. Kaspar was in the lobby when I returned. "I've had a bath drawn in your room and it should still be a good temperature. If it's not I'll send Toni up. No messages for you. We'd normally do your room acclimatisation straight away but it can wait until tomorrow if you'd prefer."

This sounded like some weapons-grade nonsense. "Room acclimatisation?"

"Yes. Digital availability profiles. Atmospheric texturing, scent and sound. Privacy gradients. It sounds like bullshit I know but I promise it's worth it."

"You're the boss. Give me an hour and come knocking."

The bath was fine: a sunken thing the size of a paddling pool beneath a skylight illuminated with that particular blend of blue and black that London does so well. I had a Scotch from the bar and worked my way through a couple of ciggies. I'd only been in my bathrobe a minute when I heard a knock. I trailed footprints on the parquet and let him in.

"Right, first things first, the bar. What brands do you like?"

The forest of bottles was that colour palette that sets an alcoholic heart aflutter: smoky green through tawny amber with the occasional rare gem of a ruby or emerald.

"It's fine as is Kas. I'm going to enjoy exploring your choices."

"OK. Room service is bespoke so you can't really go off-menu. If there's something that you think might be hard to get out of hours then try to let us know during the day. Anything you have a taste for?"

He had that British art of making almost everything he said sound slightly filthy.

"I haven't had a decent curry for what, twenty years? Could I get a proper curry-house chicken dhansak in for this evening please."

"Of course. Poppadums? Cobra?"

"Yeah, the works. I want to be able to smell the flock wallpaper on it."

"I know just the place."

He waited. He knew there would be more.

"Other diversions?" I wondered if my reputation had preceded me at all.

"We have an in-house doctor for anything you might need a prescription for, anything stronger is off limits however." He smiled. "But on a completely unrelated topic a gentleman called Jay may pop by later. He's certainly worth knowing. As for company, there's nothing we could do in-house of course but the room phone is run via an outside algorithm. You may find something of interest there. Now, privacy. Who are you at home for?"

"If they call?"

"Yes, who gets passed on, who gets your mobile number, who gets told we've never even heard of you?"

"It's been twenty years Kas, anyone who wants to talk to me, that's fine. Give it a couple of days and I'm sure that'll change." There was plenty of time to make new enemies.

"What about environmental controls?"

"Like what? Air con?"

"No, we leave that to you, though it's set to Californian resident as a default. These are more specific aural environments designed to enhance your personal spaces." This was his catalogue voice.

"Rainforests and seashores and shit?" I might as well have stayed in California if this was the kind of new-age tat that had infected London.

"They do that kind of thing, if you like, but generally those things are too... too intrusive. Try this." He pushed at a button and dialled something in.

Nothing happened. Or at least it didn't seem to. Then I caught a low buzz and what might have been wind.

"Is that it?" I asked.

"That is…" he read from the control, "the moss garden at Kyoto, recording starting at 8am."

"Does it get more exciting?"

"Not really." He scrolled through. "It's popular though. Technically it's sonically interesting because the moss makes for a very specific kind of aural decay; it's like being in a park if the park had shagpile carpeting. You sometimes hear water — I think it's carp going for the water boatmen — and the monks do some Buddhist chant thing but that's a good eight hours away."

"It's not a loop then?"

"No, well, it repeats after twenty-four hours. You can synchronise it to GMT if you want."

I couldn't hear anything from the speakers but there was a new calm to the room.

"What else?"

"They're not all so subtle," he said, flicking the wheel. "I love this one."

We were instantly, unmistakably in a train station. Announcements, wheels on cobbles, hushed hubbub. I felt my heart beat a little faster. "That might be a bit much Kas."

He nodded. "You might like this one."

The air in the room seemed to tense up. Familiar and alien at the same time. "Yeah, leave that one on, what is it?"

"Deckard's apartment from *Blade Runner*."

Once he'd gone I got to work on Kimi's recording gear. I tried adding some vocals to "The First Footprint in Fresh Snow" but everything sounded top-heavy. Fuck it. I'd call it a mood piece, stick it at the beginning of the record. Because now I have a plan. I have a place and I have a plan. I'll make a record and someone will die.

The phone was an old rotary thing with words where the numbers would usually be. It was the old magpie rhyme: the finger hole where the 1 would be read SORROW, the next JOY, and so on.

I dialled 1. It was the weather forecast, a prerecorded thing. I switched it off after the phrase "Amber Weather Warning". Spring in fucking London.

I dialled 3. A woman's voice: colourless, international. "Hello sir, how can we help you?"

"You know, I'm not quite sure, what would you suggest?"

"Well Taylor is *very* popular, and if you've been away for a few years she has a lovely British accent."

I laughed. Kaspar was *quick*.

"Surprise me." I thought for a bit. "No blondes."

"As you wish. In two hours."

Jay arrived while I was drawing on the music room floor. He had one of those unplaceable urban faces. His hair was short at the sides and militantly slicked back but still retained a cartoonish kink and green eyes popped against the suede of his skin. A spatter of freckles made him look young, a bob-a-job drug dealer. His accent was straight-up London wideboy: that lazy, sub-patois code as much a badge of his profession as the drawl adopted by airline pilots. I got him a Diet Coke while he pulled up a screen on his phone.

"OK, your obvious stuff — brown, white, pills — can be here in an hour. Same with any kind of puff. And the TLAs we're getting are off the hook."

I'm always interested in advances in pharmacology. "TLA? New to me."

He grinned. "Kind of an arms race between the chemists and five-oh. Our guys tweak MDMA until the molecules are different enough to make 'em legal again. Police find 'em, check 'em and illegalise them. We do some more tinkering. It's evolution yeah? The thing is, they all have these initials: AAX, AAY, ADJ and I can never remember them."

He gave me an expectant look.

"So?"

"So, TLAs — three-letter abbreviations." He snapped his fingers triumphantly.

I gave a polite smile. "Well it'd be rude not to. Can I ask what they actually *do*?"

"Different stuff. Euphoria mainly, plus some oil on the old mental gears. This lot is interesting though." He pulled out a plastic tub and rattled it.

"New batch. Supposed to be quite clubby, y'know, but it kind of amplifies beauty. Had a client who spent two hours just looking at the same flower. Music is fucking nuts on it. Don't go to an art gallery, you'll pass out."

Dealers rival estate agents for overselling their wares but what the hell. I took the tub. I had a ton of sleuthing work to find Saul. "How about Adderall?"

"Sure, coupla hours though, is that OK?"

"Yeah, I don't need to concentrate yet."

He laughed and stepped into the other room to make a couple of calls.

Business completed, he relaxed a little, taking in the place around him. "Bare nice fam, first time I've been in this suite. Kimi said that it was pretty nice but it's even better than I expected. What do you do then?" He looked at the stacks of books and drawings. "Writer, yeah?"

"I'm a musician. Well I was. Musician/actor/wastrel, at the moment leaning towards the wastrel portion of my oeuvre."

"I hear that. What kind of music, something I might have heard?"

Even twenty years older and four shades whiter he wouldn't have heard of Remote/Control.

"Jazz," I said. That usually killed this kind of conversation.

"Maaaaate!" he drawled, flicking a fist towards me, "that's *my* music fam. What kind? Bebop, Acid, Miles?"

Hoist by my own petard. Time to shut this down.

"Minimal ambient."

He nodded his head sagely. "Sounds intense. Who does your PR?"

I gave him a look.

"Because," he continued, "I do all that shit. SEO, social stuff, game your presence, y'know, automated SoundCloud plays. Here's my card."

A dealer with a business card — London, don't ever change. I took it: Jay Scarlett in Edwardian script and about forty different channels on which to get hold of him. He looked around once more. "I'd love to play you some of my stuff, get your opinion some time."

I gave as neutral a nod as I could. He was up, admiring the turntable.

"SRM Tech Athena. Proper."

He rifled through the collection and pulled out a Shuggie Otis record. "Nice." He spun the disc between two fingers. "Not even the reissue. Loving your taste brah. Can I put this on?"

"Another time Jay, I've got company coming over."

"Aw, you should have said." He gave me a sly look. "Want something to help the party? Viagra? MDMA?"

I wondered quite how old I looked to him.

"No, I'm good Jay, thank you for your concern."

"Anytime, anytime." He yawned and said, "Anywaaaaay," as if I'd been keeping him there, "Better get on. Good to meet you." His fist-bump was replaced with a handshake, possibly in respect to my advanced age, and in a slouch he was gone. Maybe I should have spoken to him about guns: where there are drugs there are guns, but that's maybe more of a second-date kind of question.

I fell asleep spreadeagled in the main bedroom but jet-lag shook me awake at 5am so I moved through to the other, smaller one so that I could watch the clouds through the skylight. London's greys, the city's fallback palette. Morning greys as soft as pigeon's wings with a whisper of pink in the bass end. Evening grey's off-off-white, the colour of a much-washed work shirt. The grubby midday grey that London timeshares with Tokyo. As many greys as the Eskimos have snows. The grey of tin tacks, the grey of washing-up water, the grey of old dog hair. Tarnished spoons, Seventies Jags, raw cement. I could have watched it all morning, but I had things to do.

First, breakfast on the balcony, luxuriating in the wasteful luxury of hotel food: the perfect poached eggs in the microclimate of the cloche, the day-glo juice with its paper hat, individual jams. None of that seasonal, local, sustainable rubbish here, just the very best ingredients from around the world, hot-housed and air-freighted with the urgency of a donor kidney.

The British newspapers were incomprehensible. Banks were failing or ailing as whole countries went bankrupt. Iceland, a nation that had a parliament before Anno Domini had got out of three figures, turned out to have been an elaborate Ponzi scheme run by fishermen with Ferraris. Greece, the homeland of the twentieth century's two great growth industries — democracy and homosexuality — owed more than the whole of Europe had in reserve.

Back in LA Rae had temped at Amazon for a while. The tangle of algorithms and programs that calculated prices were a patchwork of old and new code. Legacy systems from the Jurassic age of online retailing had been refurbished then forced to co-exist with sleek new beasts. Huge swathes of the code the business ran on were now incomprehensible to anyone working there. She said it was like a mythical beast that was nine parts appendix. Often she'd arrive at the morning sales meeting to find certain prices swinging wildly between bargain and boom. Used paperbacks would rocket to a price of $71,000 before settling back at 40 cents, or long-out-of-print textbooks would top the "most popular" charts. These nauseous fluctuations were like the weather: something to be endured, not controlled. Imagine how fucked *that* was, and now imagine the vast digital ecosystem of the financial markets, with its caverns measureless to man, its predators and its plankton, the jungle of competing code. It was ungraspable.

One night, coming down off MDMA, Rae said, "I always thought that when some huge computer system took over the world like Skynet, it would at least be smart. Evil, but smart evil. Instead it's going to be dumb as a toddler, and just as destructive." I always think of that when I hear about "fluctuations in the market".

Kimi phoned. I told her the Amazon story knowing she liked this stuff.

She said, "But this is exactly how life on Earth was born. Complex systems interacting, making self-replicating subsystems. Amazon will probably be the first company to become self-aware."

I was only one cup of coffee in, so I tried to steer the conversation somewhere less sci-fi.

"Aren't you supposed to be in Shanghai?"

Her Asian tour was supposed to start tomorrow.

"Chengdu," she corrected, "and yes I'm supposed to be there right now, and no, I'm not. Because of this fucking volcano."

"The Iceland one?" I'd seen something on TV but the sound had been down. It looked like a slo-mo nuclear explosion. "I didn't have you down as the nervous type, it's miles from where you're going."

"Don't you watch the news? All flights are cancelled, it's like some kind of disaster movie. Everyone's grounded. There are distraught bankers buying second-hand Eurostar tickets for four figures."

"So? Hire yourself a jet, live a little."

"Firstly, Bran, they're all already taken. Early risers and the airport shut-ins got them. Anyway, there's all the gear, the band, the projections.

We're going nowhere. I need to come over and talk to Kaspar about something this evening — you want to get dinner?"

How much did I need her? How much could I keep her at arm's length?"

"I'm off to see Saul tonight. Can we make it tomorrow? I'll have to recover from The North."

It took a while to get used to driving on the left again but the traffic around London moved so slowly that I had plenty of time to readjust. It was bright and blowy and cold: funeral weather. Skimmed-milk skies dotted with scraps of fast-moving cloud and afterthoughts of rain. The car radio was set to Radio 4 and by the time I was out of London it made me feel like I was driving backwards into the 1950s. It was a carousel of cricket, gardening, the Archers and austerity. Unlistenable plays, god and the news. I stopped twice, smoking on muddy bits of land, watching fat kids laden with food bags from the service stations. I'd promised I wouldn't use the sat-nav but after the third circuit around the Blackburn ring road flyover, with my hotel visible but inaccessible below me, I switched it on.

Saul didn't have a mobile phone — the only such refusenik that I'd come across since my return — but the tendrils of the net had found a way. I'd emailed the booking agent for a *Back to '89* rave that he was playing and said I was interested in offering Saul some work. The agent sounded bored at the very idea. Saul was "unlikely to call" but I should "come see the show". When I asked about backstage passes he just laughed.

I called him again from the hotel. He sounded amused that I had come all this way.

"I was wondering if I could catch Saul before the show."

"I very much doubt that, even if he wanted to I'm not sure how you'd get hold of him. I guess he's driving over from Hebden this evening."

"Maybe I could catch him there, do you have the address?"

His laugh was shorter now. "No idea, we're not really at the popping round for sherry stage."

He was annoying me.

"Fine, what time is he on?"

"Whenever they fancy, not before four I'd warrant though."

Fuck. I'd been hoping I could drive back to civilisation that night.

"Right. OK. And guestlist is on the door?"

There was a snort that set my phone's speaker rattling.

"No passes. Buy a ticket like everyone else you tight cunt."

"Of course, but how do I get backstage?"

"Just ask security, I said you were coming. But I wouldn't stress. Backstage is going to be no better than out front, I doubt anyone's fighting to get back there."

Fuck and fuck. Four in the morning for the show and it was 4pm now. Twelve hours to kill in Blackburn. It was like one of those tests of ingenuity where they dropped cadets into the wilderness with just a box of matches and the clothes on their back. Still something that'd be easier to achieve than finding something interesting to do in Blackburn's light industrial area.

Saul might be trickier than the others. I'd taken (however briefly) Baxter's girlfriend, and the money that I owed Kimi was a fair old chunk, but Saul had been a friend before he was a band-mate. My very public fucking-up was on his shoulders once I'd disappeared. *He that filches from me my good name robs me of that which not enriches him, and makes me poor indeed.* Well it enriched me a bit. I tried to remember the last time I'd spoken with him. January '99. "Praise You" at number one. Remote/Control a dead band walking, existing only in name and in the cold, cold hearts of our creditors.

There was a trend in LA towards less threatening bouncers — even the occasional woman, lighter on muscle and heavier on the let's-talk-about-this attitude — but this idea had clearly not hit Blackburn. The two doormen were twitchy masses of muscle with the same lopsided boxers' faces. A Doberman idled at the end of each one's leash so now four faces were looking accusingly at me, just willing me to start something.

The slightly bigger, considerably more ugly one shone a torch in my face. "Ticket?"

He was twitching in a way that sent warning shots right across my bow. A steroid-head, the drugs even now trying to tug his short-fibre muscles ever tighter. He looked blankly at me. A walking 404 error if ever I saw one.

I turned towards the light and adopted my least threatening tone. "I'm a friend of Saul's, he's playing here tonight." Nothing. I tried again only to be cut off with a low growl of "Tickets" again. I fished around in my pocket. "How much?"

"Twenty." A hand reached out from the light source and I handed over the twenty. He switched the light off.

"He's on in about ten minutes, you might just catch him before his set."

I couldn't work out what this place would be when it wasn't being used for raves. It was high-ceilinged and topped with a corrugated iron roof that reflected back snare hits like pistol shots. Doorways around the edges gave way into municipal-looking spaces: olive corridors, windowless rooms with whiteboards, disabled toilets. As I walked through the din it didn't get any clearer. Was that a cattle grid in the corner where the concrete floor sloped down? And what were the floor-to-ceiling poles that were festooned with laser lights and speakers? The music was brutally loud and so hollowed out that all I could hear was a harsh bottom end and nightmarish, cartoon vocals. The dancers flailed, eyes closed, and a row of smoke machines failed to give the hall any kind of atmosphere. What was missing from the kind of raves I remembered from the actual 1989? Young people, human interaction, that sweaty, E'd up close dancing/dry humping that for an indie kid like me had been the main attraction. Here the dancers were atomised, each lost in their own tiny forcefield.

The MC, a chubby, bald guy in a Chelsea top and bad jeans took to the mic. The music was faded hard, leaving us with his patter. "Oi oi oi OI OI OI OI."

Around me everyone danced on. If they realised the music had stopped they showed no sign.

The MC did his ringmaster thing. "Ladiez and gennelmen, legends of the early days, Survivors of Spectrum, Shoom and the Blackburn raves. Bass-bin bangers and low-end legends, I give you Kontra Band and Risk E Bizznis." No one looked up as they took the stage.

Klaxons, air horns and crowd noises filled the air. All on tape I guessed. Field recordings of those early days, made by someone who knew that it was going to be worth capturing the Summer of Love because the Winter of Hate was going to last decades.

A spray of dry ice failed to add an air of mystery to Saul and his partner clambering on stage. He looked good. Still rangy and sharp-angled but gym-fit too now: biceps like something from an anatomy drawing, veins as thick as electrical cables. A weird pattern covered his arms and neck and he wore a glistening black headdress that reached nearly to his waist. He played a cycle of ominous chords on an old Korg.

I moved closer. Beside him a bespectacled black guy with the kind of fade I'd not seen since the Fresh Prince slowly shifted his weight from one foot to the other in time to the music in his head. He held the mike in his palms, rolled it like a cigar, looking pleadingly heavenwards.

Saul stacked up thick notes in horror-movie intervals until the speakers rattled with a high-end like knives being sharpened. Not quite music, just a shriek so invasive that even the mongs in the far corner had their arms in the air, then… without warning, he triggered a huge breakbeat, and he was jack-knifing back and forth in a troublingly Hitlerian way. Up, up and away with the knives again and then — as inevitable as taxes — the bass drop, the filling of the abyss. The singer began to unwind a pretty melody, his voice as supple as a teenager's, skating across the rough surfaces of the noise. In front of me guys pogoed, made shapes in the air with fat, ringed fingers. A shirtless guy in sweatpants swallowed a couple of pills and then doubled over to throw up. On stage a snare roll drilled through eight bars, sixteen. The guy sightlessly felt in the puke for his undigested pills and swallowed them again. This time they stayed down. Eyes rolled back, fights broke out. It was fucking hellish.

The dressing room was behind the only closed door in the building. The agent had been right, it was no better here than outside, it was simply a place without the gurners. Saul was lying face down on a yoga mat between stacked filing cabinets. His shoulder blades rose and fell in time with some breathing exercise as the room vibrated to the music outside. Every ceiling panel and light fitting took the brunt of 140 explosions a minute, adding a brittle echo to the whomps of 808 kick. The singer sat in the corner with twin pillars of incense smoke rising either side of him. Even the smoke twitched in the air on the beat. He looked up as I entered and pushed a bare foot into Saul's midriff.

"Not now," he said, voice muffled by the mat.

"Your friend." I caught a whiff of West Country in the voice.

Saul rolled onto his side and propped himself up on a bony elbow.

"Well look what the cat dragged in."

Time had been annoyingly kind to him. He had one of those flat, angular faces that reminded you of sharks or those sharp-muzzled bulldogs, and his buzz-cut was as neat as an Action Man's. At some point in the last twenty years he'd broken his nose, or more likely had it broken for him. It hadn't been fixed properly and it added a quirkiness to a face that could otherwise be over-hard. He rolled himself smoothly up into a squat. Of *course* he did fucking yoga: it's what his generation has instead of philosophy. The tattered bracelets and eastern tattoos told the story of his last twenty years more clearly than any bio.

"Enjoy the set?" He looked birdlike, perched there, his head tucked to one side.

What was the safest response? "I did. Amazing reaction you were getting, tons of energy."

His partner had gone back to his book but kept shooting glances over his specs at us.

Saul pushed his chin up. "From that lot? They'd cheer a fucking car alarm if you put 138 bpm underneath it. What did you call them Andre?"

The singer folded down a page in his book. "Cyborgs," he said. "Wind them up and off they go. Eight, nine hours at a time. Pure destruction of every single thing that made this scene so beautiful."

It felt uncomfortable standing up, looming over him but there were no chairs in the room, so I squatted down myself. Again Andre shot a glance over his glasses at me. Saul had obviously said nothing good about me.

Saul switched his weight from one foot to the other. "So what brings you to the People's Republic of Lancashire Brandon? Nostalgia?"

The two of us had met in a place not unlike this, back in '88. I'd been living in the attic of an old student digs in Whalley Range, a turreted Victorian house full of nurses who'd arranged their shifts so that five bedrooms did for eight of them. Every time I went downstairs the space seemed to have shifted; rooms were divided by tacked-up sheets and beds had migrated into hallways. The only constants were the nylon uniforms drying over radiators and a fug of dope smoke. It wasn't until Vegas that I found anywhere else so totally unconcerned with any outside concept of time. Four in the morning would find girls ironing in their underwear, eating cereal and gabbing on the phone. One in the afternoon and I'd have to pick my way through slumber parties full of facemasks and vodka-laced hot chocolates.

I wasn't a student. I'd hitch-hiked my way up to Manchester to check out the scene from the music press: the Mondays and the Roses and the long-forgotten also-rans that followed them like Pig-Pen's personal miasma. I rehearsed with bands called things like the Grooverobbers and Personal Devils in the cheap mornings at Strawberry Studios and slept in the afternoons. At night I'd watch band after band after band and try to hook up with like-minded individuals. The word was about parties up in the hills. Raves, orbitals, whatever. I got a flyer from a guy at Afflecks Palace who was handing them out to anyone whose trousers were the requisite width.

I went with three of the girls from downstairs. Nurses, with nurses' glorious love for life, dancing and unmarked pills. Jammed into a Fiesta with malfunctioning heating, the windows dripping in condensation, the air heavy with bodyspray and booze sweats. When I look back I see it as in a film. A birds' eye view, vertiginous above the moors, the line of the A666 (it's true, the original Road To Hell, look it up) trickling through moorland. We swoop down, through thin clouds to a lane lined with parked cars, looking for all the world like they'd been dumped there, and a trickle of kids heading towards the noise. Saul I'd met outside on a dewy bank sheltered enough to be the designated joint-rolling spot. He'd been friendly, distracted, positive about everything while his hands and feet tapped metronomically to the beats from inside. He played guitar and keyboards, I sang; back then that was enough to form a band.

"Nostalgia? Yeah, not that. This is all a bit more hardcore than I remember." Back in '89 I thought driving fifty miles to neck unknown pills in a field was about as full-on as it got but compared with this horror show it seemed like some unspeakably innocent time.

Andre started up, "Scratch the music business and underneath it's just criminals, criminals, criminals. That's all the big labels ever were — an attempt to put some business between us and the thugs."

My cue. "Well, how would you like to get back at them?"

Saul bounced on the balls of his feet. "Tell us at the house, this place is bad for the soul."

They were on a sooty old Triumph Bonneville, so I had to get a taxi. I'd left the car behind because I'd thought the evening might get heavy but Saul and Andre were clearly clean-living now.

Everything about the cab was soporific: the warmth of the heater, the sickly air freshener, Magic FM from the front speakers. Outside looked alien after two decades of California. Drably green, littered with patient knots of rock and veined with scaly dry-stone walls. After a couple of miles burnished pools began to appear in the hollows. The road was straight and gently rising, rising fast enough to pop my ears and give me pangs of envy for everyone in the planes flying above us. *Keep. On. Moving.*

Until. We took a long, looping right-hand curve and the lowlands opened up before us. In the distance the nuclear plant puffed clouds into the massed greys of morning.

"There you go," said the driver, nodding towards it.

At first I thought he meant that Saul lived there but then I followed the line of the road down towards the entrance and saw a patch of colour by the road, a knot in the string. It was a wooden sailing boat, weather-beaten and as ship-shaped as a child's drawing, sitting amid an exact square of blue. We reeled in the short miles of moorland and drew to a stop on the gravel outside.

The square of colour was bluebells, carpet-thick around the boat in a square so precise that it must have been trimmed with scissors. The stern disappeared into the swell of the earth, its prow rearing up to vault an invisible wave. It was painted white and navy. The masts reared back, pointing tattered sails at the sky. A limp skull-and-crossbones at the front and a smiley to the rear. I bent down to scoop up a handful of the gravel: seashells, crushed and soft-edged. Saul and Andre must have heard the car pull up because a gangway lowered from the side of the boat. They stood, arm in arm, in the doorway, like minor royals getting off a private plane.

"You made it." Saul did not sound excited about the fact.

"I did. This place—" I encompassed it all in the sweep of an arm: the desiccated cacti in their gravel beds, the driftwood sculptures, the hopeless vegetable patch, "—looks amazing."

Inside was too small for even the pair of them. With me there too every action was a choreography of "after you" and "mind the windows". I sat on a low bench with my knees round my ears while Saul made tea. ("Herbal, mint, rooibos?" he asked. "Don't you have any *tea*?" I countered.) For the first time since I crossed the Atlantic I wished Rae was with me. She'd have liked the Eastern crap that barnacled the boat's walls — she knew her dreamcatchers from her mandalas — and they'd have been eating out of her hand. It all looked much of a muchness to me and I had an abiding fear that one of them would offer to read my palm.

"This is beautiful," I said, voice raised over the whistle of a kettle, "It feels like the ark."

Smiles bounced between them.

"We found it in Tintagel, you know the King Arthur place? We played a party on the cliffs there. It finished up about six in the morning and me and Saul went for a walk while the guy cashed up."

"Still owes us two hundred," said Saul.

"It was propped up on the beach there, deck gone, a hole in the side that you could walk right through, and we sat on the deck and watched the sun come up. We weren't the first there." His hand traced the wall beside him where names were cut into the wood. MO 4 AM, SKINS, hearts and crosses.

"And we sat and waited, and listened to the sea. Saul went back to argue the fee, or so I thought," he smiled, obviously in the throes of a story he'd told before, "but two weeks later we cycled out to see the reactor and there it was, with two carpenters already working on it. It's forty feet by forty feet, as close to the plant as you're allowed to live."

"Why did you buy so close?"

"Whole point of this place. It's a rebuttal. They're big, we're small. They're ugly, we're beautiful. They pollute, we grow. Everyone who visits there has to pass this place and at least gets a glimpse that there can be another way."

Weedy sunlight crept through the gaps between boards and made the dust dance. I guessed it would always be windy here. Even on a still day like today you could hear the sails flap outside.

"So," Saul's hands were wrapped around a tiny teacup, like he was trying to nurse it back to life, "What is it that you're here for?"

It didn't work, my spiel. I thought my deal was perfect. Back in the day I'd remixed Dillon Marksman, remixed him so well that a) it sounded fucking amazing and b) there was nothing left of Dillon and his fat fraud band on the track. But our manager at the time had neglected to put my name on the publishing so when the record became that rarest of beasts, a bona fide American hit, Dillon got to keep the cash (and, even more frustratingly, the credit). I'd huffed and puffed but the lawyers said his legal house was made of bricks so I ended up settling for five fucking grand. But now the winds were changing. A couple of test cases in the States made me think that I would have won if I'd tried now. It was too late for me but Saul had been there in the room as I'd worked. I'd thought his dance music background would help, but he was too slow and too wrecked so I'd done it all myself. But no one need know that. He could sue for his "half". I'd agree he was there (for half of the half). Dillon caves, and we both sleep on pillowcases stuffed with fivers. Who could say no to that?

Saul could. He wouldn't sign anything and claimed he didn't even want the money. He spouted such bullshit that it was all I could do to stop myself from slapping him.

"You can't *own* music Bran. That's where we went wrong in the first place. We were always chasing a deal and when it didn't happen then we gave it all up just because we hadn't managed to turn ourselves into a commodity. We should have been proud of that. All the while the real treasure was sitting in front of us: the music. Nowadays Andre and I give our music away for free, and we only charge for live performances. It's a small price to pay for a communal experience."

Andre beamed like a proud mother at her daughter's recital.

Saul had always had a spiritual side but we'd managed to keep it successfully under wraps in the Remote/Control days. But now he had that supercilious air that only living in an echo-chamber of two can provide. I wanted to tell him a few home truths. That it didn't matter if *he* thought no one could own music because Dillon most clearly could and did. That if he thought that Remote/Control's music was "treasure" then both his standards and his memory were slipping. And that if last night's rave was a communal experience, then so was any other collection of window-licking mouth-breathers in one place — a dole queue perhaps, or a gangbang.

I changed tack: they could donate the money, they could buy more land with it. No, no. I appealed to his vanity: the world thought Dillon created that particular piece of treasure when we both knew it was us that deserved the cosmic kudos. It didn't work.

Everyone has a key, an action or phrase or just a way of being that makes their tumblers line up and click into place. With Saul, back in the day, it used to be envy. But that key's not working any more. Perhaps it's being clean, maybe it's love. There amongst the knick-knacks and the hanging things I tried everything. I appealed to his avarice, then hit on his high-mindedness. I flattered, I cajoled and at one point I rather think I might have flirted. Nothing.

Much too late I realised that he was enjoying saying no. With ex-junkies you needed to discover where they'd transferred their addiction. Usually it was something harmless — yoga or body-building — but here, and I kicked myself for not seeing it earlier, it was denial. He was getting off on every "no".

The wheat-free bread and the black tea. No. No.

The unbleached cotton. The bare feet.

No, no, no, no, no, no, no.

No to everything. *I'm up to twenty NOs a day. I did so much NO last night I can't see straight.*

Fuck it. I should have given him an offer he could only refuse.

I'd have to regroup and try again another day. And even if I couldn't get him into court I might still need him for the record. I tried to reconnect. There was a pattern of marks at his neck and wrists, in fact everywhere that any skin was showing.

"What are those, those tattoos?" I asked him.

He had his top off in an instant (fair enough — if I had 7% body fat and pecs like a suit of armour I don't think I'd wear a shirt ever again). His left arm, most of his chest, and all of his back was covered in liquid black-blue dots, arranged in a regular, slanting pattern. I drew closer. Tears. Identical fat teardrops falling in a pattern like rain blown by wind.

People telling you about their tattoos is only a short step up from talking about their dreams. But, needs must, and I had to get back on a better side of Saul.

"Very beautiful. Tears, isn't that a prison thing?" I was confident Saul had never done anything interesting enough to land him in jail.

It was Andre who answered. "It was a Latino thing originally, one tear for every five years in prison. But they've come to symbolise any kind of incarceration at all."

Saul butted in, "In my case, drugs." He added, "Drugs can be a prison too," (in case I'd missed his thudding analogy, I suppose).

"There's one for every month I spent under the spell of intoxicants," he went on, muddying even his own metaphor. "One month clean, one month atoned for, one new tear. I have around fifty to go."

That would be a hell of a lot of tears. They'd encroach on his face and hands before he was done, which was as good a reason for a relapse as I could imagine. He was expecting some kind of response. Beyond the obvious: *in which fucking universe does the pain of a poor Chicano boy locked up for five years in one of the world's most racist prison systems equate to a month of doing blow in Camden nightclubs?* I couldn't think of anything. Instead I made a sound of vague approval and asked them about the headdress he'd been wearing on stage. The question seemed to annoy him.

"They're called war bonnets actually," he said, "Native American war bonnets. I've been adapting Muscogee designs using roadkill feathers from the roads in the neighbourhood. You know, as a nod to the local folklore about crows and magpies?"

I could see that unless I was very careful I was about to learn something about the local folklore of crows and magpies, a circumstance I was keen to avoid. The headdresses did interest me though.

"Could you make something like that, but with a beak?" I asked him.

He looked dubious. "Maybe, how big?"

I took out my notebook and sketched. Until that moment I'd been thinking that the killers would be wearing Jack the Ripper costumes but the headdresses had a sleek unlikeliness to them. They were elemental rather than cultural and I figured I owed that to myself.

The drive back was unbearable. Traffic snarled up every fifteen miles or so with never any sign of what had caused it. I tried to will myself into being another person, one who didn't mind delay and discomfort. This remaking of yourself was one of the few things I'd liked about being an actor.

At the lowest point of my time as a family man, when I'd wake up hours before Rae and the kid, lying rigid among the fluffy pillows and soft toys thinking, "How the fuck am I going to make it through another day of this shit?", I'd only survive by pretending I was preparing for a role. How convincing could I be as a regular guy? At the school gates, where I once prided myself on being the only one smoking, now I'd be the guy asking if the other dads were helping with the science project and whether they wanted to go for a coffee to discuss it. I shovelled snow for the neighbours, clipped supermarket coupons. It was a way of making those dead, white-bread days have even a sliver of meaning. I'd like to see fucking Sean Penn immerse himself a role like that. Let's see him putting in an Oscar-winning performance while waiting by the playground fence, so brain-blown by hangover that the very sky seemed to throb, with his back aching from scratch-marks that he didn't remember getting, talking to the drones-in-fleece about school projects and bake sales, without wanting to take a shotgun to the whole lot of them.

Six hours of blank roads and blank skies. Kaspar was at the door as I came in, directing various serious Eastern Europeans to strip me of my bags and coat and…

Chapter Four

The nervousness of meeting Baxter the next day was a physical thing, more like hunger than anything mental, and the strangeness of my surroundings meant the smallest sound disturbed me. I gave up on sleep and instead went online to search for any filmed evidence of my brother.

There was some live stuff which I fast-forwarded to get to his interactions with the audience (which were so short and echoey as to be practically useless) and a couple of interviews from Nineties music shows whose constant jump-cuts gave me warnings of a migraine. The motherlode though was a collection of video interviews from the early 2000s featuring Bran seated on an empty stage with an unseen interlocutor asking questions about his career, both musical and thespian. This was an older Bran, still belligerent and dismissive, but now with a tendency to opine upon the "big questions". His views were canvassed (and vigorously given) on the meaning of art, the death of the music industry, China's rise as a world power. I couldn't tell who they had been made for but they looked slick and had an impressive number of views.

I watched them over and over, practising phrases which he reused. He was fond of "You might think that but you couldn't be more wrong" and "the role of the artist is...". The interviews were a gold mine of physical tics too. He waved away questions that he didn't feel were up to his standard with a curt, mimed brush-off. The foot dangled over the other knee. Steepled fingers when he particularly liked a question (or, more accurately, particularly liked his planned answer to it). He played with his hair like a girl would. I could use all of these; I tried some out in the mirror. Steeple fingers, look to one side. His best side; *our* best side.

"The role of the artist in a connected society?"

Push hair behind ears, little sigh to express the banality of the question.

"Disruption. Running interference. Incoherence."

Switch legs. Let the mirror see the diamonds of the socks, the soles of the brogues.

"The rest, traditional roles of narrative sense and possibility?"

The hand brushing the air. Eyes to the ceiling. A glint of rings.

"Hey."

Rae was working on another screen in her kitchen so I could only see half her face. She turned to face me. "Hey, you look tired. Bad night?"

"Couldn't sleep. Though that's probably good for meeting Baxter. Wouldn't do to be all fresh-faced."

"Good thinking. Nervous?"

"Utterly. Can I run something by you?"

"Of course."

I took a breath and pushed my hair back. I leaned back and dangled a foot.

"The thing is Bax," I stretched out the name and paused to look off-camera, "You might fucking think that, but you couldn't be more wrong. We are here to destroy the music industry, not to make money from it. So, sweetheart, let's get in, get out, fuck the consequences. The rest?" I made the brush-off gesture.

"Fuck," whispered Rae. "That is spooky. I mean it's not how he was with me and Rob but if we were at a party or something? Yeah, that's just how he'd behave."

The look she gave me wasn't the most pleasant so I put back my broadest smile. "I spent most of the night watching videos of him. I think I picked up a bit."

"More than a bit, that was good. Which videos though?"

"Some thing in an auditorium, just him on a chair. Pretty serious stuff."

Rae snorted. "Oh that thing is so sad. He had it done when work was short in LA. He figured that if casting guys saw him being taken seriously as an artist on some big British arts programme then they might cast him more. He faked the whole thing. His friend Champ did the credits and stuff, he wrote the questions himself and the interviewer was another actor-stroke-alcoholic who got paid with a couple of grams. If he'd spent half the time that it took up on going to auditions he might have worked more often."

"I'm glad he did. It's like a crash course in his public persona." I steepled my fingers and looked skywards. "You call it a persona, darling, like it's a bad thing, but you couldn't be more wrong. That word, as anyone who thinks of himself as an actor should know, means…"

Rae giggled, such an unaffected sound after hours of Brandon's bombast. "What an asshole." She made a shush sign, and I saw Robin cross the background with bowl of soup in his hand. He poked his head around until his face filled the screen. "Hello Daddy, you look tired."

"Well thank you Robin."

"Daddy," he said, "Will I go all white like you?"

I ran my fingers through my hair. It was getting long. "Maybe. My parents didn't but I have an uncle who went totally white too. Would you like to look like this?"

He looked dubious, darted off, slid back.

"Did you have it forever?" he asked.

"No, when I was your age my hair was like yours, very like yours actually, then one day it changed."

He waggled his head from one side to the other and then shot off into the other room.

Rae laughed. "Not much of an attention span on that one." She looked into the screen. "God I wish I was back in bed, that looks comfy."

I spun the laptop around. "Super king-size, four-hundred-thread count Egyptian cotton sheets, according to Kaspar. Wasted on me, I can sleep pretty much anywhere."

"What I'd give…" she started. "Anyway, you can tell me the story of how your hair went white, I don't think Bran ever did."

I got myself comfortable.

"We were eleven or so. I woke up one morning, went to brush my teeth and there it was in the mirror, a patch of pure white."

I remember rubbing at it experimentally with the ball of my hand.

"Not the whole head?"

"No, you could cover the whole thing with your palm. Brandon came in, laughed like a drain for ten seconds and then realised he had the same thing. Same patch, different place."

"Serves him right. The same day?"

"Indeed. He was inconsolable at first. I've never known a kid as vain as that since, not at ten. That first day he covered it up with our dad's Just For Men but the next day there was more."

"More?"

"Yes, the patch had grown, and then there was another one. That first week I looked ridiculous, like a Fresian. Mind you, Bran was worse. The dye didn't stick and new patches were appeared all the time. He ended up piebald. By week's end I was totally white, except my eyebrows, and Bran was a skinhead."

"No!" Rae had her hands clasped over her mouth.

"He never told you? He got a friend to shave it all off. My parents were furious, this is back in the days that being a skinhead was more a political thing than a style one. I remember my mum shaking him by the shoulders, telling him 'You. Grow. That. Back. Right. Now'." I mimed the actions, the laptop wobbling in front of me.

Robin was back, perched on the tabletop.

"What's so funny?" he wanted to know.

"When your daddy's hair first went all white he shaved it off like a skinhead."

"Really? Do you have pictures?"

"Sorry Rob," I told him. "No pictures."

He did his frog impression and then disappeared again.

"But you don't mind it now?" Rae asked.

"God no. I see old school friends now and they've gone bald or grey or whatever and they just look ancient. I look pretty much the same. Brandon didn't mind it?"

"No, I think he was quite proud of it. He dyed it for a while, in LA when he was working as an actor, but I couldn't take him seriously like that."

"Yeah, Billy Idol coming along was the turning point for him back then. He just spiked it up and pretended he'd gone platinum blonde." I yawned.

"Don't yawn," she said. "It's infectious. God I'm so tired."

I did some last-minute cramming. Watching Brandon again I started to spot chinks in his armour. There was the ghost of a stutter; you'd miss it unless you knew what to look for. I'd suffered terribly as a child with a stammer, enough so that I'd seen speech therapists, and it was the one thing Brandon had never teased me about. Now I saw why. It was very slight, his stammer. I recognised it more from his avoidance techniques than from anything he said. Often his theatrical leg crossings and hand gestures came just after he'd started to say something and then stopped. It gave the impression he was considering everything he said, but I recognised it as a holding exercise while he found another path to the summit of the word that was blocking him. "The thing about the B... the English." "It's like trying to put out fire with p...p... with gasoline." I could feel those avoided words turn to ashes in my mouth: "British...

Petrol…" I had to hand it to him, he found a replacement word far faster than I could.

But with this in my locker I started looking again. His clumsiness on stage, which he presented as a kind of stoned slackerdom, was revealed in this new light to be just that: clumsiness. And a thought started to spread. *That's me up there.* There in the seconds of stutter and the rhythm of relentless foot-tapping, that's me. There, coming in at the wrong point of a song and the quiet looks between the rest of the band. His nervous laugh at the harder questions and the silences and tics. Me, me, me. I'd been there all the time, a sleeper cell in his DNA. The path not taken. There have been times in my life when a proper rage has come upon me and each time I've berated myself that it's how Brandon would have behaved. The idea that he might exist somewhere within me terrified me, but it had never occurred to me that a similar emotion might be at work in my brother.

And then an idea swept across me with the force of being shaken awake. *That's what Rae saw in him.* When they first met. Not his swagger and poise and acid and edge, but the shadow-being at the borders of his personality. I was hidden deep in his bones and seeped out of the edges when I was needed. It was me. I ran like an undertow, a silent song beating in the blood. I was the subliminal message beneath the blare of bravado; the stutter in his songs, the ghost in his machine. It made me feel better about whatever it was I was building with Rae.

There was still Robin though. Every time Rae and I spoke I wanted to ask her about him but the whole subject felt so fragile. One of the oldest parts of Umbrage was the Glaswald: petrified twigs that I'd won on a school trip that I coated with Potassium Dichromate and watered until the twigs groaned with twisting arms of bright green crystals. I'd never quite got the balance right. Once they'd coated the wood enough to look suitably tree-like the crystals would coil and metastatize until they crumbled to the ground. They always seemed to collapse at night, and the sound they made — a gentle rain of glass — played in my mind every time I thought of Robin. I shook the feeling off. Rae first, then him.

She was gummy-eyed at the monitor, her head somewhere else while the coffee brewed. I tapped on the screen.

"Baxter is due in half an hour, I was wondering if you'd listen in?"

She yawned. "Sure, I can try."

"If you hear me getting into difficulties you could buzz me on the phone so I could make an excuse to cut it short."

"Like on a blind date?"

I must have looked confused because she laughed. "It's obviously never happened to you. It's a standard thing — you get a friend to call you ten minutes into a blind date. If the guy's OK then you say it's nothing, if he's not then bingo! There's an emergency at home."

"You can tell after ten minutes?" I thought that if that were me I'd probably just about have got my first sentence out by then.

She yawned again. "The dates I've been on, Adam? I could tell before I sat down."

Baxter texted. BE THERE IN 10.

"D'you think he'll need the laptop?" Rae was sitting at her kitchen table.

"I've no idea, I don't really know what the hell we're doing." I looked at the neat wraps on the table. "D'you think I should take some more cocaine?"

She smiled. "You sound like a kids' drug warning video. Try this: shall I do a line?"

I tried it. "Shall I do a line?"

"Better."

"But should I? I definitely feel more Brandon-ish on it."

"Well that's no surprise is it? Maybe you should. There's a calmness about you, which speaking as a woman, is totally hot, but as a long-time student of Brandon Kussgarten it's way off beam."

"You're not worried that I'll turn into an arsehole? Become him?"

"It's only a couple of lines. Anyway, you know when people say cocaine turned me into a monster, or fame made me crazy, nine times out of ten they were that way beforehand. They just needed an excuse to let it out. Your brother totally used coke to say the things he thought, deep down, but knew he couldn't normally get away with saying."

She slipped back into his accent. "For fuck's sake Rae it was just the coke talking, you know how I get."

Her cheeks coloured. "Coke won't turn you into an asshole Ads, and you know why? Because you're not an asshole."

I couldn't help smiling. "Nicest thing anyone's said to me for ages." I cut out two lines and snorted one up each nostril. There was that subtle metallic drip and nothing else. I threw my head back and the buzzer went, making me jump.

Any worries about Baxter seeing straight through me disappeared as soon as he came in. He was a ball of energy, talking thirteen to the dozen, sitting down and standing up, never at rest.

"Fuck man, where've you been? No don't tell me I don't want to know. I'd either be jealous or pissed off or both. I thought you'd gone for good though and left me holding the baby."

He pulled his glasses on and examined me. I held my breath.

"Fuck's sake. Week-long bender and you still look fresh as a daisy. Not fucking fair. I've spent the last five years going to bed at ten and eating my broccoli and I look like a sack of shit."

He took his glasses off again. "This is where you say *nah, you look good Bax.* Fuck it."

I kept quiet. It didn't seem to be doing me any harm.

He sat down for the third or fourth time.

"Annnnnnyway. You got my message? Frank Isaacs. You remember him? Pompous old twat. It's good news and bad news I think. Good news is he's obviously the man when it comes to Wilsonology. If he OKs it then it's one hundred per cent kosher, fit for purpose, golden goose time. Bad news is he really knows his stuff and if we've fucked up he'll notice. I mean I think I could swing it, make it look like I was scammed too, but…"

He was up again, disappearing head-first into the fridge. "No champagne? You're slipping Bran."

I set my voice to its most acidic.

"It's in the champagne fridge to the right there. I'm not a peasant Bax."

He held up his hands in surrender. "Sorry, sorry. So, the music's all good I think."

He eyed me beadily. "The music's all good, right?"

I nodded as he popped the champagne cork.

"So that's the main thing. Sleeve and label I have here." He opened up a messenger bag and pulled out a square of cardboard and a sheet of stickers. "Sleeve's from a Jan and Dean acetate I bought in Long Beach, totally contemporaneous, if that's the word I want, and the stickers are from the Seventies but I don't think that'll matter. So…?"

I wasn't sure what he wanted.

"The pressing plant? The vinyl. Is your guy sorted?"

There was a page in Bran's notebook with a name and number and the word PRESSER underneath, I'd been meaning to ask Rae if she knew what it meant. I tamped down the worry in my voice.

"He's been out of town for a couple of days, sorry. I'll get on it."

Baxter poured a couple of glasses of champagne and chopped up two lines. "Do it. Last piece of the puzzle, man."

He was a curious looking little man. He was only five foot six-ish, but still all his clothes looked a little small. Hairy knobs of ankle and wrist showed white as he moved around the apartment and his checked shirt was tight enough to expose crescents of flesh between the buttons. His hair was an odd monk's-tonsure kind of thing and his face was saggy and unshaven with a beard line that almost reached the bags under his eyes. The only neat parts of his appearance were the lime-green trainers he was wearing; they looked brand new.

I kept silent, one foot tucked on the other knee and watched him. It seemed to rev him up further. He was up and down, putting records on, enthusing wildly and then taking them off before they'd finished.

After the third line I began to feel shaky as hell. I spent ten minutes in the bathroom texting Rae.

Her message read "PRESSER in the notebook might be record pressing guy, figures below cld b vinyl weights? Ur doing great but don't say sorry so much."

When I came out he was on his phone too. He held up his chubby hands. "Gotta go. There's a guy up in Hendon who says he's got some John's Children rarities. Wanna come see?"

I wanted him out of there. My face ached from the blank expression. "Thanks but no, I'll get on the presser thing."

He'd only been out of the door a second when the buzzer went. What had I done that had tipped him off? There were a million ways I could have fucked this up. I lit a cigarette and waited a beat before opening the door.

He was there, quizzical. He thrust a CD into my hand. "I checked it out. It's fine, you can't hear the sample anyway. You could even take it off if you wanted."

I made as neutral a noise as I could manage and only properly breathed once he'd disappeared down the hall. It took ten minutes to find a CD player among the racks of gear and another three to find the corresponding button on the amp to switch it on. This track seemed different from the first two. It was persistent and loud, and even turned low I couldn't really work out what Brandon was singing. Rae was visibly concentrating on the laptop I'd brought through.

"It's definitely him, though I can't really make it out properly. It's good though, no?"

I gave her a look.

"Can you upload it and send it to me?"

I slid it into the laptop but when I clicked on the folder icon two files popped up. One was an mp3 with the title "The Day After the End of the World" and the other was a text file entitled DON'T READ. I opened it and read a little. Then I forwarded both to Rae, telling her, "I think you're going to want to see this."

The Day After the End of the World

The below was on the document titled DON'T READ. It was properly formatted and had obviously been spell-checked.

Baxter. Fat, funny, froggy Baxter.

I proposed coming down to see him in Brighton. He countered: Claridge's, Thursday, he had a meeting.

"Are you sure you want me along?" I asked. He was cagey about how he'd been making a living. It sounded like he was buying and selling old vinyl and I couldn't imagine I'd be much use to him. Plus the idea of a born scruff like Baxter trying to fit in at Claridge's didn't sound like much of a day out.

"Yeah come," he said, "I'm meeting some people and I could do with a wingman."

For wingman read social secretary. He'd never been good with people and had a spooky ability to always say the wrong thing. There was nothing malicious about his behaviour but nowadays you'd happily describe him as on the spectrum.

I walked from Oxford Circus down into the world of money. Cars the size of boats idled outside Gucci and Chaumet, their shaven-headed drivers hurriedly putting out ciggies as the shops disgorged Russian wives and their minders. Deeper into Mayfair the shops became more oblique. What's that one, with only the security guards marking it out from the houses? Gallery? Shoe shop? Brothel? Claridge's looked the same though: trying too hard to look like it wasn't trying too hard. The Arabs of my twenties had been replaced by Chinese kids in Moschino who didn't look up from their phones as the cocktails arrived.

Baxter was in the corner on a laptop with a cup of tea. He had *that* haircut — the short-fringe-and-feathery-bits do that's been handed down through three generations of British musicians like a family heirloom. I could have told you before I saw him that he'd be in a checked shirt, dark blue jeans and trainers, it's his tribe's uniform. His only accessory was a pair of gargantuan headphones encircling his neck like one of those South African tyre punishments.

He was lost in thought, looking at something on his computer and when I tapped his shoulder he took a while to refocus.

"Hi, Brandon, lovely." He stood up and brushed crumbs off himself before we shook hands. "Sit, come on, how are you?"

"I'm good, just getting used to London again. Do I have time for a drink?" I gestured at his tea.

"After, after. Let's just get this done and then we can go to the pub." He looked nervy. "Shouldn't take too long."

"So who are we meeting?"

"New Money and this producer he's got now. Glock something?"

"Well, we are mixing with the big boys aren't we?"

Even I, with my total disinterest in the world of hip-hop, knew those two: Atlanta rappers who'd gone from gang members to CEOs in under three years.

I looked him over. His fringe was damp with sweat and his belly encroached over an M&S belt. "What are you doing for them?"

He swung the laptop round to show a screen full of waveforms. "Beats."

"Beats?"

"Beats. You know I used buy and sell old records: charity shop and jumble sales stuff. Well, after Remote/Control, I started buying up stuff that I could sell elsewhere. Old soul and funk mainly, you remember

I always liked that stuff?" I did. Driver's choice in the Transit van and Baxter taking the last leg. Even now there are certain records — Northern soul things especially — that take me instantly back to the M25.

"Anyway a couple of black guys started buying stuff off me. Always rare stuff. And a couple of the things I'd sold turned up as breaks on UK rap things. Not big records really, but you'd hear them on the radio. So next time they came around I asked them about it. It had become like currency in certain sectors — everyone wanted the breaks that no one else had. So I boned up on the producers and started emailing them with ideas. It used to be a sideline but I make more money from it now than selling records."

The idea of Baxter as a wheeler-dealer didn't sit right with me. I wouldn't buy a used beat from the man.

"It's better if I show you. Just shut up and look cool, OK?"

The music industry is stacked against black artists. Behind the scenes the business is so white that it makes international banking look like a paragon of inclusivity. But… it did mean that when the likes of Glock and New Money broke the glass ceiling they could fly first class for a weekend at Claridge's and still make it look like a high-art act of rebellion. Bare arms looped over Louis Quatorze sofa arms, a basketball video game playing on the TV. Joints in crystal ashtrays. Lucky fuckers.

They still looked more at home there than Baxter though. He was playing snippets of tracks on his laptop; nothing sounded like it belonged on a hit record to me. I zoned out and watched the video game characters waiting patiently on their digital basketball court.

"Hold up." Glock raised a hand. His eyes had been glassy for the last two tracks.

"Go back a couple, the guitar thing." The way he said "guitar" made it sound like some kind of exotic instrument.

Baxter played it again. A busy arpeggio on a guitar so electronically treated that I'd thought it was a synth the first time round.

"One more time."

Baxter hit play again.

"I dunno man. Can you Airdrop it?"

Bax opened up his laptop and typed.

Now the riff played on vast speakers propped against the back wall. Glock looped it, let it run. He slowed it slightly. There was more menace to it at that speed. A threatening lethargy. He cut it at two places, making the beat a triplet, then dropped a four-four loop under it. The down beat shifted and new rhythms appeared. Money nodded. "Loop the first one round like three times, then the second."

"Yeah?"

"Yeah."

They could hear something even before Glock made the change; both were nodding furiously.

Now the first triplet repeated, insisted. And the second was just a moment's respite before the nagging first part came back again. Glock stripped out the hi-hats, turning the drums super-dumb: an 808 kick, a handclap, tape echoes. Even Baxter was nodding now. He looked like one of those bulldog toys you saw in car windows.

New Money picked up a wireless mike and began to rap over the top. The words unearthed another rhythm hidden in the gaps between beats. His delivery shifted the downbeat again. He ignored the chord change, ramped up the tension. Both men were up on their feet and I had goosebumps. Then *click*, stop. The two guys laughed and high-fived before collapsing back onto the couch.

Money turned to Baxter. "Hells yeah we'll take that one. Good job little man."

For one horrible second I thought Bax might attempt a high-five but he just reached for his notebook.

"OK, OK. The southern soul was $1,500 each and that last one is $3,000."

"Cool, call Matt at the office and I'll let him know that's right. You wanna stay? Hang a while?"

Even Baxter could hear lack of enthusiasm in the offer. We were being dismissed.

"That's very kind but they're selling an old BBC music library up in Acton and I need to go check it out."

"Sure." They looked bored. Glock reached for the game controller. "Till next time."

In the lift down Baxter clutched his laptop to his chest.

"Good deal?" I asked. It seemed like it: the best part of five thousand dollars for finding two records.

"Not bad, not bad at all. I've had bigger. You remember that Jay-Z track about the LA Riots?"

It wasn't really a question. You could have been comatose in intensive care for all of last summer and you still wouldn't have avoided that track.

"The sample? That preacher and his whole 'I say let this city burn and twist in the wind' thing? I found that."

"What's to stop them finding those tracks themselves now and not paying you?"

"They're not paying because I found them. They're paying me not to let anyone else have them."

It was only when we found a greasy spoon with fogged up windows and solitary old guys making cups of tea last an hour that I saw Baxter finally relax. He visibly deflated, a beer belly appearing from nowhere, his chins doubling. He ran both hands through his hair and it sprang into an untidy tangle. I realised how much he'd been holding himself in check back there.

He looked around, rubbed his hands together and ordered the works. Then he started to talk. I didn't listen to everything he said. There was a dogged monotone to his voice that I'd heard before in people who'd spent too many hours in their own company, rehearsing arguments and playing them over and over in their minds. He gabbled like someone trying to get to the end of a failing Best Man's speech and then finally gulped down his cold tea.

"So that's me. How have you been? Married? Kids?"

Don't look back, never look back.

"No. I came close a couple of times but I'm not sure I could inflict myself on anyone for that length of time. When I say *it's not you, it's me* I actually mean it."

"So you're back for a while?"

I shrugged.

"I might have something for you, then." There was smugness in his tone, but something else too. Excitement?

He said, "You know the Velvet Underground acetate they found in a garage sale in New York?"

"The Sceptre Sessions?" I knew the story well. A garage sale find that had cost cents and sold for six figures. It was a post facto justification for the hours I spent thumbing through used record bins.

"What d'you think about that?" I could see he was actually interested in my reply.

"I think it's great. It's one of the great artworks of the twentieth century. It's like finding the preliminary sketches for *Guernica* in a skip."

His eyes shone. "Exactly." I'd stumbled on the right answer. "And if they did find the whatdyacallit, the *Guernica* things in a skip, what would they do with them?"

"Same thing they did with the Velvets, auction the living hell out of the fuckers."

"Sure, but first?"

"First?"

"First they'd authenticate them right?" He gestured for another cup of tea.

"Yeah of course."

"And the VU acetate?"

"I guess." I tried to remember what I'd read in the press.

"You guess wrong. Everyone wanted it to be real so we decided it was. Not even a hint of a check on it." He sat back, pleased with himself.

"Well yeah, who would fake something like that?"

He waited a beat. Satisfaction radiated off him.

"You?" I asked.

"No, not me. Though I wish I had. To be fair I don't have any proof that it was fake, but it's pretty convenient. There was nothing else interesting in that sale, no other acetates. The guy who's supposed to have recorded it is dead. The sessions were notoriously druggy."

He was talking to himself now, working himself up.

"There's simply no other artwork that you could sell, unchecked, for that kind of money. A painting would have Sotheby's in like a shot, there are people who make a living authenticating these things, but because it's just a record…" He shook his head and refocused.

"All you'd really need to fake something like that is a guy who knows how old records look" — he pointed at himself — "and a talented mimic with no morals and bills to pay."

I wasn't sure whether to be flattered or insulted.

"Sooooo… What exactly are we talking?"

"Well." He was properly smiling now, a Cheshire Cat thing. "In terms of money it would be the Quarrymen show, the one in Bootle?"

The day the Beatles met. John and Paul together for the first time. There were pictures — John hard as nails, Paul babyish and pink — but no audio.

"I thought it wasn't recorded?" I was already running through the idea in my head. How you'd get that skiffle sound, who had those vintage guitars.

"Someone could have taped it. I'd have to do some Liverpool house clearances, find a contemporary, fake a whole backstory. But." He tilted his head. "It has some difficulties. McCartney is smart, with a great memory and he's litigious."

"So not the Quarrymen?"

"Not the Quarrymen. Really it needs to be something from the studio, something fabled, but best of all something whose makers are all dead, *or…*" his grin widened, "Better than dead, nuts."

The tumblers clicked into place. The key turned. "*Smile*?"

He clinked his mug on mine. "*Smile*."

Chapter Five

"*Smile?*"

Brandon's writing just stopped there, on that last line. My voice was hoarse from reading.

Rae was nodding. "Yeah, *Smile...* you don't know what that is?"

"I don't think so."

The corners of her mouth turned down. "It's this record, or rather, it was going to be this record by Brian Wilson, the Beach Boys guy? It was rumoured to be this masterpiece that he beamed back from God after taking a bunch of LSD. But just as he finished it he had a message from on high and he destroyed all the tapes. He thought the power of the music was starting fires all over Los Angeles."

Her look said nothing. "It's like this total Holy Grail of record collectors and musicians, they try and recreate it from the scraps that were left." She turned wistful. "God the number of fucking car journeys I've spent listening to that thing. There was an official version of it released a while back but that just seemed to make the internet guys even madder."

"Why?"

"Well the guy, Brian," she said his name like he was someone she knew, "is kind of messed up nowadays. Too much acid in the Sixties. So according to the likes of Bran he just fudged his way through it. Like a moustache on the *Mona Lisa* apparently. Bran listened to it just the one time and then went back to the outtakes, it was like it didn't really exist."

She zoned out again and I let her think. "I suppose it would be worth a fortune if they could fake it."

"Is that even possible?"

"I don't know. Brandon knew those tracks inside out, and he does a pretty good Brian impression. And he has reams of out-takes from the original sessions." I watched her fingers worrying a thread on the frayed cuff of her jumper. "The thing is I'm not sure it would matter whether it was possible or not, he'd do it anyway. Just the idea of it would be enough. It would fuck off the Beach Boys fanatics. Check. He might make a fortune from it. Check. It was supposed to be super difficult to play. Check check check. And… even if it ever got out later that it was a fake, well that might be better."

That noise flitted through the apartment again: a whirr more insect than mechanical, spinning from room to room.

"Better? How so?"

"It'd prove he was talented enough to sound just like Brian *and* it'd make a fool of any journalist who'd raved about it. Win/win."

I looked through at the instruments and recording gear in the other room. They glowed with the warmth of objects handled over decades. How old was that stuff? Beach Boys-era? It would explain why nothing looked new.

"Do you think he recorded it?"

She shrugged. "Baxter seems to think he did. You've not seen anything?"

"I wouldn't know what I was looking for. A record? Tapes? A memory stick?"

"Tapes." Rae was definite. "The record's not cut, if that's what Bax was asking about. It wouldn't be digital because that would sound too modern. So it's tapes. Big ones." She spread her hands about a foot-and-a-half apart.

I carried the laptop through into the recording room. It felt church-like in the dusk, the guitars the colours of religious paintings: dried-blood reds, tobaccoey browns and tarnished golds. On the far wall I could make out a gloomy face: two eyes of spoked tape spools in a machine and a tight line of tape for a mouth. I pointed the laptop at it.

"That's it, there's a tape in it too."

I found the switch. The machine gave a sigh and feeble green lights struggled to life. I waited for the valves to thrum with heat and then pressed play. The room was filled, instantly, with a thick soup of voices, swooping and soaring and tied tight to each other. Even I could tell it was beautiful. I sat back in a chair and let it tiptoe through neat variations, adding to the room's religious air.

"'Our Prayer', this one's called," said Rae with grim satisfaction. "Track one, side one, leave it playing."

We sat there for an hour with the music playing and the light fading. She chatted about nothing: school clothes for Robin, the paths cut in shoulder-deep winter snow that made her town a maze of gleaming white walls, whether or not she should cut her hair. I felt privileged, a new immigrant to her world. At one point the music stopped and the tape flapped on its reel.

"Look underneath for side two. I hope he finished it." There was another tape and I worked out how to spool it between the two wheels. Again the burning smell of valves, old, gold light and songs that veered from the sacred to silly. I didn't want it to end.

"It's pretty nuts that Bran put all that writing on a memory stick that he knew Baxter would have. If he'd opened it then surely there'd be enough there to keep Baxter from working with him."

Rae looked dreamy on the screen. "Oh, he'd have loved that. He was addicted to risk."

She paused for a couple of seconds. "Last month I took him to a NA meeting in Reno. Things had gotten pretty rocky between us and I thought it was a good sign that he suggested it. He's always been so dismissive of those places: 'If you don't quit alone then you're not quitting', that sort of thing. So, I didn't quiz him, just drove him there and back because of his DUIs and sat in the car for an hour listening to old tapes. When he came out he looked so battered by it that I thought it might have helped. He looked *humbled*, y'know? And that's not a word I get to use much about him."

A track ended in a tumult of noise and Rae stared out, flat-eyed.

"So when he disappeared I drove out there to see if I couldn't talk to his sponsor. I know it's all confidential but if I could just get a sense of whether the guy was surprised that Bran had gone. There was no one in Tahoe he really spoke with. So, up I go to the third floor and it's like no meeting I've ever been to: the door is metal and bolted and no one wants to let me in. And when I finally collar someone coming out and see his pupils and his trackmarks I realise what the place is: a shooting gallery."

She checked the screen to make sure I understood.

"A place to shoot up, y'know? I'm there for an hour and I watch them go in shivering and come out wrecked." She shook her head slowly, more in wonder than in disgust.

"And when he did stuff like that, and he did it a lot, it infects everything around you. If a woman came to the house — any woman: Robin's teachers, a neighbour, one of the moms — I worried that it was because Bran had fucked her and he was getting a kick from her meeting me. If he ever bought me clothes I wouldn't dare wear them out in case I mistakenly went wherever he'd stolen them from. It's so *tiring*."

I didn't know what to say. We sat in respective silences for a minute as the track played on. And then the whole thing came to an underwhelming end. A wobbly synth line tailed off over huge acoustic drums, there was a silence and then, in offstage voices. "Brian?" "Yeah, that's the one."

Rae threw off the magic of the last thirty minutes. "Well. It sounded pretty real to me, but what would I know?"

I laughed, "About twenty times more than me. So what do you want to do with it?"

"What do *you* want to do?"

There's a special kind of silence after music has finished. We sat and watched each other on the screen.

"We wouldn't really be doing anything wrong, would we? If we sold it. We'd just be passing it on." There was hope in her voice but she was facing side-on to the screen so her eyes didn't meet mine.

"It's still fraud, we know it's not the real thing." I felt instantly, irredeemably square, like someone from another era. "I mean…"

She nodded. "I know. I wish I didn't know but I know." She breathed out hard. Then an odd smile crossed her face.

"You realise that if they were planning to sell it then what we've just read could have put Baxter in prison?"

It was true. There was enough detail there to make a legal case and Brandon had saved it onto a memory stick that he'd given Baxter.

Rae sat in profile like a portrait on a coin. There was something I wanted to ask her but I worried it was inappropriate.

"Do you miss him?"

She didn't pause. "Yeah, a bit. Sometimes. There's an internal Bran who's still here, telling me not to listen to Bon Jovi and complaining that the drinks cabinet is looking a bit thin; that one I could do without. But the actual Bran, I miss that other point of contact, y'know?" She stared into the screen. "When I was a kid I'd do anything to spend more time with my dad — he worked away a lot so when he was home I'd tag along everywhere he went. He used to love to rock-climb and I even went along with that a couple of times. You're literally tied together, if one falls you pull the other one down with you. I'd be up there flat against some terrifying Kansas rock-face, more worried about my nails than anything, and he'd call up to me, "Two points of contact at all times Ray-ray.' It was his rule: you always had to have two holds on the rock. Didn't matter if it was fingertips or toes, two points of contact. One was too slim a hold on the world."

I tried to keep very quiet.

"That's what I was thinking about, at his funeral. My fingers uncurling from around a spur of rock. One point of contact gone."

My phone vibrated on the table and I switched it off.

"Men don't feel that way, do they? Like they're fading away. A week after his funeral I moved to LA. Started going to castings. Found a place up in Koreatown over a dry-cleaners. All by my sweet self on the third floor and the neighbours never seemed to leave their apartments and I'd go days without even speaking to a soul. And I began to disappear. Every day I felt a little less solid. I'd go days without talking to anyone. I even did my shopping item by item just so I'd get to speak to *someone*. Once…" she shivered, "I lay down on the sidewalk, on Melrose. Just lay down with everyone walking around me, waiting for someone to ask if I was OK. So I'd know they could see me."

Without saying anything she walked to the fridge and came back with a Coke.

"When Bran came along it was like…" she mimed an explosion. "Everything turned 3D. When you see the day through two pairs of eyes everything becomes real again. But after a while he retreated into some other world and the world flattened out again. And then Robin. God, Robin." Her hands made an indistinct shape. "That was the moment. For the first time since I was a kid I was seen twenty-four hours a day. If I'm not directly in his sight then I'm in his mind. And all of a sudden I was solid again. Broken but solid. Two points of contact at all times. So I miss Bran but, I dunno, not enough."

The calm was broken by the noise of a door opening. It was only when I saw Rae rub her eyes with the pulled-down cuffs of her jumper that I realised she'd been crying.

Robin charged into the room and then vibrated to a halt when he saw the screen. "Hi Daddy." He leant in to kiss Rae and then squatted down.

"Why are you sitting in the dark?"

I looked around me. "I hadn't even realised. We were just talking."

"Can I see Umbrage?"

I gave him a look. "Don't you have homework?"

He turned to Rae. "Mommmm?"

Could he tell she'd been crying? She swiped her sleeve under her nose.

"An hour. Exactly one hour." She pulled out her phone. "I'm setting a timer."

"Daddy? C'mon."

I set up the endoscope as he chattered about school and let it run as he talked, watching the grassy uplands unspool on screen. With a child's unerring recognition for what you least wanted them to see, he waited until the Necropolis came into view before he said anything.

"What's that? Go back, go back." He was up on his elbows with his face close to the screen. The Necropolis was a spiral of glass bowls, each with just the narrowest of mouths gaping up into the air, uncoiled around a lone hill. In each bowl grew a single plant: some spindly, wooded things, some tiny jewel-like flowers. At the summit of the spiral the glass of the bowls had darkened and cracked, and pale roots trickled through the splinters. Lower down the bowls were newer and gleamed with the fresh green of shoots, while the containers on the lowest level, now beginning to colonise the flatlands, were pristine and contained nothing more than a thin layer of earth.

"What is it?" Robin's voice was rapt. What did he know of death? What did I know at that age? The brutal mathematics of pet ownership was my only experience.

"When people from Umbrage die, some of them are buried, the way we are," I said.

"Or burned up," said Robin with glee.

"Right, or cremated. But here people do something different. I'll read from the book, OK?"

I checked the screen to watch him nod.

On a ridge overlooking the inland sea, in an area called Koleman Putara, stands a knotted, stunted tree. It's black from root to branch-tip and covered in an ebony fruit with the sheen of beetle carcasses. The fruit are deadly poisonous and a white pyre of bird bones engulfs the first few feet of trunk. A songsmith from the Darks was the first to popularise this as a place to die. He rolled an oil-glass all the way up the hill and, after swallowing a handful of the shiny berries, climbed through the open neck and lay down. It's that oil-glass that sits atop Koleman Putara, blackened and mosaiced with cracks, but still home to the spiny black plant that grew out of his remains. As with most things, Umbragians are faddy about death, and it soon became fashionable to end your life here. Those who wish to die no longer have to push the glass bowls up the hill, or climb the tree for berries. Instead they take the funicular to the summit, pay a garden-hand to pack a glass with the richest of mulches and then choose from one of thousands of seed-cocktails on sale from stalls. Seeds of any growing thing from the four corners of Umbrage are on sale here: lilies that flower once a decade, voracious climbers, pungent lavender, trembling sky-thistle. But each packet also contains one sleek black bullet seed. Down they go together, death and beauty. And as the black seed releases its toxins, slowing vital processes and drawing life back, the other seeds start to swell and burgeon in the stomach; the moment when you are no longer a man, when you've become a garden, is hard to measure. Some of Umbrage's great and good are interred here. Dreamsmith Gororo, whose work sent the whole parliament into a week of unmoving sleep, is a tangle of thick vines. Westie, Umbrage ferryman for sixty years, is a simple carpet of daisies...

I stopped it there.

"So they're not really dead?" he asked.

This was the question I'd asked myself when I'd come up with the idea. A plant wasn't dead, was it, and the transformation was no more dramatic than that from a caterpillar to a butterfly. It was just a different kind of life: a concept that was comforting to me, but I had no idea how it would seem to a child.

"No, I don't think they are. A different kind of alive maybe."

"Freddie's buried in the back garden."

"Freddie?"

He pouted. "Our cat, don't you remember?"

"Of course, sorry."

He was fidgety but quiet and Rae was nowhere to be seen. I let a couple of moments pass.

"Hey, Robin, does mummy seem happier or sadder since I went away."

"I dunno." He tugged at his lower lip.

"It's OK. There's no right answer, I just wondered what you thought."

"Sadder. I dunno. Both. Sadder then happier." He looked at me beseechingly — *don't ask me this stuff.*

"Happier recently?" I asked.

"Yes, kinda. In the last week."

A twitch of pleasure. Did I do that?

I checked my watch. "That's an hour, homework time."

He jumped up, spindly legs filling the screen.

"K, thanks Dad love you," and he was gone.

There were things that needed doing in Umbrage but I couldn't keep my eyes from the screen. A blank white oblong of window that could be snow or sunlight. A crumpled juicebox. The tap dripping. Footsteps up and down stairs. Faint notes of birdsong. Umbrage sat dozing in a deep twilight behind me but it felt like a corpse on a slab. I wanted to plunge my hands through the screen into the mess of Tahoe to pick through the pile of washing on the counter and ball the socks. A blur traversed the screen: Rae, bare-legged. I coughed and her face slid into view.

"Whoops. Thought you'd gone." She sat down, one arm crossed over her bare chest. Earlier she'd told me something about her life, unasked, and now our relationship felt lop-sided. Umbrage ran through my head — the stories I had told Robin — but they were thin things compared to hearing her talk. For a long time she just looked at me with that strange disconnect you get on a screen. Then she said, "one sec," and returned in a T-shirt, holding a bottle of nail polish.

"So Baxter needed Brandon alive?" She was painting her nails and they loomed in the monitor in front of me.

"What's that?"

"Baxter. He needed Brandon to finish this *Smile* record."

"Right, yes. Though I'm still not sure why Brandon was doing all these money jobs. You'd think he'd concentrate on his own record if it's his legacy."

She examined her nails. "Who knows why he does the things he does? Maybe he just wanted to tie them all together again. Certainly if the record did come out it might put an unwelcome spotlight on them. We could try Saul?"

I'd spent an hour earlier looking for a way of contacting him but had come up with very little. "I got the number for the promoter that Brandon mentioned. I left a message but he may have burnt his bridges there. Kimi?"

"Can you face her?"

"I'm not sure…"

A noise started up from the music room. Vague sounds of someone moving around a room and then a voice. My voice. Brandon's voice.

"You left the tape running?" asked Rae.

"Yeah, I thought you said it was the end."

"It's the end of *Smile*, yes. I guess he used the half-inch tape for something else."

I walked the laptop through. Brandon's voice sounded actorly on the huge speakers. He was saying something about steam and windows.

"Should I rewind it?"

"Yeah, go back. It only just started up."

It took a couple of minutes to find the beginning but when we did the reading started with no preamble.

Daughters of the Daughters

I've transcribed this as clearly as I can. It was surprisingly easy — I have a feeling that Brandon was reading from something written down. He hardly pauses and you can hear pages being turned at some points. It's clear from the environmental sounds that the recording was made here, in At The Sign Of The Magpie, but there's no clue as to when.

Bax and I went for a couple of pints before I walked home. I took vaguely remembered streets, taking pleasure in London's illegibility. This city is so fucking unwelcoming to newcomers — young or old, black or white, rich or poor — that it's oddly democratic. You have to put the time in. On Mount Street a trio of mirror-sunglassed Arab kids drove their supercars at a walking pace. I'd seen them parked outside Claridge's earlier: three slabs of polished fibreglass that barely reached my waist, each in an eyeball-popping lipstick shade. The kids were bored, revving constantly to keep the engines from seizing up in London's snarl, staring out into space as cameraphones were whipped out at every traffic light. I fantasised idly: a bottle of vodka with my handkerchief stuffed in the top, a flick of lighter, and then of a wrist.

The whole block where the Colony Club used to be, where I'd had my first paid-for handjob, was broken to rubble, picked over by cranes and surrounded by hoardings. They promised "gracious city living" and were emblazoned with pictures of those Jurassic Sohoites — Bacon and O'Toole and Melly and Bernard — which just seemed like rubbing salt in the wound. It was their haunts that had been bulldozed.

Every couple of streets it was repeated: some memory torn down and the wreckage locked away behind hoardings. The city is made up of screens now. It was like Kimi's gig where everything vital and alive was caged in a screen. Life at one remove.

I had a vision. The city torn to pieces and roamed over by diggers, scavengers in the ashes. Birds bursting from bare trees as pneumatic drills juddered. All happening behind a maze of billboards showing what had once been there. Ornate painted screens of royal scenes around the wreckage of Buckingham Palace. Cartoon judges laughing over cappuccinos hiding the ruins of the Inns of the Court. Dickensian urchins in Shoreditch. And at the bottom of each one: SOON TO BE LUXURY FLATS — PRICES FROM £500,000.

Through Denmark Street, and the music shops that I'd haunted from the age of thirteen. Prices had gone from the exorbitant to the speculative — eighteen grand for a '53 Strat — so that what had once been toolshops for the musicians' trade were now a very specific antiques market. At Seven Dials I walked in lockstep with a girl talking tightly into a hidden mouthpiece. I reached over and touched her arm.

"Rachel? Rachel! It is, oh my God."

I'd never seen her before, obviously. Her eyes widened and she clutched her bag tighter, but she didn't say anything. I matched her stride.

"It's how long? Ten years? No, eleven."

She shook her head but didn't say anything.

"You've been alive all this time. He said you were dead, he said you couldn't live with it, but I should have known you were stronger than that."

"I don't know you." Her voice was tiny but certain.

"Of course, of course — I understand. You have to say that. I know you though. *I know you.*"

I gave her a wink and walked on.

I knew I was back in east London once the kids started to look like refugees. They were dressed in leftovers and bin ends, big kids who'd been at the dressing-up basket. The attempts at beards were particularly heartrending. They reminded me of photographs of kids playing in the bombsites, post-World War II — kings of nothing, rulers of a wasteland. They'd picked over the rubble of our culture, cloaked themselves in rags, stripped of all meaning. I saw *Thundercats* T-shirts, leather blousons in teal and burgundy, turn-ups, branded sportswear, plastic sunglasses, sweatshirts yellow and crusty at the armpits, ski boots, braces, dinner jackets.

I sat in a coffeeshop and pulled up the Brian Wilson messageboards just to see who was saying what about what. No rumblings of a miraculous find. The whole thing would put Bax in my debt, which is exactly where I like people to be. With him under the thumb, and Kimi's love of a musical game, I had pretty much a full band. I could go ahead without Saul but there would be a symmetry to the whole thing if he were involved. Technically I didn't need them but there's a reason why the best records are made by bands.

Music, if you do it right, is making the impossible come to life. For all your everyday emotions there are words: jealousy, anger, enchantment, whatever. But for those impossible tangles of feeling, "brutal femininity", "desperate ennui", well you need an older, stranger language. And it's easier for two people, or four even, to hold all these competing emotions in orbit around themselves. A quartet could to want to build and destroy and cry and laugh and give up and persevere all at the same time; a band could believe six impossible things before breakfast. I needed irritants and accelerants. I needed firewood.

Kaspar was standing in the doorway when I got back to The Magpie, staring up at the sky like it had done him some harm. I pulled out my ciggies. He was wearing a badge that read, I LOST 10 POUNDS ASK ME HOW.

"How d'you lose ten pounds Kas?" I asked.

He produced a lighter from somewhere and lit my cigarette. "I grew dreadlocks before the weigh-in, then shaved them off."

Baxter's more dynamic now than he ever was on stage; the recording gear arrived the next morning. Two sweating guys in vests swore their way up and down the spiral stairs with as-near-as-damnit the exact contents of Brian Wilson's Sunset Sounds studio, as it was back in the summer of sixty-five. Bax and I had pored over the few pictures that still existed from those sessions. Brian already a vacant, glandular toddler, ringed by unlikely instruments. There he was grinning under a fireman's hat, picking at a battered ukulele. There's Van Dyke Parks, trim as a plantation owner, struggling with a tuba. Comprehensively moustachioed session men blew, bowed, struck and strummed a wealth of instruments that would have made a good-sized orchestra jealous.

The gear was from a guy called Tony Harrison who I'd hired from back in the Nineties, when he was the go-to guy if you wanted the kind of amp that Bolan used on *The Slider*, or a 335 that had passed through Johnny Marr's hands. He'd been expensive then, but nowadays he was astronomical.

The third time I queried a cost his voice hardened.

"These are the fucking prices OK? I hardly ever lend out at all nowadays, I just find stuff to sell to bankers."

"Bankers?"

"Bankers. Hedge fund men. Property people. The art market's got too rich for them, wine's going the same way. So the next big thing is vintage instruments. Remember that black Gold Top? The one Jimmy Page used in *The Song Remains the Same*?"

I did. I'd hired it for our very last session, at a ruinous cost. It didn't make me sound like Jimmy Page.

"Guess how much I sold it for?" He didn't wait for an answer. "A hundred and fifty grand. Some French guy in Westbourne Grove. Can't play a note as far as I can tell. Not sure he even knew who Jimmy Page was. So, think on. That Strat that you're trying to beat the price down on is probably worth two Ferraris. And you wouldn't get them for five hundred a day."

I did actually get the price down. For all his faults, the man loves his guitars, and a few minutes of cooing over his war stories of Mick n' Keef and Van and Eric got me a discount and free delivery.

I couldn't play all of the instruments in the Sunset Sound pictures. Baxter was nervous, obviously, about bringing in outsiders, but we had samples of pretty much everything, and, according to Baxter, the record would probably never be comprehensively examined.

He kept pushing his glasses back up his nose, a sign that he was excited. "The great thing is that every play diminishes its value. So whoever buys it is going to play it once, if at all. If he digitises it, that first time he plays it, we can blame any artefacts on the process."

"What d'you mean, 'if at all'?"

"I wouldn't play it. I'd put it in a climate-controlled vault, make sure everyone knew I had it and just wait."

It's a strange feeling, taking apart something you love. I've lived with *Smile* for thirty years — it's probably my longest meaningful relationship. It's an odd record, only knowable through its absences. You can see its shape hidden in Brian's other records, a ghost haunting the Gothic halls of later Beach Boys. Bits of it turn up elsewhere. Some songs are finished and well documented. Some are nothing more than titles and studio time-sheets: *Danny McCrae, Wurlitzer, 90 mins @ $30 an hour.*

We started with alternate takes of the existing sections. Some of the major songs like "Heroes and Villains" or "Cabin Essence" exist in a snowstorm of fragments. There are home demoes, which mutate into slicker sounding takes from United Western Recorders, then hugely altered versions whose provenance is unconfirmable. The popular theory among the shut-ins who make up the *Smile* online cognoscenti is that the version of "Good Vibrations" that Brian re-recorded for his next record was a cut 'n' shut of two older takes, with the first half being vastly superior, so we set out to recreate the whole thing in the spirit of those first golden minutes. The playing wasn't that hard. Brian was a genius but that didn't mean he was a virtuoso. It was actually harder to get the room sounding right — that peculiar reverb signature of Brian's swimming pool (used for the guitars) and the slapdash mike placement. We worked steadily through rack upon rack of virtual units until we found something that replicated its odd mix of slapbacks and long notes. I played guitar (a glorious semi-acoustic, so worn that you had to turn it over to discover what colour it had originally been), ukulele, bass and some organ. Baxter took the piano parts and did some tuba trills.

He pottered around the instruments like an old man on his allotment. He always made a mess of dressing himself: labels hanging out, trouser legs tucked into socks. Today he'd buttoned his shirt up wrong and one checked collar flapped uselessly out of his sweater. Still, he knew *Smile* like no one else. He perched on the piano stool, lit by candles, looking like a chubby Phantom of the Opera and poured out track after track of keyboard parts. At one point, damp with sweat and glassy eyed, he played me back a song on the big speakers. It was one of those rococo harpsichord parts that unfold like a butterfly from a cocoon and halfway through, where he flubbed a descending run — a stubbed toe of a note — he looked at me in triumph. "You hear it, you hear it?"

I wasn't sure what he meant.

"The mistake. It's the exact same one he makes in 'Little Pad' a couple of years later. Nice huh? By thy mistakes shall we know thee."

We played for hours, safe inside the world of *Smile*, a world at once as infinite as a solar system and as strictly confined as a prison. When, finally, we were done for the night, an unmistakably post-coital air suffused the room. We slumped on couches, smoked and avoided eye contact.

"It's like dressing up, isn't it?" Baxter was lying on the couch with his shadowed head lolling down. "At first you feel silly then you get something from it."

I didn't want to hear what kind of dressing up Baxter Moores might do, but I knew what he meant. I was an OK actor back in my day. I liked being someone else and feeling my face move in unaccustomed ways. I liked crying and I liked fighting without getting hurt. But I never lost myself in it the way I did recording *Smile*. Once we were two or three tracks in and Brian's syrupy rhythms started calling from the deep then you just let go. Your hands were like water. Your voice tracked his like that game where you run a hoop over an electrified metal wire, a centimetre either way setting the buzzer rattling. But you stayed calm and true and you ran that wire dead through the centre until you were home sweet home.

"You're not wrong."

I rolled a joint. The street outside was a cul-de-sac and once in a while a pair of headlights threw a white frame around the window. Once in, once out.

"Bran. Why are you here?" His feet had stopped jiggling.

"I'm going to make a record."

His silence was more accusatory than anything he might have said.

"I'm going to make a record and then I'm going to go away for a while." I thought about it. "Well more than a while. And I wanted to make amends with Kim and Saul and you. And I don't really know of any way of doing that apart from this." I threw a hand towards the music room. I couldn't see his face, which made it easier.

"I'm aware my word isn't worth much." This was something I'd said before, but here, with a man whose girlfriend I'd fucked on the night I split up his band, I knew how true it was. "And I don't think there's any way of changing that. Leopard, spots, y'know."

The grunt from the couch could have meant anything.

"What little good there is in me is in my songs. If I can't put my life right out in the real world" — I threw my arms wide — "then I can at least do it in here. I know it's not a lot. But hopefully it's something."

People think we write songs to express feelings, and who knows, perhaps there are some mentally stable folk out there for whom it's true. But I think most writers, the interesting ones anyway, write songs to *create* feelings. It's alchemy; the spark of life in the automaton. In a song you can find that perfect feeling that real life is so reluctant to provide. I don't want to be like Kate Bush writing "Running Up That Hill", I want to *be* "Running Up That Hill".

He was quiet for the first time in the whole day. Just another of his grunts and a fat finger on the PLAY button again.

"Those are going to have to be finessed at home," he said, listening back for the hundredth time, swapping between his iPod and our tape. "We'll fake some mike spill and get a few of the ambient sounds in there. You can hear a train go by in one of the Gold Star sessions." He was talking mainly to himself. "I'll have to find out what make it was."

He made a couple of notes and yawned unselfconciously. The first slivers of daylight were showing around the curtains.

"Not bad. Four done. Three were easy ones mind, but a good start." He yawned and rubbed his neck. "Same time tomorrow?"

I could have gone on forever. "Sure," I said, "You sort the brass and I'll make a start on some of the stuff that we're doing from scratch."

He kept nodding, like a tic, as he packed away. "One other thing. The Theremin on 'Good Vibrations', it's not actually a Theremin."

I fixed him with a stare. Even the newbies on the *Smile* forums knew that. They could tell you all about the device that Paul Tanner had built for Brian, an odd cross between a pedal steel and a Theremin, that produced one of the most recognisable sounds of the twentieth century.

Baxter stretched. "I know who has the original."

"The one they used on tour?" That was old news.

"Nope, the 'Vibrations' one. The fucking grail, man. Tanner sold it to a hospital because he thought it had been superseded and the hospital wanted any gear that had an oscillator." He shook his head in wonder. "They were going to use it on heart patients. But it never got used and ended up in an electronics shop in Pasadena. And guess who found it there? Hyde."

"Hyde from Jackyl & Hyde?" That made sense. He was a prodigious collector of all things analogue and musical. "Yeah, I can see that. So, go and borrow it off the old gargoyle. He lives down your way doesn't he?" Bax had mentioned him at Claridge's.

"They both do. But they won't see me." I was beginning to recognise his gestures now. The hand covering his mouth like a Japanese schoolgirl — that was embarrassment.

I did know that they wouldn't see him, he'd mentioned it, but you should never pass up an opportunity to make an old friend feel uncomfortable. "Yeah, why was that again? They're such *sweethearts*."

He stared at me like he was constipated. "Their fucking records man." He looked reverent. "You should see their collection. Fuck. 'Rabbit Foot Blues' on 78. A Benny Cliff Trio single, mint in sleeve, even Kenny and the Cadets. I couldn't help pushing. I'd go down there and listen to their endless anecdotes and drink that Camp Coffee and Jackie'd play these fucking records that are like, they're like legends. No, not legends. They're rarer than that, they're like myths. They have fucking wax cylinders of Robert Johnson, Bran."

I recognised his look from NA meetings. Pure, feverish hunger. "So, what's the problem?"

"I just wanted to take some pictures, you know for authentication, and for my own... pleasure."

I had a momentary, ugly vision of him on his knees, hand down his jeans, grunting to iPhone images of 1950s rockabilly sleeves.

"They went crazy. They would have thrown me out on my arse if they weren't frail as sparrows. I've been back but they don't even answer the door."

That'd be killing him. A world-class record collection on his doorstep. Forget what they were worth, the bragging rights alone would light up his particular slice of the internet.

"Why d'you think it'd be any different for me? It's been years."

"They like you Bran, *she* likes you. Always asks after you." He approximated her faux-Texas snarl. "'What ever happened to the purdy one?' The thing is Bran I think it's the key to the record. No one's ever got close to capturing that sound, not properly. If someone came to me saying they'd found the *Smile* originals it'd be the first thing I checked."

He was right. The pierce and warble of the thing was as recognisable as a voice. If we got it right it would tug all of our inconsistencies into place behind it.

"Fine, get me the address, I could do with some sea air. Now why don't you fuck off and let me work?" I felt the undertow of inspiration and Bax was beginning to bore me.

Once he'd gone the room hummed with electricity. Those old amps vibrated and spluttered and were prone to tantrums, but there was no denying they filled the air with possibility. The centre of the music room was a bare expanse of parquet the colour of pipe tobacco. I found a packet of chalk and tried to recreate the Sigillum Dei Aemeth. A drawing pin pushed between the parquet in the centre, a piece of string. I traced the outer ring and then drew a heptagon inside it, touching at seven points. The names of the Angels of Brightness should go here I knew, but I could only remember a couple. Horlwn and Galethog were the sun and moon, I dredged that up from somewhere, but the others refused to appear. Instead I wrote in names. BRANDON.

KIMI. SAUL. BAXTER. DILLON. HYDE. I toyed with the last one. KASPAR had an excitingly Gothic set of letters but he had the feel of a Lesser Angel about him. Fuck it, I knew who'd be playing a part, even if it were an inadvertent one. I wrote in ADAM at the top tip.

Then the angles of the seven-pointed star that you drew, satisfyingly, in one zig-zagging stroke. The Sons of Light it was called, and the pentagon formed its centre was named for the Daughters of the Daughters. And then that oldest of clichés, the pentagram, sitting smugly in the centre.

It suited the overwrought nature of the room, with its candlesticks and bell jars, the portraiture and metalwork. I took a paperweight from the desk and used it as the shew-stone, tossing it mindlessly among the lines of power like I had on a hundred teenage afternoons crouched over diagrams and books. What fucking nonsense this was. Another of the puny ways we've tried to impose some order on the universe, another thin layer of ice over the abyss.

I've flip-flopped on these things over the years. I loved them in my pretentious youth. I was forever reading bloodcurdling futures for timid girls at parties. As an adult I was as sceptical as a Dawkins, holding forth for hours on the constructs that stopped people from taking control of their lives. That phase was even more unbearable than the first. It took me years to work out the power of these fripperies: tarot, Rorschach, OKCupid. They didn't unearth the hidden structure of the universe, they made one up. And, however flimsy the construct — autumn ice on black water, highwires between skyscrapers — it gave you a handhold to at least face the chasm that is everyday existence.

I tossed the shew-stone three times. Baxter, 6, Sons of Light. I let it mean what I wanted it to mean. I sat at Bax's Wurlitzer, the stool so low that I felt like Schroeder, and flicked the sixth preset. It was a husk of a sound. I willed myself into an approximation of Baxter, hunched and myopic, careless with the keys, careful with the pedals, and began to play.

"Sons of Light forget their names…" I was off. I recorded quickly. Drums, bass, guitar, vocals, while still deep in Brian-space, my fingers moving with his ragged exactitude, every trace of black and blue gone from my voice. I let the stone decide the directions. It picked out percussion, nudged the lyrics, cut an outro that wasn't quite working.

I listened back over breakfast. Kaspar came up with kedgeree, something that I always order and then remember I don't especially like, and he sat with me on the balcony as the track played.

"It's nice," he said. "Calmer than I would have expected."

"You put into your songs what you're missing in real life," I said, and then, feeling like I was back giving interviews, added, "Thank you."

When he'd gone I lay out on the balcony under the weak London morning, watching the contrails. A flock of parakeets flashed past chattering, the green of their bellies seemingly still lit by some tropical sun. They glinted like jewels.

At this point Bran stops talking. There's twenty seconds of background noise and then a track plays.

Chapter Six

I usually dream of everyday life in Umbrage. I'll be a lullaby-peddler kneeling at the bedside of a merchant's teething son, singing the secret song passed down to me through generations (while discretely dabbing a corner of cloth in essence of laudanum, just in case). Or the river will materialise around me, ferrymen's shouted conversations across the waves, the suck of river mud between bare toes and the feel of old rope on my palm. Or I'm drunk at the zinc bars, circling in eddies of beer and lies, a dream within a dream within a dream.

But here at The Magpie for two days straight I've dreamt of Tahoe. Last night I was walking through the house at night, the scene lit with that gauzy glow of moonlight on snow, and I ran my hands over the walls and window-sills, the rails and worktops, always touching, like the conductor on a dodgem car. I saw it all: the clock on the cooker set an hour slow, the recycling bin full to overflowing, the hairbands knotted with blonde fuzz. A wonderland stranger than Umbrage could ever be. I dreamt of Robin in his room. Blankets twisted around his knobbled ankle, not flesh of my flesh but something deeper, chemical keys turning in chemical locks. He wore an American football jersey rucked up under his arms, everything else in the room grey in the moongleam. His fearful, brittle rib-cage, his constellations of moles. Something half-finished stood in the middle of a workbench. A tower of white squares, covered in flaps, the occasional one flipped open to reveal hooks and hydraulics and pulleys and motors. Something written in a language that only Robin and I knew. That moves there, and that slides open, and that section drops away. Out into a corridor lined with photos, lit by a window onto frost-rimed branches and far-away car lights.

Rae's door open. Starfished across her bed, like she'd been dropped from a great height, window open to the lake. Crushed up against the sheets giving her a lopsided pout. More laughter lines than worry lines, like my mum would say. Books on the bedside table, topped with a pair of reading glasses. *Financial Planning for Dummies* with what looked like every third page folded over at the corner.

I sat on the edge of the bed but nothing moved. I was weightless. There was the faintest movement with each breath and a flutter of blood in a neck-vein to tell me she was alive.

When I woke I could still feel the pull. This room with its art and books and voice-activated TV and six kinds of bottled water was less real than the dream. The window through to Tahoe was still open but it was night there, the screen just a wall of grey. I replayed Brandon's recording to see if there was anything to be gleaned from it.

The title "Sons of Light" seemed as good a place to start as any. I googled it and waded through pages of occult sites. They were badly designed and full of photocopied images from old books. Sad, empty comments sections. Each site was different, each was the same. I recognised the obsession and desperation. I could feel the screenburn from here. "Sons of Light" yielded nothing, but I hit gold with "Daughters of the Daughters".

It was a Baidu page. I had to search again just to discover what Baidu was, but it appeared to be the Chinese version of Facebook. The page itself was a squiggle of Chinese characters, cartoon pop-ups and friend suggestions, but the waveform at the centre looked like the SoundCloud links. Underneath, in the comments, someone called CC had provided the lyrics in both English and kanji "for my Chinese friends".

I was about to Skype Rae when the familiar tone bubbled up from the laptop.

I clicked ACCEPT. "Hey, Rae, guess what I f…"

"Fucking little mother fucking *fuck*." Rae was inches from the laptop. She shot me a look and thrust something against the camera, turning my screen white.

"That evil little *fucker*." The page of white turned and squirmed. "I will *kill* him. I would kill him if he wasn't already dead."

I tried to calm her. She pulled the page away and started pacing, only in shot for split seconds. She was running a constant monologue. "Fucking… Fuck… Stupid." She slapped herself hard on the forehead, sat down and then instantly jumped up. "I can't even…"

I slowed my breathing, trying to enact some sympathetic calming effect.

"He sold the house right out from under us." She was in profile, vibrating with rage. "Sold it and didn't say a word." She read the page again in front of her.

"How?"

"How? Because I'm a fucking idiot that's how. Because I put him on the mortgage two years back so we could write off the payments against his fucking nonexistent tax bill that's how. Because I let my guard down for one, stupid, second."

"Can he do that?"

She shook her head. "He's done it."

"Can't you do anything about it?"

She gave me an evil look.

"Can you at least get your share of the money?" Her shake was almost imperceptible now.

"How long?"

She smoothed out the letter. "Six weeks. Maybe. He sold it to the bank. To the *bank*. Jesus what an idiot. It might take them a while to find a buyer, but…"

She looked around her. "Borrowed time. And renting here is ridiculous. Landlords make more from Bay Area skiers in a month than I can pay a year." Her voice was rising. "And Robin just about likes this school and I can't move him again." The words began to trip over themselves. "And the fucking moving and the deposit and the nosy neighbours."

She looked up and her eyes and nose were pink, like a baby animal's. "I can't look at you at the moment. I know it's not you, but…"

The screen went black, the speaker quiet. I thought of the bills here: the food and drink I'd been ordering, Kaspar's little treats.

There was a pause and then a small voice. "I'm still here though."

I tried to cut in. "The *Smile* money."

Silence.

"Baxter said it was a big deal right?"

"So? How much could it be? 50K? My cut's twenty-five. I suppose it would be a deposit and a couple of months' rent."

"Take the lot. It's not mine. Brandon doesn't owe me anything."

"I couldn't. I won't. Anyway Baxter has to sell it first." But there was an hopeful edge to her voice now.

"Well let's get it sold. I'll call him now. And then there's Saul's thing. The contract."

I heard a sniffle. "You don't think Bran fucked that up?"

"I'm sure he did. But it can be unfucked. I'm not him, Rae. I may not have his charm but I don't think I rub people up the wrong way as much as he did either."

The screen flickered back into life. She was low in the frame, raw and tousled.

"You don't. You're easy to talk to. But it's too much. All of this. You're not him, you don't have to make this right."

I could sense the distance between us. The dark ocean and the mountains and the leagues of rain.

"I want to." As I said the words I knew it was true. Let me be wanted. Let me be needed. Let me be seen.

"Really?" She trailed a jumper-sleeve under her nose as if she weren't on camera.

"Really. Where's Robin?"

She glanced out of frame. "Upstairs, working on something for you." She smiled the very smallest of smiles. I saw his tower of white squares, fresh from the dream.

"Good, tell him I'll call in an hour."

I had work to do.

I called Rae back after an hour. She and Robin were at the kitchen table. He looked skittish; I guessed he'd heard Rae's outburst this morning. As I talked to her he watched us both carefully.

"I spoke to Baxter. Just one little thing to do. Nothing to worry about."

I shouldn't have said that. I never understand how I can say one thing and people, rightly, assume the opposite, but her look was fretful.

"Robin, your mum tells me you've made something for me?"

"Yeah." He was torn between showing me and leaving Rae, I could tell. He fiddled with his pens.

"Go set it up. I need to talk to your mum." There was a fierceness to his look that I'd not seen before. "It's all good stuff, I promise. No fighting."

He nodded and took off. Rae pushed her chair so she was centre frame. "Nothing to worry about? That sounds worrying."

I kept my voice light. "It's good really. Just some problems getting the record actually made. Baxter's sorting his end but he says Brandon agreed to arrange the pressing. I checked the number in his notebook, the PRESSER one, and it's a studio apparently. I'm going to call them in a bit. But first, this morning, before, y'know, I was going to tell you I found another track."

"Damn. I was just going to search. Where was it?"

I sent her the link. She didn't have to tell me that we should listen together, just counted down three-two-one on her fingers. This was something different again: spindly, circling guitars over stocky drums, everything somehow in pieces, unsettled and unsettling. Brandon's voice was distant and harsh, ending lines with yelps that reverberated for seconds. They sounded like animal cries. I didn't like it at all.

"Wow, that's great." Rae shook her head. "It's like something from 1983. Not his taste at all though." She clicked play again. Her head nodded along to the beat and she mouthed a couple of the lyrics.

After singing along for a while she watched me from the screen. "What do you like? I never hear music on in the background there."

"Just the radio really. Growing up with Brandon made music impossible. Whatever I liked was wrong so I stopped trying. And now I feel like other people hear something in music that I don't."

She nodded. "That's a shame, but I get it. Putting a record on in front of Bran was a bit like being up in court." She grinned. "I can't tell you what it's like to be able to play Yaz around the house without Bran having a meltdown."

Robin called from upstairs, "I'm *readddddy*."

"Sorry, he's been talking about this for hours, you're going to have to go see. Be nice, OK?"

I didn't admit that I was looking forward to it. I said, "Of course."

Robin had the laptop in his hand. "I don't have an endoscope but mom got me something even cooler, hang on."

The picture on the screen wobbled and then went black. Robin muttered. Then an image lurched onto the screen. It was his room: the furniture had been pushed to one side, and a square table, shiny with glass or water, had been positioned in the centre. The view see-sawed and stabilised. I could see the table more clearly now. It was low and deep, with the sides partially covered. Its surface was divided up into a series of exact squares, like a mirrored chess board. The view shifted until I was looking at the table from almost directly overhead.

"How are you doing that?" I asked. The viewpoint was way above his head height.

"It's a microlight drone with an iPhone mount and stabilisers, mom got it, look."

The table zoomed closer until its surface filled the screen. Then it zoomed out again. Robin giggled to himself as he guided the drone. "That's not the best bit."

I heard the sound of blinds closing and the table became a black pool. He bent down, caught in his own camera for a second, and fiddled with something on the edge of the table. Lamps came on around the edge, bright white bulbs like runway landing lights. For a moment nothing happened — just the whirr of the drone rotors and his breath. And then a row of the squares tilted upwards. On all four sides they rose in unison, each catching the lamplight at different moments, sending streaks of light along their edges. Now they were a mirrored city wall, turning an arch from a ruin into a doorway.

"You go in here, see," Robin placed a plastic model soldier within the arch, "and then you step towards the middle." He slid the soldier one square forward and again fiddled at the table's side. There was a small handle there, as delicate as the one on Umbrage's music box. He turned it and a ring of mirrored blocks rose as one. The sides reflected light from the edge tiles and sent it dancing across the room's walls. Robin walked around the table gleefully, obscuring shafts of light as he walked.

"And then here." He placed the soldier a step closer to the middle and turned the handle again. The centre blocks rose and angled into a gleaming spire.

It was beautifully done. Through the spaces in the table's surface I could see some of the workings: Meccano and twine. Light bounced from lamp to slope to block to wall in clear lines, building another, less substantial city in the air.

"And then," Robin hooked a weight to the soldier's base, pushed him one square on and it disappeared down a hole in the centre of the city. I caught a gasp in my throat as the little figure was swallowed by the blackness. But as he fell something rose up: a spindly contraption like a nude umbrella, unfolding in the shafts of light, and each prong was topped with a sliver of silver paper, buffeted by the drone's downdraft and lit by the beams of light as the city, the whole tabletop city, began to revolve, making streams of light rotate and cross like scaffolding around the room. And each sliver of silver had the same phrase written across it in the terrible beauty of a child's writing: COME HOME COME HOME COME HOME COME HOME COME HOME COME HOME COME HOME COME HOME

I heard the door close. "Robin?" I said, but he was gone, so I sat, doubled, halved, torn watching a city of light revolve around my screen.

It was an hour later when Rae came in to retrieve the laptop. The drone had finally spluttered to a halt after one too many scuffings on the wall, and the city was still. Her face loomed into view, crisscrossed by beams of light.

"It's amazing right?" She angled the laptop to face the city. You couldn't still see the silver paper strips. They sat dark and bedraggled in the low light. I wondered who the messages were really meant for. Me or Brandon?

"He spent hours on YouTube watching engineering projects for like *college* students. I didn't think he'd be able to do it." She turned the laptop to face herself.

"You, you are a good man Adam Kussgarten." She looked me long and hard in the eyes then. "That was important to him. It was important to me."

I was unused to being looked at this closely. I forced myself to look back. Grey eyes, grey sweatshirt, pale skin.

"I feel like we're taking from you without giving back."

I wanted to shout *no*. I was getting so much back. The tethers that had so rankled Brandon, I wanted them. *Tangle me up* I thought, *tie me down*. The pull of her eyes. *See me*.

But I couldn't say it. We looked at each other for a second and then her eyes flickered to the room behind me. "So many beautiful things," she sighed. "Pianos and paintings and the *flowers*. All that booze and girls on tap and people at your beck and call. You're going to develop expensive tastes Ads."

I looked around. After the first couple of days here I hardly noticed the furnishings but it was true, there wasn't an ugly object anywhere in sight.

"I don't know. It's quite sad I think. There's something so desperate about what rich people spend their money on. This place feels like it's trying to make up for something."

I blushed: I wasn't used to talking this way.

Rae sighed. "You're right, I know. This is what you get instead of love, I guess."

That sentence echoed around my mind until my phone started vibrating in my pocket. Notifications crowded the screen, seemingly a message every couple of seconds.

"It's Baxter."

The texts mounted up.

"He says he cracked and sent Frank Isaacs mp3s of some of the *Smile* stuff. Isaacs says it's 'the most important musical find of the century'. He has a buyer right now, so if I don't sort the pressing this week he's going to freaking freak. His words obviously."

She mused. "That's great right? We might actually get some money out of this."

"*You* might. I told you. I don't want it, I don't need it and I don't deserve it. It's for you. And Robin. Call it reparations."

She laughed. "Actually Robin is technically Native American. It's a long story, I'll tell you another time."

I kept reading. "He says the stuff on Dillon's website is really funny but is it a good idea to be sticking my head above the parapet right now. Mean anything to you?"

"Dillon's the guy I told you about, with the remix? Brandon'll have been trolling I suppose. When he was wrecked he'd pose as a Dillon fan online and make fun of him. Pathetic really. Let me have a look."

Her hands clattered on the keys and a smile rose on her face. "Hey check out dillonmarksman.com"

I went onto the site. It was very slick, with sections for his musical projects, charity stuff, his "revolutionary mobile app" and mentoring work. A rotating slide show of images showed Dillon with a cavalcade of famous people. He was clinking cocktails with Steven Tyler on the deck of a yacht, placing a mortar board atop a beaming Steve Jobs, ditch-digging, still in his turquoise Nudie suit, while Sting looked on gravely.

I clicked through to the forum. It wasn't hard to find the thread that Baxter had been talking about — most of the discussions there had five or fewer replies but one, at the top of the page, titled *American XS — My Part in its Downfall* had racked up thousands of views.

"You see it?" I asked Rae.

"Sorry, no, I haven't got past the front page. Did you see the picture of Dillon and Metallica washing oil off a seabird? Fuck me, this is glorious."

I let her scroll through the pictures for a while and then she said, "OK, got it. The top one yeah? On three we dive in, right?" She beamed at the screen. "One. Two. Three."

Some Monsterism

This was one of a number of threads on dillonmarksman.com. It's by a guest user with no other posts.

Awake with the dawn. Brutal LA light filtered through the graffiti that covers every inch of the floor-to-ceiling windows in this glass box of a bedroom. The sunlight is stained with Renaissance colours — vermillion, umber, emerald — and projected across my sheets. The windows have been painted from the inside. A malevolent Mickey Mouse, crucified through his sausagey white hands, stares balefully down while cartoon B-boys spin and pose at the base of his cross. Donald Duck totes an Uzi, as tear tattoos weep from a gimlet eye. It's all a bit much after the night I've had, to be honest.

There's a scratchy noise repeating from somewhere deep in the house so I go to investigate. Broken glass litters the carpet so I feel around for the flip-flops. Flip-flops and a bathrobe like a honeymooner. Flip-flops and a bathrobe and the last of the duty-free B&H like a proper Brit abroad.

In the corridor the painting is cruder and many of the windows are starred with gunshots, and paint-gummy where they meet the floor. Here and there, through the shards of broken glass, you catch sight of the outside world. A sprinkler's arc and the trail of traffic on the I-50. The noise is louder here, like the tick of an artificial heart.

The first bedroom's door is propped open. A tangle of limbs — white, brown, yellow — more beautiful than the art outside. In the next room four black guys in boiler suits are dividing up a bare wall in pencil, preparing it for painting. It looks like a butcher's chart of the best cuts. All four give me serious head-nods. "Looking good, guys," I tell them.

Down the corridor. The carpet's an ashtray, littered with spray-paint cans and bottles. It smells of stale booze and burnt feathers. The last bedroom has its windows blacked out, sheets doubled over and gaffa-taped against any stray sunbeam. A mattress, a video camera and a discarded Spider-Man costume. Don't ask.

On Day One of the party Champ set up a DJ booth in the master bathroom. Leads snake down the stairs to speakers in every downstairs room, and even out by the pool. I poke my head inside. Somebody left a record playing last night and it's still spinning in its lock-out groove, broadcasting static straight into our dreams. *That's* the noise.

I lift the arm gently and choose the first record of the day. Something to wake up to, something to swim to, something to mark Day Five of this permanent party. I drop the needle on Warren Zevon's "Sentimental Hygiene" and feel the walls shiver to the riff.

Out onto the stairs, pitted and gritted with ground glass. You can't help but stop at the top of the staircase to take in a view that has been on the cover of *Architectural Digest* AND the *Mid-Century Masters* book, two more front covers than I ever had. The stairs appear to float in mid-air in a way that has been copied in every wannabe minimalist house from Long Beach to the mountains.

Downstairs is open-plan and expansive but the modernist vibe is spoiled by the remnants of the ongoing party. Maybe thirty sleeping people, in deckchairs and what's left of the couch, draped over armchairs or just foetal on the floor. The glass doors out to the pool have been taken off their hinges. The chandelier sits in the middle of the floor, bedecked in fairy lights, its crystal drops spread out around it like petticoats. I was elsewhere when they brought the palm trees inside but now leaves scrape the ceiling, their fronds stiff and blackened. The music is boomy and brittle, careening off all the flat surfaces inside, but no one wakes. I pick my way gently through the wreckage, human and otherwise, out to the pool.

7am and it feels like a microwave. Pulses of warmth radiate off the tiles. Someone must have brought more food colouring last night because the pool water is an even deeper red. Blood-red, jelly-red, lipstick-red. Crimson with ribbons of silver light from the slightest of breezes. I ditch the B&H and the robe. Someone's asleep on the diving board so I plant myself on the edge of the pool and curl my toes over the rim. *Bounce two-three*. The aim is to make as little disturbance as possible, which isn't my usual MO, but horses for courses.

On your toes and over, folding yourself up and then a slice into the water. In and under, a cleansing rush of cold, eyes open. It only hurts for a second. And then the bottom of the pool through layers of red. Like staring at the sun through closed eyes. Sunken treasure: coins, glass, a solitary high heel. A breath and then push off the side and through the water, thick with red, lungs complaining, pushing yourself down to feel the pool floor on your belly as you reach for the other side. Until you touch the far end, and burst for the surface like a rebirth, up into the air, into great gobfuls of air and burnt-out palm trees and bonfires and music and art. Silver Lake. 1999. Christmas Day.

But I'm getting ahead of myself. I'm a long-time lurker on this forum but a first-time poster. Like many of you here I've been reading about the forthcoming reissue of *American XS* with rising anticipation. I'm sure it's being done for the purest of artistic motives — the commenter here who said that Dillon was "a venal little leech who would dig up his granny if she provided a viable revenue stream" is being churlish, and whoever described him as "a talentless little dwarf" is just plain cruel. Let's give him the benefit of the doubt. Once the album has been remastered I'm confident that the original *American XS* will sound weedy, cheap and tawdry. I'm listening to it now and that's exactly how it sounds. Anticipation is a funny thing.

My reason for posting here is that I see that there's a forty-eight-page book, *XS All Areas*, celebrating the creation of the album. As I'm certain that my contribution to that creation will go overlooked I thought this might be a good place to explain how I accidentally inspired that deathless work. Read on…

In 1999 I was the soon-to-be-ex lead singer of REDACTED. After a showcase gig which ended in recrimination and injury I was licking my wounds at the family home of my old friend, guitarist and keyboard player, REDACTED. It was an inappropriately picturesque spot for a breakdown. His parents owned a converted vicarage in Norfolk: all honeysuckle and wood pigeons and deer nibbling at your petunias. Anyway, you're wondering where Dillon fits in. I'd had as big a night as you could have in Norwich in the 1990s and arrived back at the vicarage at the same time as the postie. Going through the mail in the hope that his parents might have applied for a credit card recently, I found a postcard. The La Brea Tar Pits on the front, and on the back:

"Hey REDACTED, Got a crazy schedule coming up. Going to be in Blighty to shoot some stuff in November. Want to come see how it's done? Or I know you said you liked the look of my house out here, want to cat-sit? That is if REDACTED aren't busy on your stadium tour ha ha. Call my agent if you're interested. Dillon."

I can feel it still. The quiet in the hallway and the blood rushing in my ears. To be gone from this fucking scene and Britain and its jealousy and its BBC2 and all those people who'd seen me fail. I went through the pockets of REDACTED's jacket. There they were, the keys to his dad's Triumph Stag. No bags, no schedule, no worries. The only ticket I could afford went via Madrid and Delhi. Twenty-four hours without a book or Walkman. At LAX I changed my last £25 into dollars, caught three buses to Silver Lake, arriving travel-crusted and hungover, to fall asleep in the doorway of Dillon's real-estate agent.

My disarray didn't seem to worry her when she arrived. "Dillon said he might have someone stopping by. I'm thankful to be honest — my assistant's been feeding the cat and she's allergic."

Readers of this forum will know the house well. It's Richard Neutra's VDL Studio, where Dillon had his home and offices for years, and even his studio once, after, like so many over-ambitious musicians, he'd crashed his cachet on the rocks of Hollywood's big business. (And by the way, I don't think Dillon gets the credit he deserves for his real estate acumen. His Malibu condo development, his renovation of Picasso's studio in the South of France, his Dublin cyber-hotels? Who says that these things aren't as creative as his musical works? Certainly not me.) Even casual Dillonites will know one view of the house. The cover of *American XS*, that iconic shot of this mid-century classic in tatters, every pane of glass smashed, the swimming pool crimson with what looked like blood, and piles of furniture beneath the windows, the wizened matchheads of burnt-out palm trees, and wide-eyed Californians in bikinis and warpaint, motorcycle leathers and baseball caps, stoned and useless amongst the rubble. It was taken there. The photo is credited to Dillon, like so much is, but he wasn't even in the country when it was taken. The photo was the work of Champ Lord, pick-up artist, airline scammer, and, at that time, my only friend west of Dublin. The devastation? That was all mine.

I spent my first day there wandering through the rooms, relishing the throb of Californian heat and the pools of shadow in every corner. The house's angles were sharp and clean with a tastefulness that veered close to invisibility. The stairs were just wooden slats and blinds threw bands of light that inched across matted floors. A sculpture of seven steel spheres, each reflecting a fish-eye view of the lounge, twisted in the breeze. Everything exuded a gallery-like calm.

I wasn't sure if Dillon had actually moved in. Boxes of unopened stuff lined every room: CDs, video equipment, clothes, an exercise bike, art propped up against the walls. I went through it all, not knowing what I was looking for, and it was evening before I hit the motherlode. Taped on the wall in an anteroom that housed the home phone was a list of numbers: food places, a drugstore, music shops, and lots of names that I didn't recognise. It was time to check out where Dillon's credit was good. Your boy did well for himself. *American XS* was a year away and he was abroad filming his Britpop movie but some of that Hollywood money must have already been flowing because he had accounts everywhere.

By the end of the week I had a routine. I slept out by the pool with a dome of smog above me. Each morning the sprinkler woke me; I rolled out of its range and watched the droplets form a perfect, personal rainbow. Sprinklers and sirens, geckoes and joggers. A slow parade of maids, gardeners and cooks, not a white face among them, chattering along the shortcut down by the reservoir. LA mornings. I took to the phones. I'd drawn a red star by all the establishments at which Dillon had credit. I ordered breakfast from the list, working my way steadily through the rota, regardless of what I had a taste for. Kim Chi Monday. Burrito Tuesday. Sushi Wednesday. Then on to the liquor store where the clerk was under the illusion that I knew something about wine. We'd chat for a while about vintages and vineyards, mouthfeel and acidities, and then he'd send a case over. Now, years later, as I have, through some unthinking accretion of grown-up knowledge, ingested at least the basics of wine, I wonder at the stuff he sold me. 1960s Montrachets into which I decanted catering size tins of fruit salad to make sangria, a Vendange Tardive from 1983 that I used for cooking.

Once the basics were accounted for — shelter, food, drink — I moved onto making money. There were two record stores among the phone numbers. From Tower Records on Sunset I ordered a ton of LA stuff that I didn't really know, like John Phillips and Chet Baker and black-and-white noir films and books on architecture and mixtapes of local rappers and low-rider videos and Orange County punk stuff and then just set it running, just to get the city under my nails. Then, for the cash, I moved on to the big-ticket items — box-sets, reissues and collector's editions — which I'd flip at Aron's Records an hour later, only making about thirty cents on the dollar but it was enough for walking-around money. Dillon's own stuff raised some cash too. His record collection went for $350, almost certainly much, much too little but I couldn't help wince at the idea that the assistant thought that the collection of hopeless Britpop rarities was mine. By the end I was begging him just to give me the money. The musical gear got a little more.

It was a kind of life. I went out every night somewhere different and only chose my back-story when I got asked. I hit on anyone who looked authentically Angeleno — let's call it research — and then heard myself explaining that I was a golf caddy, or that I designed prosthetic limbs or I manned a toll-booth in Pasadena, words that tumbled out leaving me splayed between truth and lies and desire and fear. There were scenes in the morning when I'd forgotten which role I was playing and the whole thing seemed silly and cheap and the girl was looking for her underwear and fixing her makeup in one of Dillon's mirrors propped up against the walls, asking me for heartbreakingly small investment advice or the best place to get pet insurance or anything that flowed from the lies that had been so easy the night before.

It couldn't last, obviously. I scoured *Variety* for any mention of delays to shooting on Dillon's film but it was progressing well. I caught him on MTV, the VJ asking him if he might be the heir to Ridley Scott. The sheer fucking chutzpah of his wink to camera was enough for me to order eight jeroboams of champagne from his account and distribute them to bums on the street. I was just getting going when the real estate agent called. To say that Dillon would be back in a week, on Boxing Day. She didn't need to say that I was expected to find myself an alternative manger.

That final week may, I'm sad to say, be my finest work. When my clogs are in hock and the daisies have been pushed I haven't actually achieved much. The people who remember REDACTED are scant, those for whom the music actually meant something scanter still. My acting roles were paltry things: scene-fillers, time-wasters. And the record that I have brewing at the moment? Who knows? But there's still a swathe of Angelenos whose eyes light up if you mention the Neutra House party.

To throw a party that comprehensively and minutely destroys a celebrated example of mid-century modern architecture and everything in it is, I'm sure you'll agree, not too much of a problem. But to make that destruction a slow-burn, seven-day affair, with plot twists, recurring characters and cliff-hangers, including chapters of destruction and stories of redemption, all in a city you don't know with nothing at your disposal but a handful of recently delivered credit cards, well that pal, is art. Flames had to be stoked, directed, left to rage and reduced to embers. Fresh fuel had to be introduced gently. Booze and drugs were natural accelerants but the cocktail's measurements had to be exact. Invite too many hippies, with their sound systems and hydroponic grass and acoustic guitars, and the whole thing became safe. Turn up the gas by introducing Valley meth-heads, with their air of paranoia and penchant for destruction, ups the ante but my fear was always that they'd take the place apart, brick by brick, before the week was up. Police raids were cleansing, clock-resetting things, giving me a chance to sleep and tweak the guestlist, spread some rumours. I bought a cheap cellphone and called the agent. My Dillon impression was spot on: his mockney drawl was a breeze to another Home Counties drop-out like myself. Whenever she called, and boy did she call, I would fend her off. It was "about to be dealt with", teams were "on their way", she should "leave it to me". Then I'd switch to my own phone to promise I'd hold down the fort, downplaying the stories of violence and drunkenness, the blood-red pool and the indoor fires.

It was Champ who stocked the house with the spray paint beloved of east LA's graffiti writers and spread the word of some virgin walls that needed defacing. It was Champ who convinced the younger Hollywood A-listers that this was the kind of happening that Dennis Hopper and Jack Nicholson would have stalked through in the Sixties. I brought terrifying Orange County schoolgirls for whom the drug use and chicken dancing was just a typical Friday night, and film students tired of Nineties blockbusters. I found that you were allowed to do anything in LA as long as you filmed it: prostitution became porn, destruction became spectacle.

Champ brought another spice to the mix: a bunch of New York club kids, transplanted here by promoters trying to crowbar some cool into LA's laughable club culture. When they heard of a then two-day bender out in Silver Lake where some Brit guy was *dying or something* and *like, wrecking the place* then they were in. This was much more along the lines of the high-concept, low-taste clubbing these kids liked so they moved in, dragging a long tail of dealers and stylists and pranksters to squirrel themselves away in the big, bare bedrooms of the upstairs. They nested like rats in sniffling, bitchy packs, hissing at anyone healthy looking who came too close. It was them who stained the pool red.

But, like I say, it had to be conducted. The days were for art, the nights for destruction. I rigged a mike up to the house's sound system and started each day with a holiday camp-style rundown of the forthcoming events and a blast of whichever yacht-rock monstrosity seemed most fitting. Kenny Loggins and the Doobie Brothers were staples but it was Steely Dan's "Showbiz Kids" that got the biggest cheer. Then I'd scrape the barrels of Dillon's credit in the last few stores that hadn't got the message that these were bills that were never going to be honoured. We sent doughnuts and cigars to the cops who parked outside so they'd radio in the news that "that party" looked like it was dying down. Caterers set up long tables over piles of prone bodies and Champ documented everything on one of the few things in the house I hadn't sold, a gorgeous large-format Leica camera. We walked the tightrope between police raids, booze shortages and structural damage right until Dillon was due back.

That cover picture — the pool of blood, charcoaled palms, the war-zone of the house and the line-up of those who made it through to Christmas Day — was taken by Champ, squinting into the morning sun. I recognise a few of them; some went on to be household names. I'm not there of course. I was stringently deniable. Think of me as the eye of the storm. Still, steady, invisible.

Christmas Day, once I'd showered off the food colouring and smoke and paint splatter and dressed to the sound of the party waking up, I took a cab up to Griffith Park. From there you could watch the dark spiral of smoke rising from the house. Too far to watch Dillon arrive, or to see the police turn up twenty minutes later, though sirens sounded for hours. Kudos to Dillon though. He may not have many qualities but making money from ruins is deep in his DNA. It was only weeks later that I was reading his *Rolling Stone* cover interview (headline "The Last Party — Marksman takes aim at the death of the American Dream"), where he explained how his new record was written and conceived during a week-long party that *he'd* thrown to destroy his "safe American life". Champ's pic was the cover of course, the super-8 films students had made there were co-opted as impossibly glamorous (and very cheap) music videos.

So, now you know. The concept, the look and the origin of *American XS* was mine. But like mineral water, you have to admire the man who had the sheer balls to charge for it. And the music? I can't and wouldn't want to take credit for that. But as a parting gift I want to leave you with what I left for Dillon that Christmas morning. A postcard of Tower Bridge with the note KNOW I SHOULD HAVE TIDIED A BIT BEFORE I LEFT BUT IT'S NICE TO HAVE SOMETHING TO DO ON BOXING DAY INNIT? x K, and a tape with a song I wrote for him as an act of I'm-not-sure-what. Is there such thing as a contrite fuck you? I doubt it'll find its way onto the box set so I'll leave it to the estimable members of this forum to discuss the similarities between this track (recorded a full year before *American XS*) and track twelve of Dillon's record, "Some Monsterism".

Chapter Seven

There were lots of replies, at least half remonstrating with others for engaging with the troll, which just prolonged the discussion. People speculated on the thread's author and Brandon got mentioned but plenty of others did too. As for the similarity between the tracks, there wasn't much disagreement — they were basically the same tune, but without a timeline the most common response was "so what?" That was Rae's take too.

"He's just fucking with them — I bet he knocked that up over there. If he had any way of making money from Dillon I would have heard about it. It's just one more little hand grenade thrown into the record he's making. More publicity, more sympathy."

"And the rest of it? The party? Did he make that up?"

"Not at all. I was there, just for a while. It was wild."

"Is that where you met?"

"No. Well, yes but no. I saw him, briefly, but we didn't really speak. I'd been at a party over in Malibu with a bunch of girls from the agency. Y'know, go, look pretty, pretend to be interested if some old guy talks to you about the movie business. We went for the free food." She looked around her room. "I was *so* broke. We'd go to these things and take it in turns to fill our handbags with canapés. This time it was paté and those little rice balls and a half bottle of Champagne and everything. And I was thinking 'all I want to do is get home, get my pyjamas on and eat paté in front of the TV' but the girls were all going on about this party being thrown by this crazy English guy and he's trashing the place and Flea and Johnny Depp were there yesterday. It was on the way home so what the hell."

She jumped up and opened the fridge. "Now I really want one of those rice balls." She returned with a plastic pack of carrot sticks.

"You could hear the party from a block away. The police kept coming by and shutting it down and then Bran would open up the doors again, put a record on and the next shift would arrive. So we wandered around, hoping to see Johnny Depp and watching people come out of the pool looking like Carrie because they'd coloured the water red somehow. And I was starving so I went upstairs to find somewhere to eat in peace and I went into a room and there was Bran watching the party below, though I didn't know it was him then. I was totally embarrassed because I had this bag of fish-sticks and stuff, so I said hi and he said hi and I went and sat on the toilet and ate sushi."

She nibbled on a carrot. She was looping the two tracks as she talked, one after another. If Brandon had faked his then he'd done a good job, you could hear the bones of the finished track in his acoustic version.

"Let's use it," I said.

Rae looked up mid-crunch, "Huh?"

"Let's use this track. On his record. I'm sure it's not something he meant for his swansong but who cares? We've already got what, four tracks? Five with this one. If we could scrape a record together and tie it to his killing like he wanted then who'd get the royalties? His next of kin: you."

Rae rubbed her face. "Maybe. I guess. So what's next?"

In my head I counted the steps. Get the *Smile* record made. Convince Saul to sue. Get Kimi to release Brandon's record.

"First we get the *Smile* record cut." The phrase was unfamiliar in my mouth. I opened up his notebook at the page with the PRESSER phone number. "I'm going to call and organise it. Get ready to message me if you have any advice."

She crossed her fingers.

I dialled. It rang for maybe ten rings and then there was a voice: a London accent, bored.

"Hot action. John."

"Hi, it's Brandon."

"Uh huh." A pause. A rush of breath that was probably a drag on a cigarette.

"Brandon Kussgarten?"

"I know." Another drag.

My only real tactic as Brandon had been to say as little as possible and hope the other person filled the silence, but it wasn't working here. I forced myself to relax. Everything bores you, I told myself. "So, are we going to do this thing?"

"I thought it was off. I was expecting you last week."

I remembered a line from the videos. "Something came up." I brushed imaginary dirt from my cuff.

There was another lung-filling drag. He said, "Dylan's at the Novellos thing tonight."

Unexpected names going off like bombs: Dylan. Novello.

"Um... so?" Pinching myself to smarten up. No hesitations. I should have had a line.

"So? It's up to you."

I looked to Rae onscreen. She shrugged. "Tonight then." I forced myself to lose the question mark from the end of the sentence.

"All right, fucking finally. We've got a session until ten. They're not supposed to over-run but they will. Call it eleven when I finally get rid of them. I want to be well out of there by the time you're in. Call it midnight so I'm back at home and accounted for, one would be even better. Check that Tony's asleep and use the window I showed you. You know how to use the gear, right?"

"Of course. Remind me which window?"

"Fuck's sake. Back bathroom like I told you. Right, I've done enough — it's not my fault you missed the first time. If you don't turn up tonight then I'm keeping the cash and there will not be a third chance. Goodbye Brandon Kussgarten."

A click. And nothing. My hands were shaking. Rae filled the screen.

"You were awesome! I mean it." She was on her feet back in Tahoe.

"You think so? I'm not sure what I agreed to."

"To break in somewhere and cut a record I think. You bad-ass!" She did a little dance around the table and then sat down. "Where though? How did he answer the phone? Hard Action?"

"'Hot' I think."

Her fingers flew across the keyboard. "Hot Action, London. Well not that, naturally. Ew. Oh snap."

"What?"

She read from the screen. "Hot Action is a London-based studio owned and run by Dillon Marksman. It prides itself on providing the best pre-digital recording gear in Europe. It was originally an adults-only cinema and peep show, and Marksman has retained many of the original features."

Dillon. Dylan's at the Novellos.

"Wait, the guy we were just reading about? With the house?"

"The house and the remix. This would so appeal to Bran's sense of humour. Using Dillon's gear to cut his record."

"I wonder who we spoke to."

"Well, it sounds like there's a pressing room at the studio. So an engineer?"

"But if he's not going to be there who's going to work the machinery?"

"Well Bran would have done it I expect. It is the kind of thing he knows about." She gave me a sympathetic look. "I'm not sure it's the something you could learn from YouTube."

I sensed hope fading from her. Her money. Robin's money.

"Give me an hour," I told her.

She was right about YouTube. There were odd clips showing records being made but nothing like a step-by-step guide. The machine itself looked uncomplicated enough but the jargon was impenetrable.

I cut out two lines on the back of a record sleeve and snorted them as fast as I could. I called Baxter.

"Bax. One piece of good news and one piece of bad."

"That's an improvement on your usual ratio I suppose. Tell me."

"The cut's all sorted. 1am, at Dillon's place." Brandon might have already told him but I couldn't assume that.

"Dillon? Dillon Marksman? Jesus, don't get him involved. He'll want to be part of it. The man's a talent vampire."

"Strictly speaking he doesn't know about it. I've got an in at the studio, this would be done off the books."

I could hear him relax. "Doesn't he now? How satisfying. I've always wanted to get one over on that smug cunt. You know he hired Saul and Kimi for that tour and never even called me…"

I interrupted him. "But the engineer can't be there and it's not something I can handle. You're going to have to step up."

"Do the cut? No. I left this to you because it's the kind of double-dealing that I'm no good at. I get the shakes if there's an extra carton of Marlboro in my bag at Customs."

I felt doors shutting, darkness closing in. I willed power into my voice. "No skin off my nose Bax sweetheart, I haven't staked my rep on this thing. Anyway, I've had a bit of a windfall — the money's not quite so urgent now."

He was silent for a long moment and then he started complaining. I had him.

I met him at the tube. He was wearing a huge parka with the hood down, making his face look like it was being served on a platter. He was grumbling away at me even as he came up the steps.

"I mean I've got to find a buyer, and *sell* the thing, and it's my name that's attached if anything goes wrong but does that matter to him? No, he has to drag me into every little piece of this."

I didn't have to dig deep into Brandon's personality to find my scorn: there was something intensely annoying about the man.

"Bax, always a pleasure." I nodded hello. "Shall we?"

We walked through empty Haggerston streets. It had rained earlier so London looked slick and clean and every streetlight was haloed with drizzle.

Baxter couldn't stop talking, veering between complaints about how badly he was being treated and excitement over how much money we might make. We turned right and left through suburban streets with window boxes and 4x4s, past gloomy low-rise estates with just one or two lights showing, and cut through the grounds of a hospital where green-clad nurses and bandaged patients smoked silently in the pools of neon. I'd packed the tapes in a leather rucksack I'd found in Brandon's closet and they tugged reproachfully at my shoulders.

Bruton Street was almost completely in darkness. One side was a building site where pictures of young couples in gym gear covered a billboard in front of a black hole of building work. The one light came at the end where a neon sign, retro even to my eyes, read HOT ACTION over a sunken doorway. A line of light illuminated the gap at the bottom of the door.

"So what's the plan?" said Baxter.

The rest of the building sat in darkness. A squat and complex space — as my eyes adjusted I could see that it spread over a couple of blocks — with the entrance right in one corner. I couldn't see an obvious window. I pulled up the torch on my phone and began to follow the brickwork along the street.

"Bran? You do know where we're going?"

I held up a hand. About ten yards down there were big double doors, their original colour obliterated by graffiti and stickers. I tugged experimentally at them.

"Bran. I thought you said this was sorted." Baxter's whine pulled at my nerves.

"It is, shut up, we're looking for the window."

The cone of light from the phone showed up more walls. Then an opening. An alleyway? I gestured Baxter to follow me and then saw it. An oblong of wall a shade lighter than the rest.

"Here." I felt around for something to stand on but the alleyway was empty. "Give us a leg up."

Baxter was just a shadow behind me. He steadied himself against the wall and cupped his hands. I pulled the rucksack tight and stepped into the cradle he'd made. The window pushed open and I had my shoulders through before I realised the rucksack wouldn't make it.

I dropped it down to him. "Take the tapes, I'm going to try again."

This time I squeezed through. With half my body inside I reached out my arms. Walls to my left and right but nothing in front or below. The darkness was total. The ammonia tang and tight space meant it was probably a toilet stall but I couldn't tell how far down the floor would be. I swung my arms again, hoping for something to give me a sense of distance. For a few seconds I hung there — body in, legs out, belt buckle biting into my belly — and then I just let go.

I missed the toilet seat with my arms and my head hit the rim just as my hands found the floor. Scrabbling to keep my face away from the bowl I twisted and my legs kicked at the air. For a moment I was in a perfect handstand before my legs toppled back, kicking open the stall door.

Baxter had pulled himself up and the top of his face appeared in the window before dropping down again. I put my phone on the top of the door and climbed on the seat. He looked up from the alley below.

"C'mon — it's fine."

I dragged him up and through. It took a couple of goes. I'd cut my forehead on the toilet bowl and the wound throbbed with the exertion. We turned left out of the toilet along a carpeted corridor lined with photographs.

Baxter had his phone out for light and was giving me a running commentary. "Dillon with Jack White, Dillon with Robyn, Dillon with fucking Bono. God, the man is such a tart. Is that fucking Winnie Mandela?" He stopped to take a proper look.

"Bax. Job in hand, please." I gave him the smallest of shoves. We came to a T-junction with both corridors gently curving away. "Which way?" asked Baxter.

"Right," I said, not knowing, trusting that I'd recognise something from the pictures Rae had sent me. The curving corridor had alcoves to the left; I looked in and saw it opened out onto a bigger space. It was almost a reflection of the music room at the Magpie: instruments on stands and the glint of polished keyboards.

Baxter peered through. "Must be the peep-show space. Does he really think anyone's going to wank off over *his* band? Have you heard that fucking drummer? Christ."

I recognised the room from the website. "Good. The cutting room is off the side there."

There was a light on: a blue lamp throwing elongated shadows against the curve of the walls.

"There." Baxter had spotted something. "The machine's on and everything."

He was in his element. The room was small and bathed in an icy light. Baxter threaded and adjusted the tape, listening intently through a pair of headphones that he'd brought with him. He talked under his breath to the machine — *good girl, now where's that light come from and what does it want, no you don't missy* — until he was ready. Then he pulled a plain black disc from his bag. It was smooth as a mirror and it glinted in the swimming-pool light of the cutting room.

"Beautiful isn't it?"

He spun the disc between two fingers, watching it reflect patches of blue, and then with a sigh, slid it into place on the cutting machine. We sat with our backs against the machine. Its warmth and gentle vibrations reminded me of childhood car trips. I was getting used to

Baxter's way of talking now. As long as you gave him an occasional sign that you were listening he'd happily tell stories for hours.

Afterwards he insisted on coming back to the Magpie — Brighton trains don't start until six — and celebrating. We had champagne and coke, and snacks that Kaspar sent up. While he was in the bathroom I texted Rae. WENT WELL BAX HERE TALK LATER and got an immediate reply WELL DONE!! SWITCH THE MIKE ON

Knowing Rae was listening made me less self-conscious. Baxter was back in hyper-active mood, peppering the conversation with questions like "do you remember?" and "do you ever see…", and I was out of my depth. The names meant nothing to me but he ploughed on happily.

I went to change the record and my phone buzzed. It was Rae with her reading of the situation: HE WANTS SOMETHING BUT I CAN'T TELL WHAT.

Back in the music room Baxter continued a story as if I'd not left the room, strumming on a guitar as he talked.

"Hey Bax. Was there something else?"

He tapped out a nervous rhythm on his knee. "Well, this *is* supposed to be a celebration. I thought we could call up that Sistine girl again. And someone for you too, obviously."

I very much wanted to be able to speak to Rae but there was no disguising the fact that it sounded exactly like something Brandon would do. "Sistine. Yes. Sure, sure. I can't remember where I put her number."

"Just use the batphone," he laughed. "Want me to do it?"

I gestured to the phone. "Be my guest."

I went to the kitchen and flipped out my mobile to see if Rae had any thoughts. I could hear the excitement in Baxter's voice. "Hi, it's Baxter in Mr Kussgarten's suite again. Hello Annabelle. Wonderful, thank you. We're having a little celebration and were wondering if Sistine might join us? Fantastic. I'll check."

He poked his head around the door. "Anyone special for you?"

I froze. "Thanks Baxter, no."

Half an hour later, when two girls got buzzed up, I realised that Baxter had taken my "no" to mean "no one special" rather than "no, please God, don't get me involved in any of this".

At the door they peeled off like fighter pilots. Baxter threw his arms around a petite, dark-haired girl, cooing, "Sistine, how lovely" while the other girl took me smilingly by the arm. She was a slender, Afroed woman, as tall as me even in flat shoes. When she whispered, "Hello again darling" I realised — of course — that she'd been here before with Brandon.

I offered to make some drinks to give me time to think, but Baxter was puppyish, tugging at Sistine's sleeve, and in an instant they were off upstairs, waving goodbye before I'd even put the ice in the glasses.

She sat perched on the worktop, watching me make the drinks. I heard a shriek of laughter from the guest bedroom, then music. When she finally spoke she had a surprisingly deep voice.

"So, Mr Actor, what's it to be? The same again?"

What was worse, saying yes and being led who-knows-where by Brandon's tastes, or no and be left in charge? She was tall, slender, professional looking. She terrified me.

"Yeah, same again."

That seemed to please her. "Great, great. Unfinished business, yeah?" Her accent had slipped a little and there was an unaffected smile on her face. "Shall I go on up?"

"You remember the way?"

She nodded happily. "See you up there."

As soon as she was on the stairs I unfroze the laptop screen. Rae beamed out at me. "Hello playa."

"Not my idea, I promise."

"I heard, I heard. She's cute though, are you going to leave her up there?"

"I would if I could. It'd be rude, right?"

Her smile stretched wider. "Rude, yes. That would never do." She turned her head sideways. "Look, you're single, it's Bran's money, and she's hot."

"Well, it's actually your money, technically."

She made a face. "So it is. Jesus, I hope she's worth it."

I wondered if there was an upside to the situation as I headed up the stairs. Maybe I could find something out from her. Brandon liked to talk — who knew what he might have said to her. The bedroom was blazingly lit, with all the lamps on. The girl sat, fully clothed and cross-legged on the bed, a backgammon board set up in front of her. She caught the look of surprise on my face. "Is this not what you meant?" Her legs were pulled up under her like a kid's and the dice were poised in her hand. I saw her readjust her expectations.

"Yes, of course, sorry, miles away."

I sat across the board from her, making the board slide towards me.

The goofy look was back on her face. "You know I've been practising?"

I copied her and rolled a dice, trying to remember the rules. "Really?"

"Yeah. I used to be gooooood when I was a kid." There was a hint of something European in her accent, making me think of Martinique or Guam. "An' I haven't lost like that for ages." She pulled a face. "So now it is *onnnn*."

We played for about half an hour and she won every game. For the first few she was triumphant, raising her hands after each win like a victorious boxer. "In the blue corner your undefeated champion, *Anique*."

But by the fourth game she was quizzical. "Not on your game today?"

"I'm sorry," I told her, "Things on my mind."

She stopped mid-throw, the dice on her upturned hand, "You wanna…?" There was a wariness to her that turned on and off instantly.

"No, you're good, this evening was more for Baxter."

"OK, you want to stop? Do something else?" She looked genuinely disappointed.

"No, keep playing, just don't expect me to win."

"I can live with that." She shook her head and went back to the dice. She rolled a double three and counted out her moves with glee. "And three…" She swept one of my men back to its home.

"So you are you going to watch my triumph again later?"

"Sorry?"

"The camera." She gestured up above her head. "You going to watch yourself getting beat?" She leaned over the board. "Is that what gets you off?"

Where she'd gestured, over the headboard, there was a long oblong painting of a caterpillar partway through its transformation. There had been no mention of cameras in Brandon's notebook, but that didn't mean much. I thought about everything that had been said and done in this room since he moved in.

"Oh, I switched them off," I told her.

She rolled the dice and swooped on the pieces. "Pity, you could watch your ass getting whipped again."

I didn't hear Baxter leave in the morning. It wasn't until gone noon that the combination of open curtains and a thunderous headache drove me out of the bed. I checked the door panel: climate controls, environmental profile, DO NOT DISTURB signs and, along the bottom, a row of lights, each by a tiny lettered label. BR1, BR2, K, L1, L2, and RF with red LEDs by each. I went back to the bedroom. Above the picture frame a black bar about the size of half a chopstick was glued to the wall.

I buzzed reception. "Morning Kas." I corrected myself. "Afternoon, even. I want all the camera footage from last week. Something I need to see."

"Not a problem. It's all on the Magpie app. Have you logged in before?"

Had I? "No, I haven't needed to."

"Then it'll take a couple of minutes to set up. I can send someone to help you with it?"

"No, I think I can manage that. Remind me who else can view it — maybe I don't need to even see it."

"No one." His comeback was immediate. "Just the occupant of the room and it gets deleted the moment you leave, automatically."

"Oh yeah. Great, thanks Kas."

He was right, it was pretty simple. I set up a new profile. There was nothing from that first night with Kimi but I suppose Brandon wasn't technically the occupier then, but from then on there were nine feeds onscreen at once, of every moment.

I watched in fits and starts. There were long patches where he was unmoving. Reading, or listening to music (it was hard to tell because there was no sound with the recordings) or more often just staring into space. You could fast-forward an hour without the slightest flicker of action from him. I watched the first four days, including the visits of Jay and the guitar guy. There were other deliveries too: mainly clothes but other, smaller packages too that Brandon immediately pocketed, unopened. I tried to catch his manner when he was with people to see if I'd captured his actions. The Brandon on screen was stiller than I remembered him, and less flamboyant.

When it got to the bit with Sistine and Anique, the first time round, he covered the camera in his room, the screen sweeping and fading to grey as, in the right-hand corner, Baxter humped and sweated over the other girl. Later, once they were gone, he was back to his unmoving self. The day after that he spent hours at a clunky old typewriter, pecking away at the keys with two fingers as a roll of paper shrank in front of him.

It was only later, eating lunch out on the balcony, watching the drizzle smearing the clean lines of the skyscrapers, that I realised what I hadn't seen. No drugs. No drink. No cigarettes even. I went back inside and rewatched some of it. He took a line with Jay, and he definitely handed something out when the girls were there, but in his time alone he was relentlessly clean-living. A couple of times Kas came up with food and Brandon dumped it immediately into the waste disposal. Instead he drank glass after glass of homemade smoothies, made from veg stuffed into a blender and drunk straight from the jug.

I rewound to Jay's visit. The frustration of seeing their lips move but no sound. At the end of it, after a complex handshake that I knew I'd never be able to master, he shut the door and swept everything that had sat on the table — wraps, pill bottles, blister packs — into a drawer. I paused the video and went to check. Yes, it was all still there. Only one of the wraps had been disturbed, and I guessed that was while Jay was there. The rest was untouched.

I went back to the video. He went out occasionally but when he was at home he was either making, or listening to music. He broke off every couple of hours for more of the green vegetable goop, or to do some push-ups, but the rest of time he was as studious as a schoolboy. There were no nights out. No visitors. He was home every evening. He recorded for a couple of hours, read for a little and then went to bed around 10pm.

I looked from the screen to the scene behind me. He was, I realised, neater than me, and unexpectedly healthier, at least than this new version of me. I put the video on at its highest speed, the light blooming and dying, Brandon flitting between rooms, as insubstantial as a ghost. Until, all of a sudden, the apartment was full of bodies. I backed up. There was Brandon, dressing slowly, long moments in front of the mirror. One minute, two. Just my brother, my double, in front of the glass with an unreadable expression on his face.

Then, methodically, he started to trash the apartment. He lit cigarette after cigarette and left them to burn down, mainly in ashtrays but also on chair arms and saucers. He pulled out armfuls of bottles from the drinks cabinet and half emptied them down the sink. He topped some of the wine with fresh cigarette butts. Then he spread the bottles around the flat: the music room, the lounge, a couple by the bed. Then he set about the records — transferring them from sleeve to sleeve and then secreting them all over the room. He took out one that I didn't recognise and pinned it to the wall. Then, looking bored, he casually threw kitchen knives at it until it was speared through in four different places. He went from room to room leaving disarray in his wake. He mussed up the spare bed and then went to his room for dirty clothing which he deposited on the floor. He spent a minute looking at the pattern of discarded clothes, rearranging them with the tip of his foot, smoking a cigarette for the bedside ashtray.

And then he was done. He sat in the lounge, for once without a record spinning on the player, and waited. I fast-forwarded until his guests arrived. It was the band. Baxter first, laden with bags and instruments. An embrace, genuine looking, and a drink for him. Then Saul. He got a hand-shake and then there was a long, serious looking conversation with the pair of them still in the hallway. And while they were there, Kimi, who looked tense, but had hugs for everyone, arrived on those towering heels. Her arrival seemed to be the catalyst for Saul to actually come inside.

And off they went. I fast-forwarded through most of if. They were obviously recording — for long minutes they sat in their respective headphones and nothing moved bar hands and feet. Then huddles, arguments, and laughter, much more laughter than I expected. It went on for ages but without sound it was dull fare. And then, hours later, they left one by one. Saul first, then Baxter and then Kimi, who stayed for a drink. It didn't look like Brandon and her were talking much though. After she left, Brandon started again in the music room.

I checked the timecode. 2am, 3am, 4am. He worked his way around the instruments, one by one, occasionally fiddling with the big reel-to-reel tape machine. At 6am he stopped for a while and then disappeared into the bathroom. 6.30am, 7am. Then he was out, dressing quickly with no thought for the mirror. I recognised the outfit. A black jacket flecked with grey, and wide, heavy trousers. It was the outfit from the security footage: the clothes that he would die in.

His face loomed in the top left-hand corner of the feed. He was switching off the camera above the bedroom mirror. There was a flicker of a cufflinked hand and the screen went black. He moved to the lounge. Again his face swam into view, again the square turned black. Through the music room, into the spare room, my brother's face — all business — then darkness. The last camera was by the door. I watched a screen of eight black oblongs, all bar the bottom left-hand corner. He pulled a stool into place, climbed on it and then looked straight into the camera. I felt that familiar itchy discomfort of someone looking me right in the eye and I forced myself to look back. He breathed out — something decided, something finished — winked and the screen went black.

There was nothing after that. The timecode clicked through to another day but the screen stayed empty. Even when it reached the day that I arrived it stayed resolutely dark. I went back to the final image. 7.11am. His face, filling the bottom left corner, was washed out and swollen by the lens but... But it didn't look like a man who thought he'd be dead in eight hours. There had been a spring to his step as he moved from room to room and that last, awful wink felt playful rather than rueful.

There was something else. I couldn't shake the feeling that the wink was meant for me. He'd led me here and fed me clues to keep coming back. I was in his world, following his tracks. His flat, his family and his games. How well did he know me? How much could he control? (A line from the interviews I'd studied came back to me: "Brandon, what made you choose the name Remote/Control?" Half smile, cross of the legs. "Well I'm remote. And controlling.")

I've never felt freer than I have this past week. No longer swept along by the river's flow, I'm swimming against it, and that's the only way you feel the water on your skin. But that wink said that I was right where Brandon wanted me, and right on schedule. As he paused, in that second before the wink and the dead screen, as his tractor beams locked in, I knew that look was for me, as clearly as if he'd said my name. I was still in his orbit.

What should I say to Rae about this Brandon, this monkish, bookish hermit? I didn't want to tell her. It was worse that he'd done all this while he was sober. The Brandon of the liner notes was at least adrift in a storm of addiction and magic; she could blame her abandonment on outside forces. But this was a man in perfect control.

I was overcome with a wave of revulsion for his cruelty. I wouldn't tell her. But I wouldn't lie. I went back to the start of the recordings to look for something I could give her from the tapes. Nothing. His routine was as puritan as mine had been back in Trellick Tower: everything was subsumed to the work.

I tried another tack. I rewound to the recording session. About halfway through there was a discussion. The four of them were huddled around a piece of paper. It ended with Brandon scribbling chords out on the floor in chalk. From the camera angle it was unreadable so I went back to the music room to see if any trace remained. To the right of the Dee diagram, under a side table, the work remained, smeared but legible. A block of chords: Am Gmaj7, D, Dmin, and written alongside them the words CLEAR YOUR HISTORY. Googling that phrase brought nothing but sites on how to cover your tracks online but when I put the phrase in quotes and added MUSIC it brought up a Bandcamp page for an artist called The Ashes. The track was three minutes long so I looked around for an accompanying text. Nothing. No links, no comments, just the music.

I sat at a desk looking over grimy Shoreditch chimneys, eating pickled ginger with chopsticks. There were four indentations in the desk's leather top: this was where the typewriter had sat that I'd seen him working with on the footage. I opened the drawers and found that the antique cherrywood hid a filing cabinet. Pens and pencils were up top and in the cavernous bottom drawer sat the typewriter, fed with a scroll of paper as thick as my arm. I lifted it out, paper and all. It was heavy and smelt of oil and rubber. The roll was one continuous sheet, and metres of it were covered in neat blocks of typing. I rolled it out across the music room floor and found the beginning. In capitals it read VOODOO RAE.

Clear Your History

Voodoo Rae — Act I

Champ had a precise formula for the perfect time to hook up in a bar. Some happy conflagration of desperation, pheromones and rising cab fares. It formed part of his whole playa persona: a ragtag bag of tricks for seducing women in bars, a pursuit which he carried out with a joyless professionalism. He had schedules and strategies, and flowcharts dedicated to combinations of pick-up lines and topics of conversation.

I didn't understand his commitment. He was a good-looking, personable guy with no sense of shame, which is normally a winning combination, but he had to make a competition out of it. It was as if his only real goal was to win the respect of the gurus of the Pick-Up Artist message boards which he read vociferously. The boards were, like any online space where men congregate, forests of stats, abbreviations and petty arguments, and regulars discussed their metrics like they were sports pundits.

We were in The Dresden Room, an LA institution where a desiccated old duo in matching wigs played jazz standards, badly, to an audience of hipsters, pre-clubbers and locals. It was one of those places that had swung so many times between so-bad-it's-hip and simply bad that the city had given up keeping score, and now it was just a muscle memory — somewhere that drunken feet took you at a certain witching hour. It was dark and noisy and quirky enough that you could drop in without looking like you were desperate.

Champ was at the bar dividing his attention between two groups of girls and I was trying my hardest not to be his wingman. I alternated between listening to the band and listening to him, the juxtaposition of the syrupy standards and his spiky chat-up lines jarring my happy descent into drunkenness.

A cigarette that bears a lipstick's traces
"It's pretty brave of you to wear an outfit like that"
An airline ticket to romantic places
"Although you do have a great little body. Are you bulimic?"
And still my heart has wings
"Doesn't it piss you off the way she does the talking for all of you?"
These foolish things remind me of you
"Yeah, you should definitely get a tattoo, you need something to make you interesting"

A shiver of cold air ran through the bar as two girls walked in, jackets pulled over their heads against the rain outside. A blonde and a brunette, like negatives of each other in a way too neat to be accidental. On the left: blonde with a lazy slash of a mouth, puppy-fattish enough to be a recent Angeleno. Thick eyebrows that you could see were itching to be arched. Her friend was a Central Casting Cali Goth, the exact same height with long hair in a short fringe, dressed all in black. She was wearing a Clan of Xymox T-shirt that would have been obscure even in London.

I caught a glint of recognition from the blonde. Not the animal chemistry of the quick pick-up, more that she'd recognised me from some internal database — she knew something about me that I didn't know about her.

They took seats further down the bar and turned ostentatiously inwards to deflect attention. Champ's head snapped towards them as if on a string.

He gestured at me and set off to stand between them. I waited. The longer I could stay out of his orbit on nights like this, the less shrapnel I'd take later. He sat by the blonde and asked her name; this was Rae.

His voice was brash. "Ray, like a dude? Bold choice."

This was his "negging": negative comments wrapped up in compliments. He'd explained the psychology of it to me many times. The bringing down to your level, the sense of unease, the need for approval. I'd seen it work too, but only on profoundly dumb or profoundly damaged girls, and there was a note of humorous contempt in Rae's face that I thought boded ill for Champ.

He waved me over again and reluctantly I introduced myself to her friend, hitting the British accent hard. Soon we were chatting — music, tattoos, films — as I tried to eavesdrop into Champ's conversation.

I could hear the rhythms of what they were saying if not the words. A pointed question from Champ got an amused response from Rae. He tried again, she brushed him back off. Thrust and parry. Dating as a contact sport. Meanwhile Clan of Xymox was going full Anglophile, championing long-lost bands that even the Brit-Goths had given up on: Stockholm Monsters, Dead Can Dance, March Violets. Champ was doubling down and sounding harsher, Rae sounded less amused.

Clan of Xymox was asking me whether I'd ever been to the Batcave when it all kicked off. Rae had finally had enough. I'm not sure which of Champ's insults-dressed-as-compliments had tipped the balance but the smile evaporated from her face. She leant in so she was looking up at him and took his hand in hers.

Then, loudly enough for everyone up at the bar to hear, she said, "I will go home with you right now and let you perform any sordid little act that you want, if you can say one simple thing to me, soul to soul, person to person, that's truly from the heart."

She laid her palm on his chest and fluttered her eyelashes.

Champ gawped as she started counting down on her fingers. "Three, two…"

"I… I love you?"

Even Xymox laughed at that.

Champ didn't look back as he left, which I took as a sign he didn't expect me to follow. Anyway, I was probably irredeemably tainted by his failure now; I'd be harmless to these two. As I chatted with Xymox, Rae watched me.

"We've met before." She had a way of examining you as if she were looking over a pair of glasses.

"I thought you looked familiar." She didn't. She was striking enough for me to know that if we had met then I would have filed her away somewhere.

"Before, at a party up in Silver Lake."

This happened a lot. That last party, the one that put paid to Dillon's house in the hills, the one with the fire trucks and the blood-red swimming pool and the out-of-town TV crews — well, half of LA seems to have been there. It's like the Pistols at the Free Trade Hall: if everyone who said they were there really was then it could have been held in the Hollywood Bowl.

"Oh, the *party*." I still didn't remember her. "Do I need to apologise?"

"No, you were sweet. A bit distracted. You seemed kinda dedicated to trashing the place. I'm guessing you're not there now?"

"Well, you know, the upkeep and all that." I checked her expression to make sure that she knew I was joking; sarcasm's a risky move early on in an American bar conversation.

"Yeah, who needs the hassle, right?"

"Exactly."

Rae had a car, an ancient Jetta that smelled of pot smoke and hairspray, with a back seat full of takeout litter. I squatted in the rear with my hair brushing the roof, and watched the two of them in the mirror, marvelling, as ever, at the lovely easiness of women together. It gave me a chance to look at her properly, sporadically sidelit in neon, her busy hands with bitten nails. There was something wholesome about her. In a year LA would have had its way with her. She'd be a few pounds lighter, her hair a shade brighter and that laugh wouldn't tumble out quite so unguardedly. But for now she was radiant.

Her friend kept a constant, low-level conversation going — a kind of stream-of-unconsciousness thing — and twice Rae turned to look at me as if to say *sorry about her*.

It's twenty years later and I couldn't tell you Xymox's real name or the gist of the conversations we had or which landmarks we passed, but I do remember the music. Rae was playing a mix-CD and whenever I hear any of those tracks again I'm sent crashing back to the rear seat of the Jetta. There was "Been Caught Stealing" and Rae's pretty throat bared to the glow of traffic lights as she and her friend did the barking bit. There was "Imitating Angels" by some now-forgotten LA scene band, which at the time sounded like the most vital thing that anyone had ever recorded (I've heard it since and it's not — young love is worse than drugs for impairing your judgement).

And then, on the elevated section of the 110, with tidy pockets of residential life laid out below us and a holding pattern of airplane lights stacking over LAX, with the busted air conditioning soaking us in dust and fumes and my head brushing the vinyl roof with every pothole, there was "Voodoo Ray". It set Rae and Xymox high-fiving in the front and calling out "theme tune", their shoulders hunching and releasing to some car-seat dance that only the two of them knew. I hear that track perhaps three or four times a year now and every time instantly the scene replays. The liquid lights of the LA suburbs through murky car windows, as gaudy as Vegas and as dull as Burnage. Xymox approximating the muezzin chant with her fringe bobbing, Rae waiting for the "Voodoo Ray" bit to turn and chant it through a bashful grin, the push of the hi-hats and the pull of the road.

We pulled up outside the place Xymox was house-sitting and idled there at the curb for a couple of minutes to let the track end.

The house was spacious and blankly empty. A pool steamed sleepily under outdoor lights and the furniture looked showroom new. It was oddly familiar: a particular bland Californian style that I couldn't place but that I'd seen a hundred times. Like a chain hotel with ideas above its station. Faux antique lamps and plenty of smoked glass. Art books.

"It's a porn house," whispered Rae while Xymox was in the bathroom. "Half the houses in this sub-division are. They use them for shoots. Then the owners take the profits and spend the winter surfing in Maui or whatever, so she looks after them for weeks at a time, a different house every night. It's freaking hilarious if you turn up when they're shooting, you have to pick your way through naked bodies to get to her room."

She lowered her voice further as Xymox returned. "And that couch you're sitting on? It's wipe-clean."

The night coiled itself tight around us. I shifted my focus onto Rae (mainly because I was interested in her, but also because the other girl was doing my head in. At one point she said in all seriousness, "Y'know, African-American actors get all up in arms when they cast a white guy in a black part, but every fucking vampire role on TV goes to someone who's not from the scene. I say if you haven't drunk blood for real then you shouldn't be allowed to play a vamp. Fuck, I'd be so good in Buffy.")

She started spending more time in the bathroom and each time she returned more unsteady and distant. Normally I'd bridle at this breach of etiquette — if she was holding then we should be sharing — but it was working my way. Rae and I were nesting on the wipe-clean, nose to nose in that yeah-this-is-going-to-happen stage.

She had a face that was forever on the edge of smiling, begging you to give a little push. I told stories just to see how they made her face alter. I was about to suggest a change of scene when there was a dull thud from the bathroom, a solitary, very clear *ow*, and then silence.

"You better go look," I said. "She might be indecent."

"She *is* indecent," Rae laughed, but she went to check anyway, "Don't go anywhere."

She was gone maybe twenty seconds and then called through from the bathroom, "Um, Brandon, can you give me a hand?"

The girl was sitting on the toilet, fully clothed but tilted sideways, and there was a smear of red where her temple rested on a bath tap. It looked uncomfortable. Her eyes were closed.

"Fuuuuuuuck," I whispered, as if louder might wake her. "What did she take?"

"I don't know, she only had a tiny bit of blow." She went through the girl's pockets. "Sweetheart, sweetheart?"

She shook her experimentally. The blood was a vivid red against the white of her makeup.

It was the work of a moment to haul her over my shoulder as Rae dialled numbers on her phone, trying to find someone who knew the area.

"Fuck, I can't drive in this state," she said. "Are you OK with American cars?"

I hadn't driven since I got to LA but the local streets were spookily quiet. "I'd better be, I guess."

I tried to unload the girl into the back but the booster seats and general crap made it impossible. "She's going to have to ride up front with me," I said.

Rae was giggling, despite herself, "This is so fucked up." She strapped the girl into the front seat, tucked her arms under the seatbelt and clambered into the back. She was alternating between crying and laughing. "If we get stopped now this is just…"

I took it as slowly as I dared, Rae reading directions from the back. If we cornered too fast the girl flopped against me so Rae had to lean forward and press her against the window. The lights spooled in reverse, the neon colder now. I switched the music off so the only sounds were the rush of air and Rae's urgent instructions. *Left at the end here, no next one, sorry, fuck.*

You could see the hospital from a mile away. White-light glare lit up a whole city block and ambulances idled in the car park. I was considering whether we had to park up or could just dump her on the doorstep when the girl made a noise. She let out a bovine moan, then a deep out-breath and pushed herself away from the window. There was a smear of dark blood across the glass. She looked at me, and then Rae and then out of the car.

"The fuck are we?"

I pulled to a stop.

"At the hospital, you OD'd."

She looked askance. She was, improbably, wide awake and lucid.

"*Excuse* me. I do not OD. Who said I OD'd?" Her hair was sticking up and she yawned lopsidedly. She wiped a hand under her nose and it came away red.

Rae's voice came from the back. "You were passed out in the bathroom and we just assumed…"

"I'm fucking *narcoleptic*, I've told you that about a *million* times. Fuck, if I went to the hospital every time I passed out I'd never be at home."

She shook her head. "*OD'd.* I had like three lines back there. *You* had more than me. You girl, you watch too many films."

We left her back at the porn house, lying out by the pool, staunching her nosebleed. We didn't discuss what we'd do next. Rae's house was all the way across LA, an hour of shuttered strip malls, menthol cigarettes and Depeche Mode remixes. She lived in Runyon Canyon, on a street so dark and serpentine it felt like frontier times. As the car climbed out of the basin she switched the music off to listen for coyote calls and we watched winged things flit through the twin cones of the headlights.

Rae admitted that the girl had told her about the narcolepsy when they'd first met, but that, "I thought it was just something she'd made up to make her seem more interesting, like being gluten intolerant, or a sex addict or something — one of those bullshit LA things. Why can't anyone here have an illness that they haven't made a movie about?"

We sat on her porch looking out over a pool of lights lapping against the mountains and the shore. Joy Division played from the lounge and I swam in the disconnect: skulls rolling in the surf, palm trees on fire. Rae stood up from her chair and reached out into the dark. Her hand came back clasped around a neon-bright orange which she peeled thoughtlessly. The smell was cloying in the stillness. I went inside to get more cigarettes and when I returned she was sleeping, curled up like a cat on the deck, a twist of hair shivering with each out breath, her lips wet with orange juice.

I let the record play on as the mountain ridges paled into sunrise. The air shimmered and a movement caught my eye: a hummingbird, all straight lines and clockwork movements. It hovered over the pot plants one by one, finding nothing of interest and then settled gyroscopically into a square of airspace over Rae's face. The sound of its wings was as tiny a noise as you could imagine: the sound of snowflakes hitting the ground, the sound of the hair rising on your arms. It balanced perfectly in the air, unmoving bar the blur of wings and it extended its neck so that it could reach a bead of juice at the corner of Rae's mouth. Every sound competed to be the smallest: Rae's breaths, the shuffle of wings, distant waves, distant cars.

I held my breath. The bead of the hummingbird's eye was a pinhead. Its wings were impossible.

I never really went home again.

Four neat sketches run down the margin here: a hummingbird in flight, its wings captured at different points of their arc. The wings have been partially erased and redrawn, making them gauzy against the clean lines of the body.

Voodoo Rae — Act II

I moved in by osmosis, the slow spread of my possessions through Rae's house charting our relationship. My paperbacks companionably face-to-face with hers in the bookcase. My hair in her bin after she cut it short one night. My vodka crowding her frozen peas out of the ice box. Mine became ours. Hers became ours.

My records sounded different through her stereo, with its one broken speaker, leaving certain LPs gutted and thin, runtish versions that I can never quite shake. My fingers in her thick hair. Her perfume on my collar. Her balled-up wads of gum found days later in my jeans pockets. And that house, our house finally, with its wooden walls and open windows and the way that nature encroached until it was as if we were camping up in the canyon. The smells of frangipani and jacaranda and the high notes of orange trees and the bitter musk of coyote droppings and avocados rotting on the trees mingled and multiplied with the coffee and tobacco to create a place neither inside nor out. It was two miles to the store for ciggies. Ten for petrol. Butterflies bigger than your hand flattened themselves onto the glow of the TV screen at night. We hauled speakers into the branches of an avocado tree that draped itself over the deck to play Joni and Judee and Gram and Tammy. Breakfast on the porch: roll-ups and fresh orange juice. Skies of blue and orange as bright as food colouring. Coke nights and dope dawns. And with it all the endless fascination of new love, wanting to know everything, to reach back into each other's pasts and install yourself there.

Night after night, moonlit and stoned until we were nothing more than voices, telling each other the story of who we were and where we'd been. Cicadas, wind chimes, car tyres: when I hear Rae's voice in my mind these are the background noises. Her clotted mid-western roundness, slow over a story and always a laugh for herself, a deep burble of pleasure. Every story containing the germ of the next, stories like mountain streams, talking for the very pleasure of it until I was inside her world, lost in her woods. I liked her smaller stories best: what a normal day at her high school was like, the shows her parents watched, every haircut she'd ever had.

The outside world was thin after that. These were the months of castings: modelling for her, acting for me. We'd drive the long way round, away from the city out into the hills, past the Manson house and the tweaker huts, just to get to that crest of hill where Malibu and the Pacific are laid out before you. It was always at that point that the radio kicked back into life. KDAY, the rap station with its cartoon horror music for a cartoon horror city. "Bitches Ain't Shit" and "Murder Was the Case". Rae doing her toenails up on the dashboard, ciggies and mints in the parking lot.

We went everywhere and got turned down most places. At least with acting it was a matter of interpretation. I could — and always did — argue that I was rejected because the casting agent simply *did not understand* the power of my performance. Rae's modelling was simpler and more brutal. You drove miles in a car you couldn't afford, to stand in front of a director who would reluctantly look up from his Blackberry, look right at you, for a moment, a staggeringly brief moment, certainly less time than you'd spend picking out a lobster in a restaurant, and shake his head, which meant "no, you certainly weren't a person that other people would pay to look at" so you'd drive back another twenty miles through the snarl and snark, back to the warm bubble of The Canyon and try not to take it personally.

Back to the universe of The Canyon, with its army of two. And its anthems and symbols, its sacred books and holy places. Curled around each other in the hammock as the Thousand and One Nights of Rae unfolded and the smallest possible unit of time was one side of an LP. I didn't read the papers or watch the news and I couldn't have told you what was going on in the world, but I knew, exactly, how many times Rae had managed to top up her father's vodka with water before he realised what was happening (eight) and who had been number three on the super top-secret list of "guys who I'd go to bed with" that her and Carly Jameson had made, which they were supposed to burn afterwards but Carly instead had showed around everyone in their class (Henry Winkler).

It was a life of constant little losses and rare big wins. Coke and Champagne when we got a job, cigarettes and coffee the rest of the time. I suffered jealous aches when I read in *LA Weekly* which of my compatriots were playing The Strip. Who among them had reached escape velocity: The Beta Band at The Roxy, Lush doing Lollapalooza. Dillon on Leno.

My vices were booze, women and pills; Rae's were shoplifting and open houses. She was relentless with the open houses. On weekends we'd lie in late, listening to records and eating, listening to records and fucking, listening to records and reading, until the pull of it grew too strong for her. She'd get antsy and dress up in Sunday clothes: Fifties sun-dresses and thrift-store sunglasses. Heels, plastic jewellery. Then into the Jetta, Rae with her feet up on the dashboard and a copy of the *LA Times* folded and pencil-ringed in her hand.

We'd drive for hours to wherever had caught Rae's magpie eye. We saw split-levels in Palm Springs that Frank Sinatra was always supposed to have stayed at. We kept our shoes on for fortieth-floor K-Town rat-holes, and ducked our heads into Long Beach houseboats so tiny that the owners had to wait outside. We always parked a block away to hide the Jetta with its garbage-bag side windows and scuffed bumpers, Rae doing her lipstick in the wing mirror, preparing her haughtiest face. She'd be rigidly alert through the whole visit, scanning every inch of each property like she was a camera. With that feminine radar she could extrapolate the owners' entire lives from the contents of the bathroom cabinets or the notes left on the fridge. I'd be left with the realtor, making small talk as they tried to work out if our raggedy second-hand-ness was actual poverty or some new, tech-money thing, while Rae scraped every surface clean with those watchful grey eyes. I used it as acting practice, a new character with every trip and I dropped contradictory hints about our financial standing just for something to do.

So, a year and a half into our life together, we were deep in the desert south of Vegas, where I thought I had a buyer for one of the last things I'd kept from Dillon's place, a battered 1966 P-Bass in its original case. Rae was along for the ride so when I saw a sign reading PALATIAL ESTATE — OPEN HOUSES I kept quiet. I thought she hadn't seen it but then she leant over and flicked the indicator.

"Not so fast B-Boy. A ten-hour round-trip? I get *something*."

It was a winding backroad through parched scrubland, punctuated only by gunshot-pocked road signs and uncategorisable roadkill. The AC was broken so the windows were open to that dusty, herby desert air. Cacti threw shadows up rocky outcrops: Roadrunner territory.

The valley had been brutally landscaped, with huge horizontal platforms cut deep into the mountainside so that it looked like dried-out paddy fields. It was a rough-hewn feat of geo-engineering, made all the more alien by its barrenness.

"Looks like they were expecting to do a lot more building, huh?" Rae did her makeup: Sixties kohl, scarlet lips. "It's a modern ghost town."

The road wound through platforms of earth like a contour map: the subdivisons and traffic systems were just lines in the dirt. Only one platform was occupied. A cul-de-sac of dust-blown, mock-Spanish bungalows with empty swimming pools thick with dried sagebrush and windows open to the elements.

There was no sign of human habitation. Everything rang in the dead air. The slams of our car doors were like gunshots.

Rae's *hello, anyone here?* hung in the air until a door opened somewhere inside.

The caretaker was a rangy, elastic-limbed stoner kid. His centre parting and handlebar moustache were pure 1973 Haight-Ashbury, his Air Jordans and Nike skullcap ten-minutes-out-of-date Nineties, and his tartan shirt classic grunge; he looked like a remnants bin.

As he kicked the door closed we could see into his room. The entirety of his furniture was an airbed and a bong. He smoothed down the ends of his moustache as he talked.

"You didn't think the sign looked sort of fucked? We haven't had an open house here for months. Should take it down I guess."

He had the slow cadence of someone who was very stoned or who hadn't heard their own voice for a while. Probably both.

"They stopped building coupla' years back. It was s'posed to be five hundred homes. Big ol' gym, mini-mart, gas station even." He waved his hand vaguely in the direction of the lopped off hilltops. "High-end *community*."

He looked us up and down. "Not sure it'd have been your kind of place even if they finished it. No offence."

Still, he seemed to feel that a tour was in order. We walked in silence along the main road as waves of dry heat reflected from the tarmac. The whole estate was like a picked-clean skeleton. Glassless windows were gaping eye sockets. Yawning garage doors were jaws open to the desert air.

We walked into one of the homes at random, the kid waiting outside like we might want to talk in private. The terracotta tiles were gritty with dirt, flashing me back to Dillon's place. We walked through it all without speaking, the only sound a constant whistle of wind. A window framed cowboy-film views out over the valley. Mile upon mile of levelled ground, stepped like a ziggurat with outlines of roads and gardens that would now never be. This central section was high enough that you could look down on distant birds riding thermals. Rae was bored; without human beings the place was dead to her. She pushed open the kitchen door and reared back. There was a flash of white and Rae's hand shot to her mouth. A mule deer, spooked, had leapt neatly out the open window. We watched it bolt across the lot and then pick its way gently down the hillside, nibbling at bushes.

We were three-point-turning outside the main house, the car a sweatbox after half an hour in the sun, when the kid loped back over. He went to rap on the window and made a face as he realised it was open.

Rae stopped the engine and his long, slow face filled the window. "I don' s'pose you guys want a job?"

There's a sketch here, very rough, in smudged black pencil. Three figures wearing the same kind of headdresses as the one that I found on my very first day here. They are standing around something, a something made up of rough pencil cross-hatchings, drawn so hard as to almost tear the page. It looks like a pile of rags maybe, or a rook's nest. The figures' heads are down and the heavy line of a shotgun hangs from the rightmost one's hand.

Voodoo Rae — Act III

After we moved up there everything changed. Rae waited tables and took a distance-learning degree in Makeup for Horror, Sci-Fi and Fantasy Film from the Toni Basil School for Professional Development. It wasn't unusual for me to come home from a night shift to find a squadron of giggly zombies drinking breakfast smoothies through straws so their wounds didn't fall off. I did six weeks as a stand-in John Lennon at the House of Blues's Starry Cavalcade, part of a faux-Beatles whose other three members were OxyContin-addicted Las Vegans, pancaked in makeup to disguise their Latino heritage, who practised their Scouse accents by watching episode after episode of *Thomas the Tank Engine* backstage. Seeing which way the Vegas wind was blowing, Rae and I enrolled at croupier school to learn to deal poker, which was where the big tips were. We graduated in the winter, receiving photocopied scrolls in the cleared out card-room of the Winchester Days Inn Hotel. There was one mortar board between the whole class, which we passed around for solemn photos, before redeeming our Graduate Bounty: $100-worth of chips and vouchers for three free margaritas.

We started out with shifts at the least prestigious off-Strip casinos. I enjoyed it. That white-noise jangle of Vegas: slots, bullshit conversations and roulette rattle, like an orchestra tuning up forever. It was pure anticipation. People were pulled tight as guitar strings, vibrating with the tension of it all.

They fascinated me, the actual gamblers. Not the ones who said "never bet more than you can afford to lose". That's not gambling. Betting what you *can* afford to lose is an investment, or, if you're seriously rich, just a way of killing time. One Texan guy put fifty thousand on a corner number when I was running the roulette wheel and then something caught his eye across the room and he forgot to even watch the spin. It came up 34 and I had to get someone to chase him down with his four hundred grand. Like I said, just killing time. I don't understand those people. In a town as amoral as Vegas you can do some seriously freaky shit for fifty thousand, so why waste it among the rubes? Gambling, true gambling means risk. It means the risk of losing everything, the risk of getting swept away. That's why it's addictive, because it can be life-changing either way.

In the most transient town on Earth I felt weirdly settled, out among the microwave mornings and ice-box nights and the million cicadas and billion stars. It was timeless and blank and if you lay out on the house's flat roof and slowed your breathing you could actually see the dome of stars rotate around you.

Every weekend Rae and I blagged and borrowed swag from the casino hotels: nearly new mini-fridges and last year's flat-screen TVs and erotic sculptures and hibachis and thousand-dollar bathrobes and golf carts and listening devices and nightsticks and Bang & Olufsen CD towers and sushi rolling kits. The Jetta's trunk was often so stuffed that it crunched horribly on the rear axle as we drove home through the Monday morning dawn. We were living like high rollers and hobos: pure luxury and real poverty and nothing in between. Just as it should be.

This then was the world my son was born into. His birth certificate read PLACE OF BIRTH: Wokova Reserve, Nevada. Technically the whole estate was on Native American land. It was one of the parcels of waterless, cropless, sun-blasted earth that was given to the Paiute Tribe like so many glass beads, back in the Forties when the idea that anyone would want to live out here was laughable. Then Vegas boomed and the realtors came back to clear the Paiute off the land for a second time; real Indian givers. This time it cost them a slew of charitable donations and a "heritage programme" that meant everything on the estate had a Native American name. (The hopelessly optimistic map in the entranceway listed a Winnemucca golf course and even a Nün'wa Paya Hup Ca'a' Otuu'mu cultural centre.) So Robin is technically a Paiute, though I can't think of a nationality that offers less in the way of perks.

He was born up there in the moonscape of the Sierra Madre foothills, among silence and stars, a week early while I was dealing blackjack in the old Atlantis Casino. The Atlantis was one of those rudimentary gambling dens that crowd the state line between California and Nevada. It had none of the bells and whistles of the Strip: no free buffet, no hostesses, no big-name attraction playing downstairs. It was simply the very first place you could gamble if you were coming from the south, making its clientele the most depressing in the whole state. If you couldn't wait the forty minutes it took to drive to Vegas proper then you had a problem.

And they had a no-cellphones rule which meant that Rae's texts that night, as they ran from the lightly concerned (*I feel weird but I can't tell if it's baby weird*) through rising worry (*can u come home I really think this might be it*) onwards into intelligibility (*fucksake B just be here FFS*), just set my jacket pocket jangling inside my locker.

It was only on a break, smoking outside in the starlight with the busboys, that the under pit boss caught up with me. Rae had called him in desperation.

I got home too late. Rae was starfished in the paddling pool, her body luminous in the harshness of the halogen, hands gripping the rubber handholds on the rim. A ribbon of red unfurled between her legs.

She looked frazzled and half-drowned. Her first words to me as a mother: "Where have you beeeen? I've been calling for *hours*."

She was befraggled by sweat and pool-water, her breasts floating, magnified just under the surface. Light reflected in the water made her features swim. Her hand was hot and tiny.

"No cellphones on the floor, remember? If Gary hadn't seen the *fifty missed calls* message I'd still be there."

I looked around. "Aren't we missing someone?"

"Collie has him. He was kind of gunky." She wrung her hair out. "Healthy, but gunky."

Collie was her duma, a quarter-Native-American stripper-cum-realtor who Rae had befriended in Whole Foods, whose name neither she nor Rae found as funny as I did.

"Col-lie," she called and Collie emerged from the house, with the smallest of bundles in her arms.

"Who's a good girl?" I said.

An hour later, as the water, pink with conjoined blood, gurgled down the storm drain, and the drone of Collie's motorbike hung in the air, there he was. Robin Arturo Kussgarten. Wrapped up in Rae on her Caesar's Palace lounger, her legs tucked underneath her, dusky in starlight, tired flesh in a sodden hotel robe. Robin was a tiny, scrunched-up thing in her arms — a fist, a walnut — and both of them were pink with blood and love. Their faces were trained on each other's, Rae somehow both sleepy and alert, Robin's eyes furiously shut against the indignity of the world.

Robin Arturo Kussgarten, a thing ancient and new, curled like a fat comma in Rae's lap. And Rae herself salt-skinned and grubby, like an orphan kid herself with a toy, making Robin A Kussgarten something smaller still: a seed, an idea.

I watched the lovely, hopeful tug between their two faces, linked like earth and moon, like sea and sky, like Madonna and child. But no Madonna and child ever had this backdrop: the ghost house, the contour-map town and the pale roads, set under a crow's wing of night littered with careless diamonds.

I could have watched them forever — the slo-mo blink of Rae's grey eyes and the furlings and unfurling of Robin's fists — if it wasn't for some quality of the light that made me uneasy. There was a repeating swell of darkness, almost imperceptible until you looked up into the spangle of the Milky Way, dawn-bright in the raw air of the mountains. There you saw, vertiginously far away, a wheel of blackness obscuring the moon and stars in a smooth circle. Three shadows making a lazy sweep of the heavens, darkening whole galaxies, whole nebula, with a subtle angling of a wing, three black shapes on a black background: shadows on velvet, three silent vultures.

Rae finally slept around 5am, Robin curled into her, flesh on flesh. Their faces, even deep in respective slumbers, beamed information at each other, two satellite dishes in constant contact: I AM HERE I AM HERE I AM HERE, while I smoked and watched the vultures circle as the sun freed the landscape from night.

At this point there's a drawing that takes up almost a foot of the reel. He'd cut three scraps of paper, each the rough shape of a bird with outstretched wings, from the bottom of the roll. Then he'd laid them on the paper and sprayed ink from his pen. It filled the page with hundreds of inky dots, like blood splatter. And then he'd removed the torn paper to leave three perfect voids among the stars.

Voodoo Rae — Act IV

So, Robin. Lucky even in the womb. Star-crowned. Vulture child, Indian born. Prince of a deserted kingdom. Born with a page-turner backstory on a million-dollar movie set. And blessed with what my family never gave me: fucked-up parents in fucked-up jobs in a fucked-up house on the edge of a fucked-up world. How lucky could a kid be? There's not an artist alive who didn't crawl, smoking, from some kind of family wreckage.

And this life was a gift that kept on giving. There were daily doses of drama, conflict and dysfunction to mould his infant mind. His babysitters were a revolving cast of Vegas's temporary homeless, refugees from the city's brutal gig economy trying to get back on their feet (or going down for the last time). There were croupiers between casinos who dealt endless practice hands of high-low over breakfast, even Robin in his high-chair getting his three-up, two-down. We took in RSI-stricken strippers whose box-fresh, milkless breasts had him mewling in frustration. Bus-station pimp-bait newbies, as big-eyed and helpless as baby birds, slept at the end of our bed and whined and kicked through bad dreams until Rae banished them to sleep by Robin's crib. Tarot-card readers with front-seat iguanas. Card counters. Snake handlers. What boy wouldn't want this freak show as a backdrop?

And then there was the desert. Its rhythms were older, slower. In a place where a cactus might flower once every seven years, where you can go a decade without rain, what's an hour, a day, a week? We spent days on the roof of the house where you might at least catch a breath of breeze, camped out under a tent of pilfered hotel bed sheets, reading and listening to endless records. Magazines and cigarettes and gemstone skies, flawless and bland. Shadows shrinking, disappearing and lengthening. Robin was our only clock.

As soon as he could stand he was out and exploring on a clunky metal trike that was years too big for him. Rae had found it at a heartrending garage sale in Henderson: wedding rings, baby clothes in their packaging and his'n'hers golf bags. From the rooftop we'd watch Robin as he pedalled furiously, his fireman's helmet bobbing up and down with the effort. Down the main access road he'd go, over ground so hot that sometimes you could smell the trike's rubber tyres melting, down to the main gates, then left along the far edge of the putative golf course.

Rae was nervous when he wasn't visible from the roof-top so I'd rigged up a trailer for him. Inside was a gallon bottle of water, a walkie-talkie and a boombox. Once out of sight he'd press play on the boombox so we could follow his progress in the hidden sections. Music blared from the western perimeter and through the discarded drainage pipes down into the visitors' car park. I made him mixtape after mixtape but the only one which really caught his attention was a compilation of Midlands rock, heavy on the Sabbath and Purple.

He played it so often that I could place him on the map purely by the music. If Ozzy had finished with his woman because she couldn't help him with his mind then Robin was crossing the Hunipui ballroom. If Black Betty had a child that was goddamn wild then he was skirting the catering block. And always, miles above him like a personal weather system, the trio of vultures circled, lazy and watchful, convinced that anything that tiny must surely die soon. But Robin trundled on and they rotated in the sky patiently.

He never sweated, never tanned, as if he belonged out there somehow, the accidental Native American-ness of his birth protecting him from the environment. Rae worried though. When he came back from his rounds he'd be obsessive and dreamy and shivery. He'd stop in the middle of what he was doing, frozen in thought, a sentence half-finished in his mouth, a sandwich hanging limply from his hand. But if she tried to make him stay home he threw monumental tantrums, vast symphonies of outrage that wracked his frame and left him puce with fury, wet-faced and breathless until Rae relented.

I started to work longer hours. The poker boom had crested and now there was a glut of Hold 'Em Poker dealers. Rae went back to work too. Sometimes we'd work the same room, leaving Robin in the care of countless Candys and Kittys and Sugars and Vixens. His trike rides grew longer and he was quieter at home. You'd ask him a question and he'd look back at you blankly, only to answer hours later, sometimes not until he'd gone to bed. He'd tiptoe through in his pyjamas and say, "it was Led Zeppelin daddy" or "there were forty-two of them".

Which day was it when the shark of our relationship, which until then had always moved forward, began to circle and slow? One of those desert days, surely. Until Vegas every day with Rae was unique. Even the days in bed, listening to music, were, to me, as different from each other as individual people. But in the desert, time stretched like the shadows. Your body clock slowed. In the heat of midday a word would do you for an hour, moving the chair into the shade felt like a day's work.

For Rae, I think, every day there was lit with Robin's life; she marvelled in every tiny change in him and cried for an hour the first time he scuffed his knee, but for me the changes were too slow and incremental to break the prison of the days. Friends of friends slept in unoccupied shells of the estate and then disappeared, leaving indecipherable flotsam on leaking airbeds: bowling trophies, sex toys, baby teeth. One evening I dealt to a high-roller who dropped a million while he waited for the Celine Dion show to start. Next day a college kid lost fifty bucks and wept in his seat. Rae's fashion magazines yellowed after just a day in the rooftop sunshine — relics of the almost present. Their cover lines seemed to be exactly the same each month. HOW TO HAVE MINDBLOWING SEX WHAT'S HOT IN HAIR RIGHT NOW LOVE YOURSELF AND HE WILL TOO.

Rae suggested moving somewhere more wholesome for Robin. The mountains: Alberta maybe, Denver. I wanted to stay. The thinnest of cracks in our Nation of Two.

Longer weekends. Worse weekends. Champ was back after some unspecified problems in Mexico, so he and I spent long days under his rules of disorder. No plans. No baggage. Just a spot to meet — the corner of Eddy and Larkin in San Francisco — and one of Champ's stolen credit cards. We'd go into any bar, any shop and just talk. Assume everyone, however unpromising, is the key to the next forty-eight hours. Say yes. Say yes to free Spanish classes. Say yes, you have been saved and you've seen the glory of the Lord. Say yes to a teenage house party where you buy beer and ciggies for four hundred people. Say yes, sure you're a cab, driving four drunk businessmen in suits over to Oakland to "see the natives". Say yes to police line-ups. Say yes to a third-floor Tenderloin walk-up even though your invitee has a gun-shaped bulge in his front pocket and track marks on either arm. Say yes because of that, not in spite of it. These weren't lost weekends, they were *hidden* weekends — buried even while they were happening. We were snowploughs in a blizzard of nights that I knew would only reoccur as flashbacks: mirrors, tattoos, bar-light. Blood, gold teeth, strobe-light. Weekdays with Rae and Robin were just the filling of the reservoir, ton upon ton of dead black water, straining against the dam of Friday and the moment when Champ and I removed the bricks.

Then Robin started getting sick. Fevers. Cold sweats. Sleepwalking. Shivers. You'd find him frozen, mid-gesture, as if he'd forgotten how to move, and his skin would be clammy. I found him in odd places: rooftops and basements, in dark corners. We took him to the doctor in Vegas three times and each time as we descended from the scant air he'd flicker to life. His cheeks would pinken, his eyes would shine and his chatter returned. He was fresh-faced and alert in the doctor's waiting room, bouncing onto the examination table like it was a birthday treat. Tests that cost more than I paid for my first car all said the same thing: CLEAR CLEAR CLEAR. But the drive home leeched the colour from his face and he shrank back into the seat.

We had no Wi-Fi in the desert so Rae bought a thick stack of medical encyclopedias from a pawn shop, books so old that they had entries for Hysteria and Mongoloids. His symptoms suggested dropsy or The Vapors. He might have the ague. Fainting sickness. Collie burnt burrobrush and shadscale. His room had the acrid smell of illness.

Rae and I worked more shifts, leaving Robin at Collie's. He blossomed at sea level, stuffing himself with ice cream and junk TV before wilting on the journey home.

Every day now Rae was saying it was time to go, we should find a place in LA or the mountains, but it felt like a retreat. I liked how we lived. It was rough-edged and precarious and Vegas tossed out up a never-ending churn of house guests. Everyone I met was broken and sun-maddened and manipulable and sad.

Robin got nosebleeds, Robin got migraines. His hair was like bleached cotton and his eyes were always pink. On bad nights, when he writhed and muttered and tore holes in his bedsheets, the vultures circled lower and wider, like the holding pattern at LAX, a traffic system in the sky. Rae and I rowed all the time. Arguments about little things became arguments about everything.

There were suitcases in the hallway. New contacts appeared on Rae's phone. The car was always full of petrol.

Robin, Rae: they were out of there.

Chapter Eight

I couldn't picture Robin in the desert, and I couldn't imagine him as a Native American at all, even as a technicality. Everything about him, from that pale skin so quick to take a blush to those busy, clever hands, spoke to me of a particular kind of British kid. He was someone from school who would gush over last night's *Doctor Who* and Airfix models. He would grow up to be dreamy, and clumsy, with bursts of oddly aimed enthusiasm. I knew the way things moved in his mind. I could feel the ideas that would plant hooks in him.

I pulled out The Book of Umbrage and began to write. The story flowed from the nib of my pen, tugging ideas into place behind it. Once everything was down on the page I willed the two of them to wake but the screen stayed unmoving. I sent down for breakfast and tidied up. Still nothing.

I fretted over what I'd read that morning. I didn't want to hear about good times between Brandon and Rae, even if they were years ago. I wanted my brother to be one-dimensional and hateful and gone.

It was midday before I saw the first movement: Rae in a robe, with damp hair hanging down over her face. She waved a silent hello and put a finger to her lips. There was the *tap, tap, tap* of fingers on keyboard — she had to go out but Robin would be down soon. I wanted to hear just a moment of her voice. I messaged to tell her I had something to show Robin.

After she left I made some coffee. The light from their kitchen window inched its way across the wall like a sundial. I cut myself a line and waited. Somewhere in their flat a clock was ticking. When Robin finally appeared he came onscreen in a blur of limbs too fast for the camera.

"Mom says you've got something for me what is it hi hi morning Daddy what is it?"

I opened up the Book of Umbrage and Robin sat cross-legged with his hands on his knees, inches from the screen. He ate cereal noisily.

"There's a throne," I told him, "carved from ivory, in an abandoned building called The Folly, up in the mountains. It's overgrown, but one New Year kids from the valley below dared each other to go up and explore. It took a couple of hours, but they didn't mind. It was one of those boring, grown-up days when nothing interesting happens at home anyway."

The endoscope was positioned inches from the top of the mountain and I flicked it on. A dusty path through a landscape strewn with boulders, the only vegetation wizened and black. I uncoiled it uphill until the top of a damaged tower came into view.

"When they got to the top, they set to exploring. Nature had reclaimed much of the folly. Vines forced their way through the cracks between rocks and started to work away at the fabric of the place."

I focused on a piece I've always been proud of: a row of balsa wood blocks into which I'd planted seeds. Nowadays the blocks were veined with roots that twisted them up and away from the ground.

"When they got inside they found a badger cub sleeping on the throne. They got close enough to see its little ribs rising and falling but they didn't wake it. That evening one of the boys told his father, a priest, what they'd seen. Well, I've told you how much the Umbragians love an omen" — Robin nodded furiously, spoon in mouth — "so the priest declared that the next twelve months would be the Year of the Badger. Everything the citizens did, every decision they took, would be done through the filter of badgerishness, if there's such a word."

"Badgerdom," whispered Robin.

"Badgerdom, of course. So, when they were unsure what to do they invoked the qualities of the badger: tenaciousness, patience, independence. And every year since they send a child up there to see if there's an animal on the throne."

"And is there?"

"Usually. The kid'll camp out there for days if need be, waiting. Even a butterfly, alighting on the throne for a split second, that counts. The Year of the Butterfly was a strange one. There have been a couple of years though…"

I flicked open the book again, "About twenty years back no animal was found so they continued with the Year of the Lizard. And quite recently we had three straight years of the crow."

"What are crow years like?"

I read from the book. "Craft is preferred over hard work, beauty is prized, waste is abhorred." I knew he wouldn't understand all of the words but meaning isn't always the most important part of a story.

"And this year?"

"That's why I thought of it. It's Umbragian New Year today. I thought *you* might go and see if anything is there."

His spoon stopped in mid-air. "Really? And I'll see what's on the throne? Just me?"

"Of course."

He had a nervous tic, one that I could feel the ghost of across my own face: opening his eyes wide, three times in succession, like he was trying to wake up.

"But will I really see it, or, y'know, *make it up*?" He whispered the last bit. It was the right question.

"Well, you see it but you don't see it, do you know what I mean?"

He nodded with that seriousness only children can have.

I ran the endoscope up the side of one of the hills that overlooked Au-Hav, snaking it between model trees and over pencil-thin streams. "Here's The Folly."

The whole hilltop, unlike the parched landscape around it, was thick with moss and mould. It spilled down the sides, reaching slender fingers down the grooves in the hillside's surface. Somewhere under the fuzz of vegetation was the outline of a curved spire and a rectangular base. There was a slot cut into the moss, opening out into a dark-emerald chamber with a single ivory chair at its centre. The thickness of the foliage around The Folly meant that Robin got no sight of the structure until the endoscope was almost on top of it. Then it loomed, sinuous and verdant, to fill the screen.

"It's spooky," he said, sounding delighted.

I ran the camera up the side of the spire. Near the top the off-white of the original wood showed through in places and burned bright on the screen.

"I know. It's real vegetation, most of it, not the fake stuff."

"That's so cool. It's like you expect to see birds and stuff. How comes it's not kept clean like everywhere else?"

"No one knows." I had a hunch Robin would like this story. As a kid I was fascinated by stories of abandoned cities, or mysteries like the *Marie Celeste*, and it felt like something genetic.

"It was built by a group of Umbragians who liked open spaces. They sequestered themselves up here and were pretty much self-sufficient. You know what self-sufficient means?"

Robin nodded furiously on the screen.

"They kept themselves to themselves so when a party of hikers from Dracksal, down in the valley, stopped by here there was no real way of knowing how long they'd been gone."

"No clues?" Robin's face was close to the screen.

"Well…"

Much of this morning had been given over to rewriting the clues hidden in The Folly's fabric, to make them look right for a ten-year-old. I took a length of dowling and parted some of the vegetation that hung down over the chamber. The walls, pale as maggot-skin, were covered in scratchy patterns and writing. They were something between symbols and drawings, and they covered the entire back wall.

"What does it mean?"

"Who knows? I have an idea, but maybe you could take a look."

I clicked the endoscope button to take stills and dropped the pictures into the chat box. He opened them and instantly his face slackened. I knew that look: absorption.

"Hey, that's for later. Don't forget what we came here for, the throne animal."

His hand leapt to his mouth. "I forgot."

"It's always a child who looks so I'm going to step aside. Let me know if you see anything."

I went out to the kitchen and did a line on the kitchen counter with the water running so Robin wouldn't hear me. When I got back he was staring into the screen with his face scrunched up.

"Anything?"

"I think so. It wasn't too clear."

I let him think.

"I mean I saw it but I'm not certain."

"That's OK. Tell me what you saw."

"Like a rabbit? But bigger."

"A hare?"

"I'm not sure."

"Google 'hare — H A R E' and take a look."

He typed with one finger. "That's it, that's totally it."

"Interesting. They call them jack-rabbits in the States I think." I checked the book. "There's never been a Year of the Hare before. What do we know about them?"

Robin stared as I consulted Wikipedia.

"In English mythology the hare was a trickster, influenced by the moon, wild and unpredictable. They changed sex from month to month. They're that rarest of things, a cunning animal that's not a carnivore. So, he's peaceful but tricky. He's fast, and he zig-zags and rears up on his haunches, and boxes and runs wild in the moonlight."

Robin looked unconvinced. "How do they follow that? Do they have to run around in moonlight?"

"No, but they can take the spirit of the hare. Be wild but not vicious, swift but not rigid, mad but not crazy."

Robin bounced on the bed. "Mad not crazy, *mad not crazy*," he chanted, boxing the air in front of him. It was infectious. I slapped my hands on the desk and chanted along with him until we were both facing our respective screens, shadow-boxing.

"Mad not crazy, mad not crazy."

At full volume he collapsed in a pile on the bed, shaking with laughter. He was still laughing when Rae appeared, laden with shopping.

She took one look: the ruined tower on the screen, the Wikipedia page and Robin's tears of laughter. "Boys," she said as she led Robin away.

The day spread out in front of me. I ate, I read, I repaired Umbrage's western seawall. It was evening before Rae returned. She sat in the kitchen with a mug of coffee.

"I have no idea what you said to him earlier but he has been working away in his room for *hours*. He even told me not to disturb him." She shook her head happily. "He's come in here twice all day, once to ask me a question about jack-rabbits, which in no way could I answer by the way, so thanks for that, and once for a sandwich."

"It was just a little puzzle. But I think it will appeal to him."

"Because it appeals to you?"

"Yes. Well it definitely would have appealed to me as a kid."

"But not now?" There was a trace of smile in her voice.

"Maybe a little."

I sat for a long while after that. The sound of rain on the balcony and wet tyres on the street below mixed in with Umbrage's symphony of clicks and burbles. There was a smear across the view back into Robin's bedroom. I tried to wipe it clean but it must have been on his end — he'd kissed the exact spot of the laptop camera.

I didn't feel like doing anything. I wasn't tired, or high or worried. I poured a drink from one of Brandon's half-opened bottles, a tawny whiskey that I didn't want to know the price of, and waited, content.

Hours later the screen wobbled. Rae had come in to collect the laptop.

"Can't sleep," she whispered, her face in profile on the screen as she walked down the hallway. She lay down on her bed, her pose identical to Robin's earlier.

"It's silly. I'm really tired but knowing the laptop was in Robin's room felt like I'd left a door open." She lay on her side and pushed her hair back. "Why aren't you asleep, it's late there?"

"You look tired," I said, "close your eyes."

She looked beautiful right then. Late night puffiness gave her a cherubic look and her eyes flickered open, startled, every time she began to fall asleep.

I tried to drink in the details of their life over her shoulder. Action figures left in a frozen battle on the bedside table, family photos and Rae's shoes where she'd kicked them off. Over the bed there was an old-fashioned map on the wall with a couple of jerky lines running across it.

"What's that, the map?" I asked.

Rae looked over her shoulder. "Oh."

The lines ran from England to California, and from somewhere deep in the American interior. With a start, too late, I realised what it might be.

"Brandon made it. Not long after we met. The red twine is his path across the world. The blue is me. Kansas to California. Not much of an adventure."

She turned the laptop around so I could see the map, but not her face. Where the two lines met, at a pin in Los Angeles, they were intertwined and their conjoined paths spiralled outwards around the city and then north to Vegas and on to Tahoe. Now I was closer I could see a third piece of twine, yellow this time, joining them from Vegas to Tahoe.

It was a pretty thing. I felt sick.

Rae sighed. "I'll say something for your brother, he could make you feel special. *Chosen* even. He always made me think I could make something of myself. Everyone else was an idiot, a chancer, but me? I was going to do great things. *We* were."

She hooked her little finger under the path from Vegas to Tahoe. "I mean it was probably fifty per cent ego: anyone who he had picked had to be special, didn't they? But with him at first I never worried about the future. We were going to *win*."

I cursed myself for asking. She watched the screen and I couldn't read her eyes. I didn't want Brandon to be the last thing in her mind as she fell asleep.

"Match your breathing to mine, slow down," I told her, keeping the laptop mike close to my mouth.

I breathed long and slow, and she began to relax, her eyes half-closing, then three-quarter closing and then gone.

I kept as quiet as I could. In the blue light of the screen she looked almost abstract, a snowscape with eyelashes for winter trees and a river of hair. She said something indistinct before rolling over. I wanted to reach into the scene to push her hair away from her eyes. I took the laptop into the bedroom and placed it at the end of the bed, letting her light wash over me.

The noises were indistinct. Movements and low voices. Not street sounds, something closer. Maybe it was Rae or Robin through the laptop. I felt a pang for the comfort of their home. Here at the Magpie, the *trompe l'oeil* ceiling was nearly thirty feet above me. The walk to the bathroom was longer than most of the flats I'd ever lived in.

I headed to the kitchen for a glass of water and found two men standing in the hallway, reading something by the light of a mobile. White guys, bulky, shaven-headed. For a second they looked as surprised as I did but before I could do any of the things that I'd expect to do in such a situation — scream, run, hide — they were upon me. A hand closed hard across my mouth and then something yanked at my ankles. I toppled and was hauled upside down, my hair just touching the parquet. I reached down to steady myself and my hands were kicked away. I tried again. The same thing happened. I rocked from side to side, trying to get a better view.

Someone squatted in front on me while a hand still clamped my mouth. "Hold him higher for fuck's sake. My knees are killing me."

I was hoisted higher until my face was level with his. Upside down it was hard to tell exactly what he looked like. A clean, pinkish face with skin that looked pulled tight. Stubble on his jaw and head, longer at the jaw. A blue roadmap of veins.

He took his hand away from my mouth and wagged a finger at me. "Shhh."

Experimentally he reached out and pushed me gently in the chest. I swung back and forth and he watched me.

"You know, I was hoping that Saul was wrong when he said you were back here. I didn't believe him. I said to Ron, 'He'll be long gone that one. He's got a brain in his head.'"

The other guy nodded. He gave me another shove, keeping me swinging.

"Because when we met you I thought to myself, 'Now this isn't our usual client, he's *discerning*'. It's rare that someone who hires us takes any kind of pride in what they do. It's just 'go here, do him,' like they're ordering a pizza. Like we don't have any opinions. Like we don't want to be creative with it. But you, you had a vision for the whole thing. I like that. And then, when you disappeared, I said to Ron that something must have happened to you because, let's face it, running away when you still have a payment to make is the action of an ignorant, ignorant man. And you Brandon, don't strike me as an ignorant man."

I tried to say something but he placed a finger on my lips.

"I mean you have obvious flaws, like the pills and the big mouth and I have to say, what I consider a low-level homophobia, possibly through some unresolved same-sex attractions. And also there's a fine line between creative and over-elaborate and I'm not sure it's a line you're aware of. But despite that you're not ignorant. You understand the penalties and reparations and the compoundment of interest that are involved in hiring professional people to do a job, and then reneging on that deal."

He placed his hand either side of my face.

"But now here we are and I find you're back in this… whatever this place is. By all accounts living it very large indeed, and I find myself disappointed in you."

He actually did look disappointed.

"As to what form that disappointment will take…" Here he spread his hands wide, as if he were about to catch a ball. "Well, we'll find out later, won't we? But for now. Where's. Our. Money."

Each word was punctuated with a shove to the chest.

"I don't know," I said, my words gummy with the weight of my upside-down tongue.

I didn't see his hand move at all. I just felt a single blow land, hard, above my right ear and then my whole skull started throbbing.

He said something under his breath and nodded at whoever was holding my ankles and I was lowered to the ground. My jaw felt tight and there was a low rumbling that hadn't been there before.

"All right, the safe first. I don't really want to be fiddling around in your pockets."

They walked me through to the guest bedroom, a hand on each elbow like they were helping an old lady across the road. By the time I had the picture off the wall my teeth were chattering. I shook as I entered the combination. I snuck a glance at the other guy, while the first emptied the files and envelopes from the safe. He was taller still, with the same shaved head and stubble combination, and a similar sheen to his skin, but they didn't look like brothers. More like two people trying to look like brothers.

"This is two-and-a-half thousand." He said it like it was tragic news — a fire in an orphanage — and ran the heel of his hand along the ridge of his eyebrows as if trying to shift a headache.

"Which is nothing. Actually it's worse than nothing because this looks like *remnants*." He sounded tired but there was a twitchiness to him that was making me wary.

He placed a hand on each side of my face and squeezed my cheeks. "So, my duck. Where. Is. Our. Money?"

I willed my voice calm. "I don't know who you are. I am assuming, because it has happened many, many times before, that you are in some way involved with my twin brother, my identical twin brother, Brandon."

A smile passed between them. "And you're not Brandon?"

I shook my head.

"You're the brother, Adam."

How did they know my name? "Exactly," I said but with a sense of foreboding.

"That's pretty poor. You've had a week to come up with something more convincing than that."

"But you knew he had a twin. You knew my name."

"Yeah, obviously, we know about Adam." His face was weighty with sorrow. "We know because we killed him."

Ten minutes later we were sat on the sofa, going around it again. Over herbal tea (them) and a Scotch (me) I laid out everything that had happened. The phone call, the police, my deceptions, how I'd ended up here. They listened and then talked amongst themselves and I couldn't tell how much they believed me. The quiet one seemed to be called Reggie but I didn't want to ask them about that. What I wanted to do was to ask them about something that was coalescing in my mind. Once they were satisfied that I wasn't a flight risk I tried a couple of questions.

"So did Adam's killing go as planned?"

A look passed between the two of them. "Not exactly. But the end result was the main thing."

Dominos toppled. "Not exactly? Was there something you were supposed to wear? Something you were supposed to leave?"

Ronnie rubbed at the back of his neck. "Yeah. It was all a bit complex, a bit elaborate. And you can be a bit grandiose after a couple of lines. You, him, whoever."

Reggie nodded. "There were fucking costumes and a record we were supposed to leave."

Ronnie took back over. "And a passport and a wallet, remember?"

Reggie said, "A whole fucking production."

Their voices were more similar than their faces, I realised.

"Like I said, pretty fucking elaborate. But the day before we were due to, y'know, we were out checking out the area, looking for a spot, when we see him walking home alone. And we just improvised. No fucking headdresses or whatever. But the same result. You got what you wanted."

I let it all sink in. I wanted them to see it rather than me having to explain.

"And how did you know it was Adam, not Brandon?"

There was a moment of silence.

"Stands to reason doesn't it? Over in Notting Hill by his flat. Wearing a ratty anorak, no way that was Brandon. Man was a snappy dresser for all his faults. Right where you said he'd be, too."

But he sounded dubious now. "I mean you never leave this place do you? Saul said you were like a hermit."

I tried to recreate the chain of events. Brandon tells Kimi his plan. But then he hires these two to kill me. To kill me and leave his ID on my body. To kill me and plant his record on me. The media starts up. Kimi says her bit. He's in the news. But where's Brandon?

I felt everything in my body stiffen. He's me. He goes back to my flat and waits for the police. He does what I did. He identifies the body. He waits and watches. He's Adam Kussgarten, mourning brother. Perhaps he even comforts Rae. And he gets to watch his final creation unfold. Better still he gets to see it unfold while all the proceeds go to Brandon's next of kin. Me. Him.

I was torn between a sorrow that my life meant so little to him and an admiration for the neatness of it all. And then Ronnie and Reggie messed it all up.

Gently I floated this new theory, but they were unconvinced. If Brandon's plan was elaborate, this was a step too far. They were more interested, yet seemingly unworried, by the news that the killing had been captured on camera.

"How did it look? With the duck masks and stuff? Did it look bad-ass?" The taller one, Reggie, mimed the killing again, stepping across the room quickly and placing two fingers at my temple. "Bang bang."

He regarded me thoughtfully. "Fuck I wish we had a copy. Needs considering, does this. Shall we, y'know, meditate on it?"

Reggie lit three cones of incense in a triangle around us. They sat cross-legged and held hands with their eyes closed. I didn't really know what to do with myself.

As if reading my mind, Ronnie whispered, "Just sit there and look pretty OK?"

In unison they took small bottles from jeans pockets and dropped a brown liquid under their tongues. Reggie licked his lips like a cat with a furball. I sat quietly, trying to get a handle on how my fate was progressing, and what kind of people these were. Ron and Reg. Reg and Ron. I couldn't quite place them. They had gym bunny physiques: great triangular plates of flesh up top, encroaching on thick necks, but spindlier legs. They wore identical white Ts that were so tight that I could see individual veins pulsing beneath them.

Ronnie rolled his head in a circle. I couldn't tell which of them it was who started talking first

"We were, it's true, a bit previous. You could argue without carrying out due diligence."

"Yeah, but this is Marcus all over again. Too trusting of the wrong people."

"Karmically it's a fucking mess. There aren't enough good deeds on the planet."

"But practically? Practically there's no change."

"Could argue *practically* we're in the clear."

As they whispered the quality of the light in the room changed infinitesimally and with a jolt I recognised what it meant: someone had walked in front of the camera back in Tahoe and the flat-screen TV here had lit up. I willed whoever it was to keep moving. The screen-light stayed on. I kept my eyes on Ronnie and Reggie. If it were Rae was there a way I could get a message to her? I was just formulating something to ask them that might explain the situation when I heard Robin's voice.

"Daddy?"

Ronnie jumped and wheeled round.

"Daddy? Whatchu doing?" Robin, over life-size on the vast screen, tilted his head from side to side.

Ronnie and Reggie looked at each other and Reggie whispered, "You take this."

Ronnie dropped into a crouch again, eyes level with Robin's on the screen.

"Hey buddy, we just popped in to see your daddy here, y'know, a cup of tea, a bit of a chinwag."

"Robin, go back to bed, OK?" I tried to inject some meaning into my look.

"OK," he nodded, but he seemed reluctant to move.

Reggie held up a hand. "Of course, back to bed in just a sec."

Ronnie mouthed something to him and he nodded. "Is your mum around?"

Robin looked sly. "Yeah but she's asleep. I shouldn't really be up."

"Gotcha, our secret. But she's there with you, right?"

"Yeah." He locked his eyes on me.

"That's good, just wanted to check you were OK. Your daddy is right, you should be in bed."

He gave the tiniest nod of the head to Reggie and before I could react he clasped a hand over my mouth. He lifted me off my heels and dragged me to the doorway. I was facing the bedroom but I could still hear the conversation.

"It's the middle of the night there. You guys on holiday?"

Robin would be bursting to talk, even to a stranger. "No I'm at home."

"Course you are, your daddy said. Looks nice."

I could hear the boredom in Robin's voice. "I guess."

"You'd rather be in London?"

"Yeah. Most of London was burned down in 1666 by a great fire." He slowed over the last two words and I could tell he was wondering why it was great.

"That's right. You really know your stuff. How far away d'you think it is?"

"I can check on Google maps." Even before I tried to call out I felt the hand tighten further and I was pulled deeper into the lounge.

"That's right you can. Door to door even if you know the address there."

Carefully Robin spelled out the address as he typed it in, his tongue hanging out with the effort.

"Fit... teen... Bear's Nest Road... Tahoe.... City... *Mom!* What's our zip again?"

A pause. Faint sound of footsteps. Rae's voice, too far away to be clear.

Robin turned his head. "Our zip."

And then Rae's voice, clearly now. "What's it for honey? Why are you up?"

There was a pause then she replaced Robin at the screen. Her eyes darted around, taking it all in.

"Who the fuck are you?"

Ronnie's voice was light. "Just a friend of your boyfriend's. Nice kid. Bye there."

"Where is he?"

Ronnie squatted down. "Well that's a couple of questions really. Who exactly are we talking about?"

The briefest pause. But enough. "My boyfriend."

"And would this errant beau have a name, darling?"

The same pause. "Brandon, Brandon Kussgarten."

Reggie swung the laptop around to face Ronnie and I. "Would this be the fellah?" He swung it back into place.

"Yes."

"Interesting, interesting. And would you have any idea where Brandon keeps his money? You'd be saving him some major inconvenience if you did."

Another, longer, silence. I thought the screen might have frozen. And then, without warning, Rae stepped out of eyeline.

I heard faint beeps of a phone keyboard and then her voice down the speaker. Confident, official. "Hello police, I'd like to report a kidnapping."

Her phone screen glowed in the darkness. "It's in England actually."

"Stupid bitch." Ronnie turned back to Reggie and me. He was clenching and unclenching his fists. "Stupid *bitch*."

"113 Elleworth Road E1, room 6. Yes, it's a hotel."

Reggie tightened his grip. "You think she's serious?"

Ronnie nodded, "It sounded like an international number. We have their address though now, we can come back to this."

He looked back at the screen. "Cunt," he added, thoughtfully.

He came very close to me then, close enough for me to catch the twitch in his eyes and see the spots he'd missed shaving. He looked me in one eye and then the other.

"Now I'm not certain if you're Brandon or not, and to be honest I'm past fucking caring. But you're in his house, spending his money, with his girl and kid calling you up in the night."

He spread his arms wide to encompass Brandon's stuff. "If it looks like a duck and quacks like a duck…"

Reggie nodded, as if his brother had said something unutterably wise.

"So whoever the fuck you are, you *owe*. The forty-five K we agreed and, let's call it fifteen for our not inconsiderable troubles. Our card."

He threw a business card on the floor and took my chin in his hand. "Friday, sweetie, the whole kit and caboodle — no ifs or buts, or…" He raised an eyebrow.

"We'll kill you all over again," said Reg.

I couldn't get the taste of Ron's aftershave off my face. I pulled the laptop through to the bathroom to clean up as Rae babbled.

"I just called any number I was so sure that they were going to hear the recorded voice on the other end but it worked, it really worked. Shit I have to check on Robin," and with that she was gone.

I sat on the toilet and my heart raced.

The address. Rae and Robin's address. They had that now. And I had given it to them. Even Brandon hadn't managed to inflict so much peril on them in such a short time. And it had taken Rae to actually get rid of them.

I looked around the bathroom. Its opulence was absurd. What had I been doing all this time? I'd learnt nothing of real use from staying here. I'd not got back a penny of their money. Instead I'd been playing with toys and drinking and making believe that Rae and Robin were mine. Before my intervention all that Kussgartens had done to those two was to disappoint them. In ten days I'd managed to put them in mortal danger.

Umbrage's lights twinkled and the surfaces around it were encrusted with the dust of extinguished lines and crushed Adderall. *This* is what I'd been doing while they sat in limbo, five thousand miles away.

There was a calm in the flat after they'd gone, like the silence of a platform after the last train. So, I was a dead man — what was new? I looked back on my life in Trellick Tower as if through the wrong end of a telescope. Scurrying back and forth around that shell of a flat, doing errands out of habit, answering emails, making deep ruts in my life. Twenty years and there was hardly any of it I could remember clearly. But since Rae's call each day had been as rich and strange as a novel. Moments that I'd have with me forever. There were hours even that would stay unchanging within me until I died: that first time in Umbrage with Robin, Rae's laughter through laptop speakers, our pizza dinner together.

My head rang from being held upside down. That was me right there: suspended, in other people's hands. I felt an ache in my thighs like after a long day's walking, but it was the opposite. It was an ache to run, to move, to kick out. To use and not be used.

I sat silently until Rae came back. She stared from the screen with her lower lip clamped between thumb and forefinger. Then she let out a low moan.

"Adamadamadamadamadamadam. Shit, I'm so sorry. What the hell have I done?" She tugged at her lip. "I should never have asked you. Even pretending to be him brings down a ton of shit."

I felt calm, like the room itself. I wanted to tell her that she had done nothing wrong, that she and Robin were the best things that had ever happened to me, that everything was my fault, but the words were stillborn in my mouth. No more talking.

She said, as much to herself as to me, "You could just get on a flight. They might be able to find us here but if we moved, moved state even. They don't know anything about us, our real names even…"

My heart rang at her assumption that we could be together — at any other moment this would have been the biggest news I could possibly imagine. But I didn't want to run. I tried to piece together a way of making this right.

I thought of it as an engineering problem. Timelines and deadlines and forces that needed to be brought to bear. Where were the weak points and cracks that could be widened, where were the fears that could be preyed on? Baxter would be easiest because he now had the most to lose. Saul would need some finesse, and Kimi? She was a black box to me. But there was a combination that would unlock them all. That one goes here and that one goes there until, there it was: a path through the ruins.

My stutter was returning but Rae waited patiently as I talked. I explained Brandon's real plan, as I understood it, and where it left us. I told her she should take Robin away from the house for a while if she could. I told her everything would be all right. And all the while I was sick to the stomach with my weakness and procrastination. I told her my plan.

"He has to die again."

I started to sketch it out. "He has to die again. It's perfect. We'll scrape together his record and it'll come out as planned with the backstory that he worked on. The money from *Smile*, and Saul's lawsuit if it happens, come to me, which means they come to you. And I'm the grieving brother again, managing his estate for his grieving widow."

Her voice was small. "And where would you be, afterwards?"

"There of course, if you'll have me."

As soon as she was gone I started. I had to take Brandon's anger and sharpen it to a point. I had a line, then a second, and an Adderall. I went around the flat throwing open windows to let in the dawn and I shut down the line to Tahoe; no distractions today.

A shirt torn into strips and soaked in mineral water was enough to block the fire alarms. I covered the sprinklers too, though hopefully the alarms being out would mean they wouldn't be set off.

I couldn't bear to look at Umbrage. The weight of years I'd devoted to it tugged like a riptide in the room. I called Jay for the supplies: lighter fluid, blasting caps, and a drone. I'd settled on a volcano to destroy the city. I had enough cameras to capture the destruction: a wide static, two focussed on major buildings, a hand-held and a drone cam but I couldn't do it all on my own. Kaspar's discretion made him the obvious choice as cameraman, but with the fire hazard it might be a mistake. Jay was busy. George, the architecture student, would understand where and when to film but he might try to dissuade me from such full-scale destruction. The band would be worse than useless. I was resigned to an uncomfortable discussion with Kaspar when I had a thought.

An hour later the intercom buzzed.

"Mr Kussgarten, Sistine is here."

Discrete though he was, I could hear intrigue in Kaspar's voice. Even in Bran's world 9am would be an unusual time to be entertaining hookers.

"Lovely, send her up."

She got it straight away and she worked her way around the cameras, checking their output while I mixed together the baking soda, petroleum jelly and lighter fluid. I set half aside for the volcano and distributed the rest around Umbrage, concentrating on basements and attics. Then I embedded electric motors, strapping them to every supporting strut and seabed before wiring them to a single switch, while Sistine stuffed the bigger buildings with M80s and smeared petroleum gel across the fields and grasslands. If the contrast between this meeting and our last discomforted her at all she didn't show it. In fact she threw herself into the task with enthusiasm. It was her that sculpted the main crater, rising darkly from the lowlands, barren and smooth and alien against Umbrage's busy cityscape. I packed the centre: blasting cap, gel mixture and iron filings.

I checked the feeds from each camera and went over possible high-points and spectacles. Sistine had a real eye for it; when I told her so she laughed: "In my line of work you have to know where your best side is."

We sat back on the couch to look over the city. Umbrage was as busy as it ever got. The funiculars and wind turbines and dream-sails and chain bridges were all working.

We pressed the button together.

At first, nothing. Motors vibrated at different frequencies and for a second it looked as if all we were going to get was an Umbrage that shook in a variety of interesting ways. But then the frequencies began to combine and multiply. You saw it first in the waters: patterns of waves criss-crossed and overlapped, cycling through order and chaos.

The Darks of Mols was the first piece of land to collapse. The moorland rippled like liquid and then began to tear into thick stripes of light and dark. Simultaneously the row of pylons that crossed the Darks shook their feet free from the ground and toppled gratefully onto the dark earth. A line of sparks became a band of fire that burned brightest where chasms were forming in the underlay. I brought the drone closer to catch the liquid shadows of the fallen pylons dancing across the cliffs.

There was a gentle thump like someone moving furniture in another room and then a crack as the volcano's lid broke. A vibration set all the church bells in the city trembling as one, before the volcano erupted. Shards of clay, instantly baked hard, rained down on the inland sea. A shower of sparks, fizzing like fireworks, followed and caught on the breeze, setting small fires where they landed. And then all in a rush the burning gel gushed from the crater. Firstly as a glowing orange fountain that came close to the ceiling, then as a thick delta of fire careering down the volcano's slopes.

"Bran, over here." Sistine was focusing a camera on the Necropolis where the vivaria, glued hard into the hillside, were cracking as the mountain began to shake itself apart. Trees with thick globs of earth still attached to their roots tumbled down the incline and began to clog the River Ansti.

Then everything happened at once. The towers at Treblon collapsed as one with a satisfying shudder just as a wave of flame raced across the reed-fields which were so dry as to have not needed any accelerant. I flew the drone up and down, left and right, and everywhere was mayhem. The smoke detectors remained silent, and when the inland sea broke its banks it put out most of the major fires as well as any sprinkler system would have. From then on it was a war of attrition between the deluge of new rivers coursing their way to the sea, the vibrations of the remaining motors, and the firetraps Sistine had built. Whole districts convulsed like dying animals, settling into crumpled ruins. A layer of smoke haloed the city, making the drone's images all the more dramatic and everything over a storey high was levelled. I flew in silence over the wreckage and the drone's rotors drove the smoke through the blackened skeleton of the city. The thin whirr of the drone and the steady drip of water onto the parquet were the only sounds. It took nearly an hour and by the end Umbrage was a smouldering, acrid wasteland. Its smelt of smoke and petrol, and in places the frame of the city — its long-forgotten trestles and supports — showed through the blackened ground.

Kaspar had phoned once — *is everything OK, I smelled smoke* — but I promised I was just disposing of some paperwork, which won a chuckle.

Sistine sat in a armchair, her fingers and face smeared with soot, and drank champagne from the bottle.

"Jesus, that was *fun*. The most fun I've had here," she said with glee. She caught herself. "I mean Baxter is great too…"

I waved it away. That was someone else, another time.

"So," Sistine said, eyeing the line of smoke snaking towards the skylight, "You're off, I guess?"

I hadn't explained what we were doing — one of my favourite things about being Brandon these last days has been the fact that I don't ever need to explain myself.

"Why do you say that?"

She looked at the wreckage of Umbrage, listened to the creak of cooling metal.

"I don't know, this seems kind of final. Remember what you told me that first time?"

I waited.

"About burning down your old life? Never looking back?"

I nodded. When had Brandon told her that?

"Well this looks a lot like that." She wiped soot from her brow. "Fun, anyway. Is that all?"

"I think so. Let me get your money."

The safe was empty but I still had a couple of packets of Brandon's US cash. I called through. "Are dollars OK?"

She opened the calculator on her phone. "Sure. Three hours, call it a grand. That's what? Fifteen hundred bucks?"

I counted it out. She looked young, sitting with her legs tucked under her, and I remembered an idea I'd had. "Actually there is one thing you might do for me. A picture."

She raised an eyebrow.

"Not that kind of thing, honest. A passport picture." I gave her the rest of the dollars. "There's a machine down on the corner."

She counted out the money. There was another five hundred or so, and she gave me a quizzical look. She said, "I'm not sure but I *think* it's probably only a pound."

"Call it a tip. And I do need to style you a bit."

I combed out her fringe and patted down some stray curls. I had a memory, a physical memory of the feel of my mother's hands on my face, doing the same things with my unruly hair. I looked at her.

"Could you take your makeup off, all of it?"

"You're the boss."

I texted Jay while she was in the bathroom. "Hey, a while back you said something about a passport?"

The girl who came back into the room was another person entirely. She had retreated into herself, you wouldn't have given her a second look on the street. Flat hair, plain, neat features, a country girl. She looked better in a way too, more herself.

"Like this?" Even her voice was flatter.

"It's perfect."

Kaspar was hanging around outside the door as she left. I opened the door a little — the rooms must have smelt like a war zone — and he did his best to not look worried.

"This came by courier earlier but I thought you might be otherwise engaged."

He handed me an amateurish looking magazine, shrink-wrapped in plastic. I closed the door on him and tore it open. *The Journal of Found Sound and Field Recordings Vol. XIV*. I recognised the kind of thing — the model-making world was full of magazines like this, photocopied at work, aping scholarly journals but really just an outlet for obsessions that were outgrowing their owner's living room. I flicked through articles on "Underwater Recording and Deep-Sea Sounds" and "Nuclear Bunkers: Putting the 'Radio' back into Radioactivity" and a slip of paper fell from the pages. It was hand-written, the signature illegible. I held it up to the light to read it: "Thanks for the piece — it's on page 111. Hope you get some downloads!"

Tiny Lightning

From *The Journal of Found Sound and Field Recordings Vol XIV*
"Recording Single Snowflakes: A Beginner's Guide" by Brandon
Noyes.

Field recording: individual snowflakes, 5.45am, 3/4/03, Tahoe City,
CA. 12 mins and 34 secs. Equipment: CAD Equitek E100, Sony TC-
D5, Logic Audio

This recording was made on a frozen lake behind a house in which I
used to live, in Tahoe City, California. In summer the lake was fetid and
littered with dead leaves. In the autumn it froze from edge to edge, and
by November it was as hard as iron. It became a disc of white among
the firs, patterned only by bird tracks until the locals awoke. By March
it started to thaw. Most people took the long way around but still, on
some mornings when I woke early I'd risk the walk to go and get a
coffee from the diner on Tahoe's main street.

Each step brought a response from the ice: sub-aural groans or
splintery crackling, and you had to listen to these for clues to guide
your feet. Crossing might take twenty minutes, far longer than walking
the perimeter, but it felt auspicious to start the morning with Danny at
the diner saying, "not your day to die today then?" each time I arrived.
There was a particular sound I liked too: a shudder deep in the ice with
a hollow echo that you only heard on these spring mornings. I resolved

to capture a recording of it; my old Sony TC-D5 was kept charged and ready, hanging in the garage.

One Monday in April I returned from San Francisco after a sleepless forty-eight hours, with competing chemicals fighting for control of my nervous system. Coke vs temazepam. Coffee vs cognac. Ecstasy vs agony. Amid the comedown my house looked like a prison. The curtained windows were a reprimand, a foretaste of a week of recriminations. I needed a coffee.

I picked up the recording gear and made for the ice. I walked through tussocks of snow-covered grass, under branches pregnant with icicles, down to the lakeside.

There's something hallucinatory about Tahoe; it's alive with the extremes of perception that you sometimes get on acid. Clear air lets you see for miles and the snow isolates sounds into single sources. The clean edges of things shine.

I stepped onto the ice as delicately as a fawn, which wasn't the easiest feat after the weekend I'd had. In April the ice melts during the day and then freezes over again at night, so the surface was freckled like a bird's egg, grey on white. It was pock-marked and riven with slushy cracks. I took a step and felt the ice stretch and wake. I slid to the left where the footing was surer. Each step was a minefield. When my weight sent hairline cracks sprinting deep into the surrounding ice, I had to retrace my path to try another tack.

Halfway across I looked over at the diner. The lights were still out. My chest and back were soaked with sweat even in the sub-zero air so I lay face down for a second, the ice on my face as calming in my state as a bathroom floor, and lit a ciggie. In the silence the fingersnap of the lighter gave way to the crackle of burning tobacco. I sucked in air and it rushed like a waterfall as the drugs did their victory laps around my body. Cold radiated up into the points where I touched the ice: my shoulders, knees and skull.

When I rolled onto my back the ice creaked beneath me. It was the sound of a dying thing. I set up the recorder and scraped ice from the headphones. I turned down the sensitivity and listened. It was beautiful. No wind; just silence and then, like whale song, a howl as underwater plates shifted against each other. If I moved my weight around I could make the ice move.

There, star-shaped on the ice, I drummed my heels against the cold and it felt like it was *my* body that creaked and groaned. Every movement was transmitted outwards like I was a fly in a web. I brought a heel down hard and there was a crack like a gunshot and then silvery ripples. A fissure opened up from where my foot now rested, metres long. Enough. In my state the water would be cold enough to kill me in seconds.

I lay still and let the lake settle. A noise whispered in the headphones: patter of static like distant rain. Snow had begun to fall. It fell in straight lines, individual snowflakes as clear as diamonds. A flake landed on the tip of my cigarette and hissed to its death. I thought about the singular shapes of snowflakes and the way their path through the air was written in their form; each change in temperature and every buffet of wind altered the way their crystalline arms grew — an entire history written in icy limbs.

I turned the microphone sensitivity higher. A far-off tapping and the noise of my heart beating. I needed more isolation. I slid the mike as far from my body as possible and lay still, willing my breath shallower.

A sound like a match striking. Burst and sizzle. Another. Sounds bloomed like snowdrops. *Tsscck. Tsssssscck. T-Tsscck.* I closed my eyes and let the cold freeze the sickness out of me. There was a crackle like bubble wrap. Later I found out that this was the noise of the snowflakes' electrical charge sparking into the ground, a million miniature lightning strikes, each one as unique as the snowflakes themselves. Once in a while, despite the cover, you'd hear the sound of a flake hitting the mike itself. A soft explosion that wiped out all the other sounds, clearing a path for the silence to rush back in.

The snow fell harder. On my eyelids, on my stubble. The sounds were tiny and vast like a supernova seen from earth. I tasted snowmelt on my lips and, from the corner of my eye, saw a light in the diner go on. I pressed STOP and looked to the shore. The snow had laid evenly over the ice and I was the only black mark on a field of white. Once I was upright I found it was easier to close my eyes. I slid each foot forward until my weight began to shift, letting the ice flex but not break. If I had even an inkling of that vertiginous fall, like missing a stair in the dark, then I eased back and breathed. Wait, slide left, slide right, try again. Until, lost in it, snow-blind and shivering, I touched grass.

I threw myself down and looked back over the ice. Behind me the snow had already swallowed my tracks.

The recording was made by taking the original sound source and slowly increasing the rate of quantisement and pitch correction until every snowfall had been assigned a note and a place on a rhythm grid. There was a section between 8:45 and 9:30 that I particularly liked — after that it's simply looped and the tempo increased until it made a rudimentary drum track. Feel free to use either in your own recordings — the whole piece is under a Creative Commons license.

Chapter Nine

I called Robin before I set off to see Baxter. He'd been asleep — he pawed at puffy eyes and yawned so wide I could see every one of his perfect teeth — but I knew that once I became Brandon I'd lose my connection with him. Ideally he'd have had more time with the clues from The Folly; still, if he had my DNA then he might have unravelled them. He spread his notebooks on his bed, full of diagrams, crossings-out and long lines of text. His pyjamas were too small and his thin wrists shone white on the screen.

"I think it's like a map." He pushed a scribbled piece of paper against the camera.

"This, here." He pointed at a complex symbol. "I think this is the whole of Umbrage. The circle is the lake, and this lightning shape is the ravine, and the squares at the back are the Darks."

He took the paper down and looked at me beseechingly.

I kept my face impassive. "Interesting. Go on."

"Then there's this symbol, like an eight on its side. I think it's a bee-dance thing."

How had I known that he'd recognise that? Bees and beehives were a childhood obsession of mine. I knew the bear-traps he'd willingly tumble into.

"What's a bee dance?"

"Like when a bee finds honey? Or is it pollen? It does this special dance that shows the others where to go." He opened his mouth wide again, less a yawn, more of an unclicking of the jaw.

"OK, so how does it work?"

"They have to go in a line from the waist of the eight." He looked through his notebook until he found the page he wanted and then traced a line that ran across the page.

"Right around the walls, through the columns, to here. But on the way there are all these animal pictures." He showed me jittery line drawings of bees and bears and birds. "And I don't know what they mean."

I let the silence win out for a second and gave him a sympathetic smile to let him know it was all there to be uncovered. With a start he said, "They could be the years."

I raised an eyebrow.

"They could be the names of the years. How would I find out?"

I pulled out the Book. "Does it go Badger, Magpie, Ant, Badger?"

He traced the patterns. "Yes, so it's years." He stood up and sat down immediately.

"So you have a direction, and you have time, how many years?"

He counted out loud. "Twenty-six, twenty-seven. Twenty-seven. And then you come to this symbol."

Again he pressed the paper against the screen. There was another, smaller symbol like a wheel atop a lozenge.

"And what's that?"

"I dunno. There was stuff like that in the Valley House but you never told me what it meant."

He placed it in front of him and stared down at it. "It has some of the same writing as the first one. Can you read it?"

I hadn't explained any of the Umbragian picture words. Everything had moved so fast.

"Well those two signs under the first symbol read 'Umb' and 'Rage', so I guess you were right about it being a sign for Umbrage. Those symbols are there in the second one too, but with one more added."

"Something Umbrage? Umbrage something?"

"It's the symbol for a child, does that help?"

He muttered. "Umbrage child. Son of Umbrage. Young Umbrage." His eyes never left my image on the screen, waiting for a flicker of recognition.

He stopped dead.

"New Umbrage?"

"Could be. They were going hundreds of miles on a journey that would take twenty-seven years to start another city. Could be New Umbrage."

"Where?" Robin's eyes were sparkling with anticipation.

"Who knows? Hopefully we'll find out some day. Hopefully *you'll* find out some day, I have my hands full with the original Umbrage." The machinery started to move inside him. "I do know that the angle of the bee dance is thirty-nine degrees."

I'd leave him to work out later that was the bearing from London to Tahoe. I stepped closer to the camera so he could see my eyes.

"I'm going to be busy for a little bit Robin, OK?"

He nodded warily.

"But I promise I'll be back. I promise." I tried to beam the fierceness with which I felt this across to him. "I have to go do something for your mum now, OK? And you're going to look after her until I get back."

His nod was slight but definite.

I texted Rae with the link to Brandon's field recording and wrote, "I'm going off-radar for a while but I'm always thinking of you two."

I dressed for trouble. A powder blue Gucci suit with thin gold chains at the cuffs, and an ivory shirt so soft that it felt more liquid than material. The tie was a meaty purple ("Oxblood" Kaspar called it, approvingly), as were the shoes. Not Lobbs this time but some German make that gleamed like a limousine's bonnet.

As I dressed I felt a kind of strength. Clothes like these said something about the wearer. Something about care and arrogance and power and a sheer head-spinning disregard for thrift — they put a barrier up around you that felt like armour.

And beneath the armour there was a black wire twisting up through me, pulling everything taut about it. A black wire the shape of a burned-out match, snaking through vertebrae and stiffening my neck. I had a line, another, and let everything tighten inside me.

As I walked down Brick Lane towards the tube I could feel the pull of eyes on me. Being Brandon brought a weight of attention that I couldn't get used to. You were always being measured up as something. On a whim I stopped in at a barbers on one of the sidestreets. It was reassuringly old-fashioned and smelt of leather and lemon. The mirrors were fogged with steam and it was soundtracked by the ticking of heavy scissors. Only the barber himself, with his sleeve of sea-monster tattoos and hair in a messy bun, seemed to belong to the twenty-first century. I flicked through my phone to find the picture I wanted — Brandon's first LA headshot, where his quiff was a complicated, sculptural thing, like a just-breaking wave.

The barber examined the phone dubiously. "But this is you, right?"

"Yeah, of course." I crossed my legs and did the Brandon dust brush-off.

"Huh. Mostly people bring in pictures of celebs, y'know. Actors or what-have-you." He looked at the picture again. "This is a first."

"What can I say, I have a type," I said. "And I don't have all day."

Afterwards, back on Brick Lane, where the press of Londoners was strongest, a guy on his phone bumped shoulders with me. Not hard. It was just enough to send me spinning on my axis; I didn't even fall. But in a second I was face to face with him, saying *fuck you* calmly but with a weight of intent that came out of nowhere.

His response was instantaneous. He brought his face as close to mine as it could be without actually touching. Pedestrians parted neatly for us and looked away.

He was shorter than me, but not by much, and he looked up at me with genuine fury. *Fuck. You. Too.* Each word was accompanied with a warm spray of spittle, and then we were toe to toe. Something in me was screaming *run* but the wire tightened, pitching me forward a little.

My forehead touched his, his hairline tickling at my brow and his breath warming the space between us. I felt a power — something like ignorance, something like fatalism — and I said, very clearly, *walk away little man*, in a voice that wasn't mine but was familiar, like hearing yourself on tape. And for another moment our eyes locked, and I could see a web of pink veins through the white, and a shutter-slide of pupils widening and then he was gone, just another bob of curly hair among the crowd.

I darted into a coffee shop, my hands shaking. If it had come to blows everything would have crumbled, I knew that. I would have been in a ball on the floor, hands cradling my skull as I waited for it to be over. Still. It hadn't come to that and now I felt like a knife, a point of light. Back on the streets people flowed around me like water. I was a racehorse in blinkers, a hawk mid-dive. I took the tube to Victoria, the train to Brighton.

On the train I played the tracks over and over until their rhythms were my rhythms. I must have been talking to myself too, because I found I was alone in a bank of four seats on an otherwise full train. I drank gins from the trolley that came round, three at a time, and when the attendant gave me a mournful look I repeated something I'd heard Brandon say years ago: "Don't think of it as neat gin, think of it as a very, very dry martini." I gave him a wink and a tenner tip.

Hove felt better than London, purer. There were horizons and seagulls and empty streets. I liked the push of sea air against my skin and I snapped my teeth like a dog against the sea spray. The route to Baxter's place took me down roads that were solid and pale and quiet, places of family dinners and back-garden barbecues, but once I turned off the main streets it turned drabber.

Tucked behind the Regency terraces was an unlovely industrial estate, ringed by sixties tower blocks that must have looked bright and modernist for about a week before the salt in the air stripped the paint right off the concrete and the seagull-shit turned the roofing to Pollocks. Baxter's place was in a row of garages, all padlocked bar the last, where a tiny door like something out of Alice in Wonderland had been cut into the corrugated steel. Above it, someone had sprayed *Broken Records*. I rang the bell and heard a dog barking over distant music, and footsteps.

Baxter peered out like a turtle from its shell. "Jesus Bran, you're on time? I'm not even dressed, I figured you'd be another couple of hours."

He ushered me inside and down a corridor, talking all the way.

"Remember the tour we did when we had that tour manager who used to make call-time an hour earlier than we needed to leave, just because he knew how late you'd be?"

He didn't seem to need me to answer. We turned a corner into a surprisingly comfortable looking room, three times longer than it was wide, dotted with jukeboxes.

"So you started being two hours late to compensate, so *he* starts making call-time even earlier and by the end of the tour if we needed to leave at midday, lobby call would be 9am and you'd get up at two."

I smiled. I think that was what he was after. The coke was wearing off and I didn't have the The Magpie's protective shell to bolster my Brandon impersonation.

"I'm going to get changed, there's coffee and tea in the kitchen there" — he pointed out a small side door — "and all the jukeboxes are working; have a blast."

I supposed I should play something. The nearest jukebox was finned and turquoise with a grill like the front of a car. I flicked through the tracks and picked one at random, figuring that any song that I recognised would be wrong. Something pounding and shrill burst from the speakers.

Baxter poked his head around the doorway, his hair damp. "Is that 'Nothing but a Heartache'? Great choice dude."

I had time to play two more tracks before Baxter re-emerged in a check shirt and jeans. I remembered Brandon's description of him and looked for where he might have mis-dressed himself and sure enough, there it was. One leg of his jeans was tucked into the back of a chequered sock.

"Here, come and see this." He led me through the maze of jukeboxes into another of the converted garages. The ceiling had been lowered and there were cubby-holes built into all four walls and each one contained a pair of trainers, spotlit from above like some priceless vase. It had the air of a high-end jewellery shop.

"So?" He waited, head on one side.

I couldn't imagine what Brandon's take on this might be. Impressed at the attempt at street culture? Horrified at the sheer neediness of it?

"I didn't know you were so sporty Bax," I said, finally.

He laughed. "Yeah, I know. Never really worn a pair in anger."

He was caressing a particularly garish pair, smoothing down the day-glo laces. "So what brings you here Bran?"

"Money," I said.

He raised his eyebrows and doubled his chins. "Money? Now? I told you we have to be really careful how we go about this Bran. We have a couple of people to pay first. And I'm thinking we leave it a month just in case Isaacs has it properly checked out. Insurance, right?"

I was glad that I'd snuck a quick line in while he was changing. I tried out a 180-degree turn in my mind — *don't fear conflict, stoke it.* "No Baxter, I need it now. I have outgoings."

He looked carefully at me and stopped towelling his hair. "Outgoings? Go stay somewhere cheaper for a bit, you could survive without the butler or whatever that guy is." He sounded direct but looked nervous.

"Other outgoings, Baxter. I have responsibilities."

He laughed at that too. "No Bran, you've got habits, those are very different things."

I felt a heat rise in me. "Don't tell me what I have or don't have. You didn't say anything about all this shit when we agreed to this."

His voice turned whiny in an instant. "I did. We sat in that fucking caff and I told you that it would take a while but it'd be worth it. This isn't some drug deal Brandon, this is serious, it will happen when it happens."

"It happens now. Right now."

For the first time he seemed to take in the scar on my forehead and the scratches on my neck. I probably still smelled of smoke too. He draped the towel around his neck like a boxer. "What have you done?"

"None of your business. But I made a record for you, I'm making money for you, and any minute now I'm even going to make you famous again, and what do I get? Nothing."

I was beginning to shake. *Reign it in Bran*, I told myself.

"OK, OK, I can get you an advance." He took out his wallet. "How much?"

The magic number in my head. Fifty for Rae's mortgage, thirty-five for Ron and Reg. Maybe a thousand to get me to Tahoe. "£86,000."

He put the wallet down carefully. "Bran," he said, like he was talking to a kid, "I just don't have that. I could do you five K."

I concentrated on my hands not shaking. "£86,000. Now. Or I end this."

He looked like he might cry. "Is that it? Is that what this whole thing was about?"

He sat down and his shoulders slumped. "I've been talking with Kimi most nights, you know? On the way back from whatever you guys have been cooking up. *He's changed Bax*, she keeps saying, *he's like a different person. He listens, sometimes he even cares.* But you haven't changed have you? You just needed to be someone else for a couple of weeks until you had your claws into some serious money. If that's all we were to you Bran, why didn't you just say?"

He started counting out twenties from his wallet.

"You could have just said, *I could do with the cash. I've got myself in a spot of bother*. It's what we expected. But you had to make it personal again."

He looked at the cash. "£1040. Take it and fuck off. You can have the rest when we're in the clear, every last penny."

I took the passport from my pocket. I had a sudden physical desire to hold a gun, a cold, heavy gun, just for the heft of it.

"Bax, I didn't want to do this."

That was a lie. I could feel it now, the fury. I *wanted* him to say no to the deal, to throw it in my face. He had to lose for me to win. He picked up the passport, turned it over and opened it.

"Sarah Chappell. Oh, is it Sistine? God, funny picture." He flicked though the virgin pages. "She's hardly been anywhere."

I waited a beat. Baxter was a born straight man. "Not had much chance has she? Seeing as she's fifteen."

He gave me a stuffed frog look.

"Go on, check."

He reopened the passport at the back page and read it. "Bran." His voice was low. "Shit, Bran. Did you know?"

"Of course not. I don't mind paying for it, but just with money. Not with my liberty."

"But she never said."

"Oh fine, then you're in the clear. *She never said, officer.*"

"But she seemed so…" I could see the clockwork working in his head. He blushed at some memory.

"She wouldn't say anything, would she?"

I took the passport and waggled it under his nose. "*She* probably wouldn't…" I pulled out the iPad. It had taken three different connections to download the footage of him with Sistine, taking care to cut out the less incriminating stuff. The discussion of safe words and the kiss goodbye were on the digital cutting-room floor. This was just the good stuff. I couldn't say, what with modern morals, whether it looked like consensual, but rough sex, or whether it read as straightforward abuse, but coupled with the passport it looked bad. I let the video start. I was sure we wouldn't need to get to the end.

Baxter watched as if it were someone else. He made no attempt to stop it.

"You *know* what this is. It's been edited so you must have seen the whole thing. You *know*." His expression was more wonder than anger. "This is not what it looks like."

I put my arm around his damp shoulders and felt him recoil. I let Brandon run my mouth for a while.

"Bax, Bax, Bax, everything is what it looks like. I understand, believe you me. No one is just one person. Or at least no one interesting is. I get it. Sometimes you're Baxter Moores, doting father, loving husband, provider. Sometimes you're Bax the Beats guy, friend of the stars. And sometimes you're this guy."

I pressed pause. "Big bad Baxter. Huffing and puffing and blowing down. I get it. We're all a million different people, some good and some bad and you haven't lived unless you've tried some stuff. You know that I've been there Bax. But this guy…"

I gestured to the screen. "This guy, he has to pay. Not the good guy or the family man or even the band member. Those guys get a free pass and kind words at their funeral. But this guy… he pays. Because although I understand the subtleties at play here, and I think even Sistine knows the roles we all have to play, but the general public, they're not going to be so understanding."

"Brandon." He stopped. "This crosses a line."

I smiled.

"Seriously Bran. Most of what you do falls into the category of being an arsehole. But this is evil. You understand the difference, right? What you have here, on tape, is a mistake. A bad mistake, sure, but it's not malicious. What you're doing is malicious. I was always going to get you your money. But if you take it now, like this? You're gone. Gone to the other side."

I didn't bother to reply. I was on the other side. Rae's side. Our side. Good versus evil, left versus right? I didn't have time for them.

He shielded the combination to the safe with his back, as if it mattered now. As if I couldn't take anything I wanted.

"I mean it Bran. This is where you leave us. Y'know, the world." He pulled rubber bands off a piles of notes.

"This would have been yours next month anyway. The only reason I have the cash is so that we could get paid at the same time for *Smile*."

He shook his head at the mention of the word and counted out the notes. His face was wet with tears but his voice was steadier than it had been since I arrived.

"Once you're there you can't come back. You think you're a bad guy but you're not, not yet."

He placed each note carefully, like it was worth something.

I rewound the video back to the start again and found my favourite bit. I turned the volume higher; the microphones on those little cameras were shit. "And you? You came back from this Bax?"

I watched his face go blank.

It took me nearly thirty minutes to find the car that matched the keys I'd swiped from his side table. I walked a spiral around the streets near his studio, ever widening, pressing the UNLOCK button every few steps. His car turned out to be a muscular American thing in red and yellow, easily the most conspicuous vehicle on the street.

For a split second after I started the car I genuinely thought a bomb had gone off. There was a jolt and a sound like a jet engine. It took me all of five seconds, my head jammed protectively between my legs, to realise it was the stereo. The entire rear of the car had been ripped out and replaced with a set of giant speakers which were vibrating wildly to whatever Baxter had played last.

I flapped at every button on the dashboard until it quietened. It took a while: there was more hardware than air traffic control, and I had to work my way around them one by one, getting a grip on their functions. At least half were for the stereo. Another set dealt with the hydraulics. For some reason each corner of the car could be lifted and dropped at will and after some fiddling it took me another five minutes to get it back to level.

After all this, actually driving the thing was a relief. It had been a decade since I last drove and I crunched the gears four or five times before I got the hang of it. I'd planned to head straight to Saul's but if Baxter reported this car missing then it would be spotted in seconds. I phoned Jay.

"Hey, are you interested in buying a car?" I put the phone on video chat so he could see the inside. "I'll swap this one for anything, something discrete."

"Show me the stereo again," he asked, so I panned around, showing him brand names and electronics.

He cut right to the chase. "Very nice. Is it yours?"

"Not entirely." I thought about it. "Actually, not in any way."

He shook his head. "No can do fam, which is a shame because that is quite a whip."

But ten miles down the M23 I got a WhatsApp message from a number I didn't know. I clicked it open.

"21 Marbury Road, N22. VW Camper alright?"

Marbury Street turned out to be a multi-storey car park in a quiet Wood Green street. I parked on the top floor so I could look out over the entrance below.

My mobile pinged twice in quick succession: Jay — *there in 15, top floor*. And an email from Rae.

"You seem to have lit a fire under Robin. He's holed up in his room with 12 sheets of modelling tin and a soldering iron. Are you sure it's safe for him to have? He swears you told him how to do it. Anyway, the field recordings magazine has a website and on it Bran's track is a YouTube clip, not audio. And guess what's underneath? Miss u nutgarden R x"

I lay on my back on the bonnet, letting the warm metal soothe my aching back, and clicked the link she'd attached.

Are We Going to be Alright?

The YouTube clip is four minutes' footage of snow falling while the track that we'd already heard played over the top. Underneath are a series of comments, all under the username Kissing Garden: YouTube's text limit meant he'd had to reply to himself, over and over, to fit in everything he'd written.

Kissing Garden — 15 days ago

It took at least a minute between my ringing the doorbell — turquoise Bakelite with a spritely *La Cucaracha* — and Mr Hyde answering the door. The flat behind him was dark and he was a spindly silhouette against the gloom. Back when Remote/Control toured with them he towered over me, but now, even with the rickety coxcomb of an eight-inch quiff, he was perhaps an inch shorter than me. He leaned heavily on a stick.

"Can I help you, son?"

That voice. Southern honey. On record he was as sonorous as a preacher, with the same promise of soon-to-come damnation, but in person he sounded homely. He had the unruffled drawl that pilots adopt to explain that an engine's gone down.

I thrust out a hand. "I'm Brandon, Brandon Kussgarten. My band toured with you back in the Nineties. Remote/Control?"

That ruined landscape of a face loomed out of the dark, examined my hand, and then me. His quiff toppled forwards.

"Your little record-collecting pal not with you, son?" He said "record-collecting" the way someone else might say paedophile.

"He is not, sir." The "sir" just slipped out.

He looked left and right along the walkway of the tower block.

"Well, you'd better bring your skinny white ass on inside then."

Outside might be pure Seventies tower block — the kind of hastily knocked up job-for-the-boys that sits mouldering in every big city — but inside the flat it was pure 1950s Americana. Red velvet curtains, tassled like a stripper, were drawn tight, and dim lamps threw cones of light in every corner. There were thick rugs in golds and scarlets and a drinks cabinet with an etched front holding those glasses meant for cocktails that don't exist anymore: highballs, Rob Roys, egg flips.

As my eyes adjusted I took in more. The fireplace was too big for the room and clad in faux stone — it looked like the kind of thing you'd see Dean Martin leaning against with a martini. Over Hyde's shoulder I could see the gleam of the kitchenette. The kettle was avocado, the mixer the colour of salmon mousse. The fridge was a turquoise both light and dull and the cabinets were edged in a kind of faded tartan. It didn't feel kitsch though, I'm not sure why. Partly it was just great fucking taste. There was a painting in an alcove that looked like an original de Kooning and the chairs were definitely Herman Miller. But also it was the sheer rigour of it. There was simply not a thing in the flat that dated from the past fifty years. Nothing to make the hostess trolleys and zebra-skin bar stools look out of time.

Kissing Garden — 15 days ago

"Boy from a band's here," Hyde declared, seemingly into the dark of the room. "Friend of the other one. The collectin' lad."

A portion of the couch, which appeared nothing more than a lumpy shape under a mountain of throws and blankets, peeled itself away and squealed, "Is that Brandon? Oh my sweet lord."

Jackie wasn't quite as desiccated as Hyde. One of the advantages of wearing makeup as thick as house paint since you were fourteen is that the mask remains the same whatever the damage underneath, but those miraculous legs were now just a rumour of flesh, sharp angles in a pair of leopard-skin pyjama bottoms. Her arms too were mottled and pitted like blue cheese. I remembered her on stage in Camden once, stabbing at effects pedals with ten-inch heels, her huge Gretsch White Falcon making her look elfin as she howled up into the mike. Now she looked like a breath of wind would blow her right back to bed.

Kissing Garden — 15 days ago

Jackie "Jackylline" O, is like me, a returnee. Born just down the road from here, in Horsham of all places, she made her own transatlantic escape back in 1972. According to her bio she spent her time "stripping and fruit-picking" in the Bay Area, before Hyde (real name Maurice Muscovitch) came across her modelling in a nude life-drawing class, and, without even asking her name, split up his band, the Swamp Gators, and dragged her on stage the very next night without so much as a rehearsal. As Jackyl & Hyde they made raw, ramshackle rockabilly records for an audience that would have needed to quadruple to even be considered "cult". Until, swept up in the first breathless wave of LA punk, they became something like mascots for the Black Flags and GoGos and Xs, a perennial support act howling trebly swamp blues into a tsunami of punk spittle from Orange County to Orgreave.

They had the last laugh though. With a bloody-minded resolution to never change, to never improve even, they'd outlived the headliners who were now blown to irrelevance, addiction or the morgue. They clambered their way up from outsiders to elder statesmen to national treasures by simply never stopping. We'd supported them in 1992 on a jaunt around mid-size British venues, a pairing so arbitrary that it spoke volumes for their utter disinterest in the current music scene.

Despite the mismatch, or possibly because of it, we'd had fun. Every moment of a Jackyl & Hyde set was unchanging. On every date at the midway point of the sixth song (same song, same set, every night)

Hyde dropped to his skinny knees, mic cord around his neck, and spluttered the same bible verses and dime-store pornography at an uncaring Jackie. Every night there were two encores, every night Jackie was bundled off stage at the end of the second by roadies dressed as psychiatric nurses. Even Hyde's Presleyesque *thankyuhvermuch*s were spaced out evenly over the night. This level of routine left them plenty of time to hang out. Their tour bus (a metallic Airstream of course) doubled as kind of portable Southern plantation house. There was a samovar of ice tea laced with bourbon. Bathtub speed. Twinkies and Sno-Balls.

I spent a lot of time with Jackie. She was doubly, trebly lost, but I envied her total reinvention. She'd destroyed any trace of the Home Counties girl she'd once been. If anything her accent was heavier than his, and nothing of her, from her hair to her nails to her voice to her name was original. She wore corsets that literally rearranged her organs and a kabuki mask of pancake makeup. It was glorious to watch the pair of them out in public. Him emaciated in black leather, frazzled like a burnt match, arm in arm with this bulimic Betty Page. There would have been fewer looks if you'd freed a couple of polar bears.

She hauled herself to her feet. Still skinny, still beehived, still painted like a doll; she tiptoed across the room to hug me. Her arms felt insubstantial, hollow.

"Well, let's have a look at you."

I forced myself to hold her gaze. Her eyes were bloodshot against the white paint of her makeup, and the mask was crazy paving around her eyes and mouth. But there was shrewdness there. Careful, Bran, careful.

"Well ain't you just a picture. Come into the light."

She squeezed my hand with brittle fingers and led me into the kitchen, but Hyde didn't follow. He folded himself back into the couch. The TV was bulky and small-screened and was showing a black-and-white film.

"So." She filled a kettle and lit the gas. Even the matches were vintage, I noticed, some American brand with a picture of a tiger on the cover. She shuffled slowly between kettle and tap and, from behind you could see the old woman she'd become.

"What brings you to see us honey?"

Again I sensed steel under the sugar. My intention had been to chat about old times and then drop the idea of borrowing the electro-Theremin, Colombo-style, as I left. But Jackie's gaze was unwavering.

"Brian Wilson's Theremin."

She blew on her tea. Her mug advertised the 1933 Chicago World's Fair, mine The Brooklyn Dodgers.

"Of course honey, whatever you need. Plenty of Theremins around though, and plenty more up-to-date than ours."

"I want that old-time feel though."

She knew there was more. "That's nice. We certainly got that going on."

"And if anyone were to ask about it I'd really appreciate you not mentioning that I was ever here."

"There it is." She held my gaze. "Your record-collecting friend wrapped up in this?"

Calculations running through my mind. Trust your instincts.

"He is, yeah, but you won't have to have any contact with him."

"Good, he riles Hyde up all kinds of ways. OK, OK. How much?"

Back-of-a-fag-packet calculations in my mind. "A thousand. That's not what I think it's worth, it's what I have."

"Then that'll have to do. Come on, let's visit."

Kissing Garden — 15 days ago

She took my hand again, and I realised it might be more about support than flirting. She positioned me on the couch between her and Hyde. The TV programme switched to a news report. A snowy black-and-white screen with a bullfrog of a newsreader in suit and tie. The sound was low but clear enough in the still of the room.

"Secretary of State Dean Acheson announced an agreement with the governments of France and the state of Vietnam today to provide ten million dollars of military assistance…"

I raised an eyebrow at Jackie, who winked back at me. I sipped my coffee as the news stories rolled by. Dongshan Island captured by the red Chinese. UFO pictures cause a storm in *Time* magazine. Nino Farina wins the Silverstone GP. I looked over my shoulder at the tear-off calendar on the kitchen door that I'd written off as just another wilful anachronism. It read 13 May 1950.

The news came to an end. Jackie thumbed through a worn *TV Guide*, George Burns twinkling behind an unlit cigar on the cover. I could see programmes circled in red ink.

"Jus' the Texaco Star Theatre on now hun, shall we have a little drink?"

Hyde didn't answer. He just bent his bony body upright and switched the TV off. He gestured to the radiogram in the corner.

"Put a record on would you son? Cocktail music."

The bottom of the radiogram held a rainbow of LPs in their sleeves. I barely recognised one in ten of them, though I mentally catalogued them for annoying Bax later. In the end I chose one because of the cover: a polo-necked, prodigiously moustachioed Italian staring balefully at a framed photograph of a peasant girl.

A clock chimed and two wooden figures pushed aside a flimsy door in its face. No taller than thumbs, they were still, recognisably Jackie and Hyde. Hyde in shiny black with a quiff as sharp as a stiletto, Jackie in red with cartoonish thigh-boots.

"Fan made it," said Hyde, defiantly. "Anyway, that's cocktail time."

Jackie was ahead of him. She flipped open the drinks cabinet and started pulling out bottles, singing to herself. She poured out thick glugs of Cees cough syrup from what looked like an original 1950s bottle, crusted almost black around the neck and covered in waxy purple drips. She added a cupful of Lift lemonade — I could see the slogan on the can, "it's *f-f-f-f-f-frozen*" — and handfuls of ice cubes.

There was a bowl filled with hundreds of Jolly Ranchers on the mirrored cabinet. "Which flavour, darling?"

Hyde didn't take his eyes from the shaker. "Let our guest choose, I guess," and Jackie turned to me.

I couldn't imagine it would make any difference, what with the other ingredients, so I chose at random. "Red?"

"Red it is." She used the ice tongs to extract eight or nine red sweets and dropped them in the shaker.

"Maybe you could do the honours?" she asked me.

The mixture was glutinous and the shaker made sucking noises as I worked it. Hyde watched the shaker as intently as a cat at a window. He started to talk.

"Many folks think of sizzurp as a recent thing, y'know, something that the rappers drink." He licked his lips. "But it has a rich history down there in Houston. They used to call it *lean*, because you'd y'know…"

He flopped to one side, his quiff preceding him.

I slowed down my shaking but I could hear that the sweets still hadn't fully dissolved.

"Horn players mainly, at first. The promethazine in the cough syrup meant you could blow all night, the Codeine gets you lost in the music."

"And the Jolly Ranchers?" I asked.

He licked his lips again. "Show me the man who doesn't like Jolly Ranchers."

Jackie took the shaker from me, reverently, and poured the resulting goo into martini glasses. It actually wasn't bad on first taste. Sweet as only an American drink could be but with a herby warmth that tasted like days off school. It left a thick residue all around your mouth though.

Hyde polished his off noisily and poured another while Jackie and I sipped politely. His mouth continued moving even when he wasn't drinking. He looked around the room as if it was all new to him and then settled his gaze onto me.

"I have a question for you son. Are you the director of your own life?"

His hand went behind his ear and under the thicket of his hair I saw the liverish colour of a hearing aid. He needed a fresh dye-job — there was a line of pure white along his hairline.

"Or are you a bit-part player?"

I thought the question was rhetorical, preacher style, but he watched me for an answer. His eyes were milky pools amid the crepe-paper of his skin.

"I try, sir, to be the director but the world has a way of wearing you down."

He nodded, seriously.

"You have to be constantly on guard. You must always be the director. We decided…" he flung the arm holding his stick wide, "to live in a different era ten years back. Everyone said it couldn't be done, everyone's scared of it. But it can."

His stare dared me to disagree.

"The TV?" I asked.

"Original tapes, digitised and run from an external server. Exactly sixty years to the day. Papers too."

He gestured to a thick sheaf of *Gainesville Daily Register*s in the magazine rack. The crosswords were filled in in ink.

"Food?"

"Mainly fresh but you'd be amazed what you can find online. Tinned stuff lasts forever anyway." His eyes shone. "Twinkie?"

I felt the weight of it then. The outside pressure, like being in a diving bell. "Why?"

"It's where we belong. I've always known that. I was born out of time." His mouth drooped, pulling down deep trenches that transected his face. "Why do people travel anywhere? Ever arrived in a city and thought 'this is where I belong'?"

I had. Manhattan. Melbourne. Manchester. Something in the light or the accent.

"No one mocks those people, do they? No one says 'son, you don't belong here'. Not anymore. Instead it's as if they've found something, like they've fallen in love. Well, we fell in love with a time, not a place. And then we bent reality to our will."

I recognised the cadences of a long-rehearsed argument. I could have countered that to live this way was a retreat, that it diminished life, but what was the point? There was no more chance of shifting these two from their circuit than the figures in the cuckoo clock.

"I think it's an incredible thing you're doing."

Jackie caught the doubt in my voice, I was sure. How far did she go along with this, I wondered. Coupledom is always a dance of compromises but how do you compromise with this kind of absolutism? Still, Jackie had turned her life into a cartoon long before this.

Kissing Garden — 15 days ago

"So, why should we let you use our instrument then, son?"

I didn't realise that he had heard Jackie and I talking. His quiff toppled forward and he brushed it aside.

I risked a look at Jackie. The faintest of head-shakes. *Blink once if you're being held against your will.*

"I'm making a 1960s record. Not a record that sounds like the 1960s but a record that lives in that time. Your machine is the missing link."

He nodded. "You could hire a 1960s Theremin though. That'd be contemporaneous. There a reason why it has to be Brian's?"

I looked again at Jackie. Nothing. I could say it was an attempt to make the record live the way they did. Completely authentically, entirely fake. But…

"To fuck someone over. To make money. To live forever."

He threw a bony arm around my shoulder. It was light as a bird's wing.

"Well hell boy, why didn't you say before?"

Jackie shuffled back and forth between the two rooms like a clockwork scarecrow. Did she know what a tragedy her life was, this girl who'd played live in forty-eight countries, who'd been the first crush of so many teenage boys (and girls), now locked into an orbit so tightly circumscribed that there was a path worn in the carpet between the couch and the fridge? Probably not. We don't, do we? We couldn't and still go on. Instead we pull down the blinds, delete our profiles and let the phone ring out until the world is small enough for us to feel important again.

Hyde pulled out the Theremin, in a black leather case. He examined me stolidly.

"You want to jam it out a little before you go?"

I was about to say no, I'd trespassed enough on their time, but an idea niggled at me. There was a song I'd written back in Vegas which I'd carried with me for years. It was a countryish thing with a hokey Hank Williams refrain that went, "Are we gonna be all right?"

It was a question that stabbed a black needle in me whenever I sang it, because it was part of the oldest, saddest conversation I knew. It was a question that I had asked and been asked many times before, usually in bed, or in a midnight kitchen amid a wreckage of bottles, or once on a plane, seconds before we took off, asked so seriously that it might have been a question about the flight, but of course it wasn't. Every time I'd asked or been asked it signalled the end of something, because in asking you got your answer.

As a song it was perfect in my head — small and desperate — but every attempt to record it had flattened me and the song both. But something of the mood in the flat, and the vultures circling above Jackie and Hyde that they were oblivious to, made me feel it might work here.

"Does that Tascam work?" I asked. I'd seen the old tape machine as I'd walked in, a piece of machinery the size of a cinema projector.

"*Everything* here works boy," said Hyde, tapping his cane on the floor with each word. "You got something for us?"

Kissing Garden — 15 days ago

We only did two takes. Hyde took the verses in a gravel-pit baritone, mixing up words and adding phrases, but he got the essence of it immediately. Jackie sang the refrain. On the first take I harmonised with her but the unity wiped the bleakness from the song. I asked her to sing take two alone. There was everything of her in that vocal: the pure tones of a playground singer, the frailty of a bird-boned old lady. Sussex, California, nowhere. She picked at an antique Gretsch bigger than her and the noise was so faint on the tape that it sounded like a cat scratching to get out. They didn't want to hear it back so I listened on headphones and shivered at the rightness of it all. Nothing was straight, nothing was whole. It was a broken, flightless thing.

Baxter was waiting around the corner in a beachfront cafe. Brighton was as bleak as a black-and-white film: grey skies, grey water, grey stones.

"How did it go?" You could feel the questions queueing up behind this first one. I placed the cased Theremin on the table.

"Good. A thousand for it."

"A thousand? You were supposed to be charming them, what did you do, hit on her?"

I waved him away. "We need them to be invested in this anyway. Otherwise they might talk. And they *really* don't like you."

Kissing Garden — 15 days ago

I was still cloaked in the miasma of their flat. Sweet coffee and candle wax, sizzurp and fifty-year-old cigarettes. It brought a slothfulness with it that was not just to do with the drink. I slid down the plastic chair to watch a seagull high against the blank sheet of the sky, balanced gyroscopically against the tumult. His head was steady, unmoving as the wind bent his wings and ruffled his feathers. I wished we could swap places, that I could be there skyblown, stripped clean by high winter air. Instead I was here, among the mess and baggage of other people. I plugged my headphones back in and just watched the gull.

Chapter Ten

My plan had been to park a little way outside Saul's and wait until I was certain that he was out, but that was before I saw the place. It was, as Brandon had said, easy to find. As you crested a grassless ridge on the A666 it was laid out below you, a blot on the road up to the power station, but its isolation meant there was nowhere nearby that you could park without being seen.

I stopped in a picnic area a couple of miles back from the house and watched through binoculars. I couldn't sit still. Somewhere behind me a wave was gathering, a black wave in a wine-dark sea. It pressed against the backs of my eyes as it gathered force. A wall of water, thick with trash and clammy creatures, ready to break when it made landfall. If I sat still I felt it swell and surge towards me.

"Not yet," I said, "Just let me do this and then you can have me."

I took one of Jay's TLAs and maybe it was the anticipation — the rush before the rush — but I felt its effects instantly. It was like tuning a staticky radio into the clearest 50,000-watt transmitter. I could *feel* the scratch of the bullrushes against the boat's sides as I watched them through the binoculars. I could sense the heat of the petrol cooling in the engine behind me. A radar-blip of excitement presaged a ring of starlings wheeling past. I forced myself to slow down my breathing.

Something tugged my attention off to the right. There, on the moor, great and alive in the dusk, two hares reared onto their hind legs and batted furiously at each other. It was so quiet that you could hear the pad of paw on paw. Robin's voice: *mad not crazy*.

I jumped back into the camper van, started the engine and pointed it downhill until we were doing seventy on the long slope that curved down to the boat, scaring the hares into a low-slung, scrambled escape. Then I killed the engine and let the van glide to a stop on the gravel outside. Nature had held its breath against the mechanical racket but now it returned: the mumble of bees, columns of birdsong.

They weren't home. At the far side of the boat was a porthole with screws so rusty and weather-worn that I could remove them by hand.

Inside it was musty and crowded with objects, like a teenager's room, and as I moved around I kept bumping things off walls and scraping limbs on the exposed beams. It was the perfect spot for setting off fires; there was barely an inch of space that didn't contain some firetrap. Feathers, fabrics, books, and all of them locked tight in this wooden box. I rigged up the smaller devices in suitable spots and then took up a couple of floorboards under a tatty looking rug. The big device went in here, sending up a soft cloud of sawdust as I dropped it into place. Then I tidied up, trying to make sure everything was how I'd found it, and left via the front to screw the porthole back into place.

I'd saved a smaller kit to check the wiring. There was an old-fashioned, American-style mailbox by the road and I placed it in there. Robin had shown me how to rig up a Wi-Fi game controller to flick switches. I toggled the joystick and pressed X. There was a low thump and a noise like tearing fabric as the mailbox bulged and burst into flames. Napalm dripped in fiery globules from the base, scorching the grass on the ground, and a smudged line of smoke reached for the sky.

They found me there, Saul and Andre, asleep on the wooden steps of the boat, under the shadow of the skeletal remains of the mailbox. Their voices woke me. How long had I slept?

"What's happened here? Look at the mailbox."

"It's fucking Bran. D'you think that's his van?"

Silence. "Is he *dead*?"

"This isn't good. Should we just go? Leave him here?"

I yawned, giving it some Brandonian theatrics.

"Evening ladies."

The swell in my head receded. They stayed at the end of the drive, like it was my house and they were the interlopers.

"Brandon. Are you OK?" Saul's eyes flicked between me and the mailbox.

"Fine and dandy," I told him. "Thought I'd pop by."

I sat up and placed my hands on my knees. A noise like the retreat of a wave on shingle tore across my mind and then quietened.

"And you two? Good ride?" They were dressed in day-glo Lycra. "Let's go inside."

Andre unlocked the front door and I went in first. There was a pleasing feeling of being at home here which I didn't want to lose.

"Come on, don't be shy, your mother wasn't." I flopped on a couch swathed in embroidered throws and sank into its broken base. "Sit yourself down. Andre love, why don't you make us a nice cuppa."

He didn't move until Saul gave him a look and he disappeared back into the tiny galley.

"So, Saul. Ronnie and Reggie eh?"

"Oh. Did they come to see you?"

The controller was warm in my pocket as I pressed the A button. White light roared from the right-hand side of the cabin and the bird headdress burst into flames.

It was pretty impressive. A cold glow lit the skull from within: the eyes blazed as the feathers caught and shrivelled. Saul watched in fascination as the flame burned blue and acrid smoke pooled around the ceiling.

It took Andre to realise the whole place might go up. He doused the flames with a hand-held fire extinguisher. I let the noise subside as inside me a wave picked up speed beneath a starless sky.

"Yes, Ronnie and Reggie came to see me. And guess who gave them the address?"

Saul held his hands up. "I didn't know that where you were staying was a secret."

"Fair enough. But didn't they seem, I don't know, a bit *miffed* with me?"

He was silent at that. How much did he know? It didn't really matter.

"A phone call would have been fine. 'Sorry Bran — I may have inadvertently sent a couple of homicidal goons your way.' I could have at least tidied up for them, made myself look presentable. Instead they turned up extremely uninvited and now have it in their heads that I owe them quite a lot of money, money that I don't have. So I thought to myself, who *does* have that kind of money? And it came to me. Lovely Saul. Who could just sign one little piece of paper and I'd have just enough to keep my head on my shoulders, and what's more it's money that he doesn't even want, which makes it all the easier, doesn't it?"

Saul shook his head with his eyes closed. "It goes against everything I believe and everything I've worked for. It's not right…"

I pressed B and steeled myself so that when the shards of coloured glass rained throughout the boat I didn't flinch at all. Saul was on his knees with his hands over his ears though. Andre stood holding the useless fire extinguisher at his side.

It was only once Saul had signed the papers that I told them my share of the money would all go to Robin. Leading with that might have saved myself much of the aggravation but I understood how best to use Brandon's power now. *Yes* kick a man when he's down, *yes* to the final twist of the knife. Logic and threats might be enough to tamp Baxter and Saul down for now but I needed them to keep quiet about all this when I was out of their lives too. Only cruelty, and the threat of madness, would gave me that level of remote control.

I left them tidying up in the dark, the smell of petrol and burnt feathers hanging over the boat. Once I was back in the camper van I pressed the final button. You could hear the distant *whoomph* even over the engine noise as the sails burst into flames.

I angled the rear-view mirror to watch: burning rainbows, burning bones, burning peace signs. An oblong of light as Saul and Andre came out to see what was happening. Three tongues of fire grabbing for the sky and two silhouetted figures hand in hand. It was beautiful. My heart fluttered and stuttered and I had to gasp down great lungfuls of icy air to keep me from passing out. The blaze was the only light for miles, framing the scene in something blacker than black: pure night. The boat, shimmering with flame, adrift on a sea that was sky, that was oil, that was night.

Around Todmorden when the gleam of the cat's-eyes started to trail like tracer rounds, I parked up and lay in the back of the camper. Baxter was done; I had his money and I had his compliance. Saul was cowed and the contract would give Robin something for the future. That left Kimi and the record and I had no idea where to start with her.

Instead I focused on Ronnie and Reggie. Andre said they were working the door of a rave up near Rochdale that night so I headed north. Streetlamps smeared across my vision and I swore I could hear the conversations in the cars next to me at traffic lights. As I drove I craved sleep but when I parked to lay down my heart hammered until I had to start moving again. I drove as fast as I dared with the windows wide open to drown out the static in my head.

The traffic thinned as I headed out of town then congealed again as we neared the party. Four or five to a car, their windows down with music playing, partygoers turned a country lane into a battle of competing sound systems. A lone building stood spotlit on a hillside as the traffic slowed to a standstill and people began to get out and walk, abandoning their cars on the roadside. Light shone from open car doors as people leaned in and laughed. I saw deals being done against the glow of car interiors.

A man slapped the front window, frightening me. I wound it down an inch.

"Mate, mate, mate can we use the back of your van?" He was pressed hard against the glass, gesturing behind him at some girl hanging back.

"Sorry, I can't."

He pushed his face against the glass, flattening his lips as he bellowed, "Well fuck yooooooou then". And with that he was away. I heard him a little further down the line of stopped cars. "Mate mate mate. No wait."

I drew the curtains in the back and counted out the money.

From the darkness of a small hillock I watched Ronnie and Reggie working the queue. It was mostly good-natured. Once or twice Ronnie had to put his hands on the shoulders of one of the dancing queuers to still them so Reggie could go through their pockets, but they seemed focused on getting inside. Wide eyes concentrated on the noise and light coming from the double doors and jaws worked soundlessly. I waited until the queue died down before making my way over.

Reggie saw me first. He was examining a plastic bottle of confiscated pills.

"Well, look who it isn't, the dead man."

Ronnie looked up. Back on my home turf they'd been imperious, treating the Magpie's security and my presence as negligible, nothing to be concerned with. But here, with their dogs and their people around them, they definitely looked wary. Ronnie's knuckles whitened as he tightened his grip on the Doberman's collar.

"This is a surprise Brandon, I can't stress that enough." Both of them held back.

I raised both hands. "I have your money."

A look between them: quick, hungry. "Here, now?"

I nodded. "In a van, down the lane. I had to park up because of the traffic."

"All of it?"

"Every penny."

Ronnie walked with me down the lane in an uncomfortable silence. A few stragglers were coming the other way and somewhere down in the valley kids were dancing around a fire: no music, just stick figures whirling around the flames. The walk seemed longer than the journey up the hill and I was beginning to think I'd overshot when I saw the familiar shape of the camper.

Ron looked out of place in the dolls-house confines of the VW. He perched on the built-in sofa while I took the money from its hiding place. His face was waxy in the tube-light, pale skin pulled tight over his skull, his stubble longer than his shaven head. He looked for all the world like an Action Man. I felt a nervousness from him that I didn't expect. I must have looked worse than I thought.

I counted out the money. "Here. That's everything."

He nodded, seemingly satisfied, and put the money in his jacket.

"So, we're square? And you won't bother my girlfriend? Or the boy?"

Even saying *my girlfriend* gave me a forbidden thrill. *Mine, mine mine.*

"Of course." He sounded offended. "We never would've. I don't like to have anything to do with families. Yours, mine, anyone's. Too much drama."

He perched further forward on his seat and I could see the pink of his skull through the stubble. "You can tell me now. Which one are you really?"

It took me a second. "I'm the brother. The one you were supposed to kill. Seriously."

He examined me. "Fuck, sorry about that. Never got anything that wrong before."

He looked apologetic, as if we were discussing some minor incident. "Or, I guess, sorry about your brother." He rested both hands on his knees.

"He was a cold fish that one, anyway."

"How d'you mean?"

"Well, killing your brother, I mean it's got to have some kind of karmic retribution, don't you think? On some level. Some spiritual cost. It's like a Greek myth." He ran a hand across his head. "And it just seemed like no thing to him. No thing at all. I'm glad we fucked up in a way."

"Me too."

He gave a tight smile at that. "Yeah, I bet. So, the kid and the girl?"

"His."

"And do they know?"

"Yeah, they know." I didn't want to explain about Robin.

He licked his lips thoughtfully. "So, it all worked out for you then?"

I looked around the interior of the camper, the closest thing I had to a home now that Umbrage and the Magpie were gone, felt the sting of powder burns along my fingers and sensed the dark wall of water that adrenaline was barely shoring up.

"Just peachy."

I was nearly ten miles away before the idea hit me. I swung the van around and retraced my route. When I got back to the party Ronnie and Reggie were sitting in a Nissen hut by the entrance, drinking tea from china cups.

"Hey, do you guys want to make some money?"

Ronnie pushed the door closed with his boot. The music sounded miles away.

"What kind of thing?"

"Nothing you haven't done before."

The drive back to London was a flurry of texts sent under bleak northern skies in bleak northern laybys, typing one-handed as passing lorries shook the walls of the camper. I sent a WhatsApp to Jay: *hey can u get me a Kevlar vest*, texted Saul: *lawyers will need a statement from you in the next couple of days.* And to Rae, simply: *I'm coming, hang on.*

Then it was back to driving. Talk radio, no music and a light pouring over me like sloughing off dead skin. It was only when the traffic began to snarl on London's outskirts that gravity reasserted itself. The first hints of morning framed the skyline and the idea of driving city streets weighed on me.

I pulled into a service station and parked in the far corner of the car park. Someone had left a roll of thin orange blankets in the locker so I pulled them tight around me and tried to sleep. My phone buzzed constantly on the table but I ignored it. A couple of hours' sleep would do me but when I closed my eyes I heard vast wingbeats like far-off thunder. I told myself not to be scared, to imagine those same wings enfolding me into a feathery cocoon. I willed myself into the streets of New Umbrage, my gift to Robin. I felt his hand in mine — those tiny bones — as we walked through his model: a landscape that shifted and reconfigured around us. A kernel of terror squatted in my heart, a terror for Robin and the arbitrary world we were building around him. And a kindred terror at his generation's blitheness to it all. I slept in patches. Machinery, wingbeats, hot breath under musty blankets. Phone buzz, car tyres, the beep of reversing lorries. Robin and I walking hand in hand along flagstones that flowed like liquid, only icing over once his toes touched them. A painted-on sky, dead pixels, stage-set shopfronts. Everything unslotted. Kevlar vests. Empty car parks. Coming Home.

"We're here daddy," said Robin, picking up the pace, skipping on stepping stones that materialised under every unwatched step. "Just keep on walking."

I woke to a banging on the camper door and it took me a couple of moments to remember where I was. I was damp with sweat and the slivers of window I could see through the curtains ran with condensation. I opened the door an inch to hide the table littered with wraps and pill packets, and a man in a hi-viz jacket was taking pictures of the VW on his phone.

Seeing me, he said, "It says 'lorries only' in four-foot fucking letters, mate."

I was in London for midday. Spring rain made the streets slick and the sun was low, giving the city a glassy sheen. The petrol station had cut up the last of Brandon's credit cards in front of me so I was spending cash from Baxter's pile.

My phone rattled on the dashboard — Jay's number. *10am tomorrow, 516 The Liberty Building.* Nineteen hours. My head was a black tower, an echoing well.

I parked and tried to sleep but the blood pulsed hard in my chest and my eyes sprang open at any little noise. I'd have to power through. I drove anywhere, taking whichever street looked the emptiest, until I was somewhere out near Snaresbrook on a square of back roads enclosing a paltry wood and pond. I drove around and around the four roads, turning left, left, left, left until I could have done it with my eyes closed. It wasn't enough to still the chatter in my head. It would be early in California but I needed to hear a voice that knew me.

Rae picked up on the first ring. "Ads? Is that you?"

"Hey." I propped the phone on the dashboard. "I'm just out driving. I have Baxter's money. I've got a promise from Saul that he'll sign the lawsuit. It's happening."

As I said it I felt the paranoia slip away. It's happening. I'm doing it.

"That's amazing. How?"

I laughed for what felt like the first time in days. "I'm not really sure. Fifty per cent Brandon and fifty per cent me. It doesn't matter. I just need… Just talk to me for a bit OK? Tell me something from your past."

I could hear her moving around. She'd be in bed, under the covers. "Did I ever tell you how we got here, to Tahoe?"

I tried to remember where Brandon's Story of Rae finished. "No, I've heard about LA, in the Canyon though."

"Oh man, that's missing out all of Vegas. Hold onto your hat. We were living in this weird place. It was supposed to be this totally chi-chi estate, like the Palm Springs of Nevada, but the money ran out almost as soon as they started and all that was left was one show home, thirty shells of houses and mile upon mile of levelled-off desert. There were massive earthmovers just abandoned there, seized up with sand. Technically we were the caretakers but it didn't look like anyone was ever coming back."

"Was there power and water?"

"In the show home, yes. That's where we lived. But the rest of it was just ghost town. It was all right actually. It was restful after LA and beautiful, especially at night. You could lie on your back and just watch the universe rotate around you."

I pulled the van over and parked on a yellow line. Rae's voice was blurring the edges of things. I reclined the seat and held the phone close to my ear.

"We went back to school. Croupier classes, to learn how to deal at the casinos? An actual proper school with lesson plans and whiteboards and exams and everything. It was *hard*. There's maths and these long sequences to remember and each game has little quirks and you're constantly being reminded that if you make a mistake it can cost someone hundreds of thousands of dollars. Which is a lot of pressure for ten dollars an hour plus tips. Bran was actually good at it though. I mean he *hated* being told what to do but he loved the drama of it. He used to say, 'In what other profession can you irrevocably ruin a life with the flick of the wrist? It's like being a brain surgeon.' He loved the big games, loved to watch someone fucking up their life."

I heard her moving around in the bed, trying to get comfortable.

"But it was all good. Once we graduated we took it in turns to work and we were making some money. And on the quiet days — Mondays mainly — we'd have these awesome parties. Thirty or forty people up from Vegas. Peyote and grass round the fire, music as loud as you like and everyone crashing out in empty buildings. It was free, y'know, like being a kid again. And nothing really to do except read and have sex, and what with it being twenty miles to a drugstore and Bran's total inability to plan ahead, I guess it was only a matter of time before we got pregnant."

She was quiet for a moment. "I mean, obviously never say that to Robin. I'm so grateful for those twenty miles now, without them I might never... But the minute he came into the world I suddenly saw where we were living through his eyes. And the place was just... just no. I mean for starters the heat was brutal. Once when we were there a guy from the next town, this young, fit guy, went hiking and got caught in a rockslide. Broke his ankles so he couldn't get himself into the shade. Guess how long before sunstroke killed him?"

"Um, three days?"

"Six hours. Six hours and he was dead. It's a place that actively wants to turn everything to dust."

I heard her move through the room and the sound of curtains being drawn.

"So, I went back to dealing poker. It meant leaving Robin with some pretty dodgy people, but I was desperate to get out and Brandon seemed happy enough up in the hills. I started working the cheap tables but there was such a high turnover of staff that you got promoted like once a week. And the thing is, Bran was a pretty good dealer but he *never* got tips. Usually if you dealt to a big winner then you'd at least get given one of those orange chips that they used to call pumpkins. But Bran, I guess he looked like he didn't need a tip because he'd come home with nothing.

"I was getting nearly two hundred bucks a night when it was just the locals playing, but then the Chinese players started asking for me. Voodoo Rae. They'd heard it from the other dealers who'd heard it from Bran. 'C'mon Rae, do do your voodoo'. I'd be dealing the one-five dollar game and the pit boss would come over and drag me off to one of the private rooms where it was all Chinese. Even the waiters spoke Mandarin. But I'd deal and do the calls in English and everyone seemed happy. And, the first few times, if I got a proper tip I'd stop off and pick up pumpkin pie from this twenty-four-hour bakery on the way home. I'd get back and say, 'pumpkin for all' and Robin would get the pie and Bran would get the orange chip, but I stopped after a while because he wasn't ever getting any money off his players, and I was getting a thousand every couple of nights, and it drove him crazy. So I started hiding them away. Pumpkins and Barneys. Thousands and five hundreds. As long as you didn't cash them in then they weren't too tempting but at the end of every week I'd walk out to the furthest of the empty houses and squirrel away another couple of chips. I never counted them or tried to calculate how much was there. I just dropped them in an old cash box and enjoyed the sound of them rattling around.

"And then one night we were both working and we walked into the casino and there was this air of anticipation, so thick you could feel it. And that meant one of two things. Someone famous was playing or someone was on tilt."

I hadn't interrupted. Her voice had fallen into a lovely dark rhythm, like being read to as a child. The stale air of the camper van had melted away until there was just me and a voice.

"On tilt?" I asked.

"Yeah. Like a pinball machine I guess. Huh. I've never thought about its meaning before. It's when someone loses all sense of logic and starts spiralling. They start making crazy bets. It can be kind of amazing to watch. Terrifying, but amazing. The whole room is electrified because it means a feeding frenzy is coming. And this night there are three tables playing but it's obvious where the action is. Six players in the corner table, sitting in dead silence, as everyone is watching. The pit boss comes over — this lovely, lovely man, Ernie, an old-school Vegas guy who was there when it was just gangsters and cacti — and even he's sweating because he needs someone who knows Pai Gow Poker."

"Pai Gow?" I switched off the neon tube over the bed to lose myself deeper in her voice.

"It's this Chinese poker game that's very fast moving and there's always a ton of big bets but only a few casinos played it back then. And the guy who is on tilt is this obese Chinese guy in a ten-gallon hat who is threatening to leave and go play across the road at The Sands because they're like the Pai Gow experts. But he still has a *stack* of chips in front of him and everyone wants a piece of it and luckily, because me and Bran are recent graduates, it was one of the variants we'd been taught. So in seconds the other dealer is off and Bran's dealing Pai Gow for huge money. I get the table next to him, dealing the five to twenty-five dollar regulars but to be honest everyone, the other players included, are just betting on autopilot so they can watch this guy crash and burn. And it's horrible to see, just a bloodbath. Bran deals, they bet, Ten Gallon Hat loses. Bran deals, the same thing happens. And you watch one pile of chips shrink and all the others rise. The guy who is winning biggest has headphones on so he can't be spooked and the other players are keeping their eyes down and Bran is watching Ten Gallon closely, because this is like the moment in a nature documentary where the cheetah finally gets his claws in the wildebeest or whatever. And then Ten Gallon starts talking to Bran.

"You know it's just because he can't get a rise out of the others at the table, but still it's constant. 'Fucking shitty cards from a dumb fuck dealer you smiling there fucker? You smiling? Yeah you Billy Idol. You watching, yeah, you think it's funny? I tell you what's funny fucking Eraserhead looking motherfucker this fucking hand I just lost is what ten times your fucking salary and I don't even care I lose money like that down the back of the couch.'

"And he loses again. Loses big and I'm willing Bran *please don't smile* but as he collects the cards he turns to the winner and says, 'beautifully played sir' and I don't think I've ever heard Bran call anyone sir before and then he deals the next hand and he's whistling "Eyes Without A Face".

This hand, now the guy is playing it like he's playing against Bran. The others have been forgotten, even Headphones Guy, who has ninety percent of his chips now. Ten Gallon is saying 'fucking albino fuck I see you smiling like you think it's a big deal fucking thousand dollars it's a big deal to you Billy Idol fuck' and Bran's still whistling and he has this half-smile going that's got to be a hundred times more annoying than if he were laughing and the chips are stacking up and Ten Gallon doesn't even look at his cards. He's betting blind which makes the others nervous because all the time he's been on tilt they've been reading him like a book but now who knows what might happen, right?"

Dusk had fallen and Rae's voice was soft as moth's wings.

"Still, no one's dropping out. They've all got his chips to gamble with and this could be the last time around. Bran's just singing the 'say your prayers' bit and even Headphones Guy has taken them off now so he can listen to Ten Gallon's spiel 'fucking Billy Idol albino fag fuck smile one more time I dare you' and the pit boss is watching carefully but no *way* is he getting involved, not with six players still in and this car crash of chips in the middle. And the cards get flipped over and the winner is this old girl who'd been so quiet I'd hardly noticed her. She's this little old lady with those cataract shades who I knew from before because she was a total shark. She won fifteen thousand dollars once when I was dealing Blackjack and she tipped me in homemade cookies."

I heard Rae move away from the phone. "Just getting a sweater, it's cold here."

My eyes were shut tight so I couldn't see the camper van and coke wraps and the clothes muddied from last night as I waited for the voice to tether me back to the ground again.

"And Ten Gallon stands up and stretches like it's no big thing and looks through the few chips he has left, and he's turning them over and over. And he throws a handful of them at Bran. Like five or six, right at him. They just bounce off him and he doesn't move. And everyone is quiet now. On my table we've stopped even pretending to play and Ten Gallon says, 'Don't you want your tip Billy Idol motherfucker? All you have to do is bend over.' And I'm trying to add up how much he threw, because it was a proper handful and he'd been playing with these gold chips that we don't even use on my table. Back at dealer school we roleplayed this exact scene and I was hoping the voice in Bran's head was saying the same as mine: *keep calm, don't engage, wait for the pit boss* and then Ten Gallon comes very close to Bran and whispers, but loud enough for us all to hear, 'Bend over and take it, boy'. And for a long moment I thought Bran was just going to let it go. And then he leant in very close like he was about to whisper in the guy's ear and he whipped his elbow round."

The excitement in her voice painted the whole scene for me: a chicken wing of an elbow, pow, out like a punch and I could taste the crunch of it, the pulping of lip against tooth. I made the same gesture silently to myself.

"And Bran was out of there before the guy even hit the ground. Up and walking. And I can see Ten Gallon's hand now, tens over sevens, not a bad hand really, and beads of blood on the tens and on the baize. Ernie just swept in there like he was on casters as Ten Gallon was being seen to and promised Champagne and oysters up in his suite, and that the room would be comped, and in come the waiters and the baize was changed and new cards and drinks for everyone, not just at their table but everywhere in the card room. And Ernie just shoves me into the dealer's seat and says *you're up Voodoo* and on we go as if nothing had happened. Ten Gallon with a bloody handkerchief and Headphones Guy back in his bubble of sound and the little old lady off to count her winnings. And I didn't really want to ask the pit boss about the chips because the cleaners know not to touch them so I'm dealing and trying to keep my cool but at the same time I'm exploring under the table and counting up four, five chips with my stockinged feet and wondering what denomination they are and whether we're talking five hundreds or five thousands. And, and, I need a pee, sorry…"

Every few seconds a car drove past, soaking the camper's interior in pale light, making my eyes hurt. I felt sick and my neck ached and by the time Rae came back some of the hypnotic air of her story was lost. She told me how she knew that she should have walked out in solidarity with Bran — it's what he would have expected — but instead she dealt on, the match reaching some kind of stalemate and it was two hours later after the table broke up that she managed to get the chips off the floor. Six chips in all, each one $25,000. And then her second dilemma of the night, but the pit boss had been insistent, the chips had clearly been a tip, it wasn't for him to take them, and what Rae and Bran did with them was up to her. And how, in not so many words, he implied that it was better for her to spend them on Bran and her than for him to have them outright.

I took the phone from my ear and switched to video chat so that I could watch her. The bedroom light was on, turning her into a silhouette, and she was hunched, as if the weight of dragging up the memory was tiring her.

"My legs shook the whole drive home. All the lights were blazing but Bran was nowhere to be seen. $150,000 in my pocket and more stashed around the estate. So I gathered it all up, packed Robin into the car seat and we drove. Back to Vegas to redeem the chips first. And then north on the 95. I sort of knew where I was going, sort of didn't."

She looked around the room she was in. "And four hours later we stopped to stretch our legs so I pulled off the road into this little loop of houses and there's *this* place, for sale and looking like something out of Disney. Seriously. There were cardinals and blue jays nesting and people walking dogs and you could smell pine and ozone and there weren't any fucking *vultures* in the sky."

She pulled a shawl around her. "And I was crying, just a little bit, and people kept coming over and checking I was OK and did I need anything, old people who had that look, like they'd learned how to live properly, and I could see into this house and it was so small and friendly looking. And in a flash I knew that if I went to the real estate office that this place would cost less than the value of the chips, I just *knew it*."

She looked around the room again and touched the table in front of her as if she couldn't believe it.

"And what did Bran say?"

"What could he say? Nothing. *It's your money Rae*. Really. He stayed in Vegas at first but now he was barred from working in every casino in the state and it's a company town, y'know. And it was the beginning of the end for him and me. I know it should have been the other stuff. The cheating or the missing nights or the fucking degenerates he brought around, but that night, the chips and the house and the idea that I could put something ahead of him. I think it ended something for him. Me too."

She smoothed out the bedspread in front of her. "Do you know the difference between a compulsive gambler and a normal gambler?"

I shook my head.

"They did a study on it that came out while we were working there. Most of us, if we have a near miss, y'know: 'nine, ten, jack, king, ace', or five of the Lotto numbers — then we feel bad, even a little bit sick."

I nodded to myself, the asymmetry of her list of cards had made me feel mildly nauseous.

"But there's a certain subset of people who, when they have one of those near-misses, the pleasure centres of their brain light up like it's a win. Those are the people this country's built on."

I'd never heard her so fierce. "Losing is winning, pain is pleasure, poverty is the just the waiting room of millionairedom. It's a nation of fantasists. And I just wanted to cash out. Not to pretend that our life hadn't been bet on red when it came up black. I wanted to win, just once."

A couple were arguing out in the street, louder than the traffic. Rae walked down the hall to the kitchen.

"Ads, have you been listening to Bran's lyrics?"

"Not really. Something about them just slides right past me." The occasional phrase stuck with me, but I was unsure why. But mostly they were just noise.

"I think he's leaving clues that *they* killed him. The band. Kimi, Baxter and Saul."

Poor Baxter, poor Saul. Despite it all I got the impression that they both quite liked Brandon. There was a history, sure, but nothing that deserved this.

"Didn't he say, right back when this started that there would be clues hidden in the music? I haven't thought about it since."

"A couple of things jumped out at me. And I suddenly realised it would be the most Brandon thing ever. To get the three of them to play on songs that pointed a finger at them." She chewed a cuticle. "Why do you think he's like that?"

"Like what exactly?"

"Like he has to get one over on everyone. With the *Smile* record and this, it's all about him being smarter than the people around him. It's so needy, don't you think? Kind of insecure. I mean, he's smart, right?"

I remembered Brandon at school, in class, before they separated us. He was good with words, less so with numbers. Competitive enough to do well on tests.

"He was, yeah, but one thing about being a twin is that your differences get magnified. I was the good twin so he was the bad one. I was the quiet one so he was the loud one. And I was the smart one. It didn't matter that I wasn't particularly quiet or good at first. I was fractionally quieter so our roles were set. And Brandon wasn't dumb, no. But he was the dumb one and that can be so self-fulfilling."

I lay back and looked at the pattern on the van's roof.

"My mother used to tell me something: imagine a raindrop falling on the continental divide, up in Mount Snow in the Rockies. When it hits the peak it splits — half falls left, the other right. One half follows the Columbia River to the Pacific, one winds its way to the Atlantic via Hudson Bay. Two identical molecules: two very different paths."

A phrase echoed in my mind: *sensitive dependence on initial conditions.*

"It's pretty difficult to shake."

In the dark of the van I saw a lone raindrop falling through a night sky, the peak of the mountain like a compass needle.

"Even as a grown up?"

"Of course, it's worse in a way. You're set by then. It's a long way back from the Atlantic to the top of a mountain."

"What mountain?" The voice came from off-screen.

The picture shook as Robin threw himself on the bed. "In Umbrage?"

Rae threw a blanket over him, making him squeal. While he thrashed around she brought the phone close. Her face filled the screen.

"You see. I got my big win."

Once they'd gone everything receded around me. The wall of black water was no more, replaced by an endless warm static. I spread-eagled myself on the floor, picturing myself safe in the thin line where grey sea meets grey sky. I slept, on and off until the rattle of my phone woke me. An email from Jay.

"Our mutual friend says that sleeve notes are a bad idea, especially for a track that she says you haven't managed to finish. If you were to go ahead there are certain edits she insists you make. She's included them as edits on the original document, attached here. See you tomorrow."

I opened the attachment, a Word document, and started to read.

Slowing of Light

The Word doc has comments in the margin at a couple of points, presumably from Kimi. I've included them here, asterisked at the point they were commenting on.

I listened back to "Are We Going to be Alright?" dozens of times, trying to imagine it as the last track on the record. Sometimes it sounded right. I liked the way the only answer to "Are We Going to be Alright?" was silence. And it was good that my voice was gone from the track before it finished, like Elvis in the limo with a cheeseburger and a malt while his band vamped through the last five minutes of "Suspicious Minds". But most of the time it just sounded out of place. I called Kimi.

"Hello ghost," she said.

"Hello robot," I replied.

She was in a cab. Kimi was always in a cab. Over the last week she'd called me four or five times while she was in transit, seemingly just to chat. She knew that listening wasn't my strong suit but I had the feeling that she had no one else in her life like me: so broken and unimportant that she could ditch the positive mask. With me she was funnier and crueller than she came across in public, rich with resentments that could be poured down the phone to a cipher like me. It didn't matter what I thought.

I told her, "Listen Kimi, I need an ending."

She snapped back, "I thought we had that sorted. It's soon isn't it? No, don't tell me, it's best I don't know. Or would it be better I *did* know so I could be out of the country?" The question was more to herself than to me.

"No, that's sorted…" I said, realising what she was talking about. The other thing: the actual ending.

"But you're having second thoughts? You're bottling it." She sounded a little drunk. There was a playground sing-song to her words.

(Yeah, we need to lose this whole exchange, from "Listen" to "words". I think it's obvious why.)

"Not that. For fuck's sake shut up a moment Kimi. An ending for the record. I need something that…" I wasn't sure what I needed. "I need something final."

The last track. The end of the end of the end. My "Purple Rain", my "Hurt", my "A Day in the Life".

I could hear the white noise of traffic.

"There is something," she said. "Something from forever ago. I wrote it when Remote/Control split up but I could never finish it. I've been carrying it around with me ever since. Hang on."

A car door closed. She was walking somewhere. Changes in sound: outdoors, indoors, large room, smaller.

"It's a song. Or rather it's half a song. I don't know. It's *something*. I'll Dropbox it to you."

I sat out on the balcony and watched the pigeons strut until my phone pinged. I played the track over the big speakers. It was a slow, plain-faced ballad with chords as old as the moon. It trudged along, every step as inevitable as taxes, and her band sounded like some cruise-ship combo five hours into a six-hour marathon. Kimi came in maybe a minute deep into the groove. This was pre-voicebox and her voice was rich and low as she incanted a set of long lines, somewhere between a shopping list and a sentencing.

> *Lost Boys and Hollow Men, Camgirls and the Bored, Wandsworth*
> *and Wormwood and Holloway and Ford*
> *Clothes-hidden bruises, H, E and X, Botox and Rolex and*
> *passing bad cheques*

> *Lear jets and treadmills, trackmarks and tears, safe words for caged*
>   *birds, Chopard and De Beers*
> *Crystal and Cristalle and crisis and crime, Bath salts, hesitation*
>   *marks, me my mine*

Then, after three long verses, there was a key change that swelled heavenwards until it reached a moment of balance like the second when a plane's wheels leave the ground, and then we were back into the verse. This happened five more times. Five more lists, five more swells. I got goosebumps.

I played it again. It was *something*, she was right. It went where you want music to go: inexplicable but familiar, a feeling that you knew deep in your blood but which had no name. It was impossible and inevitable. The verses twisted the feeling tight within you, waiting for one line in that tundra of the chorus to make it all come together. One little line there would finish this thing.

I called her back and told her I loved it. She had news too: she'd coaxed the whole band into coming here to record, even Saul, though I hate to imagine what she had to offer him to make him dismount his high horse. I doubt Baxter needed much convincing: he's the kind of sap who'd willingly go to a school reunion. We'd have two days here to finish the record and then, well, everything would be over. I asked her what she'd told them.

"Just what they needed to get them here. They don't know anything about your plans, *after*. Baxter's doing it because he has that soppy side to him and he thinks it might be 'cathartic'. I think he's hoping you're going to cry. Saul's just doing it because you'll be in his debt. And I said that you complete him." The voicebox turned her laughter into a series of staccato barks.

"Christ Kimi, you're making me sound like Elton fucking John here. This isn't going to be one of those Circle of Life things."

Still, it felt right to have all four of us there. You want your last ever performance to be something complete, however damaged. Think the Beatles on the Apple roof — *I hope we passed the audition* — rather than the Stone Roses at Reading.

"Hey," she said, "I did what had to be done. Your winning personality wasn't going to get us all in the same room together, was it?"

I had the news on in the background. There were only two stories — the volcanoes and the financial crisis — and they melded irresistibly. Grounded planes and Mordor skies and security guards locking up century-old banks for the final time. Lehman's, Merrill Lynch. Gone, gone. Names you knew but didn't understand, like constellations. A pall of ash, a cloud like a frozen explosion and deep below in the shadow, veins of pulsing amber. Impossibilities before breakfast. Rocks flowed like water, banks owed more money than had existed throughout recorded history and a cloud the weight of a mountain hung in the sky. Each song I recorded took a year from my life. It was a slow-motion disaster, like a car crash at one frame a minute and I loved every second of it.

Kimi asked, "So are we rerecording everything?"

I'd played her some tracks. She was a good sounding-board in that she was tough, had good ears and didn't care if she hurt my feelings. Musically she was full of suggestions but lyrically she left well alone. I wasn't sure whether that was because she thought they were unimprovable or she didn't know where to start. I chose to believe the former.

"Nah. A couple of things sound right already so I'm only going to mess with the ones that need some chemistry."

On screen a helicopter circled the ash cloud, close enough to whip the smoke into a liquid landscape. Like the ground beneath it was slowly tearing itself apart. Across the bottom of the screen stock market prices trundled past: all preceded by minus signs, all falling.

Kimi was telling the driver a short cut. The silence was a relief. When she returned she was louder.

"Do you have a title?"

I hadn't. No last song, no title. "Not yet. The trouble is that once *Blood on the Tracks* was taken, everything else became a bit of an also-ran."

She paused. "That *is* a good one. I was thinking *Suicide Notes* but it's a bit on-the-nose."

"A bit on the nose, and terrible."

She snorted. "What about *Notes from Nowhere*?"

I rolled it around. "I quite like it. Double meaning but not a pun. Sounds timeless."

I wrote it out on the pad by my bed.

"It sounds like I've heard it before. Is it something?" A book, I thought, old and leather bound.

"Of course it's something…" I could hear her frustration with everyone's slowness: the taxi driver's, mine, the world's. "Of course it's something, it's *good*. We're just picking over the rubble by this point."

A reporter stood on the fresh land under the ash cloud, silhouetted by cooling lava. Sparks rose drunkenly around him. The news crawler read GREEK FINANCE MINISTER SAYS THESE ARE THE LAST DAYS.

The next morning I played Kimi's tune over and over as I prepared the room. I'd rewritten the verses so that there was one each for the four of us, but the chorus still eluded me. Maybe the pressure was too much. It would be the last line on the final track of a record at the end of the world. I'd leave it until the tape was rolling.

I could see the paths the four of us would take written in the air. I could see the interference patterns between Saul and Bax and the distance at which I needed to hold them: close enough for friction, not close enough for ignition. I felt the dark pull of Kimi too. The gravity of her fame and the way it bent logic around her. Left to her own devices she would suck the whole project into her orbit, suck it down and crush it into something weighty and dark.

(Oh please! If I have to be an astronomical object in your tortured analogy, let it at least be a supernova, pumping heat and light into the vacuum of this project.)

I sat on the balcony and looked out at where the stars should be. Somewhere out there was *Voyager 1*, that fragile thing with its tinfoil skin and breadstick legs, travelling at 39,000 mph, speeding stubbornly through the dead unknown beyond our solar system. Hardly any of that speed was due to its rockets, though, they were just there to throw off earth's gravity. No, since then it has slingshot its way through the solar system, catching acceleration from hair-raising orbits around planet after planet, each one lending it another velocitous kick until it was the fastest moving thing for a billion miles. *(U OK hun?)*

That was the strategy I needed to take. To orbit Kimi's dark star and Saul's angry quasar and Baxter's dead system and use them to propel me onwards. I could see the path; I could taste it.

I drew diagrams on the floor. For Saul the bird, for Bax a crescent moon. Kimi I gave a five-pointed star. Its meaning depended on its orientation but that meant nothing when there was no up or down. I lit candles and drew blinds. I tuned the guitars and switched on amps, revelling in the way the valves added weight to the air.

I smoked a cigarette out on the balcony. Little deaths, big lives. The fox was back — ballerina-footed on the filthy glass of the warehouse roof, sooty at his toes, bible-black at the tips of his ears. I moved the ashtray, just an inch, and his head swivelled to bring that long snout round to face me. A quiver, a calculation of danger, black eyes. I saluted and he walked on.

White cotton shirt, black wool trousers. Sleeves rolled up like I'm Mission Control. A spritz of Aqua di Parma at the pulse points. Jugular, Ulnar. Femoral. A voice from another life, Rae studious at her makeup table — *girls wear perfume where they want to be kissed, Bran* — jugular, ulnar, femoral: the suicide veins.

For three people who'd at least been in some kind of contact over the last twenty years they seemed a lot like strangers. From Baxter and Saul's hug-turned-handshake-turned-what-the-fuck-was-that, to Bax's obvious confusion about whether Kimi had finished speaking (the lack of inflexion meant that you had to watch her eyes carefully for punctuation, and Bax would sooner wrestle a tiger than look you straight in the eye). Saul and Kimi, who I thought might bond over some kind of new-age nonsense, seemed boringly deferential towards each other. The whole room was a study in inert chemistry.

But how could it be that we four were so uncomfortable talking to each other but so comfortable playing? We were twenty years deep in other bands and new musicians, and we had nothing more to go on than my chord sheet and Baxter's *one two three four* but we clicked into place like a key in a lock. The tumblers tumbled and everyone fell into their old roles.

We tried "Clear Your History" first. We tried it slow, then faster. I didn't care about the tempo, I was waiting for something to slot into place. It took until halfway through the fourth take before it did. Something clicked between Kimi and Baxter — a dislocated shoulder gratefully coming home to its socket — and suddenly the song was a blank page again. I tried to play as plainly as possible: barre chords, no colour, but between the notes some ghost of the chemistry we'd had back in the day began to grow. Saul noodled something baroque over the top. It was pushy and stately at the same time, but you could hear him feel it work too. I pressed record for the first time, said, "from the top?" and away we went.

"Daughters of the Daughters" we did in a single take. There was something clunky about it. Everyone was reluctant to abandon the groove of the first track, trying to overlay its particular grid onto the raw data of a different tune, but it worked in an odd way. The song never properly settled but when it finished Kimi said, "that sounded like it had a stone in its shoe," and it seemed to fit. We switched tracks and when we reached some kind of equilibrium I had them go back and rerecord a couple of things.

It was so knackering being back in charge. One by one they complained that I was "telling them what to do". It was ever thus. It's not like I have any actual power over them — unfortunately — so any level of control I have is down to my powers of persuasion and the fact I'm usually right. But fuck it, if I didn't do it nothing would get done. They'd jam and chat and bitch and talk about records and jam some more and whine and go for lunch and record and delete and at the end of the day we'd be no further forward. I forced them to make choices, or if they couldn't, then to follow mine. I had to play Saul off against Kimi and then listen to her bitching before reassuring Baxter and then going off down one of Kimi's theoretical rabbit-holes which you *know* will lead nowhere but you had to indulge her otherwise when you solved the song's problems she'd still want to try it her way.

*You give yourself way too much credit, as ever Bran. Anything that works is because of your powers of persuasion, anything that's wrong is down to us. Do we have to play "count the platinum records" again to give you an idea of exactly who was driving this session?

I saved "Mythical Beasts" for the last track of the night because it was the one most in need of band chemistry. Everyone was tired and everyone was quiet, which was good; it meant less thinking and from the first downbeat it just worked.

And I was thinking… Oh Lord, don't make me miss this now. The old slow dance. The push of Baxter's drums, the pull of Kimi's bass, forever out of time but consistently, beautifully so, an unspoken conversation taking place in scraps of seconds between their heartbeats, chiding each other, *come with me come with me*, and Saul finding the spaces in between.

And I was thinking… Don't make me miss Saul's playing. As ever, lovelier than anything else about him, gentle and strong and rolling over the beat like smoke, like clouds. The beautiful mathematics of the three of them, and the geometries of vibration. Three sets of waves converging on me, collapsing down to a waveform that made fingerprints look simplistic.

And I was thinking… It's all too easy. To weave a guitar note in between the waves and then close your eyes and dance your voice across the surface, the music a slope and the tune the line that a skier takes. Oh Lord, don't make me miss this now, not now when I'm so near the end and the mythical beasts are just stories and I can't even remember how many times we've gone round this coda but we slow as one, every heartbeat a fourfold kick-drum, every kick-drum a group heartbeat, and we slow and it's ragged, ragged but together and we stop like it never was and that sound, the sound after the sound, the seconds of silence after you bring something new into the world and no one was cruel or lost or wrong or hurt and you breathe out together, as your wheels touch down, and you breathe out as one until somebody, me I guess, says, "OK, OK then."

And I was thinking… Why shouldn't I miss this now, haven't I earned it? Why shouldn't these moments be the best things I've ever done? Nine songs, nine snowflakes, made by our path through the storm — can't they mean as much as lovers and children and fortunes? The electrical charge as they hit the ground might be something so small that it wouldn't shift a needle, but these songs are special in a way that real life never turned out to be for me.

And I was thinking… don't think.
And I was thinking… disappear.

The next day, as the others set up, I asked Kimi about her track again. "So your song. It needs a chorus, right?"

"Sure. It needs something in that gap. Something to tie the lists together."

I waited.

"Something that transforms. At the moment it's just a feeling but the right line after could turn it to something alchemical. Your area, really."

"You say that like there's a right answer."

She smiled. "There is. I just don't know what it is."

The second session was all business. We started at 9pm; yesterday proved that none of us was much use before then and it's the kind of time when I start to see the machinery in action. Baxter and Kimi moved on their pre-arranged orbits like figures in a Swiss clock. Circles and ellipses interlocked and if you listened carefully you could hear the points click in and out of place. All our complex, maddening, beautiful, *human* behaviours rose from these simple paths. I took ten minutes off to "clear my head" and lay on the balcony looking up into the sky. There, beyond the atmosphere, above even the lonesome satellites and space junk, turned the oldest, slowest machinery. Power's machinery: cogs worn smooth with age, a closed system that nothing ever trickles down from. I lay there for a while listening to the three of them teeter through a tune, feeling like I'd turned a key and set them playing. They ran through "No Beauty" a few times and I listened to it come into hazy focus. Someone was misreading the chords and there was a slurred passage each time. I took a last look at the sky, feeling the weight of whatever was behind it, and came back downstairs.

The light in that room gave everything the air of a Renaissance artwork. I kept quiet in the doorway, imagining a painting: *The Recording of* Notes from Nowhere *by the Musical Group Remote/Control*. Shadows concentrated the action on a central tableau of Saul with his back to me, hunched over a keyboard, only his face lit in the cold blue of a monitor. Kimi stood in the darkness behind him, the dim glow from the skylight making her headphones glint like a halo. Baxter was sitting, his clothes dark against the cherry-red Strat stained purple in the shadows. They were still, each lost in their headphones, but I could hear feet tapping.

That feeling again, the moment of absolute rightness, of beauty alive and alongside it, its stunted friend, the knowledge that it would soon be gone. I strained to hear the ghost of the song through the thin sounds of plectrum on strings, Kimi's mumbling and the soft beat of feet. I watched this thing that I'd put together working on its own. Like my brother with his model city.

I stood in silence until Saul looked up and saw me. "Hey, Bran, what's this third chord in the middle eight supposed to be?"

I stepped into the picture, feeling self-conscious, and said, "It's a G minor," and he wheeled round on Kimi, "Told you, told you."

(I've listened back to the mp3 of "Slowing of Light", attached here. There's no G in the chord, it's an A#maj with a passing G in the bass. Just because you made it, doesn't mean you know what it is.)

We tried Kimi's song, the last song, without any rehearsal. Kimi called out the chords so that no one could attempt anything clever and I tried to catch myself by surprise as the chorus came in, willing the words to come, willing an ending that would illuminate everything that had come before — an epitaph, a headstone — but nothing came. The music was beautiful and the verses worked, but where was I? A blank space. I tucked my disappointment away. I'd try it again on my own afterwards.

Later, when it was just me and Kimi listening back on the gentlest hit of some new TLA of Jay's, I realised it was pretty good. It was rough as fuck. There were stumbles, slurs, over-complications and unexplained accidents, and on at least a couple of tracks differences in key that strayed from "jazz" into "mistake". But the songs, though I say so myself, were great, and the playing had its own dysfunctional charm.

"If you do this right you could spin your whole career. Every one of your failures can be recast as a small step towards this glorious destination."

Kimi was winding me up while she multi-tasked. She was nursing some Russian teen through an online DMT trip while putting some bass down on "The Day After the End of the World".

I'd brought a tie-line through so we could stop and start the track from over by the TV because Kimi wanted to catch the news. Bankers with five-hundred-dollar haircuts sat on New York sidewalks muttering into borrowed cellphones, their possessions in cardboard boxes at their feet. Overnight, on the streets outside each glass tower of London's financial district some newly emboldened group had painted targets and sprayed JUMP U FUCKERS across them. Champagne bars sat empty. Sushi meant to be eaten from the naked body of some girl working her way through college was thrown out by the plateful and pawn shops had stopped taking all but the most jewel-encrusted of Rolexes. And over it all the silent, waiting cloud.

She closed down the laptop and we lay on our backs, watching the smoke funnel up into the spiral staircase. I played the tracks from the beginning again.

"It's good." Her voice was aimed ceilingwards.

It was a satisfying moment and I let it hang there for a second, up among the strata of smoke, like the aftermath of a battle.

"You know good's not enough, right?"

"I know."

There's that moment on any trip, drug or otherwise, when you start your descent. When the warm fug of the moment begins to disperse.

It's the first crack of dawn, the first niggle of doubt. Kimi aimed her voice upwards into the smoke.

"What I mean is, it's good enough to be good." She laughed to herself. "It's good enough to be favourably reviewed in *The Wire* and to cause some micro-storm in some online teacup and to be hailed as a massive return to form by any journalist old enough to still remember you. And you might get it on a commercial or two, *my* involvement should at least get you that."

I still wasn't used to Kimi's knowing her worth. "But that's all it's good enough for, right?" I asked.

She looked over at me now. My eyesight was twitchy and the room was as vague as a sauna but I could make out the tautness in her expression.

She said, "It's not *nothing* you know Brandon, being good. It's better than being nothing, it's better than being bad. It's better than ninety-nine per cent of people will ever be."

Her face was dreamy. "It's better than you used to be, definitely."

"But good's not enough," I repeated.

(Bran, I can't over-stress how much we need to lose every line after this. Seriously. You must see that the whole thing falls apart if it's clear we know what's about to happen. And that's even ignoring the position it puts me in. Delete this. Double delete this.)

She just looked at me.

"If I want great, if I want a sensation, then I need the story."

"At least that," she said. "Who knows if that's even enough."

I shrugged. It was only my life we were talking about. She let the silence hang. Smoke eddies formed and recombined around the rafters. I heard her get up.

"I'm going to go, Bran. Let you do what you have to do."

Even through the voicebox she sounded sad. I went to get up.

"Don't," she said. She came over and kissed the top of my head. "Kaspar can see me out."

Chapter Eleven

The Liberty Building was a blank-faced skyscraper on the very edge of the City, close enough to Shoreditch to look out over the warren of streets but far enough away to have some peace. The silent lobby gave no clue as to whether it was offices or homes. The epauletted doorman made me think it was residential but the receptionist, with her headset and wipe-clean smile, turned that idea on its head. I told her the unit I was visiting.

She touched her earpiece. "Number 516. Miss Balloch, is she expecting you?"

So I was here to see Kimi. *Was* she expecting me? "I believe she is, yes."

There was that brief moment of blankness — the I'm-on-Bluetooth face that's unique to this century — and the smile reassembled. "Go straight up."

Kimi's place took up one whole side of the fiftieth floor. From the west window you could see the playset of the City, St Paul's and the BT Tower, and between those straight lines the silver thread of the Thames. To the east, new London. Cranes at all angles, half-built towers and everywhere the glint of sunlight on glass.

I stared out, trying to find the Magpie's rooftop and ignoring the tension in the room.

Jay was already there, setting something up on the table — a laptop, a camera, rolling papers — while Kimi talked on the phone, wandering throughout the flat. I caught fragments of her conversation. *But we're insured for the volcano stuff,* and *I saw her in Ibiza, she's too fucking thin.*

Her hair was down and shaggy and her clothes were nothing like the ones I'd seen her in on TV. She wore a shapeless T-shirt that read THIS IS WHAT A COOL DAD LOOKS LIKE and jeans smeared with dried paint. She paced back and forth, paying me no attention. Jay walked in, placed a lit cigarette in her mouth, waited, and took it back. They looked comfortable together. I heard the unmistakeable sound of a conversation being wound down and there she was in front of me. Tall, taller than me, with one hip hoiked higher than the other. The voicebox stripped any nuance from her words.

"Jay said you were around." A statement. I wondered how many of my movements he had reported back to her.

"And since a couple of his chemists have come up with a new TLA I thought, 'Well who better than Mr Caner himself to try it out on?'"

Jay took one of those cases you keep film in from his pocket and shook out three white pills. Something about their purity — the dead white of fridges — against Jay's dark palm tweaked at my nerves. The voicebox was unnerving me too.

"Fuck, I dunno Kimi, I'm a bit battered from the weekend to be honest. I was thinking more along the lines of a nice single malt and a bit of a lie down." The voice came naturally now, with its veins of condescension and boredom.

She shook her head. "I don't think so. You're ordering Kevlar vests and fake passports. It sounds like the weekend is just getting started, so I think you can make some time for me. Besides, it's a pretty short high apparently. Jay?" Even as she spoke to him her eyes stayed trained on me.

Jay did that Michael Jackson moonwalk thing across the floor to us. "Couple of hours tops. Something for our cash-rich, time-poor customers, you get me?"

"Anyway," Kimi took the pill and examined it, "where's the fun in knowing what's going to happen next anyway?"

Before switching on the camera she tied a black silk scarf around her neck, just about shielding the voicebox from view. Her hair covered her eyes and thick-rimmed glasses. The laptop showed a site: a series of webcams, men mostly, and scrolling text. I guessed this was the place she'd shown Brandon all that time ago. She typed in the details of the drug and its dose, our names — we were to be Don and Miki apparently — and that she welcomed passengers on the trip.

Jay skulked outside the sightlines of the camera, working his way through the pile of records in the living room and rolling joint after joint. "For after, innit."

I toyed with the idea of hiding the pill under my tongue but when the moment came both of them watched me so closely that I had no choice but to swallow. I felt an immediate shiver and it took me a second to realise it was just the phone buzzing in my pocket.

I peeked: a message from Rae — WHERE U @ KUSSGARTEN? — and Kimi shot me a look over the glasses.

"Phones off for a bit I think. Need you present, know what I mean?"

I nodded and switched the ringer off without answering. Instead I let Rae's morning routine run at the back of my mind as a kind of mantra. Now she's at the mirror, now she's slicing Robin's sandwiches *at an angle please mom*, now she's flapping as the oatmeal boils over. I let her day unspool as I edged across the couch until I was off camera.

Jay pushed a button and slatted blinds descended noisily across all three windows. Thin shafts of light bisected the room, making Kimi's face a camouflage of stripes.

It's an odd feeling, waiting for something to happen to your mind. I kept a watch over my thoughts like a general who was nervous of mutinous troops, and my heart hammered at several false alarms. A flutter of wings on the balcony, movements in the shadows, was it beginning? Thank god I'd been doing coke. I'd recognise the change now, the way you thought nothing was happening until it had already happened.

Kimi chatted away on the site via text. She had an earpiece in so I only saw her side of the conversations.

"No, never tried it, I'm nervous of hallucinogens."

"Like trying to drive a car, in reverse, with a shattered rear-view mirror."

"Everyone says that. I'm hotter than her though, dontcha think? She's kind of chubby." She gave me a happy wink.

The wings started up again. A rattle like a fly against a window and then a chattering inrush of air. Kimi adjusted her scarf. I turned to face her, keeping my voice low. "They must know it's you, surely?"

"Some of them, probably. They know, and I know they know, and they know I know they know. But these are people who understand you might need a holiday from yourself every now and then. You understand that, don't you, Brandon? Being an actor and all."

The voicebox flattened her intonation. Was she being sarcastic about the acting? Did she know? Something drummed against the window. Why didn't Jay go and investigate? Instead he took the needle carefully from a record and put another on.

Kimi talked to me as she typed. "You know what it's like to stand on the other side of yourself." It was a statement, not a question.

The tapping of her nails on the keyboard sounded huge. She turned back to the camera and watched some of the people on the site. I caught a glimpse of the small window in the corner that showed the scene here and moved out of shot again. She gave me a long, unfathomable look and then cocked an ear to the record playing. Something familiar, old.

"Jay! You old sap. You like this? You even know this?"

He grinned, dancing one half of a waltz. His feet traced a triangle with an elegant, sliding backstep and he beckoned Kimi with a nod. She pulled herself up, grumbling, and joined him in a slow shuffle, his head laid incongruously on her shoulder.

I felt more watched now than when she had been beside me. The green light of the laptop camera glowed, beaming the image of an empty room back to the world as they circled around together, not talking.

There was a shutting down, like being inside a concertina, as everything flattened and darkened. The edges of my vision blurred. I moved my head this way and that, keeping Jay and Kimi in the centre of the frame, making an old-fashioned painting of them. The record sounded like it was coming from another planet: *Your clothes are all made by Balmain and there's diamonds and pearls in your hair*

I heard scurrying. Tiny nails tripping beneath the floorboards and around the skirting. I followed their path: kitchen, lounge, hallway. Kim and Jay slow-wheeled, every third step bringing them back to first positions. There was something mechanical about it. Step, step, step and back. Identical each time. A film loop.

"What?" Kimi had hold of my arm, twisting me towards her. "What?"

I hadn't realised I was talking. I hadn't realised she was back beside me. The laptop camera's light glowed green. *I see you.*

"I can see the machinery." A voice. My voice? My voice.

There, behind her right eye. Delicate cog-work, thinner even than a watch's movement, ticking to and fro. I saw her cheek twitch and wondered which subtle cylinder was misfiring beneath the skin. I stood up and reached out to touch it but she reared back.

"Woah. Hands off B-boy."

I nodded but kept an eye on the spot that had moved. It might need to be debugged.

Jay danced on alone — step, step, step — and I focussed on her neck. The scarf had slipped and the voicebox glowed dully in stray bands of light. I'd deliberately ignored it before but as her eyes fluttered closed I took a closer look. It was a curved golden grill that protruded slightly from the skin of her neck, joined by puckered and pale scar tissue. It was beautifully made, I could see that now, with the fluid lines of a Bentley grill. I had to stop myself from reaching out to touch it.

We were standing face to face as Kimi tipped her head back and the voicebox glinted.

"Hey, my eyes are up here," she said, and then laughed. She pulled the scarf back up over her neck and then sang along with the record in a colourless voice.

"Where do you go to my lovely?"

I shook my head, unsure of what she meant. She was talking at the screen now but I thought the words were meant for me. A circuit of scratches ran behind the walls. The room darkened and lightened, like a giant had stepped past the window outside. She'd kicked her heels off and was my height suddenly.

"You come back here all cock of the walk, which I don't suppose is any surprise, and I think to myself, oh we can have some fun with him now, now his fangs are drawn."

She looked at me and snapped her jaw shut which made me flinch. Little noises flashed right to left behind me. I forced myself not to back away.

"Now his fangs are drawn," she repeated. "But, bless you, you realise that you don't have a lot to bring to the table any more so you have a plan and a story and an idea and I listen because, y'know, desperation can do interesting things to a man."

The screen flickered beside us and I wondered how much of this was being picked up. Jay sat in the other room with his elbows on his knees, watching. Lights brightened and dimmed, brightened and dimmed. The wingbeats slowed until they made the whole room pulse.

"And I have to say you did put the hours in, you always were a hard worker, and it's like we're building something and I'm thinking that it isn't half bad, y'know the boy's got something, now that his mind is focussed." Her voice lowered and in a whisper she said, "Death'll do that huh? Focus the mind?"

I couldn't answer. My vision throbbed like a vein. She went on, "So I pay the bills and put you right and smooth things over with the rest of the band." She examined me. "I had to pay them to spend time with you. Like you were a punter. Not something to be proud of really." She cocked her head. "And then you disappear again and I think fair enough, man probably has some things to put in order. Last wishes and all that. But three days becomes four and seven days becomes eight and I start to think you've done a runner. Which, though it's what we all expected, would be disappointing because without this thing that we have, there's really nothing to you Bran."

She tapped me gently on the forehead with a manicured nail. "Hollow man, see? Just another old white guy who doesn't know why no one is listening any more. And then you come back. Yay!" She mimed girlish surprise. "But since you've been back... I don't know. I'm sensing a lack of drive to you Bran, a lack of focus."

I couldn't work out whether the drugs were affecting her the way they were me. Her forehead and neck were damp with sweat, and between sentences her mouth seemed to move of its own accord, but her eyes were steady.

She put on a gravelly voice. "He never writes, he never calls. So I'm thinking that this little project has gone off the rails a bit." She took a step closer and placed her hands on my shoulders. "Has it Bran? Gone off the rails?"

I tried to force certain facts to the front of my mind but it was like moving heavy furniture. "No Kimi... I have not gone off the rails." I stopped and then realised I had to say more. "There are things that need to be done before the things that *need* to get done, get done, y'know?"

She didn't look like she did.

"This is a... a project where things have to fall like dominoes." I toppled a hand from vertical to horizontal. "There has to be an order, and rigour and y'know." The room seemed to empty of air, as if we were in the updraft of some vast wing, leaving me breathless.

She considered this. "Bran, it looks to me like there's only one domino that still needs to fall. It's such a little thing. I mean, I've paid, and lent, and talked and helped and there's only one thing that you have to do. And let's face it, it's the simplest thing."

She came a half-step closer — her eyes level with mine, our mouths inches apart — and placed both hands on my chest.

A stammer of light. Claws and feathers. Something trapped behind the walls.

"So simple, we all do it one day."

Her voice like machinery. Knife-lights and feather-blows.

She pushed and I rocked back on my heels, beginning to fall.

Moths' wings on a lightbulb. Bones in a mouse's nest. The floor rising up to catch me.

"The easiest thing in the world."

And then it was over. Not the sensations: the blinds still periodically darkened as if huge birds were swooping past, and my heart rate raced and slowed but I was over the hump. The world was normal with flashes of the surreal rather than the other way round and Kimi obviously felt it too. No more questions, no more traps. She leaned against the couch, blowing smoke rings my way.

Rain beat gentle drums on the windows. Jay played a game with himself, placing a felt-bottomed chess piece on the record as it spun and snatching it up again before it hit the arm. A soft tap every second under the music. *The first time* thump *ever I saw* thump *your face*. It felt like a childhood Sunday: lazy but with a shadow hanging over it.

Kimi's voice was steady. "Is it that last track that's holding you back? Still no ideas?"

I shook my head mutely. The record finished and clicked off. Jay held up two album covers. "What next Kimi?"

She fired a smaller smoke ring to chase the larger. "Bran can choose. I've got music fatigue."

Jay waggled the two covers in my direction. For once I recognised one. David Bowie, done up like a boxer. Something we'd had at home.

"The Bowie, I think." Safely back into Bran's drawl. On top of things.

But something pricked Kimi's attention as Jay moonwalked back to the record player. She held up a hand to Jay. "One sec hun." She twisted to watch me.

"Say that again Bran."

Fuck. It was David Bowie wasn't it? I could see the logo in my mind — the cassette version we'd listened to in the car. I was sure it was him. "The Bowie, darling." I tried again.

He dropped the needle. It was a track that even I knew. And definitely a Bowie song. I relaxed. It was poppy — a welcome relief after some of Jay's picks — and it sounded like car drives and workmen's radios. Kimi hummed along.

"Great guitar there. Garson or Alomar d'you think?"

I felt nauseous. I tried to brush the question off. "The guitar? Who cares about the fucking guitar. Listen to that voice."

Kimi sat up, now plainly watching me. "Yeah, the man has some pipes all right. We should skip to 'Under Pressure', now that's some singing. Which track is it?"

I rubbed my temples. "Jesus, Kimi. I can't even remember my own name at the moment. That stuff was lethal." Don't whine, I told myself.

She propped her chin on her hands. "Doesn't matter, it'll wait." She watched me.

"I might have a little doze," I told her, desperately.

"In a minute." The voice box shot the words out staccato, with equal stress. Jay watched from the lounge, aware that something was going on. She asked, "What's the only good Radiohead album, Bran?"

Silence. I actually did feel sick. My stomach churned.

"Where did we steal REM's rider again, you remember that show?"

Something twisted deep in my gut, down where there are no nerve endings. A heat rose in my throat.

"Who put the ram in the rama lama ding dong Bran?"

I held up a hand to fend her off and then stood up and headed for the bathroom. It was lined with mirrors. I knelt in front of the bowl and began to retch. A thin liquid the colour of straw.

The door opened behind me. Kimi knelt beside me and stroked my hair. "There, let it out."

My back arched but nothing came.

"The thing is," her hand was cool on the back of my neck. "I don't think you're so wrecked that you forgot how to pronounce Bowie." She said it bo-ee and I retched again. "You were kind of a stickler about that back in the day."

My head throbbed.

"Or that Mike Garson plays piano, not guitar. Or that 'Under Pressure' isn't on that album."

I spat, trying to clear the strands of acid drool.

"I mean you'd literally forget your own name before something like that."

Her touch was like someone stroking a dog: friendly, thoughtless. She took a clump of my hair and pulled me to face her, but gently. I couldn't hold her gaze.

"So what's going on?"

I wiped my hand across my mouth. I went to speak but I had no idea what to say. She looked closer. And then it happened.

"Fuuuuuuuuuuuck." The hand stopped. The voicebox quieter than ever. I heard my name, my secret name, across two small syllables. "Ad-am?"

We'd met before. I didn't remember it but Kimi did. As I sat in the kitchen, wrapped in a blanket like an invalid, Kimi and Jay examined me.

"The Venue, New Cross. It was supposed to be full of A&R because Fabulous were headlining so it was a three-line whip for getting people along. Bran introduced you as his 'stunt double'. You were nice, nervy. You liked my shoes."

It was possible. Going backstage always gave me panic attacks, I would have spent the whole time counting the seconds before I could safely leave. And she did have nice shoes.

In fits and starts I told them everything that had happened but it sounded ridiculous as I put it all together. Brandon's plan: how he was to have taken my place, the incompetence of Ron and Reg, my spur-of-the-moment decision to become him. They didn't look convinced. Finally I found the CCTV of Brandon's shooting on my phone and showed them. That was easier than trying to convince them that this wasn't some hallucinated story.

At the end of it, with Brandon just a dark smear on the ground, they went off together and talked in low voices in the kitchen. When they came back they switched everything off. The music and the cameras: dead. The blinds were turned so tight that it was like a black box in the lounge.

Kimi asked, "Why? Why are you doing this?"

I told them about Rae and Robin. I'd not said a word to anyone about them so it came out in a deluge, an outpouring like a mirror image of the ten minutes in the bathroom. I ranted about the stolen mortgage and how Brandon had betrayed them, their humiliation and poverty and my determination to use Brandon's selfishness to build them a new life.

Kimi's first reaction was, "Bran has a *kid*? Poor, poor fucker." But her features softened. "So why are you still here? You've told them what happened?"

"Of course."

She had a way of looking at you very directly. When I looked away she placed a hand on my chin and forced me to look back at her. She pushed my quiff away from my eyes.

"But there's more." Her eyes darted around my face. "You want them. You want to be with them. Is that it?"

Yes yes yes yes yes yes. Like steam escaping. *Yes yes yes yes yes*. Saying it out loud made it real. The idea was a building you could step inside and walk around. *Yes yes yes yes yes*. Yes, I want to be with them. Yes, I want to be there.

"I do, but I had things to take care of. Things of his that needed finishing so that they'd be sorted whether I were there or not."

Her smile widened. "Oh, Baxter's Beach Boys thing."

Bran's protective cloak was in tatters now. I'd vomited him away back there. I just wanted to lie there and talk it all out. "And a legal thing, with Saul."

Kimi's gaze was relentless. Her eyes searched my face for some sign that only she could interpret. "The *Smile* record is done, Baxter told me that. And Jay tells me that you've already been to see Saul. Why are you still here?"

My mouth was dry however much water I drank. "I'm not done yet. I need to finish him." I tried to hold her gaze.

"Finish him? The way it was supposed to end?"

I nodded. "There's a way. But there's another thing." Something had been nagging at me for the last few days and now, with Kimi in front of me, I could put into words.

"I want that last track done. I'm going to finish it. I'm going to reclaim it for them." The idea had come to me reading Brandon's notes. I would complete the track that had eluded him and the record would belong to me.

Kimi let out a deep sigh, as if she'd been holding her breath all this time. "And that kept you here. You risked everything for a piece of music. You're not *that* unlike him."

The rest of the night was a blur of movement. Jay was in and out every hour, constantly on the phone. After a flurry of texts we connected the Tahoe feed up to the TV so Rae could be involved. She and Kimi circled each other like cats: wary but intrigued. A call roused Ron and Reg from a warehouse party in Bethnal Green and they sat perched on the couch, clearly in awe of Kimi.

It was out of my hands. Six of us on the fiftieth floor: three unlikely couples with one thing to plan. The meat of the idea was mine, the creative touches came from Rae, but it was Kimi and Jay who made things happen. This had become a show and they knew how to put on a show.

When everything was as organised as it was ever going to be Kimi's driver took me back to Notting Hill. The post was piled high, topped with three letters from the Residents' Association: a complaint about excessive noise and out-of-hours construction work, an urgent query over the status of the registered owner, headed simply *Deceased?* and finally, inevitably, an eviction notice.

The flat was huge without Umbrage but it was empty and warm and there was a sleeping bag. I slept, unmoving, for ten straight hours. When I woke my phone showed twenty missed calls: Kimi, Jay, the residents' association. A text from Robin read simply, "We are here".

There were stale Pop Tarts in the fridge and I ate two of them raw while sitting on the toilet. My energy was returning. Not Brandon's catherine-wheel energy, spinning and spitting but never actually getting anywhere, but a builder's energy. The feeling that each brick you placed told you where the next one would go.

I had phone conversations with model-makers about stress tests and leverage ratios while I walked the Thames' eastern bridges and measured handrails. I visited sports shops and chandlers, and picked up the Kevlar vest that Jay had found me. I left Kimi to arrange the recording session, which might have been a mistake. She booked Hot Action, not knowing my history with the place. The symmetry of the thing was very Brandonesque, but whoever it was who'd left that window open hadn't sounded like he wanted to see me again. Momentum would have to carry me through.

I racked out lines in a McDonald's bathroom and took one of the TLAs that Jay had recommended. When I closed my eyes there was a noise like a river and the tick of metal feet. They pushed me onwards. I booked tickets on three different flights, allowing for the alternate ways this might play out. I sent Robin ideas for New Umbrage and as I walked I could see his streets overlaid onto London's tired old stone.

Hot Action felt very different by daylight. I followed a blinking neon sign reading **XXX ACTION INSIDE** down a dingy alley. At its end people crowded a lobby, concentrated around a table of drinks. Music was muffled by the glass frontage. I almost lost my nerve, but a combination of Brandon, the coke and those robot rhythms pulled me inside. There were too many faces, too many unknown faces, but by the back wall I recognised Kimi's blade of hair. She was a head taller than most of the men and gratefully I shouldered my way through to her. She gave me air kisses and placed a hand on my forearm with a look of concern. I faded the crowd from my mind and anchored myself onto her.

"Play nice, I didn't know that he'd be here," she whispered, and then a pair of hands spun me round.

"You talentless cocksucker."

The face was too close. Hat, glasses that were shaped like sunglasses but with clear lenses, bad skin like orangepeel and a beard that looked drawn on. But smiling, beaming even.

I looked back at Kimi and he kept talking. "You know you should have booked the place yourself, there's a special rate for unknowns."

He waited, obviously expecting a reply. A girl at his side giggled nervously. Kimi mouthed "Dillon" at me as the silence lengthened.

Finally I said, "Well I figured I owed you some back rent."

He blinked, then grabbed my arm, delighted. "Water under the bridge Brannie, forget about it. Come on, let's go and make some magic."

He steered me through the crowd, taking Kimi by the other arm. She towered above him and even I was a head taller; it felt like we were taking a kid for a walk.

We made our way through the studio with Dillon providing a running commentary. "These are the writing cubicles. We've got nearly twenty guys working here at one time, all semi-freelance. Kind of like a twenty-first century Brill Building. We do stuff for Rhianna, Katy Perry, Sugababes — all those people. I keep trying to get this cutie here to do some writing, eh Kimi?"

Her face was a mask. "That he does."

Double doors led to the old section of the studio and I recognised the layout now. Dillon had a nod and a word for anyone who walked past, as much for our benefit as theirs, I thought. He walked us along the curved corridor into the circular studio room. It looked far less sinister today. Even lit by the signs that ringed the walls — GIRL-ON-GIRL, NEW MODEL, HOT COCK ACTION — it was recognisably a workplace. A barefoot teenager was tuning up a guitar on one of the stools.

"Hey Deano, I'll take it from here." Dillon picked up the guitar and the boy scurried away.

"Good kid," he said as the boy left the room. "He's a rapper, and a damn good 'un, but I like to make sure they have a grounding in all aspects here." Again he waited. I was beginning to enjoy the awkward silences but Kimi looked pained.

"So, Kimi played me the track, it's sounding good. Didn't think you had it in you Bran."

He strummed a chord sequence on the guitar, something from the verse.

"Uh, thanks. Yeah I think we've really got something. But it's going to be the last track, and this idea just came to me." Brandon's archness was eluding me today. There was another silence.

"Here, look at this." Dillon's face lit up as he handed me the biggest mobile phone I'd ever seen. "Here, scroll down. Look."

He wore rings on every finger — ornate, gothic things — and I couldn't help looking at them rather than the screen. Skull, bird's head, eyeball.

"What do you think of that?" He was pointing to a text. Under "sender" it read NELSON MANDELA. He didn't show me the body of the message.

"Cool, I guess." I wasn't sure what he wanted me to say.

"Talking about this charity thing we did in South Africa. We put pianos in five hundred school classrooms. And, get this, all the keys were black."

He flicked through his phone. "Got one from Aretha here somewhere."

Kimi touched my arm again. "Brandon, Dillon has kindly offered to produce the session today." There was a flash of warning in her eyes.

"Oh great. That's very kind. But y'know, anyone would be fine."

Kimi was falling over herself to agree. "An engineer would do. Or a tape op even. We know exactly what we want."

Dillon waved her away. "We'll have an engineer for the grunt work. But a project like yours needs a creative to sprinkle a little fairy dust." He pointed two thumbs at himself.

"I said we'd be happy to do it ourselves." The voicebox flattened any nuance there might have been in the sentence but her eyes were fixed on me.

But there was a note of finality in Dillon's voice. "Nonsense, wouldn't hear of it."

We set up in silence. The kid came back to man the mixing desk, moving faders and patching cables. He gestured to the headphones and I put mine on. His voice was unpleasantly intimate in my ears. "Something like this?"

The track started playing. Three pairs of eyes on me. Dillon, Dean, Kimi.

Everything fluttered and strobed in my headphones, like helicopter blades. I looked at Dillon and Kimi. They seemed unconcerned.

"Yeah it sounds fine."

"No changes to the mix?"

"No, let's go with that."

Kimi leaned in so the microphone was at her neck level. "You're going to lose the organ, yeah? It's a guide."

I felt a stutter building and dark liquid rising. "Um, yeah." Trying to keep the question out of my voice.

"If I could?" Dillon's voice, not waiting for a response. "Could we roll some top off the SG? It's eating up the vocal space. Just a gnat's. And Bran? The delay on the piano? Is it printed? Because it sounds out to me."

Three pairs of eyes. Far-off helicopters. Air bubbles in thick oil.

"It's supposed to be that way." I tried not to sound petulant. Remembering something Brandon had quoted in his videos I said, "It's just wrong enough."

Dillon held his hands up. "You're the boss-man, boss-man."

There was an electronic four-count and the track started up. In the headphones I could hear beauty in it for the first time. Every line suggested the next. The melody and the chords pulled it far from home but then, every verse, back it came like a key in a lock. It pushed back at the pressure behind my eyes, balancing me on tiptoes. Up, up, on, and back. I closed my eyes and let my head hang down.

The track stopped. "Your line Bran." Dillon looked amused. Kimi, less so.

"Sorry, yes." I brought myself back. "I was, um, enjoying that."

"From the top?" The engineer's voice.

"From the top."

I'd gone back to Kimi's original lyrics. Brandon had rewritten them with a verse each for Kimi, Saul, Baxter and him, but I wanted the cornerstone of his record to be something he'd had no hand in. Kimi's chords and verse, my voice and, at its centre, in the space that he'd died still unable to fill, a line of Rae's that had haunted me since she'd first said it.

I smoothed out my lyric sheet in front of me. I should have been more nervous than I was I suppose; I hadn't sung since I was a kid. But the tide rose in me like seasickness and the inevitable cycle of chords was a gentle push in my back.

Eastern religions, signs from the deep, skin dripping oceans, too little sleep

I croaked it out. My voice sounded thin in the headphones and I felt the room's attention round on me.

Imaginary cities, cells in the sky, Astanga, the Buddha, high-life in lo-fi

I couldn't find the note. It was virtually a spoken-word piece yet still I was off-key. Kimi made a signal to the engineer and the song halted. She looked worried, Dillon intrigued.

"You OK there Bran? Big night?"

"Fine, just…" my voice tailed off. The rotor noise in my head thickened and slowed.

"Shall we try the voicebox? Like I suggested?"

I had no idea what she meant. "Sure, like we suggested."

She unplugged the lead from the mike and brought it up to her throat. On the underside of the voicebox there was the thinnest of sockets. She connected an adaptor to the cable. "Closer," she said.

I stood facing her and she placed the mike in front of me. "Speak."

I started to talk. An Umbrage story. *In the third year of the Raven, after forty days of rain.*

As I spoke she began to move her mouth silently. She pursed her lips and opened wide, her tongue tapped her teeth and all the while her eyes were on my lips. The words I spoke began to alter with the timing of her movements. They glided into a key, thickened and split, doubled and trebled and then tumbled down into something from a horror movie. It was beautiful and it was terrifying.

"Sing," she ordered, and I went back to the lyric sheet.

> *One part obsession, one pinch of denial*
> *Ambition and envy and a crocodile's smile*
> *Speaking in tongues when the machines have the mike*
> *A loop from snuff-film with one million likes*

All I provided was the rhythm, the rest was all her. The plaintive melody with its descending downwards run at the end. The repetitions and echoes, the ghostly spin-offs that thinned and multiplied and soared and plummeted. She mixed in gravel and helium, sandpaper and silk.

"OK." She closed her eyes for a second. "From the top."

We were so close that I could see every movement of her throat. She caressed and repositioned my voice and it was like being carried as a child, taken, barely awake, in your father's arms up to sleep.

> *Women are bullets and men are the guns*
> *Dark aspects, dead planets round collapsing suns*
> *Mouths are still moving long after they're dead*
> *Women are nooses, men shots to the head*

I'd emailed her the new chorus but I had no idea if she had learned it, so when we reached that point I pulled the mike close again. She was ready though and as our voices meshed she raised an eyebrow. Then, on the second time round, we were joined by Dillon. There we were, the three of us. Me gruff — a flatlining vocal that was there for padding as much as anything. Kimi, on some voice box setting that made her glide from one note to another like a violin, and Dillon with a surprisingly sweet, soulful tone. Three voices splitting and recombining, passing each other then coming together for the last word.

"This is what you get instead of love." The last word stretched out, stepping down, like a bride down church steps, hem in hand, *tap tap tap* to the final note. And again, once more.

We did it twice. Me speaking the verses with Kimi playing me like an instrument, the three of us on the chorus, and by the end the throb of blades in my head made the track sound like white noise. I was following more by Kimi's breaths than by the words and I didn't trust myself to do another take.

"That's it, I'm done."

I pushed the headphones back around my neck and Kimi unhitched the cable from her throat without meeting my eye.

Dillon nodded. "Intense. Do you want to cut it now?"

I glanced over at the machine. I couldn't look at Kimi, it felt so intimate. "No time like the present, I guess?"

Dillon pressed a button. "Deano, can you come to the cutting room?"

He pulled his stool next to mine, an inch too close. He wore a heavy, fruity scent.

"This is the way to do it, huh? So pure. Inspiration to physical product in…" he checked his watch, "Two hours. Like they did it in the early days." He fiddled with his rings.

"I've got some Robert Johnson acetates upstairs that he cut in one of those down-south recording booths. Just him and a guitar. Cost me a pretty penny." A pause. "Ask me how much."

I shrugged, "How much?"

"Half a mill. Worth it though. They're the greatest artworks of the twentieth century."

He flicked through his phone. It was a habit every time there was the briefest lull in the conversation.

"Look, Mark Zuckerberg. He gave a TED talk where he said that saving those recordings was as big a deal as saving the whale. Or something."

I felt a deep tiredness. I wanted to be done with these people and their complications.

I fingered the memory stick in my pocket. "Could you cut a whole album?"

He blinked and took off his glasses. "Sure, if you've got the masters."

I held up the memory stick. "Right now?"

"Of course right now, come on."

He walked me through to the cutting room. I caught the smell of that night with Baxter: hot metal and PVC. Kimi waited outside, talking on her phone.

"Deano, can you cue up a blank disc?"

"Sure can boss-man." I caught a hint of Dillon's voice in Dean's. Unconscious imitation or a subtle dig? Dillon tossed him the memory stick.

"Are the tracks in sequence?" Dean was asking Dillon rather than me. He looked over.

"Yeah, all set up and ready to go. Just add that last one on the end."

We sat together on a nubbly brown sofa, again slightly too close, but there was something comfortingly technical about the room — the heat and hum of machinery. Dillon alternated between listening, talking to me, and checking his phone.

"I like this one. It's kind of Beatles-y." He sang along, his voice floating over the track.

"I worked with McCartney a while back on a mobile phone launch. We did a show in Red Square." He started flicking through his texts. "I've got his number here, see?"

He blinked like it was too bright and cocked his head to the tune playing. "You think about doing this one a bit faster? Just a couple of bpm. I think it'd tighten it up some."

He tapped out a beat on the sofa's wooden arm and then turned to face me. "Maybe it needs a remix."

I wished he'd stop talking. Just holding my face the way that Brandon did was giving me a headache.

"Are you still doing remixes?"

There was nothing casual in that question. His shoulders hunched in the silence. I wanted a line.

"Nah, I told you, this is me retiring."

The tracks played on. Each one was time-stamped with the moment that Rae and I first heard them together. They came with built-in visuals: the subtle electricity of her face, the bloom of wrinkles around her eyes as she laughed, the guilty hand across the mouth, those heart-breaking nails — painted and bitten, bitten and painted — and the anarchy of her hair.

I realised that "our tune" would probably have to be "The First Footprint in Fresh Snow" which made me laugh to myself; Dillon took that as his cue.

"So, you know anything about this *Smile* acetate?"

I looked away from the cutting machine. "Acetate?"

"You're not on the forums anymore? I know your pal Baxter is. Word is he's found the motherlode. From the original tapes, whole shebang."

I was tied up in knots calculating what Brandon knew and how he'd play it with this man. "Sounds exciting."

Dillon pressed his face close to mine. His weirdly pocked and lineless face, like the surface of a basketball.

"Exciting? Exciting? It's the fucking Holy Grail. Make him come to me first if it's true."

"I will. But he hasn't mentioned it."

I don't think he realised how tightly he was gripping my wrist. "But he would come to you, I'm sure."

Kimi was out in the corridor, still on the phone. I waved to her, hoping she'd catch my distress.

Dillon kept looking directly at me as if the answers would show on my face. I forced myself to look back. He nodded at me, as if we'd decided something.

"Good man, good man. Hey, you want to see a picture of me and Mick?"

Kimi stood in the doorway. The light behind her made her look almost sculptural.

"Are you boys done catching up?"

"Just about. I'm getting Dillon's guy to cut the whole album for us."

She walked me into the corridor and shook her head.

"I know it's fun to fuck around with him but he always lands on his feet. He'll find a way to make this about him, I just know it."

I nodded. I didn't care. All that was important was movement; it didn't matter in which direction. I found an empty bathroom and did a line to quell the blood-throb in my head.

When I came out Kimi was back on her phone. Dillon drummed his fingers on the glass and mouthed, "all finished".

The acetate was still warm in its plain white sleeve. Someone had written "unnamed Kimi/Kuss project. marksman productions" in Magic Marker across the top and Kimi rolled her eyes at me.

"Let's talk as we walk." Dillon had me by the wrist again and was ignoring Kimi. His voice was low.

"What about your other little pal, Saul?" He steered me along the corridor back the way we'd come. "I hear rumblings that he might be getting lawyered up. Is that anything to do with you?"

"Why?"

"I don't know why do I? That's why I'm asking. You come back with your tail between your legs and suddenly all your little indie pals have got schemes on the go. Someone's rattled their cages. When you see him, tell him even my lawyers have better lawyers than he does."

My blood pulsed in time with each step. It was easier to channel Brandon while we were moving. *Downhill downhill.* Poison in the bones. Acid in the cells.

I reversed Dillon's grip, grabbing his fat wrist.

"Even the best lawyers in the world aren't going to stop him if he wants to sue. It's his fucking tune. He knows it, I know it…" I tightened my grip and forced my face closer to his. There was a smell of violets. "And you know it. He just didn't have the law on his side before."

His face was fifty-fifty triumph and despair. He'd been right about something he'd wanted to be wrong about.

The next day. The last day. A few hours of sleep in the ruins of the Notting Hill flat. An eviction notice was plastered on the wall outside and white tape criss-crossed the doorway. Sunlight struggled through thin curtains. The clock on the microwave flashed 00:00. And an unknown number set my mobile rattling across the floorboards.

I answered, my lips and eyes gummed closed.

"Yeah."

"It's Dillon. How much does he want, Saul?"

The light made my eyes ache and I pulled the sleeping bag over my head.

"I thought he didn't stand a chance?"

"He doesn't. But I still don't want my dirty laundry aired in court. Some of us still have a reputation you know. So how much?"

Brandon had told Saul a quarter of a million. But that was probably pumped up to get him interested. So £125,000? An idea stole over me. "He wants £66,000."

Dillon didn't bother keep the relief out of his voice. "OK, I can manage that. Weird amount."

"He's into numerology," I improvised. "It's a figure with magical qualities."

"Great, great. What a fucking muppet. How do I know he won't still sue?"

"I'll get him to sign something. I have to be out on Eel Pie Island at 5 o'clock. Can you meet me there?"

"Today? Sure. Wait, where's fucking Eel Pie Island, can't we meet at Soho House?"

"Look it up for fuck's sake. That's where I have to be. Let's get this over with."

The blood throbbed through my head in a way that set my vision trembling every ten seconds or so. I went to take a shower but the water was off.

Packages started arriving around 10am. They were from high-street clothes shops and theatrical costumiers, all already paid for after Rae and Kimi had bonded over the costumes last night. The crow headdresses were to be the centrepiece but they'd styled the rest.

I laid the deliveries out on the floorboards. FRANKIE SAYS CHOOSE LIFE T-shirts. Adidas three-stripe bottoms. Cherry-red Doc Martins. One eye each of fake eyelashes that Kimi sent over. Long black coats. It was a bonfire of symbols, meaningful on the surface, empty at its core. Perfect for Brandon.

Ronnie and Reggie turned up at noon. If they saw anything strange about trying on costumes amid the wasteland of a wrecked twentieth floor flat, under the direction of the man they were about to shoot and his dead brother's girlfriend, they gave no sign. The flat echoed to their yelps as they fought about whose headdress was nicer, and cooed over the eyelashes. Once they had the DMs laced up tight the pair of them chicken-danced around the flat, arms on each other's shoulders, throwing themselves this way and that. Then they crammed into the little bathroom preparing for the big reveal and I could hear them bickering as they made final adjustments. Their clothes laid in piles on the floor. I took Ron's phone from his jacket and retreated to the far corner of the kitchen to call Dillon.

I set up the meeting again and gave him clearer directions. He already knew where he was going but I wanted a call of a decent length to have come from Ron's number if anyone were to check his phone records later. After I hung up I sent him a text too, a text that I whittled away at until it could be read as though it had come from Ron rather than me. "£66,000 and he's dead in the water. And you're protected."

They came out hand in hand, once I'd tuned the clock radio to Kiss FM for their catwalk soundtrack. Ragged crow-men. Death in casualwear. They paraded up and down with lips set to permanent pouts and hands on hips. I cradled the laptop in my arms so Rae could see her creation, and her round of applause brought deep bows from both of them.

From the speaker her voice was full of joy. "If that's not every cool kid's Hallowe'en costume this year then I'm losing my touch."

Once they'd left I lay on the floor and watched her at work in Tahoe.

"Ready?" She turned her face sideways to look at me more clearly.

"Ready." I was. Everything was in place. "An hour until I leave, I don't know what to do with myself suddenly."

"Well, I found one more thing of Brandon's online. It just came up in a google search last night. It's comments on a video for sale on a Japanese site, I'll send it to you."

I switched over to the laptop and clicked on the link she'd sent. A hand-held video started up. People milling around a small venue, a few side-eyeing the cameraman. That low hubbub of something about to happen. On the screen Rae moved around the kitchen, singing something to herself. I clicked off Brandon's video: I could watch that any time.

OU Kids

The following is a transcription of a comment under a bootleg live video for sale on a Japanese website. The whole site is in Japanese, bar the prices and the following text.

Well, here's a surprise. I had no idea there was footage from this, the final and most ill-fated of Remote/Control gigs. I've never seen as much as a still photo of the night; by this stage a band that'd been around as long as us — two whole years of striving — was irredeemably passé. Newer and shinier bands came along leaving us on the highest of shelves and not getting any cooler. Unsigned bands, like porn stars, have to break big in the first eighteen months or accept that they're going to have to do the degrading stuff to get noticed. Hence this night, a showcase. (For those of you fortunate enough to not know what that is, a showcase is a kind of artificial gig, paid for by the band, with enough cash behind the bar to attract down that particular mix of jaded alcoholics which makes up the London A&R community, a community that will spend the entire gig up at the bar bitching about their colleagues. Thus you get the deadest of atmospheres at the precise moment the band need it to be at its wildest, making the whole point of the exercise — to get a deal — even unlikelier than before.) So why do it? Because we were fucked, broke, unhappy, hungover, bored, jealous and worst of all, profoundly in debt to the label who had given us £2,000 for a "development deal" that we — read I — had spent on clothes, booze and this godforsaken gig. This was a shameless flirt for some major label to buy out our contract.

The video's two-figure view-count is an indication of how little interest there is in a Remote/Control gig today, but for those of you thinking *what the hell is this shit* I thought I'd provide a spot of director's commentary: Ladies and Gentlemen, I give you the death of Remote/Control.

0:10 Shonky title page in Japanese. The text looks more comprehensive than the English but I'm buggered if I'm going to run it through Google Translate. It's the Borderline, just off Charing Cross Road, and it's late in 1994, that much I'm sure of.

0:20 The cameraman takes a swing through the crowd. Scant is the word I would use. Thin would fit just as well. Sparse. Patchy. Disappointing. Underwhelming. It's a mix of the less savvy A&R men who didn't realise that everyone important had already passed on us, hopeless out-of-towners, confused foreigners and Remote/Control regulars (a cohort so tiny that they could comfortably fit in a phone box). Oh, and Dillon Marksman. Look, at 0:25, that's him, with his entourage of hangers-on, doing what he does best: checking out those more talented than him and working out a way to boil down their bones into snake oil.

0:30 More crowd shots. A wild track of the camera past backs of heads onto a blur of empty stage. Get it focused dude, that's my career ending up there. The ratio of punters waiting by the stage to those queuing at the bar is around 1:12. And there's the semi-circle of doom: that patch of bare dance floor neighbouring the stage which no one dares to visit for fear of being infected by the air of decline coming from the very idea of Remote/Control.

0:45 Our intro music: Vaughn Williams' "A Lark Ascending". We'd stolen that idea (like so many others) from The Smiths, who played 'Romeo and Juliet' before they came on, lending the stage an air of drama and grandeur. Here it just sounds like someone's left Classic FM on.

0:55 The sound of a crowd erupting: cheers, whistles, a vast surge of almost sexual excitement that breaks like a wave across the audience, whipping them on to even greater fury....

1:00 ...which is all on tape, of course. It came from one of Saul's recordings of the Blackburn raves. We added the crowd noise to the classical music, hoping to get a Pavlovian response from this dog of an audience.

1:05 The lights finally lower, even if the conversations don't. There's a pitiful hiss of dry ice which makes the stage look even more barren than before.

1:12 Enter Saul, stage right. Looking, it pains me to say, fucking great. Being murderously pissed off suits him. The more street-wise among you will recognise the movements of a man who's just done a couple of pencil-thick lines backstage. (While the more emotionally intuitive of you might also guess from his rigidity that this is man vibrating with anger, possibly brought on by his old friend and band leader's admission that the last of their advance had gone on staging this fiasco, and if it didn't turn out to be a glorious success then his plan was to get on a plane, any plane, to anywhere, and never have to set eyes on the other three losers again.) He stands stage left with his back to the audience, just waiting for a knife. There's no second guitar on the first track so he takes up position behind the keyboards and plays an elegant little piano figure, waiting for....

1:30 Kimi. Kim Balloch then. Now known by a single name, like Prince or Bjork or Hitler. Look at that grown-out Mohican, the stubble on the side of her head as downy as a rabbit's ear. Her mum's pearls and Essex-girl white stilettos. She's a mess, but a hot mess, right? She straps on that white Gibson Firebird and plays root notes, up, down, up, down. Her tongue sticks out in concentration but she's in that zone where she looks so good that everything gets forgiven. Stamping in her high heels like a tantrum. Can you see what she would become even back then? She's got *something*, that's for sure. Something in the awkwardness of her movements, like she's being worked remotely. The thick smudge of her eyeliner could be affectation, could be the row we'd had backstage; she cried easily did our Kim, like it was no thing at all. If the seed of her future fame is hidden there then it was me, and the whole sorry failure of Remote/Control, that caused it to bloom. Her steel and rigour came from me. I taught her how to run a band and to bend it to your will. And if you keep watching you'll see me show her how to burn it all down too. I was a shining example *and* a cautionary tale. You're welcome.

1:45 Baxter stumbles across the back of the stage because I didn't like the lights on him. For his own good mainly; he messed up the whole aesthetic. There he is, getting comfortable, twirling his sticks like he'd *expressly been told not to*, and then "1, 2, 3, 4", and we're away.

1:50 Why did we start with this song? In my mind the drums at the beginning are huge: massed Burundi drummers recorded in Olympic Studios' stone room. Not this polite little patter. I know it's an uploaded copy of a VHS through laptop speakers but God, still this is weedy.

2:03 We're locked down. Tribal drums, Kimi's stiff-legged funk, Saul playing the little piano figure with just his left hand. All ready for....

2:30 ....no one. It's definitely my cue but nothing's happening. After the fight backstage I was probably still there, licking my wounds. Or someone else's. Was it then that it happened, me and Mel? I know it was some time that night, and to do it while her boyfriend was sweating away at the drum kit sounds like the kind of thing I might do.

2:45 The cameraman focuses on the mike in its stand like something is happening. Judging from Baxter's nervous glances stage left I must be in the wings by now. Two minutes is a long time to go around this riff, especially for an audience as uncommitted as this. And here, listening back fifteen years later, there's a nice touch that I didn't notice on the night. At 2:59 Saul alters the tune he's playing on the keyboard: it changes to "Send in the Clowns".

3:03 Here's our hero. Onstage to the kind of applause that the word "smattering" was invented for. Forgive me, but I look good, right? There are very few things that I appreciate about Remote/Control never becoming famous, but not having to compete with my younger, prettier self, is one of them. Hair looks good. Just the right side of styled. Skinny enough to enrage you if I stole your girlfriend. Clothes are on point too; I don't look like I dressed up for the gig. A bow to the audience wins not even an ironic cheer. I turn my back — to say something to Bax? No — I remember now, to do my flies up. Right in his eyeline with his furious girlfriend still backstage.

3:05 An introduction swallowed by the racket. (Though I actually said, "They say you play every venue twice, once on the way up and once on the way down. Hello Borderline, it's nice to be back.")

3:10 And I'm in. Voice sounds all right. I'm moving a bit, trying to pull the audience in a little closer, trying to fill that semi-circle. We sound OK actually. These little speakers don't capture any of the power but you can still hear that we're tight.

7:15 It's not going well. If by the second song the crowd aren't moving then they probably never will. You have to work for those moments when an audience turns, when they change from a collection of individuals into something else: a mob, a gang, a crowd. Even a third of them can be enough for a contagion to set in and suddenly every noise you make sets the puppet-strings twitching. It's an amazing feeling — truth be told it's *the* amazing feeling. To sing a line that's being sung back to you in a thousand rapt voices. To see the room bounce in time to a kick-drum. Watching hands pulled aloft by a guitar riff. Remote control: it happened a couple of brief, magical times in my whole life and I treasure those moments like others might treasure their kid's first smile.

7:30 This is not that. This is the other thing. And you can see I'm already desperate. Twisting and snarling and dancing and trying to wring some kind of power from the song, trying to transmute the lead of this lumpen audience into gold. We're three songs in and we're getting nothing back. The record companies are here to see if we draw a crowd, to see if we can work a crowd but of course they're the oil on the water that's stopping that happening. The more we try to drive the audience the more desperate we look and desperation is the most unattractive look of all.

7:25 No between-song banter. No onstage chemistry. It's effectively over here, now, but we just keep flogging the corpse of the gig onwards. We're halfway into "The Driver", which runs to seven minutes, when I turn to Saul and run a finger across my throat: not a threat but a mercy killing. End this now.

7:30 Which he ignores. The band plays on.

8:30 I signal again to end.

9:00 And on he goes. Baxter hasn't noticed anything but Kimi is all eyes.

10:15 I conduct Bax to a broken stop, my guitar swinging and feeding back. Kimi looks frozen as she slows with him. Saul pointedly closes his eyes, throws his head back and continues with the riff. Louder now and speeding it up, the chords so broken as to be squalls of noise. He turns to Bax and nods his head: *one two three four*.

Even in this pixelated darkness you can see the second of frustration in Bax's eyes before… a click of the sticks and he's back in. Kimi shrugs and starts up again and I'm left there. Captain fucking Bligh with a Telecaster.

The applause is hesitant. It's not just that we appear to have restarted a song that had already gone on too long, it's that they can tell that's someone's gone off-script. I start to sing and as soon as I find my place Saul changes key. I slide down to match it and he changes again. Kimi is white with fury.

11:30 I was pissed off at Saul back then, but at the same time this constant drone of sound he's spewing out is thankfully hiding the reality of the situation. The dry ice, the intro tape, the micro-seconds between songs: they were all there to hide the ignominy of casting our pearls so passionately before such a small audience of swine. The non-sound of an audience after a song has finished is a crushing feeling, like waking up next to someone you shouldn't. So yeah, *Sturm und Drang* Saul.

By 12 minutes you can see Saul and I are enjoying ourselves. A song finishes, Bax's drums sound like something pushed downstairs but Saul just keeps on playing, with his Madame Tussauds eyes and Ian Curtis headshake. And this time Kimi and I just glance and *bang* — we're back in with another song. Saul's still in A minor, part of the long coda to Ambulance Man, while the rest of us are in D, so it kind of works. Bax is lost somewhere in between, just a white noise of cymbals, more visual than aural. He's stiff with frustration, no improviser our Bax, but trying to follow along. And then there's some secret signal between Saul and I and we stop in unison. Jackknife of hands across strings and then stock-still like the Kraftwerk robots. The other two limp to a close and the crowd perks up. This has gone from underwhelming to disastrous and that's got to be worth watching.

13:03 Fuck knows what Saul is playing here. The video isn't clear enough to see what chord shape he's making and the sound — well you guys can hear — it's just brutal. He's slashing across the strings and every time you catch a second of melody or rhythm he messes it up again. Now, fifteen years later, I can't remember what I started singing, nonsense I guess, so low and rapid as to be a rhythm instrument. Bax starts to count in so Saul speeds up. I shout chords out at Kimi though lord knows there's no chords in this din. Every iota of tune has been bleached from this noise.

14:09 The semi-circle around us widens. Saul is laughing so hard that his cheeks are wet. The amps are on full and every time Bax or Kimi finds some kind of stability within the noise we tear it away. A couple of guys from Dillon's entourage throw themselves at the stage, hands on each other's shoulders in some kind of demented pogo. Saul turns his back and hunches over his guitar, thrashing at open strings.

14:55 Baxter and Kimi snap at the same time. Bax throws his sticks at me (and misses of course) and then Kimi gently places her bass into its stand and walks away. Her arm is around him before they even reach the side of the stage. His head on her chest like a child's. The roll of his shoulders tells you he's crying. Not that I'd known at the time. Once they stopped playing they were lost to me.

So it's just Saul and me and two guys flailing around with their beers in the air. And without the rhythm section it's about to grind to a halt until Saul reaches for a low note on the keyboard. There's a stuttering blare and then the pulse of "OU Kids" starts up. And I know none of you are here for a Remote/Control history lesson but this is the first thing Saul and I ever wrote. It relies on this brainless sequencer riff, as if "I Feel Love" had been rewritten for Nuremberg, so we could play it even if Kimi and Bax were offstage. The synth judders — I've heard more tuneful pneumatic drills — Saul tears at the guitar and on we go.

And now the two lads from the front are up on stage, my stage, lurching and windmilling like retards and one raises a beer glass high and I don't stop playing, just kick the mike stand low, near its base so it crashes into Idiot A and sends him backwards off the stage. And when his friend turns to see where he's gone it's just too perfect, and I catch him in the small of the back and send him crashing on top of his mate. Saul doesn't even turn around. And because the riff is just A and D, the kind of thing the Mary Chain would think was a little basic, you can sing anything over it. Which is what I'm doing. As Saul thrashes, head down, you can hear snippets

15:10 *When I fall in love....*

15:30 *You've lost that loving feeling.* This facing Saul, eyebrows raised, giving it the lovelorn fawn thing to hopefully get some fucking reaction from the front row. Onto my knees like Johnny Ray.

15:45 *I would rather go blind.* One hand over my eyes, one reaching for heaven. *Than to see you walk away.*

Idiot A is back. This time with a posse: Idiots B through G. As he mounts the stage Saul steps forward and without even unstrapping his guitar jabs him with the butt, sending him flat and bloody to the floor. You can't see it here but at the time there was a beautiful sight. One solitary tooth, spinning through the air in front of the band, caught in the stage lights. And this time the semi-circle does clear as his mates come to drag him away.

16:07 *I've seen the future brother, and it is murder*. Fuck I'd forgotten this. It's Leonard Cohen's "The Future" and it sounds like I'm doing the whole thing. Look at me down my knees like some lovelorn soul singer.

I've seen the future brother, and it is murder. Over and over again. Did I know I was fortune telling or did I just like the sound of the words? Probably the latter. Here come Idiots C through G though, arm in arm like it's fucking British Bulldog. The cameraman is holding the camera overhead now as the crowd moves in. Finally they're going to get a show.

I've seen the future brother, and it is murder. And like that Saul's gone. The cameraman doesn't catch his exit, the keyboards are tipped on their side, their output reduced to one single thudding note. The camera pans across the stage in search of him and then snaps back to…

Me, flailing at a guitar, ranting nonsense. At the time it felt heroic, boy-on-the-burning-deck stuff but here it just looks… sad.

I've seen the future brother, and it is murder

A bottle and then a glass are launched stagewards, beer spraying from the glass in an elegant parabola, the bottle hitting the guitar strings with an audible clang. I swing a kick at the bottle and miss. The camera shows a wall of backs. A scrum at the front of the stage like you'd get at a proper gig.

The look in my eyes there at the end: it's not entrancement, alchemy, transfiguration. It's fear of the silence that would envelop me once I stopped playing. There's the howl of a lead being pulled from an amp, a low hum and then a rectangle of light appears as Saul opens the dressing room door and I dive in. The pack are on it in seconds, the camera struggling to focus on the melee. Fists beat on the metalwork and the crowd parts to let one guy take a running kick at it, but the door doesn't budge.

21:27 The PA is switched off with a thump that sucks the air from the room. The house lights come on. As instructed the soundman plays our outro tape: Lou Reed's "Goodnight Ladies", a slice of camped-up oompah music that encourages the Idiot pack to one more assault on the dressing room door before the lights and the music and the pools of beer and hum of conversation bring everyone back to earth. It's a matter of context of course. This kind of meltdown in front of an adoring crowd at the end of a glorious career would be, though I say it myself, legendary. But when this guy does it? This footnote to a footnote? Well, it's pretty pathetic.

I've seen the future brother, and it is murder

The camera remains on the dressing room door but the director walks backwards, into the scrum around the free bar. There's no awed hush, just a babble of plans for the next party.

22:28 The camera's been placed on a table somewhere because it's steadily focused on the dressing room door. Nothing happens.

23:11 Fade to black.

So, there it is. *Une petite mort* for *un petite bande*. Kimi learning from my mistakes quite how easy it is to derail yourself. The last time we four saw each other for fifteen years. A friend betrayed. An enemy made. A ripple in a silent ocean dying down to nothing. My life.

Chapter Twelve

I watched the Japanese video later on with the sound turned down, my feet dangling in the Thames. It was grainy and Brandon looked wraith-like. I started to read his commentary but the rhythm of his words annoyed me. The closer I got to him the less substantial he was. Brandon was a tone of voice, the arch of an eyebrow, a haircut. I let the video play on while I watched a moorhen painstakingly build its nest. Despite everything Brandon said about that final gig, it was the other three that looked real up on stage: sweating and crying and bleeding and worrying. I was ready to put him in the ground.

The river was beribboned with twists of light and swifts feasted on insects. Ducks pottered about as church bells rang somewhere far-off. The island looked shady and inviting. Houseboats festooned with bikes and oars crowded the shoreline and somewhere nearby kids were playing.

I kicked ripples in the water as my phone pinged. Rae, saying she'd found the song Brandon had mentioned, "OU Kids". I didn't care. Ten tracks, eleven: what did it matter?

Dillon texted his every movement. He was at Hammersmith, he was at Chiswick, he'd be there in ten. I put my shoes and socks back on and straightened my hair.

I'd marked my position on the bridge in chalk. Once I was sure I was in the right spot I rubbed it away. Clouds scudded high over the city but here it was bright and dry. There was more headroom, somehow, out here. My reflection broke up and rearranged in the river below. White hair, white shirt, clean against the oily sky. I switched off my phone off, leaned back and watched the swallows.

I should have got Kimi involved earlier. When I explained Brandon's plan, with its double-backs and layers of cruelty, she got it straight away. By the end of my explanation she was filling in the gaps and snapping her fingers with pleasure. There on the fiftieth floor, with Rae on the big screen, Ronnie and Reggie perched on the sofa and Jay hovering, her air of mischief reminded me of Brandon's.

"I know you're only here to explain it because it all went so wrong Adam, but you have to admire the concept, no?"

I made a face.

"It is actually evil, I concede, and how he's treated Rae and Robin is unconscionable." She nodded at the screen. "But in isolation it's great. It's original, and that's something I didn't think Bran had in his armoury. This record, if it were presented the way he wanted…"

She spread her arms wide. "It could be a new kind of thing."

So with that she and Rae decided how I would die.

They dismissed my ideas to explain Brandon's latest death: a suicide note or a video explaining the whole thing.

Kimi was animated. "No no no no no. You're trying to tell a story. You want it to make sense at the end. Tie up all the loose ends. But no one wants stories like that anymore. We have to make something loud and messy and confusing and *real* and let people pick whatever they want out of it."

She counted it down. "A murder. A record. And no answers." She snapped her fingers with glee. "It's not a story, it's a Rorschach Test."

She and Rae talked quickly as my nausea subsided, testing each other out. Meanwhile Jay worked along some whole other trajectory: making phone calls that I didn't understand, speaking in a jargon so dense with acronyms that I wasn't sure if he was discussing drugs or guns.

I lay on the rug and let conversations wash over me. Rae saying, "It's like the Ripper thing, it's fascinating because you can never prove it one way or another." Ronnie: "but not too public, we're going to be pretty fucking conspicuous in headdresses and all that business." Jay cooing down the phone: "Two grams of the new stuff, smokeless blanks, and a couple of IV drips." And Kimi, walking about the flat, talking to herself. "Chuck on as many references as we can. The crows, Dillon, John Dee. Money, drugs, blood, fire, whatever. Pile them on top of each other."

I dreamt of New Umbrage, seen from below, an invert city of pulleys and chains and dark corners fitfully illuminated as the city woke. I dreamt of water and fire. And when I came to, to a room full of sleeping people, Jay in Kimi's arms like a baby, Ronnie and Reggie curled into the couch, Tahoe just a tableau on a screen, I knew what my part would be.

A raised hand in the distance. Dillon on the river bank. I made no move. A car door slammed somewhere. Kids shouting. A plane soundlessly crossing the sky. Dillon with a bag tucked under his arm, a complaint on his lips.

When the first shot hit I thought for a second that there had been a mistake. It felt so real. There was an instant shock to my chest, like being invisibly shoved. It spun me round and sent me scrabbling to my knees. The ground was filthy — gravel and fox shit — and I recoiled back. *one two three four*. Nothing. Where was the second shot? I told my head to ignore what my eyes were seeing, blood blossoming like a flower across my chest. Where was the second shot? I realised that the other blood pouch, the kill-shot, was taped over my stomach and now I had my back to the guns. I forced myself up and around.

Birdsong. Church bells. The delicious smell of cordite. The headdresses were magnificent, pitched right between the avian and the robotic. Liquid feathers flowing like insect swarms. Ronnie's shotgun rested at his side as Reggie raised his. From the corner of my eye I could see witnesses on the island, still unsure what this was. Theatre, or an advert, or actually something bad happening? Dillon was O-mouthed, ready to run. I was fucking freezing. It was important to be in shirt and trousers so that it was clear that I didn't have scuba gear hidden about my person, but the day was cold and I didn't want to look frightened on camera.

I looked up at Reggie silhouetted against the grey of the sky. Mane of feathers, curve of beak, the barrel of the shotgun. He waited. Why? Then I remembered. I dropped the record as gently as possible, watching blood smear across the paper sleeve.

My eyes raised with the shotgun, its own two pupils on mine. The beak levelled and the shotgun jerked. It made a softer sound than I expected; another invisible shove, low and deep. A sucker punch. The air rushed from my body and I pressed the button and felt the blood burst from the pouch. I wrapped my arms around myself just as Rae had taught me. Getting back up had moved me too far forward and the edge of the bridge was four or five feet behind me. If I fell back now then I'd miss the handrail. I took a step back and raised my hand, late, much too late.

At the end of things we're just bodies moving through space. Engineering problems, and not even complex ones at that. The handrail rushed to meet the back of my thigh and my weight turned the rail into a pivot. I toppled backwards, my arms reaching towards the sun, horizontal now, no noise, just the bland London sky again, before I was backwards, upside down and the noise all around me. As I fell the wire snagged on my heel. I spun right over and was tugged down, gravity and the weight combining to make me fall feet first. The wire on my heel tightening. A flash of sky but no one moving. The dark lip of the bridge. I brought my feet together but still the water slapped at my stomach and face. The trick is to make as little splash as possible. I should be able to do that.

The last thing. In Kimi's tower block in the clouds surrounded by people who were like comic-book characters, and Rae onscreen so real it hurt to look at her, and Jay saying very softly, "we're going to need some blood." Three syringes' full into a clear pouch. My blood. Brandon's blood.

The cold punched the air out of me as I reached along the wire. Robin had given me the idea. That dandelion clock at the centre of New Umbrage worked on the simplest of pulley systems. You tripped the wire, weights fell and the structure rose. Things spread apart in tandem. This morning I dropped a bag containing the lightweight breathing gear onto the river bed. A pulley wire connected it to a loop on the bridge. My foot went in the loop.

The first jolt freed the bag from the silt and pulled the wire from the bridge. I let the water envelop me until my feet touched — barely — the riverbed but the water was too filthy to see anything. I grabbed the wire from my boot and followed it, hand over hand, to the familiar shape of the mouthpiece. I'd practised this at Trellick Tower, blindfolded until I knew the shape of the mask by touch alone, holding my breath against the cold. In the sink I'd managed forty-five seconds without breathing but already, maybe ten seconds in, my lungs were heaving. I pulled the mask on, forced myself not to rush and turned the valve. Nothing. I let it run, squeezing water out of the mask until there it was: thin, rubbery air. I took a breath, another, and then fitted the goggles. Even with them on I couldn't see my hand in front of me.

I must have kicked up silt from the floor, a cloud around me like Pig-Pen. Should I wait for it to clear so I didn't leave a trail of silt? Or get moving before someone dived in to help? The sheer naked embarrassment of the latter set me walking. Short steps, holding the weight and its airtight package a little off the floor. I couldn't help kicking up mud but it dissipated around me. I toddled, inelegantly, upstream. I tried to keep the light above me even. Even light meant the same depth, meant invisibility, meant escape. Eight hundred steps I'd calculated yesterday, eight hundred steps until it was safe.

I stripped out of the wet clothes and lay for a second on the shore of the island I'd scoped out yesterday. It was two hundred metres upstream of the bridge but hidden around a kink in the river, out of sight of Eel Pie. For a moment I stared up at the sky; a dead man, a no one. I watched Heathrow planes write contrails across the sky until the sound of far-off sirens snapped me back. My hair was thick with silt and when I ran a hand through it came away filthy. I took a T-shirt and jeans from the waterproof bag and replaced them with my sodden shirt and trousers. I changed, shivering in the cool beneath the trees, and pulled a woolly hat down over my hair. I put on glasses, trainers. Nothing clothes: the sort of stuff I would have worn before this whole thing started. Then everything went into a sports bag before I pulled the rowing boat out from under the vegetation. Earwigs scuttled from underneath as I dragged it to the water. One set of sirens stopped and then another started up.

I pushed off for the south bank, the slap of oars on the water sounding loud as handclaps. Halfway across I stopped. The south bank was lined with trees — a stand of London Planes — but I could see the flash of blue lights through the trunks. A police car and an ambulance. I'd mapped the whole area and I couldn't imagine why they would stop there. It was a featureless stretch of roadside: that why I'd chosen it as the landing spot.

I let the boat drift for a minute to see if they'd move on, but there was just the blink of lights and an occasional horn. As quietly as possible I manoeuvred the boat around and struck out for the far end of Eel Pie Island instead. The houseboats here were older, and so thickly overhung with trees that they blended into the landscape. I manoeuvred quietly, gently batting at the water, until I found what I was looking for: a boarded-up houseboat with its own jetty. Through the trees I could hear voices in a shouted conversation and the same bunch of kids playing. I dragged the boat into the long grass around the untended garden and tipped it onto its side. The shouts were making their way across the island like smoke signals. Doors opened and shut and a fresh siren sounded from the south bank. I walked onto one of the main paths. It had the feeling of a well-tended campsite. Already residents were making for the bridge but slowly, chatting along the way, like the crowd before a football match. I walked with my head down, trying not to hurry.

The bridge was in turmoil. A police car and two ambulances howled impotently on the main road and I could see debris scattered across the tarmac. The island's residents collected around the entrance to the bridge but a couple were leaning over the side and taking selfies. A dinghy circled around the legs of the bridge, throwing up a wake of froth while a pair of yellow-clad policemen encircled a gesticulating Dillon. It would take some digging for anyone to connect the £66,000 he had in cash on him to the cost of Ronnie and Reggie, but some digging is what I expected.

On the main road a police car crawled up onto the grass to avoid the debris. Any second now there would be crime-scene tape and large-scale interviewing and lies to be told. I strode across the bridge, keeping my eyes on the water upstream as if I expected someone to appear. A policeman made a half-hearted attempt to keep me back but there were people joining the bridge from both sides now.

"Sorry, sorry, sorry." I walked across to the other side, turning my back to pass Dillon and the policemen. A phalanx of paramedics yomped up carrying a stretcher and oxygen tanks.

The taxi driver was chatty. I had to put earphones in just to shut him up. We headed west to Heathrow through back-garden suburbia with glimpses of the Thames through the trees.

I checked the passport again. Mine was out of date and Jay had said he'd need a day for a new one so I was travelling on Brandon's Fitzroy one. It looked brand new. The covers were stiff and the pages empty and his photo wore a wry half-smile. I practised the same look via my reflection in the window. I flicked through the pages to check for any stamps that I should know about and found, jammed deep in the fold of the middle pages, a SIM card. *Heathrow 12 miles*. Blood under my nails. Silt in my hair.

Esophobia

There was just one piece of data on the SIM card: a long piece of writing, spread across a series of texts. They were the most difficult things to transcribe as they're full of run-on sentences which lack capitals or punctuation. I've tidied them up as best I can and removed anything that I don't think is pertinent. All texts were still in the drafts folder.

5:45am. I opened a window. Partly to clear some of the gloom from the air but also to hear Kimi leaving; her brief conversation with Kaspar, car doors opening and closing, tyres on concrete and finally just the birds. Other goodbyes crowded my head. Other doors closing, other cars pulling away into the dawn. Another whole life was disappearing in the back of a long, black car. I shook the feeling off and pressed RECORD. Coming down is a great time to make a record: the gaps between things thin and you can lie back and let the universe work your strings. I rerecorded "Dead Beats" and "End of the World". We'd played them well enough but the band made them too solid and these were songs that needed the threat of collapse. I didn't listen back.

It was daybreak. A hint of reality at the edges of things and all the hazy joys of night congealing. I remembered something I'd heard on the TV and scribbled it down in my book as a possible title: *Eosophobia*, the fear of the dawn. I burnt four CDs. My only doubt was that last song and the long lacunae scattered throughout it. An inner voice told me it was fine: the gaps were pure and elegant, but deep down I knew it wasn't so. Here, at the death, I had nothing.

I wanted to be walking. I would burn through the fumes of last night and extinguish myself. I had a vision of walking to the coast, fading with every step, clouds of energy trailing behind me like a cloak, until I stepped, featherlight, off the cliff. Suede shirt, black trousers, brothel creepers.

Kaspar was on the phone in the lobby. He gestured to me to wait but I mouthed "Just going for some air," and stepped out into the dawn. Grey and gold. Smog and halogen. Stone and rain.

6:25am. It was cold enough to keep you moving fast. I took turns at random, avoiding streets I knew and letting London's backstage slide by. Left, right, right. No pattern to it. A beggar sat under the bluish light of an ATM, holding a lead but no dog. I fished in my pockets: some dollars and a baggie of Jay's TLAs. If anyone needed some beauty in his life it was this guy so I tossed a couple into his hat and dry-swallowed the others. The last hurrah of the coke leant a forward tilt to my stance, propelling me through the crowds, and a flock of suits in Old Street parted automatically for me. Into the City. It was already thick with traffic. Busses with windows wet from the sleepy breath of the dreaming shift workers: Somali cleaners and Serbian security guards and Bengali caterers and Romanian hookers and Persian croupiers and Polish repairmen. Upstream against the Mercs and the Lexuses with Radio 4 playing and backseat iPhones bringing news of which bank had gone belly-up today.

I cut north towards Barbican, past the last sad bit of London's Roman walls, shoddy and ill-lit in the lee of some Brutalist loading bay. Something in the TLAs was flyposting stray images across my mind and unspooling snippets of lyrics. An infuriating shop name — Spit'n'Panache — the cartoon splotches of vitiligo on the skin of a piebald Rasta begging from a doorway, a pigeon's tail poking out from a rustling and discarded bag of bagels, they all dropped hooks in me.

And over it all a loop of melding songs like a kid fiddling with the car radio.

Round round get around, I get around the world around the world won't listen I listen to the band on the run young hearts run free

North again. Through one of those nameless who-lives-here bits of London. Gone dawn but the street lights still on. Dead estates patiently awaiting gentrification behind their screens. The blankest of graffiti: no pictures, no beauty, just names written over names over names. Into the Angel. Rae had loved London's names. The Angel, Seven Sisters, Crystal Palace: like something from a fantasy novel.

After a third time miscalculating the trajectory of a car as I crossed the road — a smeared blare of horn, a shouted insult lost in the wind — I ducked into a greasy spoon at the back of Kings Cross. It gave me instant flashbacks to my first London life, with its laminated menus and the plastic ketchup containers shaped like tumorous tomatoes, crusted with dried product the same brown-red as old blood. I wasn't hungry but I ordered a number three — two eggs, chips, beans, sausage, bacon and fried bread — as a sop to the time I planned to spend there, and it arrived disturbingly quickly.

8:10am. I was coming to some kind of equilibrium. My heart stopped beating like butterfly wings high in my chest, and the scraps of music and conversation that were cross-fading through my mind had calmed down to something ignorable, like the hubbub of a pre-curtain theatre audience.

There were traffic lights outside the window and I watched the drivers. A business-suited woman with feline eye makeup checked her breath on the back of her hand, a van driver lit a ciggie from the end of another. The morning felt heavy and slow and I had an urge to lay my head on the Formica and sleep. The caff played oldies radio: "If Paradise Was Half as Nice" and "The Sun Ain't Gonna Shine

Anymore"; ten-second news bulletins and adverts for opticians and car insurance; "Needles and Pins", "You Can't Hurry Love". Records like clouds or rain, you couldn't imagine them being written, couldn't imagine the lyrics scribbled into a notebook, couldn't imagine the band leader saying *let's try it in three-four time*.

A Lycra-clad cyclist, exotic in lime-green and top-heavy under an insectoid helmet, balanced at the lights, micro-adjustments keeping him upright. I willed him to topple with all my heart. Hailstones the size of garden peas sprang instantaneously against the window. Two old boys sat in opposite corners of the caff, both working their way through steaming platefuls of whatever the day's special was: something brown and viscous with the aroma of cat food. I got another cup of tea and waited for the hail to subside. Two kids on bikes crossed in front of the window and one palmed something to the other without even slowing. Neatly done.

The news finished and Etta James came on. An old favourite. *I would rather, I would rather go blind... than to see you walk away.* I held my breath under its skinny spell. Like a solar eclipse it was better not to face it head on otherwise it would burn you, you had to come at it in bits. That rubbery one-string guitar part buried deep down in the mix. The girls oohing and yeahing in the background, girls who you knew were serious and beehived and lovely, who lived two bus rides away from the studio and brought their homework with them to do while they waited, with their swells and their triumphs and their fingerclicks. The horns just out of bed and late to the party, and then Etta herself, always a head-nod ahead of the beat, sounding cool and ready except on the special lines which caught in her throat like death. (When she sang *most of all I just don't wanna be free* it punched the air out of me.) I revelled in the sheer unlikeliness of it all. Two minutes and thirty-five seconds of warm Alabama air, moved this way and that by vocal cords and vibrating strings and felt beaters, trapped in a series of magnetic charges on tape and later digitised onto silver discs and sent across the ocean to be played on air, plucked algorithmically from the annals, converted again into radio waves and beamed through the haze of London skies and put back together by that radio there, sat behind the counter, the sound back in its element again, set free to strike at my eardrums. And despite all this transformation and reconfiguration it still hit me like an uppercut. My eyes wet with tears just like Etta's but six thousand miles and thirty-five years away. Remote Control.

What was my life compared with that? What was I going to do with my days that might compete? I watched the girls huddled under an awning opposite, smoking furiously, and the kids with their school jackets pulled up over their heads, and the old boys trying to make the last bit of their lunch last, and the waitress wiping down the same table again because, really what else is there to do, and the cook with his tattooed arms crossed on the counter, and the people rubbing view-holes in the condensation of the bus windows, and the endless fucking gaggle of mums with their endless fucking pramfuls of babies, and the Porsche drivers talking into headsets and the van drivers with week-old *Daily Star*s yellowing on the dashboard and I thought what the hell will I ever do to compare with this, this divine procession of tiny hopes and monumental pain, and the taste of unexpected tears on your tongue and flickering light in past-midnight bedrooms and bruises in hard-to-reach places and a loneliness like thin ice over black, black water, loneliness like animal's teeth, like a living death.

10:01am. I left a tenner on the table and left before the song could finish, striding into pinpricks of hail and the hint of sunshine at the corners of the sky. I felt righteous and feather-light. What had I been thinking? That I was important, that I mattered? My footsteps were a drumbeat and songs started up in my mind more insistent than before.

May the road rise with you, may the road to nowhere come on inside, step inside love let me find you a place there's a place for us somewhere a place we'll find a new way of living on the ceiling someday somewhere

The road rose for me. Down the hill to Kings Cross proper. Into St Pancras. For a generation just an unloved, minor-key appendix to the bustle of Kings Cross, now seemingly awake from its cocoon and thriving. Somewhere the rain got turned up a notch and I sat in the station pub there, a cookie-cutter gastro-bore called the Betjeman. I half-remembered an interview Betjeman had given, propped up and freezing in a bath chair on some bleak Sussex cliff, a million years old and posher than the queen, and his being asked "Is there anything you regret about your life?" and, fingerclick-quickly, his reply, "I wish I'd had more sex." I raised a double MacCallan to the old invert as the storm of songs swept over me.

To the centre of the city where all roads meet waiting for you, so tired, tired of waiting for my man hey whiteboy what you doing uptown top ranking say me give you heart attack waiting I'm not waiting on a lady I'm just waiting on a friend

Back south along the Euston Road. Third-division hotels that would have looked better online — *just 1 mile from major train stations and the West End* — tourists with maps blown inside out in the squall amid a steady trundle of cabin baggage on uneven pavements. Clouds hustled across a sky without a hint of blue. It was bitter in the shade, little better in the sunlight. Baker Street: rugby fans braying outside a huge pub and out into the bike lane. A thin veneer of offices and hotels to the north before estateland started for real. Paddington. Whole streets of nothing but men. Vociferous Moroccans pulling on oversized hookahs and B-movie Arab drivers leaning on German cars, always black, parked on double yellows outside god-knows-what. On Queensway a milky-eyed guy in the kind of sun-bleached fatigue jacket that back in the States would have had me clocking his pockets for gun-shaped bulges, fell into step alongside me and asked, conversationally, "Spare me a-hundred-and-forty grand for a luxury yacht?" I gave him a tenner and my head spun.

Come together as one over me, over me don't dream it's over and it never really began I know it's over the rainbow skies are blue, blue, electric blue blue is the colour of my room there's a world where I can go and tell my secrets to

2:12pm. Notting Hill. This place was already mutton dressed as lamb back in the Nineties. It used to resemble a kind of fractious Rastafarian theme park, populated by packs of horse-faced Chelsea boys for whom this was just about as much rough as they could handle and the occasional petrified Italian tourist. Now it's worse: a facsimile of a facsimile. The only black faces on show are on the murals, otherwise it's as ethnically cleansed as Mayfair (and as cruelly expensive). Onto Portobello Road. Already terminally uncool when I left. Now something like an outdoor gift shop. No Irish, No Blacks, Lots of Dogs. No-one under forty, like life during wartime. Just the same old show: men too old to be wearing army surplus jackets drinking pints in the rain, dogs eating crisps at their feet. On to the All Saints Road, my first ever stop on my first-ever trip to London. The frontline supposedly. Later it was the place for the blues clubs under fake cab offices and bike repair shops. One red bulb and ANYONE FOUND SMOKING CRACK WILL BE ASKED TO LEAVE signs. I never wanted it to end.

Another grumble of shower started up. The suede of my shirt started to pucker so I ducked into a tourist shop and bought a LONDON — UK cagoule. I could ditch it once the rain stopped. I looked up properly for the first time in hours and the broken machinery of Trellick Tower loomed a couple of blocks away. Of course. Adam would be up there somewhere fussing over his models and his plants. It felt good, the way that nothing had ever changed for him: my very own Picture of Dorian Gray.

I walked the streets around the tower safe in the knowledge Adam would be looking inwards, not out here. The weather changed channels restlessly. Hail and showers and bland black clouds. I sat in a pub opposite the tower among the market traders paying for drinks with thick piles of cash pulled from their aprons. Could I do this forever? Forget my schemes and just drift through dead cities? Walk, blown by the wind, eating with the old boys in unbranded cafes, sleeping in tourist hotels. Leave the record to its fate and turn lighter than air, a whisper of a rumour. I walked faster, wanting to be spent.

If you see me walking down the street and I start to cry the clay beneath my feet begins to crumble cos I can't help falling in love falling and laughing like a hard rain's gonna fall falling in my head like memories can't wait waiting for my man who sold the world won't listen to the band.

The lyrics coursed through me like a fever now. I was a husk driven by disease. A vase of dead flowers.

Boys keep swinging they always work it out we can work it out out of my head on the door is just dream a little dream of me, myself and I can't help falling in love again alone again or

All songs are lullabies in the end, aren't they? They're just here to send us off in the long night smiling. Sparrows in the hall, snowflakes on your tongue. Everything I saw was beautiful, everything I saw was over. An old boy struggled to his knees to tie his wife's shoe and I could have wept. A girl in dungarees added a swoop to her eyeliner in the mirror of a parked van. A teenager on a bike dumped maybe a hundred free newspapers into a bin and cycled off, rapping over his earphones.

There's a kind of hush hush thought I heard her calling my name my name is hush hush all over the world is just like the Four Tops I can't help myself I love you and nobody else could do let me live 'neath your spell on you because you're mine

And I wanted to be done. I'd skirted Trellick Tower a couple of times and suddenly it seemed so pointless. I was going there because that's what people do, right, at the end? Tie up loose ends. Fuck it, let them hang I say. We've all got the same ending coming anyway.

Keep. On. Moving (Don't stop like the hands of time) N..n..n..n...n..never stop. Keep on moving. Feeling like a shadow, drifting like a leaf. Walk this way

3:01pm. I'm outside another uncaring London pub in the rain. Why am I writing this? Who could I possibly send it to? Some random phone number perhaps. It will exist but it won't, like Schrödinger's Text Message. How can I have come this far and still want the impossible? To live beyond my death; to be loved by millions who'll never know an inch of me. Too long lost in music perhaps, where magic springs forth like water, blooms in every crack.

Heaven is a place where nothing happens. Is the whole of our heart. Is a place on earth. Where nothing happens.

Music. If I could choose an afterlife that's what I'd want to be: a snatch of song heard through a car window, the DJ talking over the top. The bassline rising up through a dance floor. A half-remembered song whispered into the ear of a child. A melody, a drumbeat, a snowflake hitting the ground. An orchestra tuning up, a rhyme for Harlem girls to skip to. A loving disease spread on the air like thistledown.

A first dance, a last waltz.

A *la la la*.

Chapter Thirteen

I was on Brandon time: everything so slow and then bursts of energy. First the sleepy tube, then the fast-forward of the train. The airport two-step of queue and questioning, questioning and queue. I sat among the tumult of passengers and watched the screens' slow countdown. So many families, so many friends. Phones clasped like lovers: *I'll be there soon*. My leftover pills and wraps were dissolving in the Thames silt; all that was left of that last week were the remnant molecules in my bloodstream. I wished I could flush myself clean, new blood for the New World. My heart fluttered with every interaction — *did you pack this bag yourself sir? Can I see your boarding card?*

I sat in a cafe and ordered mineral water. The tape that Jay had broken into the Magpie for bulged in my trouser pocket, a note rubber-banded around it. "You were right fam. Built-in recorder in the base of the phone, activated when you pressed 7. Didn't have time to listen."

Dixons sold a dictaphone that took the same size tapes. Once I'd bought that it seemed vital to use up the last of the cash, so I made random purchases. Armfuls of glossy magazines I wouldn't read, a wind-up robot for Robin, Chanel No. 5 for Rae. Miso soup and vodka. Flight socks.

The *drip drip drip* of announcements was like water torture. I walked back and forth until we had a gate, then a time, and then the long drag of sitting among strangers, watching the side of the plane and all the organisation it needed: catering trucks and the chattering air crew and the hi-viz, low-impact support staff. All the time thinking that something would — *must* — go wrong because this kind of escape isn't for the likes of me. Every time the ground staff checked their computer

screens or security beeped past on their carts, or a policeman —
festooned with armour and weaponry like this was Baghdad — made
his rounds, I thought, "I knew they'd stop me." I pressed my wrists
together surreptitiously, imagining the cold shock of handcuffs and a
truncheon in my back.

Until — wonder of wonders — the slow shrink of the city from the
plane window: real life turned to model again. Looking down like God
at the quicksilver loops of the Thames, London's signature. Eel Pie
Island would be there in an elbow of the river opposite the lozenge of
Richmond Park. With something, someone, dead in the mud beneath.

I surrendered to the no-sound, no-time, no-life of aeroplanes. I
couldn't get ten minutes into any film before it confused me but when I
tried to sleep I dreamed of a frozen black wave, ten storeys high, eyeless
sea creatures suspended undead in its cliff-face. Long minutes and short
hours unfolded around me. I watched the map: a toy plane being trundled
across the globe. I turned down biscuits and ice cream and drinks and
dinner. Instead I drank bottle after bottle of water. Every time I went to
the bathroom I waved bye bye to another few ccs of my old life.

Somewhere over Greenland I slipped the tape into the dictaphone.
Rae had texted me on my final night in Trellick Tower: "You know that
phone back at the Magpie? Did you ever try pressing seven?"

I ran the rhyme in my head, "Five for silver, six for gold, seven for a
secret never to be told."

"I never did. Hiding in plain sight, maybe?"

"It would be *very* Bran, don't you think?"

Click. "Welcome to Seven for a Secret, a project from At The Sign Of
The Magpie. After the beep, tell us something that you've never told
anyone before. Be warned, future guests will be able to access this, but
they won't know whose secret it is."

Beep.

A female voice, not one I recognised: "I have £36,000 in a savings account that my family know nothing about. They're on last chance with me, every fucking one of them. The next time they disrespect me… "

Click. "Welcome to Seven for a Secret, a project from At The Sign Of The Magpie. After the beep, tell us something that you've never told anyone before. Be warned, future guests will be able to access this, but they won't know whose secret it is."

Beep.

Silence.

Click. "Welcome to Seven for a Secret, a project from At The Sign Of The Magpie. After the beep, tell us something that you've never told anyone before. Be warned, future guests will be able to access this, but they won't know whose secret it is."

Beep.

A male voice, possibly Jay. It reminds me of him but the voice is less heavily accented.

"I light three candles every day. Every fucking day man. I put on my stab vest, I do my hair, and I light a candle for Jamie, for Jessie and for my own sorry ass. That the kind of thing you want?"

Click. "Welcome to Seven for a Secret, a project from At The Sign Of The Magpie. After the beep, tell us something that you've never told anyone before. Be warned, future guests will be able to access this, but they won't know whose secret it is."

Beep.

A male voice. A stranger. "I'm not an alcoholic. It's just that AA is literally the only place where anyone listens to me. Thank you for your time."

Click. "Welcome to Seven for a Secret, a project from At The Sign Of The Magpie. After the beep, tell us something that you've never told anyone before. Be warned, future guests will be able to access this, but they won't know whose secret it is."

Beep.

A male voice. Baxter, surely. "Sometimes, actually a lot of the time, I really, really hate music. Like can't stand another second of it. Phewwwwww, it's true."

Click. "Welcome to Seven for a Secret, a project from At The Sign Of The Magpie. After the beep, tell us something that you've never told anyone before. Be warned, future guests will be able to access this, but they won't know whose secret it is."

Beep.

A female voice, not one I recognised. There's noise in the background. "I have *no* idea whose party this is. I just followed in behind some guy in the lobby. Thanks for the champagne, stranger."

Click. "Welcome to Seven for a Secret, a project from At The Sign Of The Magpie. After the beep, tell us something that you've never told anyone before. Be warned, future guests will be able to access this, but they won't know whose secret it is."

Beep.

Brandon's voice. Possibly the same night as the previous recording, judging from the background noises. "…one minute sweetheart, I'm unburdening here. Right. First. Pluto. Pluto and Charon. Pluto's the planet, oh, about five billion miles away, out in deep deep space. Charon is its moon."

He sounded drunk. This was the only recording of him in which he slurs his words.

"Planet and moon. Rae and Robin. They're two satellites on the very edge of nothing. So far from the sun that they don't even register its pull on them. It's all about the way they dance together, both orbiting some empty point, eternally facing each other. They're locked in a frozen waltz. It's distant and cold and dark but they're never alone; who needs to be at the centre of things?"

A voice cuts in: female, indistinct. Brandon replies.

"I'm serious, if you put a fucking Arcade Fire record on in my presence I'll call hotel security. Give me a go on that."

There's a deep in-breath at this point, probably a drag on a joint because his voice is slower afterwards.

"But of course that's no secret. That's just an observation. A secret? That's where I'm heading. Back to Pluto and Charon, if they'll have me. Back to deep space, where the stars are just pinpricks, where we orbit around ourselves. I'm going back for good. I didn't know it was what I wanted until now. And in… oh… three days I'm going back."

A long exhale. *Click.*

I woke to the two fingers of the Golden Gate Bridge cresting a sea of fog. San Francisco was filmic in the dusk, drenched in a light like embers. The kind of glow that makes arriving in a brand-new city feel like a homecoming. I broke the cassette from the Magpie in two and scrunched up the tape, asking the stewardess to *take this rubbish away and burn it please love.* A chorus of electronic tones swept over the plane as soon as the wheels touched down and soon every passenger had retreated behind their phones. I dawdled through the baggage reclaim, savouring the last moments before I'd be lost once again. *They won't be there, they won't be there.* Nothing to declare: nothing could be truer. A customs guy asked to search my luggage and seemed annoyed when I said I didn't have any. I kept my head down walking into the too-bright arrivals hall, ignoring the knots of expectancy behind the barriers: kids with banners, drivers with cards, lovers with flowers. *They won't be there they won't be there.*

And then. A tiny figure with a burst of blonde thatch under a chauffeur's cap charged from the crowd and there were arms wrapped around my knees and a face crushed against my legs. I bent down to hug him like it was the most natural thing in the world. And maybe ten steps behind, holding back, there she was.

At first all I could see — the highlights reel — was that same sleepy smile, now in the flesh for the first time, like the sun coming up. Her hand was on Robin's head, and she whispered, "Hey Robbie, what do we say?" and Robin disentangled himself, stepping back with a bow that sent his chauffeur's cap falling over his eyes. "Your car awaits... Daddy." His hand was small in mine, his cap pushed back, pulling us both out into the dusk.

Now, without a screen between us, Rae was too, too much, so I watched her in slices with Robin as a bridge between us — both our hands in his, touching but not touching, talking but not talking, as we chattered with him, through him. I watched Rae in stolen glances: a spatter of freckles like the surface of a birds' egg, her shoulders hunching into a laugh, that line of silver running down from the knuckle of her neck up into tied-up hair. That voice, deeper now without computer speakers, with its folksy *kinda* and *loadsa*, and her precious hands over Robin, even in the car with me in the passenger seat. Watching her eyes and the concentration written across her mouth as we reversed, with Robin crawling forward from the back seat, his shock of blonde hair — partly my white, partly Rae's wan gold — wild and busy, and everything so bright and real and animated. Robin told a long story about New Umbrage, replete with technical terms and engineering jargon that had Rae's eyebrows jammed upwards, and in the mirror I could see her whole again and for a second her hand covered mine. I was breathless, frazzled, smitten.

We stopped at a services somewhere, Robin desperate for a pee, and Rae and I sat on a plastic bench in a fragile silence. A dark, glossy bird, like a blackbird that had been professionally polished, pecked at a takeaway bag on the ground while Rae nibbled a cuticle.

"Here." She opened up a page on her phone. It was the *Daily Mail*, the homepage. BRIT ROCKER IN BRIDGE SLAYING HORROR. The Brit rocker was Dillon, not Brandon — he was even an afterthought in his own murder.

"And you should see Twitter. It's everything from a gangland hit to a stunt for a video."

It was what we wanted, I knew, but here amid the tang of orange groves and diesel fumes and the weight of her grey eyes and the water-roar of interstate traffic and a figure bouncing like Tigger back from the bathroom, it felt like nothing. She closed the page quickly and again Robin took the lead, tugging us back to the warmth of the car. We climbed steadily and California shed its warmth as we rose. Here and there patches of hidden snow gleamed white among the firs and we rose through Western towns with taverns and diners and whistle-stop train stations and ominous water towers. Uphill again and the windows down to catch pin-pricks of icy air and no radio, no music, just Robin and the sound of wet tires on tarmac.

Mountains rose and fell: slate black, Christmas greens, skullcaps of dirty white. We curved along a thin thread of road into Tahoe City, a village really, low-rise and unfussy, and pulled up outside a house like a log cabin in browns and greens and the ground floor all garage. Sounds seemed magnified up here: ice-crunch footsteps and key-jangle loud as sound effects. Their house — the new world — opened up like origami around me. Robin was kinetic through the rooms while Rae was a warm satellite around the two of us, surprisingly a head smaller than me, concentrated in a way I hadn't expected, a beacon of light. Jet lag and comedown stretched and condensed time into pulses but Robin was insistent, "You both have to see it *right now*."

We stepped into a space so like my childhood bedroom that it made me ache. Posters and diagrams were blu-tacked a third of the way down every wall, the furniture was pushed to the edges and even the bed cowered in the corner. Everything was a mere adjunct to the model that filled the centre of the room.

New Umbrage had grown huge and sleek: a square white plain divided into hundreds of geometric tiles like a solar panel array. Whatever he'd been working on was hidden somewhere underneath. Rae and I sat on kids' chairs up against the wall as Robin wound up the robot that I'd bought him at Heathrow. Had he asked me for it? I couldn't remember. The room filled with his babble and the warmth between the two of them. Everything he said, even when it was meant for me, was channelled through Rae. When he sat between us Rae felt closer, not further away, like a force field had engulfed us all.

He tugged at Rae's sleeve. "Mom, the lights."

For a second all was night. I heard Robin place the robot somewhere in the middle of the room and then scurry back into place between us. His breathing was ragged and it blended with the whirr of the toy's clockwork. I placed a hand on his head and saw a square light up.

The robot was just a black block on a shadowed landscape and its progress was painfully slow. It walked one square and then another, the ground lighting behind it, leaving a tiny trail in the room's blackness. Now, on square three, the land began to rise beneath him on hidden hydraulics. Simultaneously faint lights sprang into life along the edge of the table. They rotated as the toy strode on, each step setting off mechanisms beneath the ground. Walls, some dark as the room, some prettily mirrored, hoisted themselves out of the table and threw shadows across the walls. The room shuddered with slow transits: skyscrapers loomed and fell, bare trees reached skywards and then shrunk back into the earth, lights like snowfall drifted down into oblivion. And through it all the lone figure marched inexorably. There was something primal about this little machine dwarfed by the walls around it: like a horror film it didn't matter that you knew it wasn't real.

The ground beneath him rose hydraulically, tugging neighbouring tiles into new configurations. Whole districts unfolded: ivy-strewn walls, fountains that sounded like bells, painted shop-fronts. The robot was raised, rotated, shunted and dropped, and with every inch the world reconfigured with him at the centre. How had he *done* this?

I reached down to touch Robin's shoulder; he was asleep, just a dead weight in my arms. So heavy, so light, so real, with that crust of dry skin around his lips and an insect bite blooming behind a rosebud ear and our respective hands on his head, touching but not touching, just in the same place at the same time and after all who can ask for more than that? Night bird sounds and the faint whirr of the robot, Robin's featherlight breathing — heartbreaking teaspoons of breath — and the city of New Umbrage unfurling like a flower.

Still it walked on. Canyons blossomed, whole districts crystallised and crumbled. The lamps brightened until the room was wet with flowing light. Some spring hidden beneath a square caused whole villages to bloom and wither on the other side of the city: villages like fireworks, like mayflies. The robot was near the centre now, each step saw the land beneath him rise. Now it was a gleaming ziggurat, clean as a new car, with one lone smudge of movement at its centre. The clockwork was winding down and progress was painstaking. I felt Rae's hand squeeze mine as it took its final steps.

At the centre it stopped, seemingly hesitant before taking a last step. And here was Rae at last with nothing in between us — no screen, no intermediary, no remote control — and we breathed together, her hand tightening in mine as the robot teetered and the square beneath it rose and twisted to deposit him on a staircase with walls leaping alongside it, up, onwards to the summit where it waited for a beat, an eternity, before the ground before it opened up, and then the same mechanism that had dumped me in the Thames and risen me up, spilt and dropped. As the robot descended it was covered over by a crystal spire, faceted and filigreed, trembling as it slid into place and the lights turned in unison to focus on its sides, and as they did it scattered the light and the walls shivered with falling motes, slowly tumbling particles, like snow.

Rae's face was rapt, lit from without and within. Her face tiger-striped with fierceness and shadow, and her lips were like nothing, like a puff of air, whispering, "Shall we?"

I hoisted Robin over my shoulder. Oven warm and awkward in my grasp, I carried him down the corridor to his room. Every window showed a snow scene like a line of Christmas cards.

I laid him out on his bed in the corner and brushed his hair out of his eyes. He let out a long sigh and turned away from me. I sat there for a while and listened to his breathing, watched the fluttering of his eyelids and the pulse at his throat.

When I got back to the bedroom Rae had brought the crystal spire in to sit in the centre of the room. The walls swam in shards of light: now diamonds, now crescent moons, now tracers. She was cross-legged on the bed and looked submerged, tattooed with light. I sat, carefully, next to her, the ancient bedsprings rolling her into my orbit.

"Is he sleeping?"

"He didn't even stir."

He. Him. Robin now. Mine. Ours.

I rise with the sun these days, I can't help it. Even with the blinds pulled tight the sun squeezes itself through the gaps and calls to me. I'm up, I'm up, I'm tight and buzzing like a guitar string as my foot taps to some unheard beat.

120 bpm. 808 kick, claps on the 3 and 4

I make a coffee and sit on the porch. It almost always snows at night here, like it's some municipal service, and every morning I wake to a brand new world. In a couple of hours the three of us will have scribbled life's sentences across this blank page. A set of tyre tracks and a line of tiny footprints shadowing mine. Chainsaws will call to each other across the valley against the music of falling icicles. But for now it's just me and the birds.

Prophet V, arpeggiator, filter opening all the way

I feel electric, incendiary, overflowing, but a slow tide pulls me back together. My brother. The dark moon and his retrograde orbit: Charon to my Pluto. Finally, unknowingly, he gave me everything that I needed to walk a straight line in this crooked world.

Filters off, sub-bass pulse.

I lean backwards out over the porch, just far enough that the tardiest flakes of snow alight on my hair, my face, my tongue, until I'm wet like I've been weeping. Leaning out until I'm balanced halfway between home and the abyss. I swim in it all — cold air and dark water and the graveside stillness — before I pull myself upright, brush off the snow, and go inside to wake my family.

Acknowledgements

Anissa, first and last and always.

Thank you to Tariq Goddard for being both guiding light and cautionary tale, and to Will Francis for his immediate and unwavering passion for *The Ruins*.

Thanks too to Johnny Daukes, Julie Clark and Catriona Ward for reading early drafts without laughing and to Josh and Rhian at Repeater for editing the later ones.

Graeme Webb created the beautiful cover image and Georgina at Watkins kindly wrangled my design into shape. Rick Hornby put flesh on the bones of the book's music — if he'd been in Remote/Control then they would have been huge.

Thank you to the boys in the band — Brett, Simon, Richard and Neil — for the everyday magic of a life making music (and for the luxury of a bass player's schedule).

And to my brother, Richard for his advice and encouragement along the way.

Finally, thank you to Mica and Lorien for their tireless research into the perils of twinhood.

Repeater Books

is dedicated to the creation of a new reality. The landscape of twenty-first-century arts and letters is faded and inert, riven by fashionable cynicism, egotistical self-reference and a nostalgia for the recent past. Repeater intends to add its voice to those movements that wish to enter history and assert control over its currents, gathering together scattered and isolated voices with those who have already called for an escape from Capitalist Realism. Our desire is to publish in every sphere and genre, combining vigorous dissent and a pragmatic willingness to succeed where messianic abstraction and quiescent co-option have stalled: abstention is not an option: we are alive and we don't agree.